# CRY OF THE HEART

For Laura.

**BOOKS BY MARTIN LAKE**

**NOVELS**

A Love Most Dangerous
Very Like a Queen

*The Viking Chronicles*
Wolves of War
To the Death

*The Saxon Chronicles*
Land of Blood and Water
Blood Enemy

*The Lost King Chronicles*
The Flame of Resistance
Triumph and Catastrophe
Blood of Ironside
In Search of Glory

A Dance of Pride and Peril
Outcasts
The Artful Dodger

**SHORT STORIES**

For King and Country
The Big School
The Guy Fawkes Contest
Mr Toad's Wedding
Mr Toad to the Rescue

# MOTHER AND SON
*Grasse, France, August 1942*

Rachael Klein squeezed herself into the alleyway. She held her breath, praying that none of her pursuers would hear it. Her heart hammered so loudly she feared it might echo off the walls.

And then her son sneezed. She placed her hand over his mouth and nose.

'Hush, David, we mustn't let the nasty men hear us.'

'But you said it was only a game.'

'It is, darling. But we don't want to lose, do we?'

She put her finger to her lips despite the terror which seized her.

Evening was coming. The town was quiet now, with few people out and about. She tilted her head, seeking for any noise. And then she heard it. The heavy thud of marching feet followed by the sound of hammering on doors.

They must be at the top of the town now, making their steady, implacable progress through the little streets and passages. The police knew where every Jew lived, of course, and these were the houses they investigated first. But they also knew that many French people were sympathetic to the Jews and might well seek to hide them. It seemed likely that they would have a list of such people and would soon be knocking on their doors as well. Not that this concerned her, for she had only been in Grasse for a year and knew very few people.

Yet now she had to find someone to help her.

She stepped out into the street. At the same moment a policeman came out of a side-road and ordered her to stop.

He was an older man, past the age he should have retired, with a weary, disgruntled look.

'Where are you going, Madame?' he asked.

'We've been for a walk,' she answered. Her throat was clenched so tight her voice sounded stiff and strangled. 'It's so stuffy inside. Now we're going home.'

He held out his hand. 'Papers.'

She opened her bag and made a show of searching through it. If he saw her identity card she would be doomed.

'I don't seem to have them,' she mumbled. Then she took out a carefully folded letter.

'I have this. A letter from the war office. My husband was a doctor in the army. I don't know if he was captured or killed or escaped with the French forces to England.'

The policeman grunted. 'My son was at Dunkirk. He's still a prisoner of war.'

'I'm sorry to hear that. I hope he comes home soon.'

The man looked older still now. He pointed at the name on the letter. 'Klein?'

'My husband is from an old Alsace family. I'm from Dijon.'

The man looked dubious but opened the letter. Caught in one of the folds was a roll of banknotes, far more than his monthly salary. He held these in his right hand, in front of her face, while he read the letter. She did not take back the notes.

'Everything seems to be in order, Madame,' he said. He gave her the letter which she quickly put in her bag, closing the clasp with conspicuous deliberation. She looked at him with an expression as neutral as she could manage.

The policeman glanced around, then put the banknotes in his pocket. 'Make sure you keep your papers with you next time,' he said. 'On your way.'

She nodded in thanks and started off. But she had only taken two steps when he reached out and stopped her. 'We're taken all the Jews into protective custody, Madame Klein. If you know of any Jews tell them to co-operate.'

'I'm not sure if…I don't know any.'

He stared at her impassively. 'I'm sure you don't, Madame. Be on your way now, as quickly as you can. Good luck.'

Then he turned and slipped away.

Rachael stepped back into the alley. She thought she was going to vomit.


## MOTHERS AND DAUGHTERS
*Grasse, August 1942*

Viviane Renaud peered into the jar on the mantle-piece. It contained five hundred francs, the last of their savings. She closed her eyes and felt the familiar thump of a headache which nowadays constantly lurked in the background. She needed to buy some shoes for Celeste. There were holes in both of them and with autumn coming, packing them with paper would no longer be enough. She made up her mind and took out fifty francs.

Out of habit she glanced around to make sure that the room was neat and tidy. There had been a time when her friends would come to the house for a chat and a cup of coffee but it rarely happened now. And if anyone did come it was with some terrible, unresolvable problem.

She glanced at the picture of Maréchal Pétain above the mantle-piece and stroked it gently with her thumb. It was the same look that she once gave to the portrait of the Madonna in her mother's house. She no longer prayed to the mother of Christ but could not remember when exactly she had stopped. Perhaps she should start again she thought, even as she knew that she would not.

The Church bell tolled six o' clock and she ran her fingers through her hair. She was twenty-five years old but she felt much older. She examined herself briefly in the mirror. Despite the exhaustion in her eyes, she took some comfort that her face looked closer to twenty than fifty. Her good looks were strained but they had not yet deserted her. Her mother always said that she was tenacious although this was criticism rather than praise. Now she was relieved that her appearance shared some of this tenacity. She was ageing better than most of her friends.

'Come on, Celeste,' she called. She heard the clatter of her daughter's feet on the stairs.

Her spirits lifted when she saw her. Celeste's skirt was too short for her and her blouse was patched but she looked as pretty and as lively as ever. She couldn't remember a time before the war, could not, like Viviane, yearn for better days that seemed never likely to return.

'We're going shopping,' Viviane said.

Celeste pulled a face.

'Shopping for some new shoes for you, ungrateful girl.'

Celeste's eyes grew wide and she gasped with pleasure. 'Can I have some red ones, Maman? I so want to have red ones.'

'We'll see.' Today, Viviane thought, she would do her best not to disappoint her daughter.

She shut the door behind her and took Celeste's hand as they made their way down the narrow lane. They lived in the Vielle Ville, the old town of Grasse, a maze of streets nestling on a hill, with steep steps, twisting alleys, little courtyards and dozens of paths leading only to dead ends. She knew almost everybody in the old town, from the oldest grandmother to the youngest child. She could not imagine how people could be happy living elsewhere.

It was the last week of August and the heat beat off the footpaths cruelly, the paper-thin soles of her own shoes doing nothing to keep it at bay. Viviane hugged the shadows between the high buildings where the sun did not reach. This is like my life, she thought, the life of all the people of France, tip-toeing out of sight.

She peered into the window of the only clothes shop still open. The clothes inside were looking more tired with each month although the prices rose, nonetheless. She walked past and headed for Madame Canet's tiny little shop on the Rue des Moulinets. She pushed the door open, surprised, as always, that Madame Canet had removed the bell which used to welcome customers with such a merry tinkle. Now it felt as if people could enter in only the most furtive manner, fearful in case they were seen or heard.

The familiar smell hit her. Old clothes, worn shoes, stale moth-balls, a few shreds of pipe tobacco tied up in paper, laundry soap, cheese, wine with twists of linen sealing the bottles instead of corks and still, remarkably, the ghostly scents of perfume which Madame Canet used to sneak home when she worked in the perfumery.

'Bonjour, Viviane,' Madame Canet said, her voice gravelly from a lifetime's dedication to Gitanes cigarettes. 'I hope you don't want food, I've little left other than cheese and an old sausage which has less life than my husband.'

Monsieur Canet had died the year before the war but Madame Canet still referred to him as if he had just popped out of the shop for a moment.

'I've used up most of my ration card for the week,' Viviane said. 'I've come for a pair of shoes for Celeste.'

Her daughter helpfully held up a foot to the old lady.

'So that's a foot is it? Madame Canet said with a chuckle. 'I never realised that's what they were.'

Celeste giggled at her joke.

'I haven't got much that will fit her,' Madame Canet said.

'Anything to see her through the winter.'

'But it's summer now, Maman,' Celeste said. 'And I want red ones.'

The old lady laughed. 'We have black and brown and none really suitable for summer. Nor for winter, come to that.'

She bent down and rummaged behind the counter. Viviane and Celeste exchanged an amused look as Madame Canet gasped and groaned like a pan on the fire. Finally, she stood upright, her face red with effort and slapped two pairs of shoes on the counter.

'They're horrible,' Celeste said.

'Don't be so rude,' said her mother. 'Try them on.'

Celeste did as she was told although her face sulked bitterly. 'They don't fit,' she said after trying the second pair.

'Too big or too small?'

'One's too small, the other too big. And there are nails sticking out of the sole.' She crossed her arms angrily.

'We'll take the big pair,' Viviane said, reaching for her purse. Then she stopped, colouring a little. 'How much, Madame?'

'What do you have?'

Viviane opened her purse to show the fifty francs.

Madame Canet snorted. 'It's not enough.' Then she sighed. 'You can have them for forty francs.'

Viviane kissed her hand in thanks and then reddened, realising what she had done. 'It's been a long time since I've had my hand kissed,' Madame Canet said. 'Thank you.'

The church bell tolled the three quarter hour as they left the shop.

Across the street, Viviane saw Sylvie, with her daughter Monique. Sylvie and she had been friends since they were toddlers; friends and rivals at school, for jobs, for clothes, for boyfriends, for husbands, even for the first one to get pregnant.

'Viviane,' Sylvie called. 'I'm dying of this heat, let's go up to the cathedral and get some air.'

They wandered along the streets in the direction of the Place de la Poissonnerie. Before the war this would have been thronged with people but it was empty today. People stayed home more now, weary of walking streets with nothing much to look at and little money to spend in bars or shops. Besides, the city lay hot and heavy in the heat, like a slumbering beast, twitching with memories of might have beens.

The sound of their feet echoed against the walls of the houses, the girls' a fast staccato, the women's a duller, more plodding noise when, in truth, it should have been as lively as the children's.

It was a relief to climb up the hill to the cathedral. A few old ladies shuffled into its vastness, whether from need for God or desire for coolness, Viviane did not know. She had long ago decided she was an atheist, much to her mother's distress, and nothing she had experienced in the last few years convinced her that her decision was incorrect.

On the far side of the cathedral were a few benches which looked out over the countryside to the south. Their teacher had told them that Grasse was known as the balcony of the Mediterranean and they could see why from here. If there were a God, Viviane thought, and he wanted a balcony, he would surely have placed it here. They could make out the sea in the distance and the blur of Cannes beside it. A slight breeze blew off the sea, hot still, but making them feel cooler than when they were in the city.

They sat for an hour, talking about their children, about their own childhoods and the difficulties of everyday life. Neither talked about their menfolk. Sylvie's Louis had been fighting in the north on the day France capitulated and had been a prisoner of war for the two years since.

Viviane's Alain had been more fortunate. He had been in the army but was a mechanic and avoided the fighting. When the Maréchal had signed the surrender, he stole one of the staff cars, crammed eight of his friends into it, and drove south. He sold the car in Marseille to a gang of petty thieves who had more money than sense and cleared off home to Grasse. The car was too large and too noticeable and the police impounded it within two days.

'Do you want to share a ciggy?' Sylvie asked. Viviane nodded. She did not particularly like smoking but cigarettes were hard to come by and so she always took a puff or two if it was offered.

'It will be good when the war ends,' Sylvie says. 'Then we can have American cigarettes and go dancing again. Perhaps we'll be liberated by the Americans. Such tall boys and dripping with money. They can teach us the jitterbug.'

'Do you think the war will ever end?' Viviane asked. 'One of my husband's friends says that the Luftwaffe have flattened London and are doing the same to New York.'

Sylvie shrugged. 'Let's hope he's wrong. I've never met an American. It will be a shame if they're all killed before I get the chance.'

She took a deep drag of her cigarette as they watched the western sky grow pink.

'The girls are growing up,' Viviane said suddenly, nodding towards where Celeste and Monique were playing some hopping game.

'But too skinny,' Sylvie said. She sighed. 'I suppose I shall have to look for more money when the weather cools off.'

Viviane did not comment. It was no secret between them how Sylvie earned her money when things got desperate.

'We can lend you some,' Viviane said, although this was a lie. 'If Alain has a good month in Marseille.'

Sylvie smiled in thanks.

Just as Viviane refrained from discussing how Sylvie earned money, she never asked about Alain's business activities. Such things were best left unsaid.

'It's getting late,' Viviane said. 'We should get back.'

Sylvie's eyes went to a man loitering in the distance. 'Will you take Monique to my mother's?' she asked.

'Of course,' Viviane said. 'But be careful.'

## HELP ME
*Grasse, August 1942*

'Come on, David,' Rachael whispered, clenching his hand tightly. 'Quiet as a mouse now.'

She slipped out of the alley into Rue Vielle Boucherie. And then she saw her. A woman crossing the road with a little girl skipping behind her. The girl had a pair of shoes dangling from her neck by their laces.

Rachael's hand went to her mouth. She watched the woman and child for a few moments. The woman paused and listened to something the girl said. Then the girl giggled loudly and the woman reached out and brushed her fingers through her hair. They looked happy together. The woman appeared to be good-natured and kind. It was enough. It had to be.

The woman and child continued down the street.

Rachael took one last swift look, her heart hammering with indecision. Then she made up her mind and hurried after them.

They stopped some way down the street while the girl bent to stroke a cat. Rachael seized the chance and approached.

'Madame,' she said, 'please help me.'

The woman turned to her with a nervous start. 'What's wrong?' she asked.

Rachael took a deep breath. 'The Police are after me.'

She cursed herself for saying this for it would immediately arouse suspicion. Why would anyone flee the police unless they had done something wrong? Any law-abiding citizen would turn her in. This woman had only to call out and the police would come running.

But the woman did not look horrified. Her eyes narrowed, more with curiosity than suspicion. 'Why are they after you?' There was no hint of accusation in her tone.

'I've done nothing wrong,' Rachael said. Tears began to form in her eyes. 'Apart from being a Jew.'

The woman stifled a sob.

'But why are the police looking for you?'

'They're rounding up all Jews and sending us to Germany.'

'But not French Jews, surely? The government will protect them.'

Rachael shook her head. 'But I'm not French. I'm German. We fled the Nazis in '37. We thought we'd be safe in France.'

'But the Germans occupy the north. This is the Free Zone. You're quite safe here.'

Rachael shook her head violently. 'Not anymore. Premier Laval has ordered that all Jews be taken to camps, even in the Free Zone. Children included. They say the Nazis haven't demanded the children but Laval is offering them up, nonetheless.'

'But Maréchal Pétain —'

'Is doing nothing. He doesn't care. Not for the likes of us. Not even though my husband joined the army. He was a surgeon.'

Sympathy raced over the woman's face. 'Where is your husband now?'

Rachael shook her head. She had no idea, had not heard from him in the two years since the fall of France.

Then she took a deep breath. 'Madame, you must help me. Please. I beg you.'

'But what can I do?' The woman looked around in alarm, in case anyone was near, in case anyone might be listening.

Rachael pushed her child towards her. 'Take my little boy. He's only four. He'll be no problem. He's a good boy.'

'But I don't have enough money to feed my own family.'

Rachael scrabbled in her purse and handed over a thick wad of notes. 'It's my life savings. Use it for the child.'

The woman looked at the money and then at the little boy. She shook her head. 'I don't want your money.'

'You must take it to pay for David.'

The woman took a step backwards. 'I don't want the boy, either. It's too dangerous. If what you say is true then it will be a crime to hide him. It will put my family in danger.'

Rachael wept now. 'Please take him. You look kind. I can see that you love your daughter.' She fell silent, wringing her hands. Then she gasped and looked behind her. The foot-beats of the police were getting closer. She turned to the woman in anguish once again.

The woman opened her mouth and Rachael almost wept, certain now that the woman would refuse once again. But she fought back the tears and stood mute, her whole body pleading.

'You won't tell?' the woman asked, at last.

Rachael's heart thrilled with fragile hope. 'Not even under torture,' she said.

The woman looked horrified at her words. Then she reached out and took David's hand.

Rachael thrust the money at her. 'Thank you,' she said, hardly able to speak now. 'What's your name?'

The woman shook her head.

Rachael understood immediately. 'Of course.' Then she bent to kiss her son on the cheek and strode out of the street towards the line of police.

The little boy started to go after her but Viviane held his hand tightly. 'Maman's only gone for a little while,' she said. 'She's gone for a baguette. I'm going to look after you.'

Then she opened the door to her house, shepherding David in ahead of her.

'Who was that?' Celeste asked.

'A friend,' Viviane answered.

She stared into her daughter's face. 'Celeste, you must never tell anybody what has happened.'

'Not even Auntie Odette?'

'Especially not her. Nor Uncle Roland.'

Celeste shrugged and stared at the little boy who was beginning to snivel.

'Get a cup of water for him,' Viviane said. And then she glanced at the roll of notes in her hand and gasped. There must have been twenty thousand francs. It would be enough to feed the boy for many years. Then she bit her lip. How could she get food for him without a ration card? Without papers?

She bent down to the little boy and began to rifle through his pockets.

'What are you doing?' he wailed.

'I'm looking for your papers,' Viviane said, forcing brightness into her voice. 'Did your Maman give you any papers to look after?'

The boy shook his head.

Viviane stiffened. There was the sound of feet pounding on the street and then a hammering on the door.

'Open up,' cried a voice.

She put her fingers to her lips and gestured Celeste to take David into the kitchen. 'Don't either of you come out,' she hissed to her. 'And keep silent.'

She waited until Celeste had closed the door behind her, quickly brushed her hair and made her way to the door. The hammering grew more intense.

'There's no need to break the door down,' she said, throwing it open. The policeman was young, barely twenty.

'Pardon, madame,' he said, 'but have you seen a woman and a boy sneaking around nearby?'

Viviane shook her head.

'You're sure?'

'Certain.' She gave him a smile. 'What has she done? Has she been selling things she shouldn't?' She stepped closer to him. 'You can tell me.'

The boy reddened. 'No, I'm not at liberty to.'

'Never mind,' Viviane said. 'I know you can't. I was only teasing you.'

The boy swallowed. 'If you see anyone you must report it.'

'Of course. Shall I report to you?' She touched him on the arm. 'Or to my brother-in-law, Capitaine Boyer?'

The boy stiffened. 'I did not realise you were related to the Capitaine, madame.' He bowed. 'Please forgive me for troubling you.'

He turned on his heel and hurried off. Viviane closed the door and leaned against it, her heart pumping fast.

Now what do I do, she wondered.

Slowly, she made her way to the kitchen. Celeste had sat David down with a cup of water and was telling him about her best friend, Monique. He looked terrified, on the verge of tears.

'How about some supper?' Vivian asked brightly.

'Yes please,' Celeste said. 'You'd like some supper wouldn't you, David?'

The little boy nodded but did not speak.

There was half a baguette in the pantry, bought yesterday and now hard and dry. Viviane sliced it thinly, poured a little milk into a saucer, and soaked the slices in it until they had softened a little. Then she put half onto a second saucer and placed both in front of the children. She would not eat tonight.

Her mind raced, anxious about how she was going to get enough food for the boy when she barely had enough for the family. The sooner her husband returned home, the better.

In the meantime, she thought miserably, she might have to go to her parents.

'Come on children,' she said brightly, time for a wash and then bed.'

She poured some water into a basin and watched as Celeste gave herself a quick rub down. 'Your turn, David,' she said.

'But I always have a bath before bedtime,' he said. 'And where's Maman?' He gave Viviane an imploring look. 'You said she'd gone to the shop.'

Viviane couldn't think what to say.

'Perhaps David's Maman's gone to his auntie,' Celeste said. 'Have you got an auntie, David?'

'Auntie Ursula.'

'Well that's it then,' Viviane said, kindly. 'She's gone to see your Auntie Ursula.'

'But why?'

'She didn't say.'

David heard this with suspicion. 'Will Maman be back soon?' he whispered. 'Auntie Ursula lives a long way away.'

'She won't be back tonight,' Viviane said. 'Tonight you're going to sleep in Celeste's bed.'

David nodded, his face wobbly with distress.

She took the children up the stairs and tucked them both into Celeste's bed. She kissed her daughter on the forehead. She wondered whether to do the same to the boy but decided not to. She snuffed out the candle, shut the door behind her and went downstairs.

She flung herself into her chair and wondered what on earth she had done.

She went to bed eventually but sleep eluded her for a long while.

She dared not dwell on what she had done in taking the boy in. She must have lost her mind. It was such a risky, foolish thing to do. She had placed herself and the whole family in jeopardy.

To take her mind from such thoughts, she went over all the food she had in the house. A few tins of peas, a chunk of saucisson, an old brie which was oozing so much it seemed like butter, a bottle of olive oil, two tomatoes and half a pepper. If she bought bread tomorrow, there would be enough for two days.

Perhaps I should take him to the police she thought as she finally drifted into sleep. But it was a troubled sleep, with dreams about houses which she could not leave because they had no doors, rooms full of strangers with staring eyes and a clock with hands which raced around the dial.

She woke, sweating from the heat. The city streets beyond her window seemed to pant like a wild beast.

The image of David's mother came into her mind. What must she be going through now? What horrors await her? Perhaps she would go to prison or be sent to a factory to work.

But no, surely she was wrong. The Maréchal would not allow such a thing. It was all a terrible mistake which he would rectify in the next few days. Or perhaps it was a rumour set running by the English or the Americans, a rumour designed to blacken the Maréchal's name. These things might happen in the north, she decided, in the part of France occupied by the Germans. But not here. Not in the Free Zone.

# THE FAMILY
### *Grasse, August 1942*

Viviane got dressed quickly. It was very early, five in the morning, but she knew that she had to be out soon in order to get any chance of buying food. She pressed her ear to her daughter's bedroom door. Celeste was singing quietly and in the background came the sound of faltering humming from the little boy.

Viviane felt sick, a flood of nausea which swelled across her stomach and then, just as abruptly subsided, then swelled once again. What had she been thinking when she took the boy? How could she jeopardise them all in such a way?

She pushed her fingers through her hair and hurried down the stairs to the living room. She was horrified to see a little backpack by the table. Where had that come from? It must belong to the child. He must have brought it with him when he entered the house although she could not for the life of her remember seeing it. She picked it up and put it on the table. Inside were neatly packed clothes, of good quality, some tiny children's books and a teddy bear. He must have been distraught last night not to have asked for it.

At the bottom of the bag was a picture. It was of Rachael holding a baby beside a short, dark man with pencil moustache and wide grin. She turned it over. Someone had written on the reverse, 'Our new family, June 3rd, 1938. Aaron, Rachael, David.'

So that would make David four years old. He was small for his age but bright and articulate. I hope he doesn't remember too much of his old life, she thought. It would be bad for him and dangerous for us. The sooner he forgets his family, the better.

She racked her brain to recall Celeste at that age. How much had she known at the time, how much did she communicate? She remembered her ceaseless chatter but not what it was about. Probably little more than endless questions and comments on whatever was happening around her.

A smile came to her mouth. Not so very different from now in fact. Her heart welled up with love for her child. And was replaced just as swiftly with terror for her.

She closed her eyes, aware that she now seemed to accept that she would keep the boy, despite the risks. 'No,' she whispered. 'I haven't made up my mind yet.'

What would be the punishment for hiding a Jewish child? If Rachael had been right then the Maréchal's government was working with the Germans. And the Nazis were said to hate the Jews. She groaned a little.

But then she heard the patter of feet coming down the stairs, Celeste already dressed and David in the underpants he had worn in bed. He looked desperate and glanced around the room. 'Maman?' he asked.

'She's not here yet,' Viviane said. 'She must still be with Auntie Ursula.'

David wailed in despair. Celeste looked distraught. Viviane, without thought, stepped over to the boy and picked him up, hugged him close and rocked him gently, crooning nonsense words all the while. After a little he stopped crying and looked up at her.

'I'm hungry,' he said.

'Then I'll go to the shops and get some bread.'

She told Celeste to help David dress while she went to the bakers. Celeste grew fractious at this for she loved going to the baker with her mother, to gaze at the bread and the increasingly rare sweet bun or tart.

'If I don't go this minute there won't be anything left,' Viviane said. 'So you just do what you're told and I'll be back in a moment.'

She grabbed her purse and unlocked the door, peering up and down the street nervously before stepping out. She shut the door behind her and, after a moment's indecision, decided not to lock it. Celeste would do as she was told, she was certain of it, and to lock the children in was too risky. There had been several fires this long, hot summer and too few firemen to put them out.

She turned right and made quickly for the Place aux Herbes. There were already a long line of market stalls setting up although there were pitifully few items being loaded onto them. Her husband's place stood vacant as it had for the last three weeks. She sighed, angrily. She knew that he was working hard for them in Marseille but she missed him. She needed him here, immediately, more than ever.

The boulangerie already had a queue of half a dozen women outside the door. She took her place in the line, nodding at the old lady in front of her. There was only the most subdued conversation and she felt suddenly bereft.

In the past, before the war, there would have been lots of talk: about how slow the queue was, how much the shopkeepers were charging, gossip about neighbours, about how young people were so loud and had too much money, about how bad or good the mayor was, according to a person's politics. How the perfume factory was going from bad to worse or good to better, according to the position one's husband held in it. About the forthcoming dance or fête. About the doings of the church and how Father Sebastian seemed to be turning senile, and the fine young priest the bishop had sent to assist him. The priest who seemed to be perpetually blushing because of the looks that women gave him, women who should have known better, did know better, but could not help themselves.

She neared the counter and was relieved to see that there were three baguettes still on the shelf. 'There's no more,' Monsieur Blanche called to the women at the back of the queue. 'I'm baking again later but there won't be much even then.'

Madame Couset stepped up to be served and Viviane held her breath. She had plenty of money and was known to brazenly attempt to buy anything left in the shop. But before she opened her mouth, Monsieur Blanche held up one finger. 'One baguette only, today, Madame,' he said.

'That's all I wanted,' Madame Couset said, although no one in the queue believed her. She almost flung the money at Monsieur Blanche and strode out of the shop like a woman who had endured the foulest of insults.

The old lady next in line bought half a baguette and smiled sweetly at Viviane as she left.

'A half or a whole one, Viviane?' Monsieur Blanche asked, his eyebrows raised.

'What do you think?' she asked.

The boulanger grinned and wrapped a slip of paper around a whole baguette. It was hot from the oven. She paid the money and smiled sweetly at Madame Dernier who was immediately behind her in the queue. She would have to content herself with half a baguette she thought.

'Is your husband still away?' Madame Dernier asked, with a glance at the baguette, insinuating that Viviane had no need of a whole one.

'Yes. But I'm expecting him back today or tomorrow.'

The woman stared at her coolly, unconvinced.

Viviane ignored her and walked out of the shop. She gasped in alarm at what met her eyes. Celeste was standing on the far side of the place, holding David firmly by the hand. Even worse, her sister Odette was marching towards them.

She flew across the cobbles, dodging through the stall holders who were busy setting out their wares, banging into two old men who moaned at her for being so clumsy. But she was too late. Odette had approached the children and was already questioning Celeste.

'Hello,' Viviane said breathlessly, as she reached them.

'Why is Celeste out on her own?' Odette demanded. 'And who is this boy?'

Viviane forced a smile. In the hours she had lain awake she had come up with an explanation.

'He's the son of my old pen-friend, Simone Legarde,' she said. 'We started to write when we were at school.'

'I didn't know you had a pen-friend.' Odette's tone was hard and suspicious.

'You don't know everything about me,' Viviane said.

'So why is her son here?' Odette said.

Viviane took her to one side and lowered her voice. 'Because he's an orphan. His parents died in an air-raid.'

'Where?'

'Where they lived.'

'And where's that?'

'Near Paris,' she said desperately. She was sure there had been a big allied air-raid on the automobile factories west of the city in the spring, raids which had killed many civilians.

Odette looked unconvinced but decided to let it go for now. 'So why is the child with you? Why isn't he in Paris?'

'Because Simone had no family, nor her husband. Her friend brought him here and asked me to look after him. It's better than him being taken to some orphanage.'

'And you agreed?' Odette asked in astonishment.

Viviane nodded. Antagonism to Odette was flaring with every word her sister spoke.

'Well, we'll see about that,' Odette said. 'We're going to Maman's.' She grabbed Celeste by the hand and marched off.

'What's it to do with Maman?' Viviane demanded, hurrying to keep up with her.

'If it involves Celeste it involves Maman.'

'Celeste is my daughter.'

'Then you should have better regard for her.'

Viviane swore quietly.

'And speaking like that in front of her is part of what I mean.'

Viviane gave her a filthy look and then her heart quailed. Where was David? She turned to look behind her and she gasped. He was nowhere to be seen. She started back the way she had come, her feet stumbling on the cobbles. And then she saw him, sitting in a gutter, howling in distress. Two old women were hurrying towards him, arms wide with concern.

She flew to him, plucked him up and mumbled words of comfort. Out of the corner of her eye she saw the look in the faces of several women, disgusted that she had left such a small child.

'No better than she should be,' one of the women muttered. 'Her mother must be ashamed.'

She ignored them and hurried after her sister, desperate not to draw any more attention to herself.

She reached her parent's street just in time to see Odette stride into their house, comfortable, confident, pushing Celeste ahead of her. She glanced up the street, caught a glimpse of Viviane and slammed the door behind her.

Viviane stared at the door angrily as she marched up to it. She hesitated on the door-step, the familiar lump in her throat. But then she took a deep breath and walked in.

'What's this Odette's told me?' her mother demanded, hand pressed angrily against her hip. 'What's going on?'

'Good morning to you, as well, Maman,' Viviane said.

'Enough of your cheek, young lady,' her mother said. 'Odette says she found Celeste wandering the streets on her own. And who is this child?' Her finger pointed like a stick at David's face, making his face pucker up.

'He's the son of my old pen-friend,' Viviane said. 'She and her husband died in an air-raid and one of her neighbours brought him here for safe-keeping.'

'Where was this air-raid?'

'Near Paris.'

Her mother's face took on a look of disbelief. 'And this neighbour came all this way, crossed the border from the Occupied Zone. To bring him here? To you? I don't believe it.'

'That's your prerogative. But it's the truth.'

Her mother's eyes drilled into her face. Viviane knew she could not withstand such piercing scrutiny for long and she turned towards Celeste.

'Have you kissed Grandmaman?' she asked.

'Yes,' Celeste answered, brightly. 'She said we could have breakfast here.'

'That's very kind, Maman,' Viviane said. She held out the baguette, hoping she would not take it.

Her mother snatched the bread without a thank you and flung it on the table.

'So what are you going to do about this boy?' she demanded.

Viviane rubbed her forehead wearily. 'I don't know. I haven't thought.'

'That's no surprise. Well, you need to think, at once. You can't look after the child so what are you going to do with him? Send him home?'

'He has no home, it was destroyed by the bombers.'

'Then he should go to an orphanage,' Odette said. 'The nuns at the convent will take him.'

Viviane did not reply. She was not a believer, but she didn't think it right that a Jewish boy should be brought up by Catholic nuns. On the other hand, it might be the best solution.

'Or won't your Satanic beliefs allow you to send him there?' said her mother.

If there was one thing which caused Viviane to adopt one path instead of another it was the views of her mother. No sooner had her mother taken one stance, then she would take the opposite. She took delight in opposing what her mother advocated and it was a response she no longer tried to control. Sometimes, when she was being charitable, she thought that her mother acted in the same way to her.

'It's nothing to do with my beliefs,' she snapped. 'It's what's right for the child.'

Her mother sighed. 'Has he got a ration card?'

Viviane shook her head.

'And yet you think it's right for the boy to go hungry and poorly clothed? How on earth do you think you can support him without a ration card or money. And with such a feckless husband as yours.'

'Keep Alain out of it, Maman.' Viviane was aware of the anger in her voice.

'I suppose the fool is all for keeping the child.'

'He's still in Marseilles, Maman,' Odette said. 'With his seedy friends, no doubt.'

Viviane did not respond. Arguments about Alain took a well-worn, predictable path and one she had never yet negotiated successfully.

'Leave the girl alone,' came a gravelly voice from the kitchen.

Her father came into the room, in his vest, with a towel around his neck which was bleeding from the blunt razor he had just used.

David stared wide-eyed at him. He was on crutches, and his right leg swung above the ground, trousers tied just below where his knee should have been.

'Had an eyeful, young feller?' he said.

'Where's the rest of your leg?' David asked.

'In Verdun,' he answered. 'Along with my dreams.'

'We don't want to hear about your war, Georges,' his wife said. 'This one is bad enough for all of us.'

'The boy looks as though he might be interested.'

David took a step closer. 'Were you a soldier?' he asked, his eyes shining with excitement. 'My grandpa was a soldier but he died in the fighting.'

Viviane's throat clenched in fear. David's grandfather would have been in the German army, not the French.

She ruffled David's hair fondly. 'Let's not talk about war and horrible things,' she said. 'My mother has a pussy cat, called Gingembre. Would you like to see her?'

David nodded.

'Take him into the yard,' Viviane told Celeste. 'See if Gingembre is there.'

'She will be,' her father said. 'Lazing in the sun. Just like all the females I'm responsible for.'

He lowered himself into his chair. 'Now, Viviane,' he said, 'what are you getting your mother all vexed about?'

Viviane told the story about her pen-friend once again. She had the uncomfortable feeling that he believed it as little as her mother did. When she finished, he reached for his pipe and began to clean it. He worked slowly, carefully but, although he seemed to be concentrating fully on the job in hand, his wife and his daughters knew he was carefully thinking things through.

Finally, he put the pipe on the table next to his chair.

'Are you sure you want to take the boy?' he asked.

'I have an obligation to my old friend.'

'I don't even recall you having a pen-friend,' her mother snorted, glancing at Odette for support.

But her husband held up his hand for silence, all the while staring thoughtfully at Viviane. 'And, even if you believe that you have an obligation to your friend, do you want to take the boy in?'

'Yes.'

'It might be for years.'

'Nevertheless.' She gave a quick nod.

Her father picked up the pipe again, sucked on it, then began to pack it with some shreds of tobacco.

'Have you thought about what your mother said?' he asked, finally. 'About how to feed and clothe the boy?'

For a moment, Viviane did not know how to answer. Then she rummaged in her purse and brought out the rolled up bank-notes. The family stared at the money in astonishment. Then Georges whistled.

'The boy must have been greatly loved,' he said. 'You'd better be sure you can live up to that.'

'I'll try, Papa,' Viviane said.

Her mother snorted with contempt but realised that this was now an end to the matter.

Georges turned to David. 'Would you like some breakfast, boy? With some honey from my brother's bees.'

David nodded eagerly.

'We're all victims of wars,' Georges said, although as much to himself as to the others.

## GERARD PITHOU
### *August 1942*

Viviane could not wait to leave her parents' house. Despite eating little the day before, she could barely swallow the few bits of bread she put in her mouth. Finally, her father beckoned her to give him a kiss. 'You're a foolish girl,' he said. 'But a good one.'

She smiled and called Celeste and David.

'Au revoir, Maman,' she said.

Her mother nodded curtly and looked away. Viviane made for the door. The ordeal was over.

The streets were filling up with people now, housewives searching for any shops with food to sell, men lounging on street corners, a few people sitting over coffee or wine at one or other of the cafes which still remained open.

She cursed that all her bread had been eaten by the family; she had planned on it lasting for a few days. Perhaps she would go back for more later today. But no, she thought, Monsieur Blanche will be suspicious that she'd eaten so much. In the past, before the war, he would not have cared how much anyone ate, as long as they paid. But now he had to pay heed to rations and regulations as well as having his own finely-tuned belief in giving people fair shares, no more, no less. He was a good man and without him, she felt sure they would have been much hungrier.

One of the market stalls had a small mound of peppers, onions and two courgettes. She could make a stew out of these, she thought, and reached into her bag for some money. Fruit and vegetables were still off ration although they were in short supply and she always took the opportunity to buy some, when she had the chance. She could not remember a time when she had last eaten a good piece of meat.

She paid for her purchases and hurried home. The sooner she got David off the street, the better. She realised that she would have to tell Celeste the story about his parents dying in an air-raid without him over-hearing. And firmly tell her not to repeat the story to him. At least, not for the present.

They spent the day in the house, not an unusual thing in the heat of the summer. The children played in the tiny back-yard, laughing with pleasure at their games. Viviane had to go out frequently to tell them to keep quiet, fearful that the neighbours would hear David's voice and grow suspicious.

Time after time, she counted out the money that David's mother had given her. She had never seen so much. She kept doing the sums in her head. It would feed and clothe David for a couple of years, she thought. Would that be enough? Could things really stay so bad for so long?

Most people thought that once Britain was defeated the Germans would moderate their demands and things would get back to normal. There would be more food on the table, regulations would be eased, perhaps the Germans would even end the occupation of the north and France would be whole again.

But Britain refused to surrender.

The Nazis claimed that London had been destroyed, that the Royal family had fled to Canada and there was looting on the streets of Britain.

But whenever Alain listened to the broadcasts from the BBC the British never admitted to any of this. They remained defiant. And now, since the Americans had joined the war, almost exultant.

She put her head in her hands. She couldn't see what would be for the best, for the allies or for the Germans to win. She just wanted this horrible war to be over.

She looked at the money once more. It might be enough to feed and clothe David but how would she buy the things he needed if he didn't have his ration book? There was the black market, of course, which was, after all, how Alain made most of his money. But that was normally only just enough to keep starvation at bay. And David was going to get bigger and hungrier all the time.

What would happen if the war lasted another ten years, she thought, the panic beginning to build in her throat. She could never keep David a secret for that long. Never even feed him.

A heavy knock sounded on the door.

'Who is it?' she asked, trying to quell the anxiety in her voice.

'It's Gerard.'

She sighed. Gerard was one of Alain's oldest friends. She slid back the lock and let him in.

He was a big man, tall and broad, and very ungainly. He seemed to fill any room he was in, and she always felt anxious for her few ornaments when he moved about.

He was always very polite, punctilious in fact, although he sometimes seemed nervous in her presence. Occasionally she caught him staring at her which made her feel both amused and a little uncomfortable. But she would immediately chide herself for such a reaction and never mentioned it to Alain. Celeste was very fond of him because he spoilt her terribly.

'Is Alain here?' he asked.

She shook her head. 'He's still away.'

'He must be doing a good deal of business.'

She smiled. 'Let's hope so.'

He did not answer and the silence grew heavy. 'Do you want some coffee?' she asked although she had little left.

'Thank you,' Gerard said and threw himself into a chair which creaked in complaint.

She came back from the kitchen a little later to find he had left the chair and was standing at the window staring out at the yard.

'Who's the little boy?' he asked with a frown.

'The son of one of my friends,' Viviane said lightly. 'It's not very good coffee, I'm afraid,' she added quickly to divert his attention.

'We must all make do in these troubled times,' Gerard said. 'Did you read the latest announcement from Monsieur Laval? It seems that the relève is not working as well as it might.'

'I don't know what the relève is.'

Gerard looked surprised. 'The plan to release one of our prisoners-of-war in exchange for every three men who volunteer to go to work in Germany.' He shook his head bitterly. 'There are too few patriots nowadays. Not enough men are volunteering to go so our soldiers must continue to be captives.'

'And you?' Viviane asked. 'Have you volunteered?'

'Not yet.'

Viviane nodded but made no comment.

Gerard gestured to the window. 'Why is the boy with you? Where is his mother?'

Viviane took a deep breath. 'She's dead, I'm afraid. And his father.' And then she told him the story she had concocted.

'And you've informed the authorities?' he asked.

'Not yet. I'll wait until Alain comes home. It will take hours at the Mairie and the police station and the children will fret if I take them with me. Alain will tell them.'

'It will be necessary.' He frowned at the boy. 'He's very dark,' he said.

'His father was as well,' she said. 'I think he may have been from Corsica.'

Gerard drained off the coffee. 'If you want, I could go to the authorities for you.'

Viviane put her hand on Gerard's arm and gave it a squeeze. 'I wouldn't want you to go to the trouble. And Alain will be home soon.'

Gerard nodded, drained his cup in one loud gulp and made for the door. But as he stepped over the threshold his glance strayed once more to David.

'I won't forget, Gerard,' Viviane said, shutting the door behind him.

She looked through the window at the children. They were shrieking even more loudly now. Perhaps it would be best if she took them out. They could go for a walk in the countryside to the north of the town.

She rapped on the window. 'Come on, children. We're going for a walk.'


### DOROTHY
*Grasse, August 1942*

'Maman,' Celeste cried, 'there's a sick lady here.'

A car was parked awry against the side of the road. She grabbed Celeste and David and raced over to it.

There was only one person in the car, a middle-aged woman, slumped against the driving wheel. Viviane pulled open the door and shook her. She groaned, then lifted her head and stared at Viviane with glassy eyes.

'Madame?' Viviane said. 'Are you hurt? Did you crash?'

The woman shook her head. 'Neither. I just blacked-out, fainted.' She groaned once more and rested her head in her hands. Her voice sounded slurred and her accent a little hard to understand.

'I should get you to a doctor.'

'No need,' the woman said. 'It's a health problem, darling, not a crash. It happens all the time. I think I may have forgotten to take my pills.'

She looked up and smiled at the children, gazing wide eyed at the car. 'Nice kids,' she said.

'My daughter found you, madame. She brought me to help you. Please let me.'

'You wanna help me?'

'Of course.'

The woman shuffled into the passenger seat. 'Then drive me home.'

'But I've never driven a car before —'

'Nothing to it,' the woman said. 'You just put your foot on the gas pedal and steer the wheel. I'll do the clutch and stick.' She beckoned to the children. 'Hey kids, fancy a ride in an automobile?'

Viviane tried to object but the woman would not be contradicted. Although still a little confused, she was very clear in her instructions on how to drive.

A few minutes later Viviane was driving, white-knuckled, along the road leading out of Grasse.

'It's only a couple of miles,' the woman said.

'What's a mile?'

'Distance. Two miles is four kilometres, I guess.'

Viviane looked horrified at having to drive so far.

Ten minutes later the woman told Viviane to turn into a driveway. She did but steered too wildly and the woman had to grab the wheel to straighten the car up.

'Go easy, girl,' the woman said. 'It's not a race. My name's Dorothy, by the way.'

Viviane nodded. For the moment she couldn't even recall her own name. She got out of the car and gave her hand to the woman who waved her away and made for the villa.

Viviane stared at it in amazement. It was a grand villa. She had never seen such a magnificent place. There were half a dozen rooms downstairs, each of them as big as the ground-floor of their own little home. It was beautiful yet rather overwhelming.

'Welcome to Villa Laurel,' Dorothy said. 'Come into the garden-room and I'll order some tea.'

The room looked over a beautiful garden with a view to Grasse and beyond to the sea. The furniture in the room was astonishing. The sofa and chairs were covered with the most exquisite fabric, a large table polished until it gleamed and a huge chandelier caught the sunlight in a thousand sparkles.

Dorothy rummaged in a drawer for a bottle of pills. She swallowed a couple and slumped into a chair.

A young woman entered the room, carrying a large tray. She gave Dorothy a look of concern.

'Afternoon tea,' Dorothy said. 'With cakes.' She beamed at the children who rushed over to the young woman and stared wide-eyed at the food on the tray.

Viviane guessed that Dorothy was in her early fifties. She had chestnut coloured hair streaked with grey, cut short with considerable flair. She had a pleasant face, rather round and soft but with sharp nose and even sharper eyes. She must have been pretty when she was younger, although now her skin was dry and lined.

Her clothes, while casual, were of the finest quality. She wore a short linen jacket with a white silk blouse, highlighted by a bright red scarf. Instead of a skirt she wore a pair of slacks which must have been more practical for driving. Her shoes were light tan in colour and low-heeled.

She regarded Viviane with interest and a hint of amusement. She appeared to be completely recovered from her black-out.

'How are you, madame?' Viviane said.

'Absolutely fine. I just needed to get the horse-pills inside me.'

'Horse-pills?' Viviane shook her head in confusion.

'It's a figure of speech.'

The young woman gave Dorothy and Viviane a cup of pale tea and the children a lemon drink and then made to leave the room. But she paused as she opened the door and gave Viviane a thoughtful almost anxious look before closing it behind her.

'Is she your daughter?' Viviane asked.

'My servant. Marie. A nice kid.'

Viviane had never met anyone with a servant before. She hid her surprise by taking a sip of her tea, which was delicate and refreshing.

'Madame —' she began.

'Dorothy,' the woman said firmly. 'I don't hold with all this formality.'

'Is that because you're from Paris?'

Dorothy looked surprised. 'I'm not from Paris.'

'But your accent. And the way you act.'

'No, darling. I'm not even French. I'm American. From New York. And California.'

Viviane gasped. She had only ever seen Americans on cinema screens.

'So why are you here?' She knew she shouldn't be so intrusive but could not stop herself asking the question.

'It's a long story.'

'I like stories,' Viviane said.

'Can we play outside?' Celeste asked. Her mouth was full of cake. David had two, one in each hand.

'Of course, honey,' Dorothy said. 'Play on the grass and keep away from the pond. There's a cat out there called Groucho who loves being tickled.'

She got up, opened the door to the garden and the children raced out.

'I still don't know your name,' she said, smiling at Viviane. 'And I haven't thanked you properly for helping me out.'

'Viviane Renaud. And there's no need to thank me.'

Dorothy laughed, a warm, deep chuckle, and held out her hand. 'I'm Dorothy Pine,' she said. 'I hope we'll become friends.'

Viviane did not know how to answer that. It was not a thing any French woman of Dorothy's age would even think to say. She ate the last of her cake and took another sip of tea. She was burning with curiosity.

'You said it was a long story, Madame Pine...sorry, Dorothy.' She put her cup on the table beside her. 'I have the time.'

Dorothy looked at her thoughtfully. 'Well that's good, then. I don't get the chance to talk with intelligent people much anymore.'

She poured herself another cup of tea and replenished Viviane's cup. 'Tell me, Viviane, do you like the movies? Films?'

'Very much. But we rarely get the chance to see them now.'

'Well, honey, I've spent most of my life working in films. It was Charles who got me my first job, Charles Chaplin. I'd written a play off Broadway which he saw and he invited me to California to write the scripts for his films. Well, not scripts exactly, because they were silent films. I wrote the explanations of what was happening between scenes.

'That might seem easy work but getting the nub of the story and communicating it in a few words was a real art. And it paid, pretty well. I made a decent living for ten years.'

She stared at Viviane. 'Are you sure you want to hear all this?'

Viviane nodded and Dorothy shrugged before continuing. Viviane could see that she was pleased to do so.

'Well, then came the talkies. Suddenly every movie studio was desperate for writers. I was on the spot and well-respected. The work fell into my lap. I wrote, let me tell you, dozens and dozens of films in those first few years of talkies.'

'Are your films famous? Would I have seen them?'

Dorothy shook her head and grinned. 'They were mostly pot-boilers. Second features, sometimes even third. But I was also brought in whenever a big-name Eastern writer couldn't get the script right. I was never credited for this, because the studious didn't want to admit they'd hired a famous turkey and besides, I was a woman. But I helped some hot-shot guys get their names on the credits.'

Viviane was enthralled. 'And did you meet many stars?'

'Met them, partied with them, loved them. But then I had the bad luck of being introduced to Sebastian Pine. He was a lovely looking guy but no actor, even though he yearned to be. He was a stuntman, and not a particularly good one. But he was a charmer, at least at first, and he won my heart and we married.'

She picked up a cake, looked at it thoughtfully, bit off a chunk and swallowed it with barely a chew before continuing.

'Unfortunately, Sebastian charmed lots of other women as well as me. He charmed the clothes off many a young starlet. And then he started drinking and taking drugs. And finally, he started beating me.'

Viviane was wide-eyed at this.

'He hit me because I was more successful than he was, I guess.' Dorothy shook her head, wearily. 'Anyhow, after he broke my arm, I finally had enough. I left him and bought myself a little place in Oakwood, as far as possible from Sunset Strip where he hung out. I learnt to type one handed and kept on churning out the scripts.'

Viviane started to ask a question but thought better of it.

'Were you going to ask if I was rich?' Dorothy asked. 'Most people do?'

Viviane nodded, embarrassed that her question had been so transparent.

'Well, darling, I was rich enough to buy this place. I was sensible, you see, I never bought stocks so when Wall Street crashed it didn't do me much harm. I just saved and saved my cash.'

'And what about your husband? Did you see him again?'

'Only in passing. And then something bad happened to him.'

She took another sip of tea before continuing.

'I said he was a stuntman and not a good one at that. One day, the studio asked him to do a stunt which lots of the more experienced guys refused. But Sebastian was an idiot and thought too highly of himself. He did the stunt, it went wrong, and his back was broken clean in half.'

Viviane gasped.

'Sad, but he survived, although he had to use a wheel-chair. His bitch of a mother came west to look after him, because I certainly wasn't going to.'

She laughed. 'The old cow, who was sharper with money than the Rockefellers and Vanderbilts combined, decided that the studio was at fault for her darling son's accident and determined to sue. She didn't need to, for she was rich as Croesus already. She was widow to a rich man and when the Crash came, she figured that people would always need gas and a place to eat so she bought up lots of gas stations and diners at knock down prices.

'But despite her wealth she smelled the chance of wringing money from the studio so she set to work. Three years it took and then, just before it went to court, the studio decided to cave in to avoid any bad publicity. They settled quietly, and Sebastian suddenly found he was a rich man. But not for long.

'A week after the money had been paid into his account, his mother was wheeling him in the Hollywood Hills when she had a heart attack. A doctor was on the scene but he was too late to save her.'

She chuckled to herself. 'Sebastian was now one of the richest men in California, not only having the settlement from the studio but also all of his mother's wealth as well. One of the richest men in California for all of sixty seconds.

'For while everyone was attending his mother nobody noticed that Sebastian was unwillingly undertaking his final stunt.'

Dorothy leaned forward in her chair, pleased that this story was enthralling Viviane every bit as much as her scripts had enthralled film-goers.

'The road where his mother died was steep,' she continued, 'very steep. Her hands had slipped from the wheelchair, of course, and it began to trundle down the hill. It quickly picked up speed and Sebastian began to holler. Some folk said he sounded scared, others that he was chortling with joy at the speed and the danger.

'Anyhow, he didn't stop at the junction and his wheelchair careered into the oncoming traffic. He was hit by a truck and killed instantly. Do you want to know something ironic?'

Viviane nodded.

'The truck was owned by the studio which had just paid him off. Suspicious, you might say. Even worse, the truck was being driven by a useless distant cousin of the studio boss. Let me tell you, Viviane, it did not look good.'

'So what happened?'

'The studio took fright and they paid me a goodly sum to agree that I would never take any legal action against them. And, although I was separated from Sebastian, I was still his wife so I inherited everything he owned, his pay-off and all his mother's gas stations and diners.'

Viviane's gaze went around the room.

'But just remember, honey,' Dorothy said in a rather sharper tone, 'I bought this villa out of my own money, out of the money I'd earned writing scripts. Not a cent from him or his ma paid for this.'

'Of course,' Viviane said.

'Not that what I inherited doesn't help,' Dorothy added with a smile. 'I lead a pretty good life, or at least I did until this war came.'

'So why didn't you leave when the war started? A lot of the English did.'

Dorothy shrugged.

'Britain was at war with Germany. America wasn't. I figured it probably never would be and besides, it wasn't easy to find a way of getting back to the States from here. I was feeling quite content until that madman Hitler declared war on the US. More fool him, I say.'

She poured them both a third cup of tea, which Viviane thought delightfully extravagant. 'So I'm stuck here for the duration as they say. I just hope that Mr Churchill and Mr Roosevelt get a move on and liberate us before things get any worse.'

Viviane felt deflated by her words. 'Surely they can't get worse? The Maréchal won't allow it.'

Dorothy frowned and rose from her chair. She went over to a sideboard and poured two large glasses of cognac. She thrust one towards Viviane who took a sip and sighed with pleasure. It was excellent.

Dorothy gave Viviane a rather pitying look. 'I fear you've got a rather exalted view of your Maréchal Pétain if you think he's gonna protect you from the Nazis.'

Viviane was shocked. 'But he's our President. And a war-hero.'

'Listen, honey, the world is like a school playground. Pétain and Laval may once have been big kids in the playground but then a bigger bully with a Charlie Chaplin moustache came along. He's the one calling all the shots, now. If Hitler says jump, Pétain and Laval will ask how high.'

The noise of the children chasing a cat floated through the open window.

'Nice kids,' Dorothy said, aware that her comment had deflated Viviane and wishing to make amends.

'Thank you.' She gave a weary smile.

'Are they both yours? They don't look alike.'

'Yes they are,' Viviane said quickly. 'Celeste takes after me, David after his father.'

Dorothy stared at her, thoughtfully. 'Well, what do you know,' she said. 'That's nice.'

She doesn't believe me, Viviane thought in panic, wondering what she could say to make it sound the truth. But before she came up with the answer, Dorothy began to speak once again.

'Do you believe my life story, honey?' she asked.

'Of course I do.'

'Well maybe you shouldn't. Maybe I was spinning a yarn. I'm a writer after all.'

Viviane looked shocked. 'But why would you do that?'

'People tell lies for all sorts of reasons, to make themselves look better than they are, because they like fooling people or just for the fun of it. Or in order to survive.' She leaned over and touched her arm. 'If you ever have to tell lies, Viviane, just make sure they're convincing.'

Viviane felt the breath catch in her chest. The American had seen through her concerning David. Straight away.

'I need to go, madame,' she said.

'Of course. I'll drive you.'

'There's no need.'

'But I insist.' She got to her feet and picked up her purse. 'I hope we can be friends,' she said. 'You and your husband. And your delightful children, of course.'

'I hope so, too,' Viviane said, although she was desperate to flee from the American.


## A SURPRISE
*Grasse, August 1942*

The door was open when she arrived, which shocked her. She had got used to locking it since the war, because of the danger from looters. Perhaps the strain of David was already beginning to tell on her.

She walked into the house and gave a cry of pleasure.

Alain was sitting on his usual chair, with a bottle of wine in front of him. He leapt up and pulled her into his arms and she breathed in his familiar scent of warm skin, leather jacket and cigarettes.

'You've been gone so long,' she said.

He nodded. 'That's true. But it was a very profitable trip. My contacts proved even better than I hoped, Viv, much better. They were very keen to do business, I can tell you. He pulled a packet of cigarettes from his pocket.

'Lucky Strike,' she said. 'American cigarettes. How did you get them?'

He tapped his finger on his nose and then chuckled. 'To be honest, I'm not entirely sure. And with the men I was dealing with, I soon learnt not to ask more than the minimum of questions.'

Then he glanced over her shoulder and whooped with delight. 'Hello, angel. How's my beautiful girl?'

Celeste giggled and clutched his leg. He reached down and pulled her up with one hand, dragging her into the hug. 'Home sweet home,' he cried.

'Does David get a hug too?' Celeste asked.

He stared at her in confusion, then at Viviane.

'There's David,' Celeste said, pointing to the door.

For once, Alain was lost for words.

'You can't keep him.' Alain said after a sparse meal. He spoke quietly but there was no mistaking that he had made up his mind. No mistaking his determination.

'Do you think I don't know that?' Viviane said. She angrily scraped back a lock of her hair but it slipped down her forehead immediately.

'There's Celeste to think about,' Alain continued.

'I'm not a fool,' she snapped.

Her eyes slipped from her daughter to the little boy on the couch. He was sleeping, contented, innocent. But he was a danger to them all.

'The Maréchal's prudence has kept the Germans off our backs.' Alain said. 'We would do well to copy him.'

Viviane nodded. Maréchal Pétain was the father of the nation, she knew that. If it weren't for him her father would almost certainly have died in the Great War, another sacrifice of blood at Verdun. And now the Maréchal was keeping the Germans at bay, a sure shield for France and its people.

Her thoughts slipped along these well-worn tracks. Over the last few years they had become a litany in her mind, almost a talisman, a token of hope. But then she thought, does the Maréchal know what his government is doing to the Jews?'

'We cannot keep a fugitive child,' Alain continued.

'He's not a fugitive,' Viviane cried. She was astonished at the strength of her feelings, at the words which flooded from her mouth. 'How can a child be a fugitive? How can he be a criminal? Look at him, Alain, he's tiny, fragile, vulnerable. How can we think he's a danger? How can we even think of surrendering him to the police? To the Nazis?'

Her words were manifestation of her pent-up frustration and fury at the long years of privation and hopelessness.

Alain stared at her in silence. She thought for a moment that he looked bitter, accusatory. Perhaps he did although as the silence seethed between them she sensed his look begin to change.

'But what about Celeste?' he murmured at last. 'If we are condemned for taking in this child, then what will happen to her?'

'Trust me,' she said.

'And food?' he continued. 'We have little enough to feed ourselves. How will we feed him?' He took a step towards the sleeping boy. 'Did his mother give you ration books for him?'

She shook her head.

'Papers?'

Again, she shook her head.

'I know his name. His first name at any rate. It's David.'

Alain sighed. 'Thank heavens for that. It might have been Moses or Aaron.'

He made the sign of scissors in the air. 'Has he been…?'

'Yes.'

Alain shrugged. 'North Africans are also circumcised. Perhaps we could pass him off as one of them.'

Viviane began to relax. Alain's practical nature, his love of problem-solving, was beginning to combat his doubts about the child.

But then she began to panic. Did this really mean they would keep the child? That they would put the family, all of them, in danger? That they would run the risk of discovery?

She realised that until her explosion of temper part of her had hoped Alain would persuade her to hand the child in to the authorities. Now, that sensible choice was drifting further out of reach.

'Are you sure?' she asked nervously. 'About keeping the child?'

Alain shook his head. 'Not at all. And I don't think you are either. But I can't see us giving him up to a life in prison.'

He gave a crooked smile. 'But we'll have to come up with a good story. A very good one.'

'I have a story,' Viviane said. 'I'm not sure how good it is but I've told my family already.'

'So you won't be able to change it without Odette and your mother getting suspicious?'

'Exactly.'

He opened his arms widely. 'Come on then. Tell me the story so I can remember it.'

She did so with a heavy heart, knowing that it was full of weaknesses and that he would have been able to fabricate something much more convincing.

But when she finished, he beamed at her.

'That's pretty good, Viv. Especially when you think how rushed you must have been to come up with it.'

'You don't think we should change it? Or add to it, perhaps?'

He shook his head. 'We can't change it now. And the simpler the better. It doesn't matter that it's a little fantastic. The whole world has gone crazy, what's a little extra madness about your pen-friend matter in comparison?' He rubbed his fingers on his lips. 'Did you really have a pen-friend?'

Viviane nodded. 'But we only wrote two letters each. Simone's writing was very hard to read and my letters were full of ink-blots.'

'Have you kept hers?'

'Possibly. Why?'

'Another bit of proof, should we need it.' He rubbed his hands together. He was beginning to get excited about the intrigue.

'There's something more,' she said. She opened her bag and pulled out the wad of money Rachael had given to her.

Alain whistled in astonishment. 'That's a lot of cash. A lot.'

'It's enough to feed the boy for several years.'

'It's a start.'

'Do you think we'll need longer?' Tears began to well in her eyes. 'Oh, Alain, how long do you think this wretched war will go on? Will Celeste ever have a normal life?'

He took her hand in his. 'General de Gaulle says we will be free one day. And the British are still fighting.'

'But Gerard says London is in ruins.'

'I wouldn't put too much faith in what Gerard says. And even if the British are defeated there's the Americans.'

'Gerard said that the Luftwaffe are bombing New York as well.'

Alain shook his head. 'I can't see that, Viv, it's too far away.'

'Not even with secret weapons?'

Alain sighed. It was getting more difficult to stay optimistic.

'Let's not think about all that,' he said. 'Let's think about our future and how we make the best of it.' He pulled another wad of notes from his pocket. 'And see, you're not the only one with a pile of banknotes.'


## MAJOR WEISER
### *Paris and Dijon, September 1942*

Major Ernst Weiser swallowed the rest of his wine in one mouthful; a waste because it was a fine Burgundy. His eyes were gripped by the lorries careering along the road towards the north-east. Lorries packed with people.

'The French are taking them to Drancy,' his friend Otto Mundt said.

'Jews?'

'Yes. And then on to the work camps in the east.'

Weiser raised one eyebrow. He had little liking for Jews but he suspected that they would be worked to death in the camps. He'd always favoured sending them to Madagascar but when he argued this once too often his commanding officer advised him to keep such views to himself. He had done so ever since, scrupulously.

'The French are keen to help us in this task,' Mundt said.

'They know what's good for them,' Weiser said. 'The more they co-operate, the better life will be for them. That old fool Pétain understands that, at least.'

The last of the lorries disappeared, leaving a smell of diesel and something else lingering on the air.

Weiser sniffed. 'Shit and piss and vomit. And terror.' He shook his head, wearily.

'Are you surprised?' Mundt asked. 'They're civilians and they must be terrified.'

'I pissed and shit and vomited at Leningrad,' Weiser said. 'As did you, I recall.'

He raised an eyebrow. 'Yes, but even at the time I was proud that I could claim it was good Aryan waste matter.'

'Careful, Otto,' Weiser said. 'Walls have ears.'

Mundt shrugged, unconcerned. 'I suppose Hitler's made us great again. Better than the old Kaiser did at any rate. Better even than Napoleon achieved for the French.'

'It was we who defeated Napoleon,' Weiser said. 'Blücher cut him down to size at Waterloo. The French still hate us for it.'

'Let them hate.' Mundt swigged the last of his wine and gestured to a waiter to bring another bottle. 'As long as they continue making such excellent wine.'

Their food arrived shortly after. Weiser had ordered a steak, cooked rare, with green beans and fried potatoes. Mundt's was a delicate river trout with little peas and carrots.

'The French know how to cook,' Weiser said.

'Except they get little food to cook with anymore,' Mundt said with a chuckle.

Weiser glanced at the passers-by. They were skinny, many with sunken cheeks and dark eyes. A quarter of the food produced in France was shipped off to Germany, leaving the people on the edge of starvation.

Weiser examined the steak on his fork. This, presumably, came from French farms. He put it in his mouth, savouring the excellent taste. Such was the fate of conquered people the world over. And such was the reward of their conquerors.

'I've got some disappointing news for us both,' Weiser said when they had finished their meal and were sipping some cognac.

Mundt's eyes widened with alarm. They had already spent two winters in the horror of Russia; surely that must be enough for any man.

Weiser shook his head, guessing what was going through his friend's mind. 'Not as disappointing as you fear,' he said. 'We're being sent somewhere warmer. Burgundy, in fact.'

Mundt sighed in relief. 'I like Paris but I'm sure I'll manage in the land of wine. How did you wangle such a good posting?'

'I didn't.' Weiser's face became more serious. 'I'm guessing that we're not being sent for our health.' He slapped his friend on the shoulder. 'Certainly not your health, with so much wine close to hand.'

Mundt laughed and took out a pack of cigarettes. He struck a match but did not light it. His face changed, looked perplexed, confused. 'Ernst, how did you know about the posting and I didn't?' he asked.

Weiser passed a piece of paper across to him. 'Because I've been promoted, Otto. I'm now an Oberstleutnant.'

'And me? You said we're both going south. Am I to serve with you?'

For answer Weiser passed another document over. 'I asked for you especially, heaven knows why.' He smiled. 'You're to be on my staff. My aide-de-camp.'

Mundt clicked his fingers to a waiter. 'Champagne,' he said. 'We've something to celebrate.'

'And then I must write to my wife,' Weiser said. 'Hilda will be delighted to hear the news.'

Dijon was the most beautiful city Weiser had ever seen. He was the officer in charge of the city and his headquarters were in the old Ducal Palace. The courtyard outside contained a range of military vehicles: armoured cars, trucks of all sizes and half a dozen motorcycles, two with side-cars. Soldiers stood to attention in sentry boxes on either side of the gates while others hurried across the courtyard on ceaseless errands.

His personal office was spacious, with high ceilings, polished wooden floor and sturdy old furniture. There were some paintings on the walls but these were overshadowed by two huge Nazi banners on either side of the fireplace. A photograph of the Führer hung on one wall, in his eye-line. Another sat upon his desk, glaring at him.

For a moment he contemplated putting this in a drawer but the palace also contained the office of the Gestapo and the headquarters of the SS so to do this would have been unwise.

He paced up and down the office, from side to side and from front to back, noting the number of steps scrupulously, neither adding to them nor subtracting. He would tell Hilda and the children the number of steps he took. The children would be proud that their papa had such an imposing place of work all to himself. His own father would be less proud, of course.

He put all his belongings in the centre of the desk and then set about placing them where they would be close to hand. His father's writing case he placed on the right, complete with ink-well and slots for several pens and pencils. His spectacle case went to his left and beside that a magnifying glass which was useful in scrutinising detailed maps. A German-French dictionary was placed beside the telephone which he pulled closer towards him, within easy reach.

On the far side of the desk he put a map of France and maps of Dijon and the surrounding area. Next to these he placed a copy of Melancholie, a romantic novel by his ancestor Ernst Keil, who he was named after.

He stood up and surveyed the desk from behind the chair, then strolled around it, examining it from every viewpoint, particularly that of any subordinates and superiors who might be visiting.

He sat down in a seat drawn up opposite his own chair and moved a few items in order to give a better idea of order and efficiency. Then he went back to his own seat and gave the desk a final scrutiny. He sighed with pleasure and then placed the picture of the Führer face down on the desk.

He was going to enjoy his new position. And enjoy being in Dijon.

There was a knock on his door and his adjutant entered. He looked angry and uncertain.

'My apologies, Oberstleutnant ,' he said. 'There is a man demanding to see you. He is most insistent although he is only a captain.'

'A captain?' Weiser said in surprise. 'What makes a captain think he can demand the attention of an officer two ranks above him.'

'He is a Hauptsturmführer, sir,' the adjutant said, 'a member of the SS.'

For the moment, Weiser said nothing. He did not know his adjutant well and decided it would be safest if he kept his thoughts about the SS to himself.

'Send the Hauptsturmführer in, please,' he said.

Almost immediately, the door was opened and a man entered the office. He was young, in his twenties by his appearance, good-looking although with eyes which seemed distant, as though they were searching for something not of this world.

Weiser waited for him to salute but he waited in vain.

'Good morning, Oberstleutnant,' he said. 'I am Hauptsturmführer Barbie. I am the SS officer with responsibility for Dijon.'

'And I am the Wehrmacht officer with responsibility for it,' Weiser said.

Barbie shrugged, as if that was of little concern to him.

He sat down in a chair without Weiser's invitation.

'Now,' he said. 'Let me tell you about my view of Dijon.'

## TANTAMOUNT TO SLAVERY
*Grasse, September 1942*

Roland Boyer read the paper once again. It was about the new law, called The Law of 4 September on the Use and Guidance of the Workforce. Boyer gave a bleak smile. You could never accuse the Government of not being explicit in the naming of its laws. Nor anything less than explicit in their demands.

The relève was not working. Too few people volunteered to go to work in Germany, even if it meant the release of French prisoners-of-war. Fewer than 100,000 had volunteered, in fact, and the Germans were demanding far more. Prime Minister Darlan had refused to send more than that number of skilled workers to Germany and the Germans insisted on his dismissal and replacement by Pierre Laval, Darlan's rival. Laval's new law meant that all able-bodied men aged 18 to 50 and single women aged 21 to 35 were obliged to do any work that the Government deemed necessary.

Boyer shook his head at this folly. He could see that this would mean trouble on the streets and he was a mere provincial policeman. Why couldn't Pétain and Laval see the same?

There was a sudden noise in the office outside. He leapt from his chair, assuming that the tumult was caused by someone angry at being arrested. Not a hardened criminal for they were always compliant, but some hitherto pillar of society who had been arrested for trading on the black market or some other misdemeanour.

He walked into the outer office and stopped dead in his tracks. The noise was not caused by members of the public but by his own men.

'What is the meaning of this?' he cried.

His voice had the desired effect and the shouts and yells calmed down.

'It's because of this, Capitaine,' said Sergeant Lassals, one of the most experienced on his force. He waved a paper in the air but Boyer had no need to look at it to realise that it was a copy of the new law.

'It's an outrage, Capitaine,' Lassals said. 'Every man and woman to be subject to the Government.'

'The French Government,' Boyer said sternly. 'The Government of France.'

He knew he was on tricky ground here for even some in his own force had doubts about Maréchal Pétain's government. He suspected that some were even supporters of General de Gaulle, a man denounced as a traitor.

'But every man and woman —' continued the sergeant.

'Not every man and woman,' Boyer said, snatching the paper from Lassals's hand. 'It exempts married women, for example.'

'Well that's a relief,' cried Gendarme Villiers with heavy sarcasm. 'At least married women will be allowed to live at home to feed their children. While their unmarried sisters will be forced to work on the roads. Or sent to Germany to slave in factories making weapons.'

Boyer gave him a nasty look. He had always suspected that the man was a socialist, possibly even a communist.

'Button it, Villiers,' Lassals said, anxious in case the young man talked himself into a disciplinary charge.

'But this is tantamount to slavery,' Villiers said.

'I'll teach you the meaning of slavery, unless you show more respect to Capitaine Boyer,' the sergeant said.

But nevertheless, he turned to Boyer with an aggrieved expression still etched on his face. 'Are we expected to enforce this law?' he asked.

'A law is a law, sergeant,' Boyer said. 'Whether we agree with it or not, our clear duty is to enforce it.'

These words subdued any inclination on the rest of the men to continue their protest. Some even went so far as to give Villiers a look of harsh rebuke.

'Tantamount to slavery,' Villiers repeated.

For once Boyer chose to ignore it. 'Now get back to work,' he said. He gave Villiers a meaningful glance. 'And let's have done with any socialist sympathies and Stalinist notions.' He strode back to his office.

'Careful boy,' he heard Lassals say to Villiers. 'The Capitaine is a good man and he likes you, but don't push him too hard or you'll suffer the consequences.'

Boyer sat at his desk and rubbed his neck irritably. If even his own men were infuriated by the new law, how would the rest of the population react? He read the details of the new law once again. He sympathised with the Maréchal but wondered, not for the first time, if he wasn't going too far to appease the Germans.

'Bloody Churchill,' he muttered. Like many Frenchmen, Boyer believed that were it not for Churchill's intransigence the war would have ended two years before and France would now be free.

'And damn bloody Attlee.' Boyer had a particular dislike for the leader of the British Labour party because he had demanded that the King should make Churchill Prime Minister. He was convinced that Attlee was a communist and that Churchill danced to his tune.

He glanced at the clock. Time to go home.

He sighed, wondering how Odette's day had been. At least, as a married woman, she would be spared being registered for any work the government deemed fit.

He stretched wearily but then stopped. But what about Viviane? Was she married or merely living with Alain? He certainly hadn't been invited to a wedding but knowing the relations between the two sisters that was no great surprise. And perhaps the family had forbidden her to marry a man with Gypsy blood.

He worried at a loose tooth with his tongue. If Viviane and Alain weren't married, she would be classed as single and eligible for the work obligation. He read the new law swiftly, fearing it might be too late for her now.

Then he took a deep breath and his rigorous and analytical brain ran through the law yet again, even more carefully. No, there was enough ambiguity within it. There was no indication of a date by which women must have been married in order to avoid the work obligation, no long past deadline that Viviane may have missed. Nevertheless, it would be sensible to arrange things as soon as could be, today if possible.

He would call in on Viviane on his way home and tell her that she should get married. The Mayor would be happy to do it this evening if he requested it, which was just as well. Better to be on the safe side.

He cleared his desk and reached for his cap. He would have to hurry. And he mustn't be seen to have told her about the new law. Who will be their witnesses, he wondered? Probably her old friend Sylvie. He paused on the threshold. She was little more than a prostitute now, he thought sadly. And such a lovely young woman.

He knocked at Viviane's house on his way home, pretending not to notice the fluttering of the curtains and how Viviane looked out of the door with uncharacteristic caution. Not like in the past when she was one of the most vivacious and daring women in the town.

Too vivacious, too daring, just like her friend Sylvie. Had they been a little less wild he might have asked one or other of them to accompany him to a dance and then who knew how things might have turned out.

The door opened a crack and Viviane beckoned him to enter.

'To what do we owe the pleasure?' Alain asked loudly from his chair.

As usual Roland could not be sure whether he was being friendly or insulting. Or maybe he did not know how to behave in civilised company, his mother being the daughter of a Romany elder.

Roland placed himself on a hard chair. 'I've come to find out if you two are married.'

Viviane looked astonished at his words.

'What business is it of yours?' Alain asked in an indignant tone. 'Or are the lick-spittles in Vichy seeking to control the morals of France now?'

Roland's eyes narrowed. 'I advise you not to be so disrespectful to the Government of the republic,' he said.

'Roland is right,' Viviane said, quickly. She did not want to antagonise Roland at the best of times, not so much because he was a policeman but because Odette would hear of it. Now, with David in the house, she was even more anxious to keep Roland sweet.

Her heart clenched suddenly. Is that why he was here? Had he heard about David and come to seize him? Seize her as well for sheltering him?

'The reason I ask why you are married,' Roland continued, his voice now less friendly than at first, 'is this.' He took the legal notice out of his pocket and handed it to Alain who read it with increasing astonishment.

'I was right to call them lick-spittles,' he said, passing the paper to Viviane. 'They do whatever the Nazis want and more.'

Viviane shot him a warning glance and then began to read the paper. She gasped and stared at Roland. 'We're not married,' she said. 'Does that mean I'm eligible for these regulations? Will I be sent away to work? To Germany perhaps.'

Roland took the paper from her and replaced it in his pocket. 'First of all, please remember that I haven't shown you this. I haven't even been here.'

Alain gave him a grudging nod of thanks.

'And now you must come with me to the Mayor,' Roland said.

'What?' Alain cried. 'Are we to ask that old fool for help? You talk nonsense.'

'It is not I who talks so foolishly,' Roland said. 'We are going to the Mayor to ensure that Viviane becomes a married woman. Today, the very day the law has been announced. It will be foolish to wait until tomorrow.'

Viviane turned in mute appeal to Alain.

Alain sighed but gave a nod. 'Fetch the children,' he said.

Then he turned to Roland. 'Will you come with us? Be my witness?'

Roland's mind moved fast. He felt strangely moved to be asked by Alain but it might look as if he were complicit in this hasty subterfuge. But then again, what would be so peculiar about asking Viviane's brother-in-law to be a witness? After all, they might claim that the wedding had been arranged long ago. And in any case, if he had to ask the Mayor to perform such a ceremony, his complicity was already apparent.

'I shall be honoured,' he said. 'But Viviane will need a witness as well.' He coughed. 'It might be best not to ask Odette.'

Viviane nodded. Her sister loathed Alain and rarely troubled to hide it. 'We can call on Sylvie on the way to the Mayor,' she said.

'Excellent.' Roland got to his feet. 'We must hurry. Monsieur Bernard will not be so amenable if he's delayed from his supper.'

The Mayor was not amenable in the slightest and grumbled and tried to put them off. It was only when Roland insisted in no uncertain terms that he acquiesced and led them to his office. Fortunately, he had not read the new law so had no idea of the reason for haste.

'I suppose she's pregnant?' Bernard whispered to Roland as his assistant prepared the records.

Roland shrugged which was confirmation enough for him. The gossip would run like fire around the town tomorrow. Roland suddenly realised this and was disquieted by it.

'Monsieur Mayor,' he whispered. 'I would view it as a special favour if you tell no one about this wedding. Stupid gossip does not sit well with my role, does not help me support you in your vital work.'

He raised one eyebrow at the Mayor, a plea, a threat, a bargain.

'Of course, my dear Capitaine, of course.' The Mayor brushed his fingers across his lips as if he were wiping sauce from them. He gave a nasty smile. 'But your wife will know, of course.'

He pretended surprise. 'Why is she not here, come to that?'

Inspiration struck. 'That is why I don't want you to breathe a word about the ceremony,' Roland said. 'Odette thinks they are already married. She loves her niece Celeste and would be distraught to find out she is illegitimate.' He placed his hand tightly on the Mayor's arm, very tightly. 'I would deem it a special favour if you help me keep our little secret.'

The Mayor sighed, annoyed that his chance to spread a little mischief would be curtailed. But it would not do to cross Capitaine Boyer, he thought. These were dangerous times and he needed all the friends he could get.

He conducted the ceremony as speedily as he could. His dinner was in the oven. His wife was equally keen to be finished and the paper-work was soon complete and the unwelcome visitors out of the way.

Viviane glanced at the marriage papers in Alain's hand. Neither of their families had wanted them to be together so this perfunctory ritual seemed appropriate. She experienced a tiny frisson of pleasure at it. But most of all she felt relief that she was now safe from being forced to work by the Government, or even worse, sent to Germany to do so.

Alain shook Roland's hand. 'Thank you,' he said. 'We're very grateful.'

'I did it for Celeste,' Roland said.

The he glanced at David. 'You are happy taking in the child of Viviane's friend?'

'Not happy, but it is necessary.'

Roland grunted.

'In these strange times we must all do things we would not normally do,' Alain said pointedly.

Roland's tongue prodded the loose tooth, pushing it backwards and forwards although he knew he shouldn't weaken it.

'All the boy's paperwork is in order?' he asked. 'Ration book, birth certificate.'

'Of course. Do you want to see them?

Roland shook his head. 'It's not necessary. Not at the moment, at any rate.'

'Will you join us for a drink?' Alain asked. 'To celebrate the wedding.'

'One drink only. Then I must go home.'

'Odette…?'

'Yes, Odette.'

## WEISER AND MUNDT
*Dijon, October 1942*

Major Otto Mundt smiled at a pretty civilian typist as he strolled through the Wehrmacht headquarters. It was a beautiful autumn day with a sky which believed it was still summer. The leaves were turning gold, however, and a few had already fallen. He tried to banish the thought but the memory of the bitter winter warfare in the Soviet Union leapt into his mind. He shuddered. He dreaded winter now.

'Does it get cold here?' he demanded of the girl.

'Oui, Major,' she said. 'Very cold.'

He stared at her, thoughtfully. Perhaps she might keep him warm in the coming months. She blushed and glanced away which served only to pique his interest still more.

'Oberstleutnant Weiser is waiting to see you,' she said, nervously.

He chose to ignore her words. 'Do you live in Dijon?' he asked.

'Oberstleutnant Weiser…'

'Yes, yes.' He flashed her a winning smile and walked towards his friend's office. But then he paused.

'What's your name, girl?'

The girl blushed even more. 'Lisette, sir.'

'A pretty name,' he said and rapped upon Weiser's door.

'Where the hell have you been?' Weiser cried. It was almost a snarl.

Mundt was taken aback. He had never seen his friend like this before.

Weiser rubbed his hand upon his forehead, as if it bore an irritating rash. He gestured Mundt to sit but did not speak, merely toyed with a pen.

'Damn this headache,' he said at last.

'You should go to a doctor,' Mundt said. He paused. 'Is that it? A bad head is making you like a raging bear?'

Weiser sighed and flung his pen down.

'Not the migraine. It's Barbie, the SS bastard.'

Mundt raised an eyebrow. 'What now?'

'He's arrested two dozen Jewish men. He accuses them of stealing and arson.'

'And is there any proof?'

'None which would satisfy you or me, Otto.'

Mundt frowned. He disliked Barbie intensely, more for the arrogant way in which he treated his friend than anything else. But he realised that, despite being only a captain, the young man was a rising star in the SS and wielded a power far higher than his rank warranted.

'So what will happen?'

'There will be no trial,' Weiser said. 'Barbie has informed me, informed me would you believe, that he has all the evidence he needs. The men will be executed today. And I am supposed to have responsibility for the city.'

'And what do the French say?'

Weiser snorted. 'They've already been in my office, protesting. I don't much care what happens to the Jews but I care about the repercussions.'

He stared out of the window. The biggest surprise he had discovered since coming to Dijon was how the French authorities were getting ever more difficult concerning the Jews. They trod a fine line between acquiescence and defiance but they were definitely proving a thorn in his side. They seemed to have discovered a new determination to protect their Jewish citizens.

'Perhaps you should leave it to the SS and the Gestapo,' Mundt said.

'Really?' Weiser's voice cloyed with sarcasm.

'Maybe.' He cocked his head and regarded his friend quizzically. 'We're soldiers, Ernst. I think you should leave such matters to the Gestapo. Don't get your hands dirty.'

Weiser glared at him but finally gave a tiny shrug. 'Perhaps you're right,' he said.

'I am, I think.' He sighed. 'God, why are the Jews such a problem?'

'Isn't that what Pontius Pilate asked?' Weiser said. 'Before washing his hands of everything?'

'I've always thought that a fable.'

Despite the casualness of his words, Mundt looked troubled by the conversation.

Weiser raised an eyebrow, pulled two cigarettes from his case and flicked one to Mundt. It was Turkish, rather mild but aromatic. Mundt struck a match, lit his friend's cigarette and then his own.

'When do you think the war will be over?' Weiser asked, quietly.

Mundt was shocked at the question and his eyes darted around the room as if it might be filled with invisible Gestapo officers. Then he took a deep pull on his cigarette and began to relax.

'Soon, I should think. The war in the east is going well?'

Weiser nodded and extended a map on the desk. He had sketched the German army's advance on it. 'The army has captured most of the Russian oil fields and is at the gates of Stalingrad. I doubt the Soviets have any resources or stomach to fight on.'

'And then we'll sweep south through Persia and join the Japanese in India. That will be the Soviets out of the war and the British Empire on its knees.'

'It can't come soon enough for me, Otto. I miss Hilda and the children. Hans will be eighteen in January. I don't want him fighting in Russia.'

'It won't come to that. The war will be over by next spring, mark my words.'

'And the Americans?' Weiser asked.

Mundt flicked the ash from his cigarette into an ash tray. 'I don't think we have anything to fear from them. They have little appetite for war and, besides, our yellow friends are keeping them busy in the Pacific.'

'And if the British surrender,' he continued, 'which they're bound to with all their shipping losses in the Atlantic, then the Americans will give up as well. They can't fight us on their own.'

Weiser frowned. 'You're so sure the British will give up?'

'The U-boats will guarantee it. Hardly any allied ships get through to England now. The population must be starving. Churchill will be overthrown.'

Weiser lit another cigarette. He always felt better talking with Otto, an eternal optimist. He, on the other hand, felt a tide of pessimism sweeping over him, threatening to send him plummeting who knows where. He took a heavy drag on his cigarette.

'But in the meantime I have to deal with the likes of Barbie.'

Otto leaned forward, his face suddenly grave. 'Listen to me, Ernst. Do not attempt to fight against Barbie, or anyone else in the SS or Gestapo. You'll only come to grief.'

'I suppose you're right,' Weiser said at last. 'It's just not right for a jumped-up little swine like Barbie to have such power.'

'He could be worse. Like the criminals and perverts rampaging around the east.'

'Perhaps you're right. Maybe we should be thankful for small mercies. As should the French.'

'In the meanwhile,' Mundt said, 'we should learn to enjoy ourselves more. The grape harvest is about to begin. There will be plenty of good wine to enjoy.' The image of Lisette, the young typist came to his mind. And more than just wine, I hope, he thought with anticipation.

## WHISPERS IN THE STREET
### *Grasse, October 1942*

It had been a trying month. David had cried each morning for an hour on waking and then, periodically throughout the day. Viviane had tried her best to encourage him out of it but she found it hard and she grew increasingly resentful. Celeste was the one who helped him most, letting him play with her toys, encouraging him to take part in games with her friend Monique and even cuddling him and wiping his face when he was at his most weepy. She's a better mother to him than I am, Viviane sometimes thought.

But gradually, as the days passed and there was no sign of his mother returning, David appeared to grow more accustomed to the fact. He asked her every day when his maman would return but by the end of September he sobbed only on waking and at bedtimes.

One day, he stood rapt as Alain tinkered with his motorbike, pointing out bits of the machinery and demanding to know their names. He even helped mop up surplus oil around the engine and as reward Alain took him for a ride on the bike, seating him in front of him with one arm wrapped around his chest to keep him secure. David was delighted and could not control his laughter and his joy.

When they returned, he seemed a different boy, almost, following Alain around the house and asking when they go could out on the bike again.

Viviane felt overwhelming relief. 'Maybe he'll settle now,' she said. 'But be careful next time you take him out, Alain. We don't want him having an accident nor too much attention drawn to him.'

This was easier said than done. Generally nowadays, people were wary of asking too many questions. But not everybody. Busy-bodies existed in Grasse as much as any town but those who relished gossip were now in their element and thrived.

Much of the talk was about those women who managed to persuade the shopkeepers to sell them the best food. Bribery was the most common explanation for this, although a few hinted that more than money paid for the purchases. Working men might grow suspicious of any work-colleagues who had more cash for wine or cigarettes. Older men would look suspiciously at younger men and ponder why they weren't prisoners of war, or dead from the battles of 1940.

But most venomous were the whispers and innuendo about young women whose husbands were prisoner-of-war or dead. They received a pension from the government, it was true, but this was pitifully small. Most had to try to find employment, something difficult for those with young children. A few, like Sylvie Duchamp, earned their money in more scandalous ways. The gossip concerning this had become so wearing that a few women grew brazen about their activities although most were ashamed and kept it secret.

On the other hand, there was less resentment of Alain than there had ever been. He had often been sneered at because his mother was Roma and he had fought many a playground battle with boys who taunted him by calling him Gypsy or told him that he would grow up to become a thief.

When he began his market business he got a reputation as a sharp operator, which was true, and a cheat, which was not. But since the start of the war, the skills which had been so derided were now admired. Alain could lay his hands on things which other traders could not and he was applauded for it. Many a vehicle was kept going on the engine parts which Alain produced from his stores, many a shopkeeper was able to sell black market wine, cigarettes, food and clothes because of his contacts. Even the police turned a blind eye to his activities, and not entirely because Capitaine Boyer was Viviane's brother-in-law. Alain showered every policeman with gifts and inducements and they suffered a collective short-sightedness because of it.

'Greasing palms seals even the biggest mouths,' he told his friend Gerard on more than one occasion.

Perhaps it was because of this, or because most people preferred to live and let live, but Viviane found her fears of gossip about David unfounded for the most part.

This was not true in her own family, however. Her mother and sister could not look at David except maliciously and never spoke to him. It was her mother's friends who cast the most baleful glances at her when Viviane walked took the children anywhere. And it was Odette's few friends who were keen to ask who David was and where he came from. The foreign boy was the epithet which they used most often to describe him. Foreign to Grasse, some might charitably imagine they meant. Foreign in other ways, was a more accurate interpretation of their words.

Some went even further than tittle-tattle on the streets.

Roland Boyer called to his wife when he arrived home one evening.

'I'm making your omelette,' she called. 'It will be ready in a minute.'

He grunted and sat at the table.

'Jeanne Greuze came to see me today,' he said when she appeared.

Odette could sense his anger and decided on a strategy of appeasement combined with threat. She threw the plate on the table.

'What's it to me?' she asked, her tone challenging. She pushed the bottle of wine to him but did not pour it.

'She wants to know about the boy who is staying with Viviane,' Boyer said. 'Or more accurately, she demands to know all about him.'

Odette tilted her head in a non-committal manner.

'And what did you tell her?'

'I told her it was none of her business.' Boyer was still seething at the bitter tone of the woman's demands.

'Perhaps she thought it was her business,' Odette said carefully. 'If she believes there's something suspicious about the boy being here.'

'What is there to be suspicious about? Viviane told us what happened.'

Odette did not answer but her silence was more than eloquent.

'You don't believe her, do you?' he said.

'Viviane?' Odette snorted. 'I rarely believe her. A lifetime of knowing her has taught me that.'

Boyer poured a glass of wine. 'I wish you two would be friends,' he said. 'Aren't times hard enough as it is?'

'We're sisters,' Odette said. 'I choose my friends. I didn't choose her.'

'I wonder if she feels the same about you?'

'She does. She makes it abundantly clear. And she hurts not only me but Maman and Papa as well. What with sleeping with that Gypsy crook.'

'Her husband, you mean.'

Odette looked at him in astonishment.

'Husband? What do you mean?'

'They're married. I've seen the papers myself.'

Odette pondered this news for a while before replying. 'And was this anything to do with the law that unmarried women are available for any work the government demands?'

Boyer shrugged. 'And what if it is? The law is most explicit. Viviane is married and the law does not relate to her.'

Odette threw her arms in the air. 'You are a slave to the law. If the law told you to wear a skirt or strangle your wife would you do it?'

'I doubt a skirt would suit me.' He swallowed his wine. The omelette was, as yet, untouched.

'Well,' Odette continued, 'I for one think that Jeanne Greuze was right to come to the police with her suspicions. It's a pity, perhaps, that she didn't talk with someone more willing to listen.'

'Listen to what? There is no substance to her insinuations. None whatsoever.'

He began to eat his omelette and went over the interview in his mind. Jeanne Greuze had not exactly accused David of being a Jew, but she pointedly wondered why he hadn't been seen in church, why he was so dark, why his accent was a little unusual.

'You're convinced that there's no truth in what she says, then?' Odette said. Her tone was less strident now, more conciliatory.

'Absolutely convinced.'

'Of course, husband.' She paused. 'You will have seen the boy's papers?'

The omelette almost stuck in his throat. He swallowed it with difficulty.

He had considered asking Viviane to let him examine the boy's papers but decided not to. The less he knew, the better all round. He had told himself that it was not a police matter and so not his responsibility to pry.

He took a long sip of his wine. 'This omelette is excellent,' he said. 'I don't suppose there are more eggs?'

Odette shook her head. She was watching him like a cat eyes a bird.

She realised that he was not going to respond so she risked a more direct question.

'So what did his papers say? Is Viviane telling the truth for once?'

He did not answer for a moment.

'More or less,' he said.

'More or less?'

He nodded, slowly. 'David's mother was, indeed, Simone Legarde. And she was killed in an RAF raid in Paris. But the boy has no father. He's illegitimate.'

Odette's eyes narrowed. Celeste, of course, was also illegitimate but Odette had long realised that any gossip about this would incur the wrath of her father. But the boy was a different matter entirely.

'That's why we must not talk about David's background,' he said. 'It's not fair on the boy.'

Odette gave a nod, as if she acquiesced.

He congratulated himself on this subterfuge. Fight fire with fire, he thought.

## VISITING DOROTHY
*Grasse November 1942*

Roland Boyer's belief that the lie he had told Odette about David's father would quell all further rumour was sadly mistaken. Odette never spoke about it to him directly, it was true. But her friends now added the word bastard to their insinuations about the boy. And the word snaked across the town.

Viviane grew desperate about it, her nerves taut and ever ready to fray. 'I wish we could get away,' she said one day.

'We can't,' Alain said, pausing in his reading. 'The government won't let anyone move now, not without a reason so strong even they can't challenge it.'

'We could say your uncle's ill,' she said.

'Stefan? He's as strong as a bull. Everyone knows it. Besides, I've no idea where he is, he could be anywhere. And I can't see you living in a caravan.'

Viviane kissed his hand. 'I don't know. I might be quite the Roma princess. And Celeste would love it.'

'I'm not sure about David, though. He prefers motorbikes and cars. Do we know anyone with a car? He would love to sit in one.'

Viviane shook her head. Then she gasped. 'I do actually. Do you remember that American lady who had a fainting fit?'

Alain looked confused.

'You do. It was soon after David came to us. She had a black-out and I had to drive her car home.'

Alain nodded. 'Oh yes. Sorry, I forgot.'

'She lives in a grand villa just outside of town. She knew Charlie Chaplin.'

'She was an actress?'

'No. She wrote films. Like someone who writes plays for the theatre.'

Alain grew more interested now. 'She must be rich.'

Viviane shrugged. 'She has a big house.'

'Perhaps you should go and visit her, Viv. It would get you away from the town and all the tittle-tattle for an hour or two.'

'I couldn't,' she said, although part of her would have loved to. She did not want to intrude on a stranger and she guessed that Dorothy's friendliness was merely because she had helped her when she was unwell.

*********************

It was a few weeks later, at the beginning of October, that there came a knock at the door. Alain was at the market and Viviane grew alarmed. No one knocked on her door unless it was official. Her friends would just walk in and her neighbours would call out before opening the door.

'Celeste,' she said. 'Go in the yard and take David with you.'

'But I want to see who it is.'

'Do as I say. And keep your voices down.'

Another knock sounded on the door, a little louder this time. Viviane glanced at the mirror above the fireplace and tidied up her hair. She took a deep breath and threw open the door.

She recognised the young woman on the doorstep although she could not remember how or where.

'My name is Marie,' the woman said. 'I am Madame Pine's maid.'

'Of course,' Viviane said. 'I'm sorry, I couldn't place you for a moment.' She looked alarmed. 'Is Madame Pine ill?'

The girl shook her head. 'She is quite well. But she wondered if you would like to visit her, with the children.' She gave an apologetic smile. 'She gets lonely. She needs to have company.'

'Why me?'

Marie shook her head. It was a mystery to her, as well.

Viviane was surprised at how the invitation lifted her spirits. 'I would love to come,' she said. 'Thank Madame Pine very much. When did she have in mind?'

'Tomorrow?' Marie said. 'If you say yes, I'm to buy some wine and cakes.'

'That will be wonderful.'

'At three in the afternoon, then,' Marie said. 'You know how to get there? It will take an hour to walk.'

'Of course.'

The next day, with all of them dressed in their finest clothes, Viviane and the children knocked on Madame Pine's door.

Alain was in Nice, negotiating a supply of flashlights and bulbs which, because of the black-out, would be in great demand in the winter months.

The door opened and Marie gestured to them to enter.

Viviane was more at ease now. The last time she had been here she had been shaking with anxiety about Dorothy's blackout and, even more, because of having to drive her car.

Today, the long walk had been relaxing and good for the children. David had asked endless questions about the trees, hedges and birds which made her think that he had probably been brought up in a city or large town. He was fascinated most by the holes in the banks beside the road; the dens of rabbits, weasels and mice. He peered into them and sniffed the pungent scents of fur and flesh which rose from within. His face was bright with pleasure and he wanted to linger and watch for any animals to appear. Eventually, Viviane had to raise her voice to make him come away.

'He's a bit grubby,' Marie said, pointing to David's knees.

'He was looking into burrows,' Viviane said, which seemed explanation enough.

Marie showed them into the garden room once again and they sat by the window. Viviane took out a handkerchief, spat into it and hurriedly rubbed at David's knees. Then, for good measure, she turned the handkerchief over, spat once again and wiped his face. She looked inquisitively at Celeste who backed away at the sight of the handkerchief.

'Not after you've wiped it on David,' she said in alarm. 'He ate a worm.'

Viviane turned to David. 'You didn't?'

David nodded. 'It wasn't very nice.'

'You must never do that again, you naughty boy. You'll be ill.'

He looked chastised for all of ten seconds. Viviane had to suppress a smile.

'How's the boy been naughty,' came Dorothy's voice from the door. 'What's the little fellow been up to?'

'He ate a worm,' Celeste said.

'Did he now?' Dorothy hunkered down beside David. 'Was it a big one or a little one?'

David stuck his thumb in his mouth. 'A little one,' he murmured.

'They're not the tastiest,' Dorothy said. 'Next time try a long one but make sure you cook it first. Hey, maybe we could share one next time you come.'

David looked at Viviane, unsure what to say to this.

'She's only teasing,' Viviane said. 'She doesn't really want to eat worms. And nor should you.'

Dorothy laughed, threw herself into a chair and glanced at Marie. 'Could we have tea and lemonade, please, Marie? And those delicious cakes you bought in town yesterday.'

Marie nodded and left the room. She was disappointed for she wanted to hear the conversation between her mistress and the woman from Grasse.

'Now, darling,' Dorothy said to Viviane, 'I want to know how things are with you.'

'Things are good, madame,' Viviane said.

'Dorothy,' she corrected. 'And I've heard on the grapevine that they aren't too good for you.'

Viviane was immediately suspicious. And defensive. 'What do you mean?'

Dorothy shrugged. 'That there's been gossip about the boy.' She turned towards the children. 'Hey, Celeste, would you and David like to go see if Groucho wants to play? He may be snoozing in the sunshine somewhere but he won't mind being woken. He's not much more than a kitten and he likes to play.'

Celeste took David's hand and headed for the garden.

'I don't know what you mean about gossip,' Viviane said, stiffly.

'Oh, I think you do. If I've heard rumour even out here, then I dread to think what you hear in the town.'

Viviane paused before answering. She could see there was no point in trying to hide things from Dorothy.

'People always talk,' she said with a shrug. 'It is, let's be fair, unusual for anyone to take in an orphan child of a friend. People are bound to talk.'

Marie brought in the tea and cakes and Dorothy thanked her. 'Sweetheart,' she said, 'could you go and help Lucile with the supper. Take some cakes with you. You bought more than we need, I think.'

Marie thanked her and left.

'She always buys more than I ask for,' Dorothy explained. 'I don't mind, I can afford it, and she adores cakes.' She shrugged and smiled. 'I let her get away with murder, actually,' she said.

All the while she was engaged in these pleasantries she was watching Viviane intently.

Viviane smiled. Her stomach was rumbling at the sight of the cakes and it was all she could do to refrain from reaching for one. 'I'd better call the children,' she said.

'Let them play for a while.' Dorothy poured the tea and passed Viviane a cup. 'I guess you're right, darling. People are bound to talk about what you did.'

She raised her cup to her lips, sipped it and returned to the table. 'Especially if the boy's a Jew.'

Viviane's cup rattled in the saucer. She felt as if she had walked into a trap. 'Who says he's a Jew?'

Dorothy raised one eyebrow. 'That's the word on the streets, honey. That you took in a Jew. It's only a rumour, of course.' She paused a moment. 'And some of the gossips say you did it for money.'

Viviane flushed red, a deep shade which covered her face, her neck, even her chest.

'All righty,' Dorothy said quietly. She got to her feet. 'Would you like something stronger than tea?'

Viviane nodded, unable for the moment to speak.

Dorothy went to the sideboard and poured them both large measures of sherry. 'It's surprisingly good,' she said, handing Viviane a glass. 'Considering it crossed the Pyrenees on mule-back.'

Viviane took a larger gulp than she intended.

'Don't worry, honey,' Dorothy said. 'Your secret's safe with us.'

For a moment Viviane meant to argue, to say that Dorothy was wrong about David, completely wrong. But she knew there was no point.

She said nothing for a while. Apart from Alain, nobody knew that David was a Jew. Yet the burden of keeping the secret had begun to wear her down. This stranger's forthright discussion of it was disconcerting, alarming even. Did she mean to denounce her to the authorities? What would happen to the boy then? And to her and Alain and Celeste?

Yet, at the same time, now that the issue had come into the open, she felt a little relieved. There was no more sense in hiding the fact. She could not close this box now.

'You can trust me,' Dorothy said quietly. Her tone was unlike any she had used hitherto. It was calm, gentle, compassionate.

'Promise?' Viviane asked, quietly.

'On my mother-in-law's grave,' Dorothy said.

Viviane gave a sigh. 'How did you hear? About David?'

'Tradesmen come to my house. I sometimes shop in town.'

'And they talk about me?'

'Only my friends. Monsieur Blanche, the baker, and old man Corot.'

'Corot the butcher?' Viviane had never been in Monsieur Corot's shop for his meat was the most expensive in town.

'They're good people. You might be wise to get to know them.'

'I know Monsieur Blanche. I buy my bread there.'

'He made these cakes.'

Viviane stared at the plate. 'I haven't seen anything like these for years.'

Dorothy smiled. 'It's a special order, honey.'

Viviane stared at her. So she must have been confident that Viviane would come to the villa. Her suspicions were immediately roused. Why was this? Why had she asked her? Marie's explanation that she liked company now appeared rather hollow.

Perhaps it would be best to try to hide these thoughts. If Dorothy was a friend then it would be churlish. If she were an enemy then showing any antagonism would merely make things worse.

'So you've heard these rumours only from Monsieur Blanche and Monsieur Corot?' she asked, trying to hide the nervousness in her voice.

Dorothy shook her head. 'Not just them. My cook Lucile lives in Grasse. She's my eyes and ears. Very useful these days.'

'So, madame,' Viviane said, 'if you don't mind me asking, what else have you heard about the boy?'

'Ooh, very formal. You must be fretting.' Dorothy gave her a sympathetic look and sipped her sherry, allowing herself time to think. 'There's not a great deal else, Viviane. Some people think the boy's a Jew, others don't. A few are bitter about this, but they're just trouble-makers. Most are either sympathetic or don't care one way or another.'

'And you?'

Dorothy touched her gently on the knee. 'I hate Hitler and all his works. I despise him. And I don't see why anybody, least of all little children, should be persecuted because of who they were born to.'

There was an unforced honesty about her words. Viviane sighed and closed her eyes. She felt a solitary tear fill one eye and she wished that her handkerchief wasn't so filthy.

'Have a cake, darling,' Dorothy said.

'I think I will.'

She chose an eclair. The chocolate was not particularly good and the cream had been mixed with something rather cloying, margarine perhaps, but it tasted lovely. She'd never been partial to cakes in the past and never thought to seek them out. Now, shortages meant it was too late to develop the taste for them.

'I don't think there's anything to worry about,' Dorothy said.

Viviane shook her head. 'I'm no longer so sure. I never imagined that Maréchal Pétain would agree to arrest children but he did. And the Nazis are animals.'

Dorothy didn't reply. She knew from various sources that the Nazis had definitely not wanted to take Jewish children. The Vichy government had offered them up, nonetheless, partly because they did not want to take care of thousands of parent-less children but also to curry favour with the Nazis. Best not to say this to Viviane, though, she thought.

Then something struck her. 'You have papers?' she asked. 'Papers for the boy?'

The eclair suddenly tasted vile in Viviane's mouth. She shook her head. 'No.'

'Then you must get them. And as soon as possible. It will be a sure proof for the child.'

'But his papers will show he is a Jew.'

'Not the real ones,' Dorothy cried. She looked at Viviane as if she were an idiot. 'You'll have to get fake ones, forgeries.'

Viviane shook her head. 'How can I do that?'

'From what I hear, your husband should be able to arrange it.' She paused. 'I'm surprised he hasn't thought of it already.'

'Alain doesn't have much patience with authorities, with regulations and papers and such-like.'

'Well he'd better learn to. The right piece of paper can be worth its weight in gold.'

In that case, Viviane thought, there may be a problem. But then she remembered the money that David's mother had given to her.

She would ask Alain to try to get papers. They had rarely talked about who he did business with but she suspected that some were on the fringes of the criminal world at the very least. If anyone could help them, surely they could.


## WHOSE BASTARD?

*Grasse, November 1942*

Odette Boyer listened to her friend Jeanne Greuze with only half a mind. She was relating her usual tales of who had bought more butter from the shops, who had been sold a better piece of meat or fish, who had been allocated two baguettes instead of one. Normally this was of the utmost interest but now Odette had other things on her mind.

Since he had come home with the news of Viviane's marriage, she had grown increasingly suspicious of Roland. He was hiding something, she knew that. A woman did not stay married to a man for thirteen years without realising when he was lying.

The problem was that Roland was a consummate policeman and, as such, adept at withholding information whenever he believed it necessary. She felt sure that he was doing so with her.

Her mind gnawed at how he had forbidden her to gossip about David because his mother was unmarried.

'Whose bastard is he, then?' she murmured to herself.

Jeanne stopped her complaints mid-flow. 'What did you say?' she asked.

Odette was surprised, not realising that she had spoken aloud. Now a cold smile came to her face. 'The child my sister has taken in,' she said. 'I've found out he's a bastard. Only I don't know who the parents are.'

'I thought the mother was Viviane's old pen-friend.'

Odette's lips pursed. 'Do you really believe that? Would you, dear Jeanne, take in the child of a woman you had no contact with since school days? Who you've probably never actually seen?'

'I certainly wouldn't.' Jeanne hugged herself with pleasure as she leaned closer. This was far more interesting than talk of baguettes and butter.

'And would a child be taken across France,' Odette continued, 'crossing the demarcation line to boot, just so a stranger could take care of him?'

'It does seem implausible.' Jeanne became hesitant now. She had a brother who she didn't particularly get on with but she would never cause him real problems. It was different with Odette and Viviane for they loathed each other. A little shiver came over her as she wondered if either sister might actually wish the other harm.

The more Odette thought about it, the greater her doubt grew. She gave a sudden gasp of certainty. 'Of course the child hasn't come from Paris. It would be impossible. He must be from somewhere nearby.'

'Sylvie Duchamp opens her legs to all and sundry,' Jeanne said. 'It's likely her bastard.'

Odette pondered this. Jeanne might well be right. Viviane and Sylvie were as thick as thieves, always had been. But why would Sylvie seek to offload her son? And why would Viviane take him in?

'Sylvie wouldn't want a young child around,' Jeanne continued. 'Not when she's...engaged in business.' Her eyebrows almost shot off her brow.

'Perhaps,' said Odette.

Somehow, however, this did not quite ring true. Surely, if Sylvie had given birth to a son it would be common knowledge? Such things could not remain secret in any town or village. No, the child could not be Sylvie's.

And then it came to her. Of course. It was blindingly obvious. Her breath was almost sucked from her body.

Why hadn't she realised this before? She felt dizzy at her own failure to realise the truth.

The child must be Alain's, fathered on some hussy who he had met on his travels. She had always suspected he bedded whoever he took a fancy to. He had persuaded Viviane, or threatened her, into taking the boy in. For the briefest moment she felt sorry for her sister but such feelings were so attenuated by a life-time's dislike that it flamed for only an instant before dying.

Jeanne grabbed her by the hand, her face bright with excitement. 'Odette, do you know who the parents are?'

Odette's eyes narrowed. 'I have my suspicions. But, like you, my dear, I'm not one to engage in tittle-tattle.' She gave her friend a smug smile and departed.

Jeanne watched her go, seething in fury, her mind a cauldron of questions about the boy's parentage and resentment that Odette had not shared her suspicions. And then she smiled. For she too, imagined that she might have the answer.

Odette hurried off to her mother's house. She threw open the door, took off her coat and hung it on her accustomed hook.

'It's me, Maman,' she called. She tried to keep the note of triumph from her voice.

'Hello, dear,' her mother said, offering her cheek for the ritual kiss. 'How is Roland? He must be so busy nowadays. I never see him.'

'I hardly see him, either. He is happier with his cronies at the police station than at home with his wife.'

Marthe gave her a sympathetic look and went into the kitchen, returning shortly afterwards with two cups of lukewarm coffee.

'Maman,' Odette began, 'what do you think about that boy that Viviane is looking after?'

'He seems a normal enough child,' Marthe said. 'A little reserved, perhaps.'

'But don't you wonder where he comes from?'

Marthe frowned. 'Didn't Viviane say he was an orphan? The son of her old friend?'

'Pen-friend, Maman. Don't you think it odd that a little boy should be sent across the whole of France to be brought up by his mother's pen-friend?'

'I hadn't really thought.'

'Well think about it now.' Odette could barely keep the irritation out of her voice.

Marthe sipped at her coffee. 'I suppose it is a little odd, now I come to think about it.' She frowned suddenly. 'Do you think Viviane is lying?'

'Why do you seem so shocked? She's hardly knows the difference between truth and falsehoods.'

Marthe did not answer. There was much in what her eldest daughter said.

'So who do you think the boy belongs to?' Marthe asked. 'One of her friends? Sylvie Duchamp perhaps?'

Odette shook her head, sat back in the chair and sipped at her coffee. This was a moment to be savoured, more especially as it kept her mother on tenter-hooks.

'It's obvious, Maman,' she said eventually. 'The boy is Alain's bastard. He's always away, on so-called business. Now we know what that business entails. He must have girlfriends from Marseilles to Menton.'

Marthe blinked repeatedly, her mind galloping over this new information. She had never trusted Alain, never liked him. She always said he wasn't good enough for her daughter. Now she had been proved right.

And then she gasped. 'The mother must be a Gypsy.'

Odette hadn't thought of this but it seemed a possibility. She gazed at her mother, annoyed that she had reached this conclusion before she had.

'She's probably one of his cousins,' she said, eager to outdo her mother in vitriol. 'There's enough of them, and Gypsies like to breed with their own kind.'

She gave a dramatic pause. 'And he's always been far too close to his sister.'

'Don't be so filthy,' Marthe cried sternly. 'I won't have such ideas in my home.'

Odette shrugged, content that she had planted the suspicion in her mother's mind. 'We'll never be certain, that's for sure,' she said.

Both women fell silent, pondering what they had conjured up. Their dislike of Alain waxed stronger with every second, thickening and strengthening like a scab on a wound.

'So what do we do now?' Marthe asked finally.

'It's Viviane's business and not ours,' Odette replied. 'We do nothing. For the moment.'

A moment later, Georges Loubet stomped in from the kitchen, put on his coat and grabbed his crutches.

'Where are you going?' Marthe said in alarm. He rarely ventured out lately.

'I thought I'd go to the bar,' he said. 'I need the fresh air and company.'

'But you've got company here. With me and Odette.'

'Male company. Sometimes a man needs to talk with his friends.'

He shut the door behind him and looked through the window as he passed. A little rumble of discontent sounded in his chest. He cared for both his daughters of course, but he found that he liked Odette a little less with each passing year. He blamed it on the war. It brought out the worst in people, set friend against friend, children against parents, sisters against sisters.

He passed the bar without as much as a glance. His old friend Jacques called out to him but he called a curt hello and did not stop.


## GEORGES INTERVENES
*Grasse, November 1942*


Georges hammered on Viviane's door.

'Papa,' she said in amazement. 'What's wrong? Is Maman ill?'

Georges shook his head. 'She's fine, there's no cause for alarm.'

He followed Viviane into the house, wondering what he was going to say, wondering what he actually wanted to say.

She was the youngest child and, although he rarely admitted it, had always been his favourite. He loved her wild, rebellious streak even though he knew it created problems for her mother. And, as she grew older, it increasingly caused problems for her: at school, at work, within the family.

Odette, on the other hand, had always been harder for him to love. More serious, more austere, more calculating. She was a pessimist rather than an optimist, and rarely given to any spontaneous act. In many ways her character chimed more with his mood, ever since the first war had taken his youth and hopes.

And perhaps that was why he liked Viviane the best. She was like the promise he had lost, the dreams which had been snuffed out on the killing fields of no-man's-land.

He settled himself into a seat while Viviane poured him a glass of wine.

He went over in his mind the conversation he had overheard between his wife and daughter. He burned with shame at how they had relished Viviane's predicament. They should have supported her, not denigrated her. If the boy was Alain's bastard she should be pitied, not reviled.

He watched David playing in the yard. He was dark, it was true, as dark as some of the Gypsies who travelled the byways of the region. Like Alain and his mother, in fact. But then again, many French people had dark complexions, olive or tanned, especially in the south.

He sighed to himself. Could Odette's suspicions be true? Could the boy really be Alain's son? A son, perhaps of a Gypsy mother? He dismissed out of hand any notion that Alain had slept with his sister or even a cousin. But some other woman? It was possible, especially for a man of Alain's ebullient, larger than life nature.

'So why have you come?' Viviane asked.

'Can't I visit my daughter?' he countered.

She raised an eyebrow. 'You never do. Is there some problem?'

He pursed his lips. How to say it? If the boy was Alain's bastard then she should be praised for taking him in. Few other women would do so, although it did not greatly surprise him that Viviane would.

He thought to talk about it in a circumspect way, be gentle and cautious.

He opened his mouth.

'Is David a bastard?'

Viviane did not reply for a moment. 'What makes you say that?'

He berated himself for his clumsiness and gave a little shrug. 'I've heard rumours. That is all.'

'Odette? Roland?'

He did not reply, not even with as much as a gesture.

'I thought so,' Viviane said.

He frowned. How could his silence give him away so readily?

'I've told you already,' she continued. 'David is my old pen-friend's son.'

'But his father? You've never mentioned his father.'

'I didn't know his father. Why would I?'

He exhaled a huge breath.

Viviane's mouth opened wide. 'You think he's Alain's child!'

He held his hands up in front of him, as if to shield himself.

'How could you Papa, how could you?'

He began to mumble, meaningless words over which he had no control, but stopped himself almost immediately.

'It's not you who says this, is it?' Viviane said. 'It's Odette.'

'It doesn't matter who said it,' he answered. 'If you say it's not so, then I believe you. As will your mother.' He paused, wondering what to say next. 'The boy's papers should prove he's legitimate. Prove who his father is.'

Viviane did not reply.

His heart lurched. So Odette had been speaking the truth.

He watched his daughter as the spirit went out of her.

'Don't fret yourself, child,' he said. 'It's noble of you to take the boy in, courageous. Not many women would do it.'

'He's not Alain's child.'

He shook his head wearily. 'Then whose child is he?'

'His parents are Jews. He's a Jew.'

Georges stared at her in utter horror.

Finally, he spoke. 'Are you mad? Those bastards in Vichy are hunting down the Jews. They're doing the Germans work for them. You're in terrible danger.'

'I know. But what else could I do. David's mother was being hunted by the police. She begged me to take him. What else could I do?'

Georges closed his eyes. This was madness. This was terribly, dreadfully dangerous.

He looked up and gazed into his daughter's eyes. He realised at once that it would be futile to try to argue against her. She had made up her mind. The wild, rebellious child.

'What do his papers say?' he asked, finally.

'I have no papers. And what would they say? That his parents are Jews. That he is a Jew. I have no papers.'

He reached out and took her hand. 'Then we must get some.' He reached for his wallet and gave her a thousand francs, all that was in there.

'I have enough money,' she said. 'David's mother gave me lots.'

Georges brushed away her attempt to give it back. 'And now your father gives as well.'

'We have to get identity papers and a ration card for David,' Viviane said to Alain when he returned home.

'I have contacts,' Alain said. 'I can get clothes for the boy.'

Viviane sighed. It was true that Alain's adept use of the black market had kept them better fed than many in Grasse but she foresaw a different problem.

'I know you can get clothes for him but that's not good enough.'

She told him about what her father had said.

Alain frowned. 'Maybe you're all worrying too much.'

'You don't know this town like I do,' she said, fiercely. 'You don't know women, either. People will see he is dressed well enough and fed well enough but they will begin to wonder why I never use a ration book for him. And then the police might hear and they will ask for his identity papers.' She picked up a comb and dragged it through her hair. 'I wish his mother had given us those as well as the money.'

'The papers would have a yellow mark on them,' Alain said. 'To show he is a Jew.'

Viviane frowned. 'I didn't know.'

Alain poured himself a second cup of coffee. His mind began to work at the problem, and his love of thwarting authority began to flame.

'He will need a ration book and a birth certificate,' he said. He sipped his coffee thoughtfully. 'And a record of baptism as well.'

Viviane looked shocked. 'Baptism? You even refused to allow Celeste to be baptised.'

Alain gave a rueful grin. 'Celeste is not a Jew. David will need all the documentation we can get.'

Viviane took his hand. She suddenly felt sick to the stomach. 'Should we baptise Celeste as well?'

'There's no need. She's French.'

'But if the police discover that David is Jewish, they might decide that Celeste is his sister and she would be in danger.'

'Roland would never let that happen.'

'I think you're coming to put too much faith in Roland,' she snapped. But, to be honest, she was more worried about what her sister might do. Or her mother.

'Roland is a stickler for the law,' Alain said. 'He lives by the book. There's no harm in him.'

'But if the book changes? If the law changes?'

She could hardly believe what she was saying. She had always had faith in Maréchal Pétain, always thought of him as the father of the nation, a shield against the Nazis. Now, she was beginning to have her doubts. Doubts she was reluctant to entertain.

'It's the Maréchal's deputy I don't trust,' she heard herself say. 'Pierre Laval is like a little German, he's the one who is betraying us.'

'I don't trust any politicians,' Alain said. 'Laval's no better nor worse than any of them. At least he used to be a socialist. Unlike Pétain.'

'Maréchal Pétain saved us at Verdun,' Viviane said.

It was a while before she spoke again. 'And I believe that he's saving us now. Or trying to.'

Alain shook his head violently. 'There's no point in putting our faith in politicians, officials or anybody else. We can only put faith in ourselves, and in our friends.'

She looked at him thoughtfully. 'Gerard was around here when you were away.'

'He's a good friend.'

'He calls here more when you're away than when you're here.'

Alain shrugged. 'He's probably keeping an eye on you.'

'That's what worries me.'

Alain glanced at her, mystified by her words. Sometimes he couldn't follow the flow of her thoughts. Most times, in fact. Nor of any woman, now that he thought about it. Including his daughter.

'Anyway, I shall get the papers. I have contacts in Marseilles.'

'Forgers? Criminals?'

He put his fingers to his lips. 'I don't ask questions. That way I don't get answers I might not want.'

She brushed his hair. 'Be quick then. And be careful.'

## PURCHASING PAPERS
*Marseille, 11 November 1942*

Alain peered out of the dirty window which looked over the port. Somewhere over there lay the island of Corsica which was where the two men in the room hailed from. The man sitting behind a table was called only by his nickname, Le Taureau, the bull. He was one of the biggest bosses in Marseille. His fingers were said to be more numerous than the tentacles of a jelly fish, and more dangerous. Alain had never met him before today.

His contact was Gabriel Chiappe, a man as tiny as Le Taureau was large. Chiappe was head of one of the gangs which specialised in smuggling, and he and Alain had engaged in deals together for many years. As much as possible in such a business, they liked one another.

'Marc Ferrant can provide the papers for my friend,' Chiappe told Le Taureau. 'He is diligent and efficient. And there will be no trace back to us.'

Le Taureau stared at him in silence. Alain sensed Chiappe's nervousness, something he had never witnessed before.

'That is good,' Le Taureau said at last. 'I piss on the fools in Vichy but the Germans? They are a different matter.'

'The Germans are a long way north,' said Alain lightly.

Le Taureau turned his gaze on him. His eyes were like that of a basilisk. Ice-cold, unblinking, barely human. Alain's heart froze.

He allowed Alain to dangle from his gaze for a little while before turning his attention back to Chiappe.

'Do it,' he told him.

'Good,' Chiappe said, reaching for his hat.

'The cost?' Le Taureau said.

Chiappe opened his hands. 'Ten thousand francs is usual.'

Alain swallowed a gasp. That was half the money David's mother had given them. He forced a smile on his lips. If it had to be, it had to be.

'Not enough,' said Le Taureau. 'Fifty thousand.'

'That's impossible,' cried Alain. 'I don't have that much.'

'And this is my concern?' Le Taureau said. 'Tell me how it is.' His cold eyes held Alain's in an icy grip.

'Maybe twenty thousand,' Chiappe suggested.

'I've said the price,' Le Taureau said. 'Forging papers for Jews is risky.'

'I didn't say the boy's a Jew,' Alain cried.

Le Taureau gave no response other than to gesture to the door.

Alain and Chiappe paused at the top of the stairs.

'Can you do it for less?' Alain asked.

'Yes. If I want to end up as a corpse in the sea. What Le Taureau says is the law in our world. I'm sorry, my friend.'

Alain sighed. 'Then the least you can do is to buy me a good lunch.'

'Gladly.' He took Alain's hand. 'Truly, I'm sorry.'

Now what?' Alain wondered. How could they protect the child?

He stayed the night in a little hotel in the back streets of the old part of Marseille. The owner, Monsieur Guizot, knew him of old and allowed him to put his motorbike in a little lean-to in the yard. He spent much of the night tossing and turning in the chill room, missing Viviane and worrying about what they should do next. The last thing he remembered, as he finally drifted off to sleep, was that he would have to let the boy take his chances in an orphanage.

He was hungry when he woke and, leaving his bike in Guizot's safe keeping, went towards his favourite cafe near the port. The day was cold and dreary with a fierce mistral wind screaming across the sea, lashing the waters into turmoil and sending rubbish on the quay-side cascading across the streets.

His eyes were wet and raw from the buffeting wind, his ears ringing with its shriek, and he was glad to duck into the warming fug of the cafe.

The owner gave him a grudging nod, the most acknowledgement he gave to even his most loyal customers.

'Coffee and some bread,' Alain said, squeezing himself behind a tiny zinc table. He glanced through the patina of dirt on the window. The quay was crowded with men: stevedores with leather jackets, porters dragging laden trolleys or striding sure-footed with parcels balanced on their heads, fishermen throwing their catches onto carts, and a small scatter of loafers who braved even this dire weather to idle contentedly and watch other men work.

The owner plonked a bowl of coffee and a plate of bread on the table. There was a tiny scrape of margarine to one side of the plate and a smear of what may or may not have been jam beside it. Alain spread the margarine and jam thinly, a gloss much thinner than the grime on the window, yet still it covered less than half the bread. He tore a lump off with his teeth, expecting it to resist but the bread was fresh and surprisingly good. He might have more, he thought, for such rare delights were worth seizing and he had an eight-hour ride home, perhaps longer with this wind. He glanced at the clock above the bar. Half past seven. If he were lucky, he would reach Grasse by evening.

He sipped his coffee which was hot and sweet but then his hand shook so suddenly he almost spilt it. An old man had silently taken a seat across the table from him, even though the cafe was virtually empty. The cafe owner had disappeared from his perch behind the bar.

'You are Alain Renaud?' the man muttered, barely moving his lips.

'Who's asking?' Alain said.

'A Corsican friend suggests you go to the Capuchin Monastery,' the man answered. 'Ask for Father Benoît.' He pressed a piece of paper into Alain's hands and slipped out of the cafe.

Alain glanced at the piece of paper. It bore an address and was signed with the letters, G.C.

'Thank you, Gabriele,' he muttered.

It took Alain an hour to find the monastery and by then the sky had grown an ominous black. He pulled on a bell and heard its dull clang echoing from the other side of the door.

He waited for a while, glancing occasionally at the sky, wondering if anybody had heard the bell and, if they had, whether they would come to answer it. But eventually the door creaked open and a young friar peered out. He was dressed in a brown tunic with a hood pulled back untidily on his neck. He was little more than a boy, judging by the sparse hairs straggling on his chin. He did not speak but merely stared at Alain.

'I've come to see Father Benoît,' Alain said.

A look of alarm crossed the young man's face but he swiftly composed himself and took on what he probably imagined was a look of calm. Alain thought it looked more vacant than anything.

'What do you want with the father?' he asked.

'I want his help.'

The friar nodded and cleared his throat. 'And who sent you?'

'Gabriel…' Alain said. He was about to say his surname but suddenly thought better of it and stopped himself. 'Gabriel sent me.'

The friar's mouth opened in astonishment. He stared at Alain in silence for a while, then peered at the street behind him as if searching for someone. He stared at Alain in awe, opened the door a little more and crooked a finger for him to enter.

They were in a narrow corridor with several doors on either side. Three religious paintings hung along either wall with a large crucifix on the wall to the right. A staircase was at the far end, leading to an upper floor.

'Gabriel sent you?' the boy repeated.

'That's right. To see Father Benoît.'

'Then come with me.'

The boy hurried off, his sandals echoing in the empty corridor, a curious slapping sound as if a wet fish were being beaten. At the end of the corridor he made for a small door to the left. Alain could see that he was almost shaking with excitement.

He opened the door and beckoned Alain to follow. There was a steep flight of steps immediately in front of them. The walls echoed with a noise of clattering and thumping and the hum of human voices from below.

The young man ran down the steps and waited at the bottom.

Alain joined him and looked around in surprise.

They were in a large cellar, which must once have served as a storehouse. The roof was low and vaulted and hanging from it were a line of very bright electric lights. To one side of the cellar were two small printing presses, worked by two elderly friars.

Along the left-hand side were half a dozen small tables, even more brightly lit by lamps, with two young friars and four nuns bending over them with the utmost concentration. At the far end of the cellar, examining a document under the glare of a light, was a middle-aged friar with a long, straggly beard.

The young friar gestured to Alain and led the way to the man, who glanced up, irritated. He was in his late forties, Alain judged, with long nose and deep eyes of a sharp intelligence.

'What is the meaning of this, Lawrence?' he demanded of the young friar. 'Why have you brought a stranger here?'

'He was sent to us, Father,' the boy said, making the sign of the cross. 'By Archangel Gabriel.'

The older friar stared at him in silence for a few moments, a range of emotions chasing each other across his face: anger, incredulity, exasperation and finally a weary acceptance.

'I doubt the archangel would visit us here, today,' he said, not unkindly. Then he patted the young man on the shoulder much as a man might a dog who had brought him his most comfortable shoes. 'Yet who knows. Back to your duties, now Lawrence. I will deal with our visitor and you must forget all about it.'

He gave Lawrence a conspiratorial look which made the boy flush with excitement.

'I am Father Benoît,' the friar said, holding out his hand to Alain. 'You do not look the sort who an angel would deal with but…' He held out his hands, as if even that might be possible.

'I was given your name by Gabriel Chiappe,' Alain began.

'I don't know the man,' Benoît said.

'Well he knows of you.' He glanced at the printing presses. 'I asked him to forge some papers for me, for a boy I have taken in. Gabriel's colleague, his boss in fact, wanted to charge me far more than I can pay. But Gabriel gave me your name so…'

He left the rest of the sentence unsaid.

'Forgeries?' the father said. He gestured to the printing presses. 'These are but copies of prayers and sermons.'

Alain glanced at the paper on the desk. It was a baptism record. He raised an eyebrow.

'The church baptises children, my friend. You must know that.'

'I'm not a church-goer.'

'May I ask why not?'

'I'm part Roma. We are not very Christian.'

Benoît tilted his head thoughtfully. 'So who do you worship? Allah? Shiva? Nature gods?'

'Money chiefly,' Alain said, 'and great men in our past.' He sighed. 'Some of my relatives also worship Sara e Kali.'

'Saint Sarah the black,' Benoît said.

Alain shrugged. He had little interest in such matters.

'Will you sell me forged papers or not?' he asked.

The friar stared at him for a long time. Alain felt abashed by it, almost intimidated, but he refused to lower his eyes.

'I will sell them,' the friar said. 'Although you may not like the price.'

Alain's eyes narrowed. Priests were more avaricious than crime-bosses, he thought. 'How much?'

'No money. But you must promise to keep the child. Keep him safe.'

Alain gave him a suspicious look. 'That is why I am here.'

'Then the cost will be easy to bear, my son.'

He picked up a pen. 'Tell me the name of the boy and his parents.'

'He's a Jew.'

'Of course. Why else are you here? I mean the name by which you wish him to be known.'

'David Legarde, His mother would be Simone Legarde.'

Benoît noted this down. 'And the father?'

Alain frowned. Neither Viviane nor he had thought of a man for his father.

'Shall we say Henri,' Benoît said. 'A good French name.'

Alain nodded.

'The boy's place of birth?'

'My wife said that Simone lived near Paris. Close to the Renault factory where she died in a bombing raid.'

'You have an intelligent wife, Monsieur.' He bent and wrote carefully, muttering to himself, 'Place of birth, Boulogne-Billancourt.'

He straightened up.' I will need to check the churches in that area. Perhaps one that was damaged in the raid. Where the records may have been destroyed.'

He held his hand out to Alain who, to his surprise, found himself kissing it.

'Return this evening, at ten,' Benoît said. 'The documents will be ready by then.'


## THE END OF VICHY FRANCE
*11 November 1942*

Weiser rubbed his eyes wearily. It was only twelve hours since he had received the order to join the invasion force. He glanced behind him at the motorised column stretching into the distance. They had covered over four hundred kilometres and were crossing the River Rhone into Avignon.

It was a pity that they had outrun the tanks, Weiser thought, but General Blaskowitz was adamant that they move as swiftly as possible. He was racing for the Mediterranean Sea and would brook no delay. He was confident that the tiny French forces would be unable put up much resistance.

His optimism appeared to have been justified. As they hurtled through villages and towns the only French people they saw were bewildered and terrified citizens. One Gendarme in a village near Valance had single-handedly tried to stop the approaching column but a bullet had ended his defiance.

'That's a big place,' Mundt said as they neared the Palace of the Popes.

'I expect we'll take it over,' Weiser said with a grin. Despite his fatigue he was exhilarated by the headlong ride and the chance of yet more conquests.

'So where do you think we're going?' Mundt asked. 'And why?'

'You're like a child going on holiday,' Weiser answered. 'I've told you all I know. 'The army is taking over in the south. Just like in the north.'

Mundt offered Weiser a cigarette. 'And you still don't know why?'

Weiser shook his head. 'But I'll know soon enough. The General has called a conference for senior officers. It will start as soon as the column has reached Avignon.'

Weiser was astonished at what he learnt at the conference. The war had taken a bad turn.

A few days before, the Allies had invaded the French territories in North Africa. Almost four hundred ships had landed seventy thousand British and American troops in a huge arc stretching from Casablanca to Algiers, a distance of fifteen hundred kilometres. The Vichy government's French forces had offered only token resistance in a handful of places; many had instantly gone over to the Allies.

'Because of this, Hitler says the French cannot be trusted,' General Blaskowitz told them. 'As of today the French Government will, in reality, cease to exist.'

He pointed to the map of France. 'We are heading for Marseille which I expect to take by this evening. Our next objective is Toulon where the French fleet is moored. At all costs we must prevent the fleet from sailing out of port and joining our adversaries.'

'Do we expect any opposition from the French?' a colonel asked.

The General shook his head. 'There are very few French soldiers in the south. But if the police are all as courageous as that lone Gendarme then maybe we should be worried.' He gave a raucous laugh, which the others joined in.

He leaned over the map and quickly outlined the route the army would take into Marseille, pointing out the areas with bottlenecks and potential resistance. He was in his element; the last time he had led an army in such an operation was the invasion of Poland. The conference lasted only twenty minutes but before he walked to his vehicle Blaskowitz called Weiser over.

'I hear good reports of your work in Dijon,' he said.

Weiser looked mystified, wondering exactly what had drawn the General's attention to him.

'You're a tough yet fair commander,' Blaskowitz said. 'You do your duty efficiently. You also put that scum Barbie in his place. I was glad to hear it.'

Weiser failed to hide a smile. It was no bad thing to have a man like Blaskowitz take notice of one.

He suddenly recalled something he had heard about the General. Rumour had it that he had opposed the worst atrocities the SS perpetrated against the Poles and was refused his rightful promotion because of it. Despite this, his undoubted skills as a commander had now led to his being picked for the invasion of Free France.

'I want you to take and hold Aix-en-Provence,' Blaskowitz continued. 'It's got a strategic importance as well as being very beautiful.' He paused and glanced around. 'There's an internment camp for dissidents and Jews ten kilometres from the centre. It's under the command of the Vichy government at the moment but the Wehrmacht will shortly have responsibility for it. See that this is done in a way which brings credit to the army and not to the SS.'

Weiser clicked his heels and saluted.

The General reached into a pocket and gave Weiser a letter. 'I'm making you an Oberst. You'll have need of the rank.'

Weiser found Mundt chatting to a group of drivers beside the column. For a moment he envied his old friend for being only a Major. The letter confirming his promotion weighed heavily in his pocket. He took a deep breath. It was an honour to be an Oberst. He would make sure he earned the General's faith and trust.

'We're going,' he said to Mundt, jumping into his car and gesturing to his friend to join him. 'Where to?'

'Aix-en-Provence. We're to take it and hold it.'

'Who's in command?'

'I am.' Weiser handed him the letter as the car moved off.

'Congratulations,' Mundt said. He was delighted for his friend. 'I doubt I'll ever catch up with you now.'

'Who knows what the fortunes of war may bring to you as well as to me.'

'Lots of wine and pretty girls, I hope.' Mundt leaned back and watched the waters of the Rhone rippling in the November sunshine.

'And what happens once we've taken Aix?' he asked. 'Is a Major allowed to hear this from his Oberst?'

Weiser chuckled. He could rely on his old friend to keep his feet firmly on the ground.

'The army will occupy the whole of France west of the Rhone,' he said, 'and the Italians will get east of the river.'

'So we'll do all the fighting and the Italians will get the prize,' Mundt said.

Weiser smiled and gave a nod.

'Trust the Italians to get the Riviera,' Mundt said. 'Lucky bastards. So we should enjoy it while we can.'

## COLLECTING THE PAPERS
*Marseille 11 November 1942*

Alain returned to his hotel and booked for an extra night. He spent the rest of the day visiting his usual contacts, using the time to try to arrange some deals. This proved harder than usual. The traffic from North Africa had inexplicably dried up a few days before and the port appeared to be handling goods only from France and Italy. This was poorer trade for Alain, foodstuffs instead of cigarettes and fancy goods, but he did what he could.

He ate a sparse supper of fish-stew and stale bread before making his way to the monastery. The streets were empty and unlit and he found his way by occasionally switching on a small hand-torch. He fingered the flick-knife in his pocket. He knew better than most how dangerous these streets could be. Despite the knife he had no relish for a dispute with street-fighters and hoped that any such would recognise him before an attack. After all, he had been dealing with the most powerful gangs for ten years now and that counted for something.

His footsteps echoed on the walls on either side, almost as if they were the sound of pursuers. If anyone pounced on him he would have little chance to fight them off. He would shout out the name of Gabriel Chiappe, say he was his friend, and keep his fingers crossed that his attackers were not the Corsican's enemies.

The streets near to the monastery were the quietest yet and he found himself moving into the centre of the street, away from the buildings. The moon rose, not yet full, and cast a cold light over the streets, enough for him to pick his way forward without the need to use the torch.

Finally, he saw the monastery ahead, breathed a sigh of relief and hurried towards it, putting out of mind, for the moment, that he had an equally worrying journey back to the hotel.

He had almost reached the monastery when he heard it. A deep-throated roar of vehicles pounding along the streets. There was a blare of lights and then, flooding into the space in front of the streets, came half a dozen motorbikes followed by three large lorries. The canopies of the lorries were flung back and men leapt from them to the ground.

At first Alain thought they were police and slunk into the shadows. Then his mouth gaped wide. They were wearing military helmets, not police ones. And they were shouting in German, not in French.

A moment later an armoured car nosed into the square and an officer climbed out and directed some men to the door of the monastery. They hammered on it for a while and, when no answer was forthcoming, laid a charge and blew it to pieces.

For a moment, Alain was rooted to the spot, too scared and too fascinated to move. Then he realised the danger, pushed himself against the wall and tried to calm his breathing. The soldiers were now spilling into the monastery. They must have heard about Benoit's work. He could hear the noise of their calls and then the sound of machinery being smashed. That was the end of the friar's operation, he thought bitterly. The end of the friars too, probably.

The German troops were now engrossed solely on the monastery. He took a few steps backwards, waiting for the moment when he could safely slip away. His heart was like a piston in his chest.

And then he saw a solitary friar race through the grounds of the monastery, holding a large bag. He darted through the darkness, sure-footed in his knowledge of the place. He made it to the street and then turned, heading in Alain's direction. He'll get away, Alain thought.

But then a soldier happened to glance up and saw him. He was ordered to halt but this served only to make the friar run more quickly. Three soldiers raced out of the monastery grounds cutting across the road to block his escape. He hugged the bag close to his chest and held out one arm as if to fend them off.

The soldiers seized him, yelling at him with a nervous aggression. One dragged the bag out of his arms and this seemed to enrage the man. He tried to wrestle it back and landed a punch on the soldier's chest. In an instant, all three men retaliated, knocking the friar to the ground with savage blows and then kicking him as if he were a piece of rubbish littering the road. He held his hands over his head, screaming in terror but still the soldiers kicked and stamped.

Then, to Alain's amazement, the man leapt to his feet, grabbed the bag from the soldier's grasp and fled towards him. The soldiers chased after him, reaching him a mere half dozen steps from Alain.

The moonlight shone on his feet and Alain recognised him. Lawrence, the young friar who had opened the door to him only this morning. Lawrence recognised him too and thrust the bag into his arms.

'Save the papers, monsieur,' he cried and turned to face the soldiers. Two smashed into him, flinging him to the ground once again. The third leapt at Alain, taking hold of the bag and trying to drag it back. Instinctively, Alain pulled hard on the bag and for a few moments, he and the soldier engaged in a desperate tug of war.

I must be mad, Alain thought, and then he let go of the bag. The soldier was still pulling on it ferociously and now, with Alain no longer struggling, he fell back onto his comrades.

Alain wasted no time. He turned and fled back the way he had come. He had no concern for any criminals roaming the streets now.

He ran in a daze. Time seemed slow, time seemed fast, his feet like lead, his feet like wings. Finally he stopped and tried to calm his breathing so he could listen better. He could just about hear the cries of the soldiers and the continual noise of metal being broken. He closed his eyes and then vomited against a wall.

He wiped his mouth and realised that he was a dozen steps from the hotel. He slipped inside and locked the door behind him, fetching a chair to jam against the handle, a futile gesture he realised even as he did so.

He would leave Marseille before dawn.

## DOROTHY STEPS UP
12 November 1942

'Papa's home,' Celeste called to her mother.

Viviane hurriedly pulled the last of the washing from the line and rushed into the house.

'Did you get the papers?' she asked.

Alain shook his head and sat down. 'I nearly did. And then things got very bad.' He went to the cupboard for a bottle of cognac and some glasses, slumped down in his chair and held his head in his hand.

'Tell me,' she said. She was fighting to keep the nausea down.

He told her how Le Taureau had put an end to any chance of getting the papers from his contacts and then how he had been more successful in approaching Father Benoît. Until the last moment.

Then he paused and took a large gulp of cognac.

'So what happened?'

Alain took her hand. 'The Germans have invaded. They've overrun the south of France.'

She shook her head in disbelief. 'But why? Maréchal Pétain said we would remain free.'

'The old fool was wrong.' He poured another glass of cognac. 'I've seen the German tanks roaring through Marseille.'

'And the papers?'

'The Germans must have heard about the monastery and its work. They destroyed the whole operation, printing presses included. I don't know if any of the friars even survived. At any rate, that's an end to any hope of getting papers from them.'

He placed his chin in his hand and stared out of the window. 'It's a shame. Father Benoît was a good man.'

Viviane nodded, although she did not much care whether Benoît was an angel or a devil. All that mattered was that he had offered to provide the papers but could not do so again.

'Why do you think they invaded? The Germans?'

'I know why,' Alain said. 'I heard it from my friend Gabriel just as I was leaving this morning. The Allies have invaded North Africa. American and British troops landed in Morocco and Algeria a few days ago. The Germans know that this means the end of Pétain's control of North Africa. Presumably they don't trust him to hold the south securely anymore.'

'Against the Allies?'

They're only eight hundred kilometres away, Viviane.'

'That's a long way. And across the sea. Surely, they would never be able to invade France from such a distance.'

'Probably not. But who knows?'

Viviane clutched Alain's hand so hard he winced.

'Do you think it will mean the end of the war?' she said. 'Will we be free once again?'

Alain sighed. 'I don't know, Viv. Pétain managed to keep the French fleet out of German hands. Now, they'll be certain to take it over and then even the Royal Navy will find itself harder pressed in the Mediterranean.'

Viviane heard this news with dismay. 'Do you think the Allies will give up? Do you think the Germans will win the war?'

'Who knows what to believe. All I can say is what I saw with my own eyes; that the Germans are now at the coast. My friend Gabriel, who has his ears close to the wind, says that this will be the end of Pétain and his puppets. Hitler will be our master now.'

Viviane's hand went to her mouth. 'What will that mean for David?'

'I don't know,' he said.

He looked away, wondering how to tell her what he had been thinking on the long journey back from Marseille. Things would be too dangerous from now on. They would have to give David up.

The clock on the wall suddenly seemed to take on a life of its own, echoing from wall to wall as if it were now deciding all their fates.

Viviane stared at Alain with growing disbelief. He was not answering. He had already made up his mind. He would say they had to let David go.

'Alain?'

Her voice shook him out of his thoughts. This was not right. The Germans invading, the whole monstrous war, none of it was right. A sudden anger seized him and he swallowed the rest of the cognac in one gulp.

'What I do know is that I'm not going to let those bastards win. No little shit is going to destroy my family and take the boy away.'

He squeezed Viviane's hand. 'Don't worry. I'll get the papers. Even if I have to forge them myself.'

Viviane swallowed the lump in her throat.

She got to her feet and went to the picture of Maréchal Pétain on the wall. Very deliberately, she unhooked it, took it out into the yard and threw it into the trash.

Viviane decided to unburden herself to Dorothy. Not that she had any real hope of getting help from her. Before Germany declared war on the United States she may have had a little more independence but now that the two countries were at war, Dorothy was as vulnerable as any other person in France. Perhaps even more vulnerable. But, apart from Sylvie, the American was the only person who she felt she could trust. And she had to talk to somebody.

Dorothy was sympathetic but not encouraging. 'I won't lie to you, Viviane,' she said. 'The German take-over changes everything. I've even thought of leaving France.'

Viviane looked crestfallen at the news.

Dorothy gave a humourless laugh. 'But that option is now completely ruled out. I'm stuck here for the duration. And my enemies are about to come knocking on my door.'

She saw the effect her words had on Viviane who was struggling to keep the tears from her eyes.

'Cheer up, darling,' she continued, as brightly as she could. 'Things are never as good or as bad as we think they might be. And I've got plenty of money, which will stand me in good stead.'

Viviane nodded although she was only half listening. Her mind was fixed on how to get David's papers. And what would happen to him if they failed.

Dorothy stared at Viviane. 'How much will it cost?' she asked.

Viviane shook her head in confusion. 'How much will what cost?'

'To forge David's papers.'

'More than we have. It's out of the question.'

Dorothy gave a grim smile. 'No, it's not darling. The mighty dollar still has some punch.' She leaned back in her seat. 'I've got a safe stashed full of Greenbacks. Get that man of yours to go back to his cronies with enough money to pay all they demand.'

For a moment Viviane was speechless.

'I couldn't do that,' she whispered at last.

'Of course not. But I think Alain could. Just view it as a loan. I'll get it back from David when he grows up and becomes a tycoon or whatever.'

Viviane burst into tears. She couldn't believe that Dorothy had made such a generous offer. Nor that it meant as much to her as she now realised it did.

## RETURN TO MARSEILLE
*Marseille 16 November 1942*

When he returned to Marseille Alain found the Germans well and truly entrenched. All the main junctions had barricades and soldiers patrolled the streets with wary faces, their rifles constantly at the ready.

He found Gabriel Chiappe in his usual haunt, a down at heel cafe on the quayside, with a clientele who hid themselves behind clouds of cigarette smoke.

'I hadn't expected to see you back so soon,' Chiappe said.

Alain frowned, 'Nor did I, Gabriel.'

He bought two glasses of wine and told him what had happened to Father Benoît.

'So what now?' Chiappe asked.

Alain glanced around to see that no one was paying attention then pulled out a roll of notes.

'Dollars,' Chiappe breathed. He gave a little whistle. 'Almost as good as gold,' he said. 'Where did you get them?'

'Never you mind. I want you to go back to Le Taureau and say I want his agreement to forge the papers. Unless you can do it without him knowing.'

'I can't piss without him knowing,' Chiappe said. He stared at the dollar bills. 'I'll go and see him immediately. I'll meet you at the La Samaritaine at noon. You can buy me lunch there.'

Alain was at the brasserie at a quarter to twelve. He felt sick, knowing that all his and Viviane's hopes might be dashed at any moment.

Chiappe arrived a little after twelve. His face gave nothing away.

'Well?' Alain asked.

'Le Taureau is happy for the deal to go ahead.'

Alain clapped his hands in joy.

'But there's a difficulty,' Chiappe added. 'Le Taureau is demanding double what he said before.'

'But why?'

'It's riskier now that the Germans are here. I see his point of view.'

'A hundred thousand francs,' Alain said. 'That's ten times more than the usual price.'

Chiappe shrugged.

Alain hesitated for only a moment. If the rich American wanted to act so charitably, who was he to disappoint her?

'It's a deal,' he said.

Chiappe said it take a couple of days for the forgers to do their work. Alain bought them both lunch and went back to his usual hotel.

He expected there to be an atmosphere of gloom and despair but far from it.

Guizot, the owner of the hotel, wiped the counter with vehement energy. 'Those filthy Bosch have bitten off more than they can chew in trying to conquer Marseille. We'll make them shit in their beds, see if we don't.'

He was either prescient or in the know, for that very night a German patrol was ambushed and killed. The motorbike and sidecar had been dismantled and scattered across the city within an hour of the incident, hidden in cellars or cannibalised onto vehicles in plain sight.

The Germans responded by killing four citizens who lived in the house opposite where the bodies were found. Nobody knew if they were innocent of the deaths or complicit. To the Germans it did not matter. They believed it would prove a deterrent.

The second night two more patrols were found dead.

'I wonder how this will end?' Alain wondered, quietly to Monsieur Guizot.

'As it always will,' he answered. 'In rivers of blood.'

Alain frowned and paid his bill. 'I might not be back for a while,' he said. He meant that he doubted he would ever return.

'Then good luck, my friend,' Guizot said. 'I hope that you have more success with your plans than you did last time.'

Alain's heart felt like stone. This was dangerous talk, and he feared it might be deadly.

He met Gabriel Chiappe in a cafe on the port. He looked wary but in good spirits.

'You seem pleased,' Alain said to him.

'With the German occupation?' He shrugged. 'Some of our businesses have been hit, smuggling for example. But the Germans have plenty of money and our bars and brothels are booming. Do you know any girls who might be interested in working for me?'

'A few. But they're in Grasse.'

Chiappe pursed his lips. 'Maybe I'll come and visit you there, one day.'

'Oh no. I deal with you in Marseille and Marseille alone. If you came to Grasse, you'd scare the children.'

Chiappe chuckled and glanced around the bar casually. 'Talking of which.' He pulled an envelope from the inside pocket of his overcoat and slid it across to Alain. 'Birth certificate, baptism certificate and ration card. I even threw in the birth certificate of the boy's mother. There's no charge for that, my friend.'

Alain slipped the envelope into his coat without opening it. Then he slid another envelope across the table to Chiappe.

'One hundred thousand,' he murmured. 'How much do you and your boys get?'

'You wouldn't want to know and I wouldn't want to tell you. Let's just say that Le Taureau will be very happy with his cut. As I am with mine.'

Alain drank off the last of his coffee.

'Thank you, my friend,' he said. 'If there's anything I can do for you...'

'Yeah, yeah,' Chiappe said with a dismissive wave. 'As if there's anything you could possibly do for me.'

'These are strange times, Gabriel. You never can tell.'

And without another word, he left the cafe, climbed onto his bike and rode off.

He had only gone two kilometres when he was stopped by a German patrol.

'Ausweis,' the soldier demanded.

Alain looked blank.

'Die Papiere,' the soldier said. 'Your papers.'

Alain nodded and passed him his papers.

The German examined them with a thoroughness which was alarming. If anything proved the necessity of getting papers for David it was this.

The soldier stared at his bike. 'You are the owner of this motorbike?'

'Yes.'

'You have proof?' The soldier was leafing through the papers once again.

Alain gave him the paper-work for the bike.

The soldier studied it, although he could not read French well. 'All is in order,' he said, handing the papers back. 'On your way.'

Alain hesitated. 'Tell me, friend,' he asked, 'why have you come to Marseille?'

'I am not your friend. And we have come to complete our conquest of the French.'

Alain smiled. 'I appreciate your honesty, Monsieur.'

The soldier looked at him with cold eyes. 'On your way,' he repeated.

Alain kicked the bike into life and rode off.

He did not stop even once on the long journey home.

'Have you got them?' Viviane asked before he'd taken two steps into the house.

He grinned and passed her the envelope.

She looked aghast. 'You've not even opened it. How do you know they're in here?'

'I know Gabriel,' he said.

She darted him an angry look and tore the seal of the envelope. She studied the documents and gasped. 'They're all here. And papers for his mother.'

'That was a gift.' He gave her a hug. 'The boy's safe, now. Thanks to that mad old American.'

'Perhaps you should come and see her.'

'Perhaps I should. I have two bottles of 1921 Medoc. I think I'll take her one.'

## SEIZING CONTROL
*Aix-en-Provence 25 November 1942*

Colonel Weiser climbed out of his car and looked around. The Fountain of the Rotonde was directly in front of him, its waters jetting above the basin, catching the autumn sun in a thousand joyful sparkles. Since being a student, he had wanted to visit Aix-en-Provence. But he had always imagined himself coming in happier times, as a solitary traveller perhaps, discovering the beauty of the Mediterranean region, or later with his growing family, maybe camping in the nearby countryside or staying in some cheap and friendly boarding house.

He had never imagined he would come at the head of an invading army, nor that he was to lead the administration of the city.

The capture of Aix had caused no problems. A number of the French troops offered resistance but the local commander saw that to continue would be futile and within a few hours ordered his men to surrender.

And now, Weiser was waiting to meet him and the civic dignitaries. A lot would depend on this first meeting, he thought. Whether the occupation of the town would be cordial with a minimum of trouble or, as more likely, with constant headaches and hindrances.

Five roads led from the Rotonde, every one of them lined by trees brimming with leaves of red or gold or copper.

Weiser straightened, seeing the line of cars nosing their way towards them. 'Here comes the welcome committee,' he said.

Otto Mundt nodded to the junior officers who deployed their men, ready for trouble.

The cars came to a halt, although the drivers did not turn off their engines, and half a dozen officials stepped out and walked nervously towards them.

'Welcome to Aix-en-Provence,' said the first official as he held out a hand.

Weiser refused the offer. A conqueror must remain apart, superior. But Mundt shook the man's hand without thinking. It felt like a mackerel on a fishmonger's slab, wet, cold and slimy. He did not bother to hide his distaste, wiping his own hand on his coat.

'Are you the Mayor?' Mundt asked. 'This is Oberst Weiser, who will be in charge of the city.'

'Alas the Mayor is indisposed,' the man said. 'I am Marcel Joubert, his Deputy.'

'That's not good enough,' Mundt muttered.

'He has a virus,' Joubert explained. 'Vomiting, diarrhoea.'

Weiser said nothing, wondering if this was the first example of the petty obstructionism he feared he would face.

'I wish him a speedy recovery,' Weiser said.

A few of the officials looked at him in surprise, astonished that a German could be so sympathetic. But the Deputy took it in his stride. He nodded, dolefully and then a winning look came over his face.

'Your quarters are being prepared,' he said. 'They are the best in the city. I am to lead you to them.'

'One minute,' Weiser said. 'I hear rumour that there is a camp nearby. At Les Milles. Where your Government interned people they considered undesirables. Intellectuals, dissidents, Jews.'

Joubert's eyes narrowed. 'That is now almost empty.'

'And the inmates?'

Joubert licked his lips, nervously. 'The authorities, in Vichy, ordered that they be sent to your country. To other camps.'

'I hear that Jewish children were sent as well.'

Weiser saw Joubert's Adam's Apple leap up and down, as swift as dice thrown in a game. He inclined his head in a gesture that could be interpreted in any number of ways.

'The Reich did not ask for these children,' Weiser continued. 'The French volunteered for them to be sent.'

'By the Prime Minister, Pierre Laval,' Joubert said. 'In Vichy.'

Weiser stared at the man for a long while. 'And locals delivered them up. Men like you, perhaps.'

Joubert did not know how to answer. Again he sought safety by trying to appear uninvolved. 'By this time the camp was being run by Rodellec Porzic, the Intendant of Police in Marseilles.'

Weiser's face grew cold. 'Tell me, Monsieur Deputy, who is worse, the Pied Piper or the king of rats who capers beside him, joyful that it is children and not rats who are going to their doom?'

'Alas for these times,' said Joubert.

The air hung heavily over the meeting.

'I do not wish to see this camp,' Weiser said, abruptly. 'I wish it to be closed. Immediately.'

'And the few inmates who are still in the camp?'

'Do with them as you wish. As long as they remain in France.'

Joubert looked jubilant at the news. Weiser and Mundt exchanged glances, questioning the sincerity of his reaction.

'Now escort the Oberst to his headquarters,' Mundt said. 'And see that the camp is closed.'

'As you command,' said Joubert.

The Wehrmacht were given an impressive headquarters by the city authorities. Mundt was content. Most of the managers were middle-aged men who were dedicated professionals and followed any instructions quickly and efficiently. There were a dozen women, mostly typists, and he selected the prettiest to be his assistant.

'She's not very good at typing,' he explained to a fellow officer, 'but she has a lovely face and gorgeous eyes.'

'Why employ her as your assistant, though?' the man responded. 'Just strip her naked and take her over your desk. If she satisfies you, send her back to the typing pool and summon her whenever you have an itch. If she's no good just sack her. But there's no need to employ her.'

Mundt pondered his advice but ignored it. He liked to be surrounded by beauty.

A few days later the itch grew strong and he summoned the young woman to his office. 'Lock the door,' he ordered.

She did so and turned to face him, face white with fear.

'Clear the desk,' he said. 'Then take your clothes off.'

The act proved swift and perfunctory. She said no word nor made no sound, throughout. He blushed as he climbed off her, feeling rather ashamed.

She put on her clothes hastily, her face averted in shame. He understood this, for he felt the same.

'This will not be the last time,' he warned her, forcing himself to sound hard and harsh.

She nodded and fled from the room, racing past an officer who was striding towards the colonel's office. He glanced at her in surprise, then rapped once on the door and threw it open.

Weiser leapt to his feet, ready to yell at whoever had the temerity to disturb him in such a manner.

Then he saw who it was and gave the Nazi salute. 'General Blaskowitz,' he said.

The General touched his cap and drew up a chair.

'I hear you've ordered that the camp at Les Milles be closed,' he said. He was a man known for getting straight to the point.

'Yes, my General.'

Blaskowitz considered this carefully. 'I understand,' he said, finally. 'But may I counsel you to be circumspect. You don't want to get yourself a reputation.'

Like you have, Weiser thought, although he did not say it. It was common knowledge that Blaskowitz would have been made a Field Marshal were it not for his fierce and vocal opposition to the worst excesses of the SS in Poland.

Weiser offered the General a cigarette but he refused it. 'Is Aix calm?' he asked.

'It is,' Weiser said. 'There was opposition when we first arrived but it was trifling. The Mayor has removed himself to the hospital but his deputy is proving compliant and effective.'

'Good. Then Aix can spare you for a few days.'

'As you wish, General.'

Blaskowitz stared at him thoughtfully before continuing. 'You will recall, Colonel, that the British Royal Navy attacked French ships in Algeria in 1940 and put five of them out of action. It led to a great deal of anti-British feeling amongst the French, which was of benefit to us, of course.'

Weiser nodded, although he thought that any benefits had been slight, at best.

'May I?' Blaskowitz indicated a map of the region and tapped his fingers on the town of Toulon.

'This is where the rest of the French fleet is berthed,' he continued. 'Three battleships, seven cruisers, eighteen destroyers, twenty submarines and dozens of other craft.

'Grand-Admiral Raeder believes that the Pétain government and the French Navy are still incensed about the British attack and will not allow the fleet at Toulon to fall into the hands of the Allies. He thinks that this sentiment will lead them to hand over their ships to the Italians.

'Hitler believes otherwise. He fears that the French will set sail for North Africa and put the Fleet in the hands of the Allies. He has sent secret orders that we are to seize the fleet. It will be a great prize. And it may tip the scales in the Mediterranean. Perhaps even make the English and the Americans sue for peace.

'The ships will be given to our navy?' Weiser asked.

'Unfortunately, no. Hitler wants us to hand them over to the Italians.'

Weiser heard this without comment. He had no experience of the Italians apart from the rumours that they were poor soldiers who would have been annihilated in the Desert War if Rommel had not come to their aid. If he ever thought of Mussolini it was with contempt.

'I want you to go with General Keppler to Toulon,' Blaskowitz continued. 'You are to liaise with the Italian forces there. General Keppler is not noted as a diplomatic man and we need to maintain the friendliest of relations with the Italians. You are to leave immediately. The attack on the port will start in thirty-six hours.'

## DIVIDING UP THE SPOILS
*27 November 1942*

General Blaskowitz had made it clear that Weiser was not to be involved in the attack on Toulon so he had stationed himself on the hills to the north of the city to wait for events to unfold.

General Keppler informed him that the operation would start at 4:00 am with tanks and armoured vehicles pouring into the port from east and west. Weiser gave his orderly instructions to be woken at 5:30 to give him time to wash and shave before the light grew bright enough to witness events.

Now, two hours later, he watched open-mouthed with shock. The French had scuttled their ships. Some had their sea valves opened and were already sinking. Others had suffered catastrophic explosions, destroying armaments and fuel.

A thick pall of smoke rose in the morning air above the harbour.

Weiser shook his head in disbelief and summoned Otto Mundt to join him.

'We're going down to the port,' he said.

'But the General told you not to join the attack —'

'The attack has failed. We're going to see why.'

Weiser stared at the ships still burning in the harbour. It was now evening and Keppler's troops stood beside their tanks, watching as the ships blazed. It reminded him of Berliners watching their homes burn after a bombing raid. They were shocked, numb, could barely believe what had happened.

So much for General Keppler's much vaunted military prowess. The operation had been a fiasco.

Had he seized control of the French fleet the Allies might have been reluctant to launch an invasion across the Mediterranean. But the scuttling of the ships had ended any hope of thwarting them.

A feeling of foreboding gnawed at him. The war appeared to be entering a more dangerous phase.

A corporal approached and asked him to attend a conference with the General. He signalled to Mundt to join him.

General Keppler was sitting at a table with his staff officers. They were all silent and shocked. Like the Eastern Front, Weiser thought. Three Italian officers were also there, a Brigadier, a General and an Admiral. Weiser and Mundt were instructed to sit next to them.

'It was a fiasco,' began the Italian Admiral. Dismay and disappointment were etched upon his face.

Keppler looked at him as if he were some disgusting insect.

'The French were forewarned,' the General's adjutant said. He glared at the Admiral as if it were he who had personally given them the warning. 'They had plenty of time to lay charges and prepare the sea valves for opening.'

The Italian soldiers glanced at each other. The Brigadier appeared to show some sympathy towards his German counterparts but the other, a Major-General, showed a trace of satisfaction at the outcome. He had suffered more than enough contempt from the ever-victorious Wehrmacht not to feel a twinge of pleasure at their present chagrin.

'Seventy-five ships scuttled,' continued the Admiral. 'It is lamentable.' He threw his arms in the air. 'You may have lost the war, Keppler. The ships would have made us the masters of the sea.'

'They would have made the German Navy masters of the sea,' said Keppler icily, 'but, alas, the Führer intended to donate them to you Italians.' He turned to his adjutant. 'I doubt Italian prima donnas would have known how to use them.'

'How dare you!' cried the Admiral, leaping to his feet.

'Hush, Leonetti,' said the Italian General. 'There is no need for friends to quarrel.'

The Admiral pointed to the dock where the ships were still burning. 'Beyond that pall of smoke lies the Mediterranean. And beyond that lies vast American and British armies. It took them only a week to conquer Morocco and Algeria. How's that for a Blitzkrieg? They could conquer Tunisia in as little time and then they will be less than three hundred kilometres from Sicily.'

'Enough of this defeatist talk,' Keppler said. 'What's done is done.'

'And Italy is the loser because of your failure.'

General Keppler clenched his fist.

'Careful, Admiral Leonetti,' the German adjutant warned. 'The Führer will not be pleased to hear how you insult one of his commanders.'

'And Il Duce will not be happy at this German failure,' replied the Admiral before storming off.

'And we are to give you the southern half of France?' Keppler said to his adjutant. 'Folly.'

He marched off, leaving his officers staring at the table.

Weiser and Mundt departed from the conference in silence. They did not say a word until their car was heading west towards Aix.

'So much for the Pact of Steel.' Mundt said, lighting a cigarette. 'Tell me, what use are the Italians?'

Weiser shrugged. 'As Keppler said, they produce the finest prima donnas for the world of opera.'

Mundt laughed, swallowed too much cigarette smoke and choked.

'But seriously,' he continued, when he had recovered his breath. 'The Italians are to be given the French Riviera? General Blaskowitz should move east to the border.' He gave Weiser a dark look. 'Perhaps even on to Rome.''

'The Führer wants to keep Mussolini sweet, Otto. There's nothing we nor General Blaskowitz can do about it.'

'Why does Hitler mollify him so much? The man's a buffoon.'

'The English say that about Hitler, don't forget.'

Mundt raised an eyebrow. 'True. Except Hitler's anything but a buffoon. Mussolini would be better employed in a circus. Not as a lion but a chimp.'

'You'd better keep those thoughts to yourself,' Weiser said.

Mundt did not speak for a while, staring out of the window at the unfolding landscape.

'Will we have to leave Aix?' he said at last. 'My assistant is a pretty little thing.'

'You should try to control your urges more, Otto.' Weiser opened his cigarette case but then thought better of it and put it back in his pocket. There was enough smoke in the car from his friend's cigarette.

'No,' he continued. 'You can keep your playmate for a little longer. The Italians have been promised everything east of the Rhone but Blaskowitz tells me that we are to keep hold of some strategic areas, including Marseilles and Aix.'

'Not Toulon?'

'I don't know. But I doubt the High Command will want our forces to clear up a dock with so many burning hulks. Nor a town incensed by the destruction of their fleet. Best leave it to our Italian friends.'

'And what do you think about what the operatic Admiral said? Do you think the Allies will invade Europe?'

Weiser shrugged. 'Personally, I doubt it. The Allies may have gained some of North Africa but it's little more than sand and palm trees. I think we got the better bargain, occupying the rest of France. Even if we have to share some of it with Mussolini.'

'It's worrying, though.'

'I worry more about the Eastern Front. About the Russians.'

Otto looked at him in surprise. 'But we've almost defeated them, Ernst. Stalingrad will fall anytime soon and we've reached the Caspian oil fields. The war is as good as over.'

Weiser laughed. 'I applaud your optimism, Otto. I just fear it's misplaced.'

Mundt glanced out of the window. 'It's only the failure to take the French fleet that makes you talk this way,' he said, at last.

'That and the fact that the Americans have started fighting.' He lit a cigarette and stared at the tip. 'I wonder what that will mean for us all.'


## A HAPPY CHRISTMAS
*December 1942*


Alain was in Cannes, negotiating food purchases for Christmas. He could easily lay his hands on oysters and Guinea Fowl but Foie Gras was difficult to come by and he would be able to charge a premium price for it.

He smiled to himself. The Italians had moved into Grasse at the beginning of December and they were already making their presence felt. They had far more money than the French and they were keen to spend it. His chief aim was to help himself to as much of it as possible.

There had also been a marked relaxation in the snooping of the French police. They were angry at how the government in Vichy had been overrun and wanted as little to do with the occupying forces as possible. His brother-in-law, in particular, seemed highly disillusioned.

The last wholesaler he visited was Jean Ribot who dealt in wines and spirits. His shelves were almost bare.

'Have you sold everything?' Alain asked in consternation.

Ribot nodded. 'The harvests were good this year. But the Germans are like locusts. They bought a million bottles of the finest Bordeaux and the same with Burgundy.'

He took a few steps to the front of his store, checking there was nobody else within earshot.

'And it's got worse since last month,' he continued. 'I used to get a lot of stock from the Languedoc but now the Bosch are squatting on that. And I always got some Algerian supplies. But since the Yanks invaded, nothing has come from over there.' He took Alain's arm. 'But for special customers, I have a few bottles.'

'At a special price, no doubt.'

Ribot grinned. 'We do what we must. Come, let me show you.'

'Do you think there will always be shortages of wine?' Alain asked as Ribot led him to a room at the back of the store.

Ribot nodded. 'The Bosch are winning in Europe, make no mistake. Russia is all but conquered. The British are exhausted and have no stomach for any more fighting. I think the Americans will march east to Egypt and then take over India. It's a new world, my friend, and not, I think a hopeful one.'

Alain felt his stomach grow cold for a moment but he shook himself out of it. 'I don't agree. I know the Americans.' He thought about Dorothy and her kindness and opposition to the Nazis. 'They won't betray the British.'

'The British betrayed us,' Ribot said. 'My brother died at Dunkirk just so those cowards could flee the battle. They deserve all they get.'

Alain thought it best to say no more. He took three cases of mixed bottles at prices he would have walked away from in the summer. But he consoled himself that they would prove to be some of the best wines available in Grasse. He doubted the Italians would want them, for they were already importing their own wines, but he felt confident he would be able to sell them to the wealthier families of Grasse, even at this inflated price.

Yet his despondent thoughts returned as he carried the wine to his motorbike. He lowered the cases into the sidecar and lashed them in securely. Every day brought some new turn to life, some good, most bad. He climbed onto his saddle and kicked the bike into life. Perhaps he'd keep the best bottles for himself. He deserved a little pleasure.

He was surprised to find Dorothy sitting in the living room when he got home.

'To what do we owe the pleasure?' he asked.

'I'm not sure it's a pleasure,' she said. 'I'm down in the dumps, if truth be told. Thinking about those poor American boys who are fighting and dying in North Africa.'

'But they may yet save us, Dorothy. Them and the British.'

'Let's hope so,' she said.

Then she shook her head, wearily. 'I've heard your General de Gaulle is in a rage about what's happening over there. It seems that some American General has recognised Admiral Darlan as head of the French forces in North Africa and de Gaulle thinks it should be him.'

'That's typical,' Alain said, with a sigh. 'We quarrel amongst ourselves instead of fighting the enemy.'

He glanced at Dorothy with curiosity. He wanted to ask her how she had found out such news but knew it would be unwise to. The less anybody asked about such things the better.

'Are you sure it's Darlan?' he asked.

'Yes. Six months ago he was Pétain's Prime Minister, and a friend of the Nazis. Now he's Roosevelt's and Churchill's pal and the ruler of the French Empire.'

Viviane came in with two cups of coffee.

'You're back,' she said to Alain. 'I didn't hear you come in. Was it a successful trip?'

'In parts. The worst news is that the Germans have taken most of the wine. I only managed to get three cases.'

He gave a sudden grin and went out of the room and across the street where he stored his goods, returning with two bottles of wine.

'These are good bottles,' he said, uncorking one of the bottles. 'Let's drink a toast to the American and French soldiers in Africa.'

'But I made coffee,' Viviane said. 'It will go to waste.'

'Better than letting the wine go that way,' Dorothy said, gratefully taking a glass.

Viviane hesitated for a moment, aware that they were drinking wine they could sell for food and other essentials. But she thought it had been so long since there had been anything to celebrate that she took it, nonetheless.

'Dorothy, did you tell Alain why you've come?' she asked.

Dorothy shook her head. 'I was just about to. My car's playing up, Alain. Monsieur Vernet at the garage says it needs a new carburettor but he can't lay his hands on one. I thought you may be able to.'

Alain frowned. 'I should be able to find something in Marseille.'

'I don't want you going there anymore,' Viviane said, quickly. 'It's too dangerous.'

'In that case I could try Nice. It won't be so easy but I'll have a go.'

'I'll pay whatever it costs,' Dorothy said. 'I can't do without my car.'

'You'll pay nothing at all,' Alain said. He picked up the other bottle and gave it to her. 'And this is also a gift.'

Dorothy smiled and put it in her bag. 'The one thing my mother taught me was always to accept a gift graciously.'

She raised her glass in the air. 'To the Allies and to victory. And the hottest place in hell for Adolf Hitler.'

They chinked glasses and took a sip.

'This is very good,' Viviane said.

'And the other bottle is for Noël,' Alain said. He gave a huge grin. Despite the fact that he considered the existence of Jesus to be childish nonsense, he still looked forward to celebrating the story.

Dorothy clicked her fingers. 'That's the other reason I came,' she said. 'I want you and the kids to spend Christmas with me. I've got plenty of food and gifts for the little ones.'

'That's really kind,' Viviane said. 'Are you sure?'

'Positive. It will be the best Christmas I've had for the last three years.'

'Then I shall provide the wine and oysters,' Alain said. 'Noël is a time for celebration.'

It seemed likely to be the best Christmas since the start of the war. Dorothy had told them they could stay overnight which excited Celeste beyond anything. She took to calling the villa a palace. 'And you're the princess,' Alain said, swinging her in his arms.

They used the motorbike and sidecar to get to Villa Laurel, leaving home at three in the afternoon to make sure of the daylight.

Celeste watched her father anxiously as he tied a case of food on the back of the bike. Now that Christmas Eve had arrived, she was less enthusiastic about spending the night at the villa. 'What if Papa Noël doesn't know where to find me?' she asked.

'Maman wrote to him yesterday to tell him where you'll be,' Alain said.

'Did he write back?'

'He did, yes.'

'Can I see the letter?'

'I'm afraid not. A fairy flew into the house and took it back to Papa Noël.'

This, more than anything, convinced her of the truth of his words.

Alain lifted her into the sidecar, squashing her in next to David. Viviane climbed in behind them.

'We're on our way to the best Noël ever,' Alain cried, kicking the bike into life and heading out of town.

Dorothy and Marie had gone to a great deal of trouble, digging out an old box of decorations which, although frayed still looked splendid. A small tree had been festooned with ribbons and underneath was a basket with wrapped sweets. Celeste had never known anything like it.

Dorothy had spent a fortune on food, making great demands on Alain's black-market web. They sat down to supper at six o' clock, as traditional a Christmas as they could conjure. The table was laid with a fine linen cloth, with three candles casting a warm glow.

The bottle of wine which Alain had given to Dorothy lay open on the table but, to everyone's delight, he had brought a bottle of champagne.

Marie brought in the food and served them, then took her place at the table, which surprised Alain and Viviane.

Dorothy noticed their reaction. 'Marie lives here,' she said.

Marie blushed a deep red and began to serve the food.

The meal was superb. The oysters were tasty and the foie gras rich and satisfying. There were no capons to be had anywhere so instead they had a roast rabbit with olives, green beans, potatoes and a delicate mustard sauce. There was a delicious young goat's cheese to follow and then, to the children's delight, a real Bûche de Noël.

'I've not eaten so well for years,' Viviane said.

'You're very welcome,' Dorothy said. 'And anyway, Lucile did the cooking and much of the food was provided by Alain.' She passed him a bottle of cognac.

'Now it's time for bed,' Viviane said to the children. 'Thank Madame Pine for a lovely supper.'

Celeste was the first to do so, giving Dorothy a loud and wet kiss upon the cheek.

'Do you think Papa Noël will be able to find me here?' she asked.

'I sure do, honey. One of his people dropped by today to say everything was hunky-dory.'

Celeste had no idea what hunky-dory meant but seemed satisfied by the phrase. She headed for the stairs, eager to get to sleep so that Papa Noël could come.

'You too, David,' Viviane said. 'Thank Madame Pine.'

David approached nervously and touched her on the knee. 'Thank you for a lovely Hanukkah,' he said.

Alain and Viviane exchanged baffled glances. What on earth did he mean by that?

But a look of alarm crossed Dorothy's face although she hid it immediately.

'Thank you, David,' she said. 'You're very welcome. But there's a new word you must use instead of Hanukkah. You must now say, Noël. Do you think you can remember that?'

He nodded with great seriousness.

Dorothy took his hand and followed Celeste up the stairs.

The children hurried down to the dining room next morning. Celeste squealed with excitement. Beneath the tree was a small pile of gifts, wrapped in old Hollywood magazines, the best paper that Dorothy could now lay her hands on.

Celeste skipped with excitement. 'Papa Noël,' has been, she called to her mother.

Viviane hurried down the stairs, anxious in case Celeste opened the gifts before the adults arrived.

She needn't have worried. Marie was standing guard in front of them, her arms folded and a stern look upon her face.

'You get no gifts until after petit-déjeuner,' she said. 'And then, only if Madame Pine lets you.'

'But Papa Noël left them for us,' Celeste said, her lips beginning to wobble in distress.

Marie gave a wide smile. 'Well in that case, maybe you can open one of them now.'

She glanced at Viviane who nodded in agreement. 'Just one, though.'

Marie selected one of the gifts and handed it to Celeste who began to tear it open.

'Careful, darling,' Viviane said. 'Madame Pine may want to use that paper again.'

Inside was a small bowl decorated with flowers.

'It's beautiful,' Celeste cried.

Marie beamed. 'It used to be mine,' she whispered to Viviane. 'My favourite uncle gave it to me when I was your daughter's age.' She guessed that Celeste would find it as enchanting as she once did.

'Now, take your places at the table, children,' she said.

'What about David?' Celeste said.

'Oh yes,' Marie said.

Viviane tensed, aware that Marie now sounded less enthusiastic. But she bent and picked up a little package and gave it to him. He unwrapped it eagerly. It was a scuffed and ancient tennis ball.

Viviane's stomach crawled. It was a second-rate gift, compared to what she had given to Celeste. Did Marie suspect something about David? Had she given him the worst gift she thought she could get away with? If she had, it was not to be wondered at. Many French people were antagonistic to Jews. Most of them had been more circumspect about it before the war but now they saw no reason to hide it. If Marie was of the same mind, then they were in terrible danger.

Marie blushed a little. 'It may look worn out,' she said, 'but it actually belonged to my uncle. He used it at Wimbledon and the Davis Cup and he said it brought him luck. He gave it to me when I was a little girl.'

Viviane sighed in relief. The battered old ball was actually a gift of the greatest generosity.

Dorothy appeared and took her place at the table, her face glowing with excitement.

Viviane fussed over the children, her fingers like thumbs because of her anxiety about Marie. Would she betray them, she wondered.

Alain arrived and sat next to her, giving her a puzzled look at her obvious distress. She felt his hand reach for her knee.

'I'm alright,' she murmured. 'Just hungry.'

At that moment a delicious smell hit their nostrils and Marie walked in bearing a steaming tray.

'Croissants, bread and home-made jam,' she said. 'But please don't ask for more, that's all there is.'

Alain bit into one immediately. 'They're delicious,' he said.

Marie blushed. 'I made them myself. With real butter.'

'It is very generous of you,' Alain said. 'It must have taken you hours to make them.'

'More than you might think,' Marie said, a little prick of pride behind her eyes.

'What a charming surprise,' Dorothy said. 'We're very grateful, Marie.'

It was the best breakfast that any of them could remember. The croissants were sublime, the bread soft and doughy and the jam superb.

'Did she make the bread as well?' Alain asked.

Dorothy nodded, her mouth full of croissant.

The meal was finished very swiftly, but not too swiftly for the children. As soon as Dorothy and Viviane gave the word, they fell on the presents.

Most were utilitarian, new clothes and a box of buttons each which they would be able to play with and could be used to replace those that went missing.

But best of all were the ones that Alain had put furthest out of reach. Celeste got a copy of 'Black Beauty' and David a set of little spanners and a hammer.

'Isn't Père Noël clever,' Alain told him. 'Now you can help me mend my motor-bike.'

'Yes, Papa,' David said, staring at the tools in wonder.

Viviane's heart raced at the word. She turned to Alain and saw tears form in his eyes.

'Happy Christmas, everyone,' Dorothy said. 'Happy Christmas.'


## THE ITALIANS ARRIVE
*Grasse, 4 January 1943*

The Italian authorities arrived in Grasse on January 4th, 1943, a small military unit which ensconced itself in the Town Hall. It was headed by Capitano Emilio Marinelli, a man who had planned to retire in 1941 but, to his fury, kept having the date deferred. He thought that he might well die before the war ended.

Although he came from a tiny village in the centre of Basilicata, he had a holiday home in Sorrento and spent most of his days worrying if the plants in the little garden would survive without his attention. He occasionally remembered to worry about his wife who was often sickly from a range of ailments which baffled her overtaxed doctors. He could never be sure whether they were genuine complaints or figments of her and her doctors' imagination.

Marinelli was a small man and given to corpulence. He blamed his lack of progress on this and the enmity of nameless officials. Had he been taller, slim and from Rome, he was convinced he would have been a Colonel by now. His bitterness was only consoled by the delights of the table. He considered himself an epicure, although a discriminating one. He was particularly partial to fine French food. He also preferred a Burgundy to a Barolo or a Cahors to a Chianti. He had been reprimanded for this by a superior officer who had insinuated that such tastes were virtually treachery.

His posting to France was, therefore, something he considered a blessing. He would have preferred to be sent to Bordeaux or Burgundy and was even prepared to risk being sent to Lyon despite it being a hotbed of the Resistance. But Grasse was pleasant enough he thought and the local wines light and refreshing.

He spent his first three days in Grasse organising his command and showing the Mayor and his officials, in no uncertain terms, that he was in command now. They seemed to acquiesce in this remarkably easily which aroused his suspicions. Were they pleased that the Italians had taken over their town or just dismissive?

He experimented with how he dealt with them, at one time pleasant and professional, at others friendly and complicit, on occasion brusque to the point of aggression. Nothing he did seemed to change their attitude to him. It was as if he were an irritant that they knew they must endure before he eventually disappeared, like a summer mosquito or a winter ailment.

He reflected on this bitterly for a whole two hours but then the smell of a mutton stew wafted into his window and he went off to dine. The meal was so delicious that he left the brasserie in good humour and decided to explore the town.

He took three soldiers with him, two of them callow young men who had only recently been in school. The third was Fabio Salgari, a sergeant of mature years who had fought in Abyssinia and on the eastern front and could be relied on in an any emergency. He also appeared to like Marinelli, an emotion few of the command shared.

They tramped the streets for an hour or two. Despite his appearance Marinelli had a good military mind, and his early experience of maps and logistics enabled him to ascertain the salient features of any landscape with barely a glance. By the time they had traversed the street a couple of times he had a good idea of the areas where any insurgencies would have advantage, potential death-traps and also the places where he could best deploy his forces to dominate and over-awe the city.

Finally, he saw an épicerie, one of the largest food-shops in Grasse and told the young men to wait inside while he and Salgari entered the shop. The scent of sausages, cheese and herbs played over them.

The owner eyed them suspiciously as they approached.

'I am Capitano Marinelli,' he informed the man.

'I guessed as much.'.

Marinelli's eyes narrowed. Was the man being disrespectful or was he simply a fool? He glanced at Salgari who stared at the man with blank expression.

Marinelli picked up a dried sausage and sniffed it. 'This smells good,' he said.

'Wild boar and mushrooms,' the shopkeeper said. 'I can give you a good price.'

Marinelli smiled. The shopkeeper realised that as the head of an occupying force, the Italian captain could take whatever he wanted, paying nothing or, at best, leaving a few coins which were a fraction of the price.

Marinelli, however, played a different game. He was well aware that if he did that the best foods and wine would be hidden from them. He decided instead to offer what he knew to be a reasonably fair price.

The shopkeeper told him the price of the sausage and Marinelli agreed it. Then he bent to examine the bottles of wine on the racks.

'All Provence wines,' Marinelli said. 'Have you nothing better?'

'The Germans have bought up most of the best wine,' the shopkeeper said. 'This is as fine as you'll find in Grasse.'

'No Bordeaux, no Burgundy, no champagne?'

The man hesitated for a heartbeat. 'Not in my shop, nor any shop in the town.'

'But judging from your demeanour, there is another source of supply.'

The shopkeeper nodded. 'Perhaps Alain Renaud has a few better bottles.'

Marinelli grinned.

Viviane froze at the heavy knocking on the door. She looked about wildly. Alain was in the storeroom and Celeste and David were playing with her dolls in a patch of sunlight on the floor.

The knocking came again, louder and more insistent.

She wiped her hands on her apron and hurried to the door. The Italian officer bowed politely. He appreciated attractive women almost as much as fine food.

She stared at him, her face like stone. She heard the children playing behind her but dared not call to quieten them, for to do so would only serve to focus his attention on them.

'You have children, signora,' he said, craning his neck to peer around her.

'Two,' she mumbled. 'A girl and a boy.'

'I congratulate you,' he said. 'I have three sons. They are good boys but my wife yearned for a daughter in vain.'

To her surprise he opened a wallet and showed him a picture of a woman with three children. 'I took this photograph myself,' he said proudly. 'At our holiday home in Sorrento.'

Viviane stared at him in surprise. Surely only rich people had holiday homes.

'Would I be right in thinking that you are Signora Viviane Renaud?' he continued.

Viviane nodded. She was too afraid to speak in case her voice gave her away.

'And is your husband here?'

She gave a nervous cough. 'He's in his storeroom. Across the street.'

'Grazie, Madame.' The little man turned on his heel and marched across the street. The two young soldiers leered at Viviane until their sergeant sharply told them to go with the Capitaino. He then gave Viviane a little bow and followed them to the storeroom.

Alain was rummaging in a chest at the far side of the room when he heard footsteps. He closed the lid and covered it with an old rug.

'Signor Renaud?' said a voice from the door.

Alain glanced around to see if there was anything incriminating on show and hurried to the door.

'Can I help you?' he asked. He made his voice friendly and relaxed, a skill he had learnt while still a youth.

'The shopkeeper in the epicerie said you are a whole-seller of good wines,' Marinelli said. He had actually said something more insulting but the Italian thought it politic not to repeat it.

'And what of it?'

'I like good wine,' Marinelli said. 'Italian wines, of course, for they are excellent. But I tend to prefer French wine.'

Alain stared at him, thoughtfully. 'And this has brought you here…?'

Marinelli laughed. 'To buy some of your wines, of course. If you have any.'

'Some. But I'm afraid that your allies have bought up most of the best wine.'

'Perhaps they are also connoisseurs.'

Alain raised a sardonic eyebrow. 'I have some good Provencel wines. Bandol, Billet.'

The Italian did not answer, as if he were unimpressed by such names.

'And some Cotes de Rhone,' Alain said, slowly, watching the Italian's face narrowly. 'And a few Chateauneuf du Pape, three Gigondas and a couple of Bordeaux.'

Marinelli beamed and held out his hands. 'I think we understand each other, Signor Renaud,' he said.

Renaud gave an equally fulsome smile. This one, he thought, might be very useful to know.

# THE MARSEILLE ROUND-UP
*Marseille, 22 January 1943*

Alain parked his motorbike in the lean-to behind the hotel. He had tried to get Dorothy's car parts from Nice but without success. His best contacts were in Marseilles so, reluctantly, he had returned here. He had no intention of telling Viviane he had come here, however.

He strolled into the hotel and glanced around. There were two old men huddled over their wine in a corner. Monsieur Guizot stood behind the bar, polishing a glass with a filthy rag. He glanced up, saw Alain and grunted in greeting. He poured a generous measure of wine into the glass and shoved it across the bar.

Alain took a sip and nodded. 'Good stuff, Sergei. Where did you get it?'

Guizot tapped the side of his nose and shook his head. Some things were best kept secret. 'You want a bed?' he asked.

Alain nodded. 'Is there room?'

Guizot gave a bark of a laugh. 'I had a travelling salesman stay here on New Year's Day. Nothing else for the last three weeks.'

One of the old men glanced up and then bent once again to his wine.

Guizot leaned over the bar and spoke in little more than a whisper. 'What are you after, Alain? There are slim pickings since the Bosch arrived. They've clamped down on almost everything and I hear that trade from Algeria has dried up completely.'

'I'm after some parts for a car.'

Guizot poured himself a glass of wine and waved it in front of Alain's nose. 'You're paying for this, right?'

Alain nodded.

Guizot took a glug of wine. 'Vincente Bardin deals in car parts,' he said. 'Your friend Chiappe knows him.'

'Where can I find him?'

'He has a little garage in Rue des Ferrats. Just beyond the port.'

Alain swigged the rest of his wine and made for the door.

Vincente Bardin was suspicious of Alain and refused to sell him anything. It was only when Alain mentioned that he was a friend of Gabriel Chiappe that he relaxed his guard a little.

'If you know Gabriel, bring him here to vouch for you. If not, piss off.'

Alain found Gabriel in one of his favourite haunts, a bar on the quayside with half a dozen male customers and rather more young women. A young blond eyed Alain as he entered and slipped towards him as smoothly as a leopard.

'It's other business I'm seeking,' Alain said.

The woman touched him on his chest, hand light as a feather, and gave him an amused and knowing look.

'I'm thirsty,' she said. 'Want to buy me a drink?'

'A coffee for the lady,' Alain called to the barman.

'You're a funny man,' she sneered at him angrily, striding back to her former seat.

Chiappe signalled to the barman for two beers and beckoned Alain to his table.

'Louise is a good girl, Alain,' he said. 'Clean and very obliging. You could do a lot worse.'

'I prefer better. And she's waiting at home for me.'

Chiappe chuckled and offered Alain a cigarette. 'So what brings you back to Marseille?' he asked.

'I need a carburettor.'

Chiappe frowned. 'You can get them anywhere. Even in Grasse.'

'This is for a Chrysler Imperial.'

'American.' Chiappe stared out of the window, his brow furrowed in thought. 'Vincente Bardin should have one.'

'Bardin sent me here to bring you to his garage to vouch for me.'

Chiappe gave him a look of surprise and gestured to a man who had been sitting silently at the back of the bar. Chiappe whispered in his ear and the man left the cafe.

They had not quite finished their beer when the door crashed open. Bardin almost flew in, propelled by a shove from Chiappe's accomplice.

Chiappe's face was incredulous. 'You wanted me to come to you?' he demanded.

'I didn't think he knew you,' Bardin began, pointing at Alain. 'I didn't mean —'

Chiappe nodded to his accomplice who slapped Bardin across the face.

'Do you have the part my friend requires?' Chiappe asked.

Bardin reached inside a bag. 'It's pretty rare. Not cheap.'

'It's no price, you worm. You disrespected my friend and me.'

Bardin licked his lips, nervously. 'I'm honoured to give such a gift to your friend,' he said. He placed the carburettor on the table and took a step backwards.

'Au revoir, Vincente,' Chiappe said. 'And be more careful in the future.'

Chiappe drained the last of his beer.

'Come on, Alain, you can buy me some lunch.'

They strolled out of the bar and headed in the direction of La Canebière where the best restaurants could be found.

'Is it my imagination or is the town very quiet?' Alain asked.

Chiappe gave him a shrewd glance. 'You've noticed? There's something brewing but I don't know what it is. It makes me uneasy. I've heard that trains loaded with police came down from Paris in the middle of the night. Not right into the city but to the little stations beyond.'

He stopped and murmured in Alain's ear. 'And Paul Carbone has gone missing.'

Alain glanced around nervously. Carbone was one of the most powerful gangsters in France. Even Le Taureau was afraid of him. 'Is he dead? Will there be a gang war?'

Chiappe shook his head. 'It's stranger. Rumour has it that he's given himself up to the Police.'

Alain looked disbelieving. 'Why on earth would he do that?'

'I don't know…' Chiappe stopped mid-sentence and then hurried to the side of the road, frantically beckoning Alain to join him.

Racing down the road were a stream of armoured vehicles, with two Panzer tanks at their head. On either side ran columns of German soldiers interspersed with French policemen and even some members of the newly formed militia, the Milice française.

A few brave souls ventured out to try to reason with the French police but they were gunned down by the soldiers. Bystanders fled at the sight of this, almost trampling each other in their desperation to flee.

Alain felt himself being grabbed by the sleeve. 'Come on, you fool,' Chiappe yelled, dragging him into a small yard.

There seemed no end to the men clattering down the street. Alain peered out and saw that the soldiers were fanning out along the port while the police and Milice hammered on doors, dragging out the occupants whether men, women or children. Any who tried to resist were savagely beaten. Alain could not believe what Frenchmen were doing to their own citizens.

'There's no way out of here,' Chiappe said. 'Let's just hope we're not seen.'

He spoke too soon. A member of the Milice paused at their hiding-place to take a breath. He glanced into the shadows and saw them. A wide grin crossed his face and he told them to come out. It was the last thing he did. Chiappe stepped forward, as if to obey, and plunged a knife into his heart.

'You bloody fool,' Alain said.

'Shut your mouth and help me get him out of sight.'

Chiappe took off the militia-man's uniform and put it on over his own clothes. 'Pass me his gun,' he ordered Alain. 'You're to pretend to be my prisoner.'

He hustled Alain out onto the street. It was utter mayhem.

Long lines of people were now being forced up the road in the direction of the train station. Chiappe forced his way into the throng. Police and Milice guards were enjoying their work. Marseille had always had a reputation as a criminal town and these men were convinced that they were clearing out a nest of vipers. They attacked anyone who tried to remonstrate with them with chilling brutality.

'And they call me a law-breaker,' Chiappe murmured quietly.

At that moment a fierce hubbub broke out to their left. An elderly man was bundled out of his house, followed by weeping women.

'My father's a rabbi,' cried one of the women. 'Don't let them take him.' A member of the Milice punched her in the mouth and dragged her to the side of the road where he was joined by two others who kicked her where she lay.

'We've got to help her,' Alain said.

'Are you crazy? We'd end up just like her.'

They continued along the street until where the road turned left towards the train station. Here the sheer press of people stopped their progress. Chiappe seized his chance.

He pushed Alain to the side of the crowd and then headed towards the Théâtre du Gymnase. 'We must hurry,' he said. 'Our best chance is to get away while there's still chaos on the streets.'

They slunk through the narrow streets to the east of the theatre until the tumult of the round-up had quietened. Then Chiappe pulled off the Milice uniform and hid it behind a rubbish bin. 'I don't think this will be a healthy uniform to be wearing now,' he said.

He glanced up at the streets. 'We should walk for a kilometre, keep to the quietest streets. Then we'll steal a car.'

'My bike is at Guizot's Hotel.'

'It will have to stay there. It's too dangerous to go back into the city.' He did not wait for an answer but led the way deep into the back streets.

After half an hour he found a battered old car and cranked it into life. The owner of the car leapt out at the noise but Chiappe casually pulled out a gun. 'I'm borrowing it to go to a funeral,' he said. 'Best make sure it's not yours.'

The man fled back into his house. Alain climbed into the passenger seat and they were off.

'Where are we going?' Alain asked as they reached the outskirts of the city.

'I thought I'd drop you home,' Chiappe said. 'It will be nice to meet your wife and family.'

# THE JOURNEY HOME
*On the road to Grasse 23 January 1943*

The car struggled along the hilly roads leading to Grasse, its little engine complaining all the way. They stopped at the edge of Brignoles for the night, checking into an auberge owned by a man as noisome as his rooms. He didn't seem to be concerned that they had no luggage and insisted they joined him in a drink at the bar.

'Have you heard the news?' he asked, spitting into a glass and wiping it away with his fingers. He poured them small glasses of rough cognac.

Alain shook his head, leaning back a little to avoid the man's rank breath.

'The police and militia are clearing out the scum in Marseilles,' the innkeeper said. 'Not before time, if you ask me. My son's in the militia and he's taking part. He's a good boy although he's got himself into trouble a couple of times. Being in the militia should help sort him out.'

'I've never been to Marseilles,' Chiappe said. 'Too dangerous for me, with all those smugglers and gangsters.'

'The militia will sort that lot out,' the innkeeper said. 'And the Germans will teach them what's what. France has needed a kick up the arse for years if you ask me. Filthy socialists and Jews deserve what they get.'

Alain raised his glass. 'Here's to the Maréchal,' he said.

The man's mouth pursed. 'The old man's a has-been. Laval's the man for the times now. It won't be long before Hitler welcomes France as an equal. And then we'll see what happens to England and the Russian scum.'

'But what about the Americans?' Alain asked quietly. 'I hear they and the English have conquered Algeria.'

'Lies.' The man spat on the floor. 'England's finished, bombed to smithereens. Their king has fled to Canada and Churchill has been locked up in an asylum.'

He poured them another glass each. 'And now that we've taken back control of the whole country, we'll use our fleet to help the Germans invade America.'

Chiappe nearly choked on his drink. 'But the fleet has been scuttled. We've no ships left.'

'More lies.' He glanced at Alain. 'Is your friend a member of the Resistance? If he's a Jew he's not welcome.'

Alain shook his head. 'He's an ex-sailor. He helped scuttle the ships.'

The man looked at him with contempt. 'You bloody rumour-monger. You're not welcome here.' He reached for the telephone on the bar.

There was a sound like a car backfiring. The innkeeper looked shocked and his hand went to his chest. Blood began to stain his already stained apron. Then he slid to the floor.

'Why did you do that?' Alain asked.

'He was going to betray us. Besides, he stank to high heaven.'

'But if the body is found —'

'It won't be. There are plenty of hungry dogs who will enjoy the feast. Come on, we'll lug him out the back.'

Alain shook his head in disbelief before helping Chiappe move the body. The growls of dogs and other creatures went long into the night.

They were on their way the next morning. There was no food in the inn and precious little money. Chiappe pocketed what there was in the till together with some bottles of spirits.

'I doubt the old bastard will be missed,' he said as they drove through the town.

Alain nodded. He gave no thought to the innkeeper. His mind kept going back to what he had witnessed in Marseille. It was not what the Germans did. That was to be expected. It was how the police and Milice behaved which chilled him most. The guardians of the people had become their enemies.

Chiappe, on the other hand, seemed not to reflect upon it at all. He had, after all, survived numerous gangland wars.

They got to Grasse late in the afternoon. The sun struggled to get through rank upon rank of ominous, grey clouds. Chiappe decided it would be best to abandon the car and drove it into a wood. He stopped only when he thought it could not be seen from the road.

Alain opened the bonnet and began to pull out any parts which might fetch a price in the market. Chiappe laughed at his enthusiasm for the task. 'We don't change our natures, old friend,' he said. Then he turned towards Grasse and grinned.

A shiver of disquiet ran through Alain. Although he was his friend, Chiappe was a seasoned criminal. His coming to Grasse might prove dangerous for the town and Alain would be blamed for it. He felt like a shepherd might do when bringing a wolf home to meet his flock.

The rain started before they reached the town and when they got to Alain's home they were drenched and cold.

Viviane looked overjoyed to see him and caught him in her arms.

'You've been gone so long. I wondered what had happened to you.'

But then she caught a glimpse of Chiappe and her face darkened.

'This is an old friend,' Alain said. 'He's staying the night.'

She looked at him in consternation but then forced a smile on her face and shook Chiappe's hand. 'You are welcome,' she said. 'I'm afraid I can't offer the sort of hospitality you might be used to in Nice —'

'I'm not from Nice. I live in Marseille.'

Viviane gave Alain an angry glance. 'You promised you wouldn't return to Marseille. It's too dangerous with the Germans there.'

'I couldn't get Dorothy's carburettor in Nice. She needs it.'

'Not enough for you to risk your life.'

'You've already heard then,' Chiappe said in surprise.

Viviane stared at him. 'Heard what?' Her voice was cold and fearful.

'About the round-up. The Germans and Milice have attacked the old port area and are taking its people away. I've no idea where or why.'

Alain sighed. 'We were quite safe,' he said. 'We were well away from any trouble.'

'Then why is your friend here?' Viviane asked.

Chiappe smiled. 'I'm not keen on the Germans,' he said. 'We thought it best if I made myself scarce.'

If he thought this might appease Viviane he was mistaken. 'So you are a wanted man. Will I find the Germans hammering on my door next?'

She glared at Alain. He had endangered all their lives. If the Germans came then David might be taken. All of them might be taken.

'Gabriel is not staying here long,' Alain said. 'If you must know, it was he who helped me escape from Marseille.'

'But you said you were in no danger there.'

Alain struggled to find an answer.

'That is true,' Chiappe said to Viviane smoothly. 'But it was rapidly becoming dangerous. Arrests, examining identity papers, beatings and who knows what else to follow. I thought it best to bring Alain back to his family.'

'And for that I'm grateful –'

'But only grateful enough to let me stay one night.'

'We understand each other perfectly, Monsieur...'

'Call me Gabriel, please. I am an old friend of Alain.'

Viviane gasped. 'Gabriel. You're the man who got David's papers.'

Chiappe inclined his head.

Viviane grabbed his hands and kissed them.

'You're very welcome, very welcome.'

'You are drenched, both of you. Alain, get some towels for Gabriel and change your own clothes. I'll get you some supper.'

Viviane lay speechless in bed that night while Alain related what he had witnessed in Marseille. He had been reluctant to tell her the details for fear that it would alarm her too much. But she soon made it clear that any evasions and half-truths would only exacerbate her fears and he told her most of what he had seen.

He did not mention the young Jewish woman being kicked half to death by the Milice nor the fact that Chiappe had killed two men during their escape. Some things were best left unsaid.

When he had finished, she crawled into his arms, her breath hot against his cheek.

'What is happening to the world?' she whispered.

'A madness,' Alain said. 'A sickness, a fever. But like all maladies it will pass in time.'

Viviane heard what he said and prayed that he was right. 'But some maladies can kill,' she said at last.

Alain squeezed her hand. 'But in this case, I think only those who are foolish or careless will die. We must make sure that we are neither of these.'

We must, she thought. Although maybe that path had been lost forever when she took in David.

They made a sparse breakfast of coffee and dried bread the following morning. Chiappe had only coffee and two foul-smelling cigarettes. The children looked at him with wide-eyed amazement, as if he were some visitor from a distant planet. Perhaps, in some ways, he was.

'I've been thinking, Alain,' he said at last. 'You and I should go into partnership. I didn't say yesterday but I recognised quite a few of my old colleagues being arrested by the police in Marseille.'

'Why was that?' Viviane asked, her voice cold and suspicious.

'We are black marketeers,' he said. 'We keep the wheels of France turning, we keep the bellies of our children fed. The authorities do not like us for it because we are more popular than them.'

She was not sure if she believed this. For all his smoothness and courtesy there was a hard and dangerous air about him. But surely Alain would not have dealings with anyone too dubious? He called Gabriel his friend and they certainly acted as if they were. And he had helped Alain escape from Marseille.

'What about it, my friend,' Chiappe continued. 'You and me as partners?'

To Viviane's surprise, Alain seemed less than enthusiastic about the suggestion.

'I don't know, Gabriel. Grasse is a small town. I'm not sure it's the best milieu for you.'

Chiappe chuckled at his careful use of milieu, the word the police used to denote the underworld of mobs and crime.

'I don't mean here,' he said. 'Christ, but I'd be bored to death here. No, I mean to move to Nice. Once I've set myself up there, we can continue to do business as before. But as partners, fifty percent.'

Alain gave him a shrewd glance. 'Why would you want to do that?'

'Times change. Only the swift and the clever will thrive.'

Alain gulped. His words were similar to the ones he had used to Viviane in bed. 'It's a fine offer, Gabriel,' he said. 'I'll think about it.'

'Don't think too long. There are others who will jump at the chance.'

Alain nodded. As long as the Nice mobs were willing to accommodate him, he was likely to do well in the city. It was smaller, there were less opportunities, but also less cut-throat competition. And with Marseille in the hands of the Germans, it would be a safer bet for him to trade there from now on. The more he thought about it, the more attractive Chiappe's offer seemed.

'I won't think too long,' Alain said. 'When will you leave?'

Chiappe laughed. 'I never outstay my welcome. Just tell me how to get to Nice and I'll be on my way.'

'I'd take you on my motorbike,' Alain said. 'If I still had it.'

'Some petrol will do,' Chiappe said. 'Don't forget I left my car on the edge of town when it ran out.'

They left within the hour. Alain brought along the parts he had removed from the car the night before while Chiappe carried a bag of food and a can of petrol.

'I'll take you by the back roads,' Alain said. 'We don't want to be stopped and questioned.'

He spoke too soon. On the outskirts of the town they were stopped by an Italian soldier who looked little more than a child. He must have sensed something dangerous about Chiappe for his hands shook with anxiety as he examined his identity papers. 'Thank you very much,' he stuttered nervously as he handed them back, hurrying away as soon as he had done so.

'You still have it,' Alain said to Chiappe with a chuckle.

'Have what?'

'The aura of menace. Like James Cagney.'

'Do I? I hadn't realised.' Chiappe gave a smile of pleasure. He had always known, of course.

They reached the car without mishap. Chiappe filled up the tank while Alain replaced the engine parts.

'Don't forget my offer,' Chiappe said. 'And don't leave it too long until you say yes.'

Alain touched him on the arm. 'Tell me one thing, my friend. Why do you want me as a partner? I am a small fish after all.'

'Because I trust you. And trust will soon be the most important currency in France.'

**CHOICES**
*Grasse, 1 February 1943*

Alain took only a week to decide on Chiappe's offer. Part of him wanted to accept because in a world going steadily more criminal it seemed that criminals like Chiappe might thrive better than most. But Viviane was adamant that he should have as little to do with him as possible. And going into partnership was out of the question.

'What if Chiappe's arrested?' she demanded. 'What if you're incriminated? Do you think that once he's caged he won't sing like a bird? And then what will happen to David? To us? To Celeste?'

She knew that the intimation of any danger to Celeste would make up Alain's mind. He threw up his hands in surrender.

The next day he took David with him when he went to Dorothy's to mend her car. She was delighted to see them but gave Alain a knowing look.

'Something wrong?' she asked.

He frowned. 'Yes, plenty. Are you a witch to read this with only one glance at me?'

'Nope, I'm a scriptwriter.' She touched his hand. 'Leave the car for a little while. Come and tell me what's troubling you.'

She called Marie to look after David while she took Alain inside and gave him a coffee and a cognac.

Dorothy was a skilled questioner and Alain had soon told her what he had seen in Marseilles. He included the attack on the woman.

'So you escaped with this mobster friend of yours?' she said, when he had finished. 'That must have made things a little easier. I don't suppose he was too fussy about what he had to do in order to make his escape.'

Alain smiled. 'You really are a scriptwriter, Dorothy. But not all shady characters are like Bogart and Cagney.'

'Don't bet on it.' She poured him a second glass of cognac. 'So where's this friend of yours now?'

'He went to Nice. He thought Marseille might be a bit too hot for him.'

She snorted. 'I think he might be wrong there. The Nazis and the mob are as alike as Satan and Beelzebub. They'll get along like old pals.'

'As long as they stay away from Grasse. At least the Italians are human.'

'Civilised as well. I think they like the good life. Emilio Marinelli is a sweetie.'

Alain glanced at her. 'You're on first name terms, I see.'

Dorothy gave him a reproving look. 'I invited him over for a soiree. He's a great fan of Hollywood films. When I told him I knew Chaplin and Laurel and Hardy he was all over me like a rash.'

Alain did not say anything for a little while. When he spoke again it was in a low and troubled voice. 'What they did in Marseilles, the Germans, the police and the Milice. Do you think it bodes ill for David?'

Dorothy sighed. It was a question she had asked herself since the Germans had taken over most of the south and she still had no clear answer.

'I think it might if the Germans occupied east of the Rhone. But I don't think they will. For some peculiar reason Hitler still supports Mussolini. Maybe it's because Benito was the first Fascist to take power and showed Hitler what he might achieve. I think he's still a little enamoured of him, a touch of hero-worship if you like. Because of this, he'll let Il Duce have his little empire.'

She took a swig of her coffee before continuing. "It's not an easy place to occupy for the Krauts, in any case. All mountains and barren narrow valleys. And the flesh-pots of the coast might prove far too enticing a temptation for stern Aryan warriors.'

Alain sighed. He had no idea if Dorothy would be proved right or wrong. But increasingly he craved certainty. And this odd American woman certainly offered that.

'I'd better get on with fixing your engine,' he said.

'And then you'll stop for some lunch, I hope.'

Alain collected some tools from the garage and began to work at the engine. As if by magic, David appeared and squatted beside him.

'Do you want any help, Papa?' he asked.

'No thanks,' Alain said. Then he stared at the little boy, thoughtfully. 'No thanks, son.'

David gave a huge grin.

Alain cursed to himself, wondering whether he had done the right thing in calling him son. Presumably the boy had a father somewhere. Was it fair that he should pretend that David was his child? Was it right? Maybe he should have corrected him when he called him Papa, not colluded with him.

He shook his head. Such things were beyond him. Maybe the boy had more wisdom in this matter than he could hope to find.

He was putting the carburettor into the engine when a car swept up the drive. An Italian insignia fluttered from the side window. It screeched to a halt and Capitano Marinelli stepped out. He watched Alain for a moment and then marched over to him.

'You are Signora Pine's mechanic?' he asked.

Alain straightened. 'No. Just a friend.'

Marinelli gave him a thoughtful look and then peered into the engine. 'What is the problem?'

'Nothing much. Just dirt in the engine. I've cleaned it.' He slid the old carburettor out of sight beneath the car. If the Italian saw it he might ask where he had got the new one from. Such items could only be bought on the black-market and Alain did not want to arouse any suspicions concerning that.

'It is a fine car, is it not?' the captain continued. 'Signora Pine is a woman of great taste.'

'Very much so.' Alain was growing nervous at the Italian's desire for conversation. The less he had to do with him the safer he would be.

'You have known her long?'

'Quite a while.' Alain suddenly realised why he was so interested. 'Madame Pine's a friend of my wife rather than me,' he said.

Marinelli looked relieved. 'You have a wife? That is good. I'm sure she is beautiful.'

'Very much.'

'And this must be your son.' Marinelli turned to David, touching him on the head. 'He's a beautiful boy.'

Alain nodded. 'He takes after his mother.'

Marinelli smiled and crouched down beside David. 'And what do you want to be when you grow up?' he asked. 'A mechanic, like your father?'

'I don't know.' David's face grew serious. 'But I don't want to be a rabbi.'

Alain's heart almost stopped. Marinelli rose from his crouch and stared at him with sudden, deep suspicion.

'You mean rabbit,' Dorothy called from just behind them.

'He doesn't like them,' she explained as she joined them. 'It's my fault. I read him some Brer Rabbit stories and he didn't like them.'

'What is Brer Rabbit?' Marinelli asked.

'I guess the French would call him Frère Lapin.' She made the sign of rabbit ears above her head. 'What would it be in Italian?'

'Fratello Coniglio,' Marinelli said. He gave a little smile. 'I would like to read these stories, Signora Pine.'

'I'll have to dig them out for you, then. I hid them away from David.'

She gave a winning smile and Marinelli beamed, all thought of David completely dispelled.

'Anyway, Captain,' she said, 'to what do I owe the pleasure of your visit?'

'No specific reason, Signora. I like to keep an eye on people who live outside of the city. You cannot be too careful.'

'And I'm very grateful. Would you like some cognac? Or something bubbly, perhaps.'

'That would be very pleasant.'

She took his arm and started back to the house. She had taken only a few steps before she turned and gestured Alain to leave. He needed no second instruction. He grabbed hold of David and hurried down the drive.

'Tell me again, exactly what happened,' Viviane said.

Alain groaned. He'd told her several times already. He felt like he was a schoolboy being interrogated by a teacher. Patiently, he repeated what David had said about not wanting to be a rabbi, how Marinelli reacted and how Dorothy had flirted with him to distract his attention.

'But he'll remember that David used the word rabbi,' Viviane said. She wiped her hands continuously as if washing them.

Alain took her hands. He could still feel them writhing beneath his grasp. 'We don't know that,' he said. 'He might believe what Dorothy told him about the rabbit stories.'

'I'm sure he can't be that stupid.'

'Maybe not. But a man who is losing his heart is half-way to losing his mind.'

He tried a grin, saw it was beginning to work and then clutched his heart as if in the throes of passion. 'Bellisima Signora Pine, I adore you,' he cried in a ludicrous Italian accent. 'And I believe it if you say the moon is cheese and Mussolini a clown.'

Then he kissed Viviane all the way up the arm, to her neck and then her cheeks. She giggled like a teenager.

'You're silly, Papa,' Celeste called from the back yard.

'He's very silly,' Viviane said. 'But he's lovely.'

She hugged him. Sometimes he was the only thing which made her feel safe and hopeful.

## THE MILICE
### *Grasse, 20 February 1943*

It was a week later and the weather had turned wet and windy.

Viviane was sitting in the living room, darning one of Celeste's socks. She hummed quietly to herself. She felt less worried than of late. Six months of keeping David under wraps had taken a toll on her but now that the Italians had arrived, the burden had lifted a little. She thought it strange that foreign invaders appeared to pose less threat to her than her own Government but it was true. And, to be honest, the Italians were not that foreign. Many of the locals had Italian relatives and some of her friends from school spent summers in the villages over the border.

Alain was sitting at the table, poring over a list he had just made of his contacts in Grasse, Cannes and Nice. They did not make up for the more extensive network he had built in Marseilles but there was nothing else for it but to work at developing things in new towns. And then he smiled. The Italians might prove the best contacts of all. And the friendship between Dorothy Pine and Emilio Marinelli could well be the best place to start.

A quiet knock sounded on the door. Viviane and Alain exchanged glances. Hardly anyone knocked in Grasse. Most people just opened the door and called out. Or, just as likely, entered the house and sat down. Before the war, they might even have helped themselves to a glass of wine or a pastis.

Viviane told Celeste and David to go upstairs and be quiet.

David trotted up quite contentedly but Celeste was truculent. She had heard the knock at the door and wanted to wait to find out who it was. Only firm words from Viviane made her leave.

Alain waited until the children had disappeared and opened the door.

'It's you,' he cried, flinging the door open. 'What's with the formality?'

Gerard Pithou slouched into the room. As usual he blushed deeply on seeing Viviane.

She raised half an eyebrow. She had always had her fair share of admirers but Gerard was not one she particularly relished. He was hardly the stuff that dreams were made of and he was gauche and uncomfortable in her presence. Nevertheless, she smiled sweetly and invited him to sit down. He was a good friend of Alain's and she always treated him in a friendly manner.

Alain had already poured Gerard a glass of wine and was thrusting it into his hand. He took one large gulp and all but emptied it.

'Top up his glass,' Viviane said, in as pleasant a voice as she could manage.

'Why are you looking so cheerful?' Alain asked him as he poured the wine.

Viviane glanced at Gerard. She could discern no trace of cheerfulness about him, merely an impression of febrile excitement.

'I've joined the Militia,' Gerard said. 'The Milice.' He pulled back his coat to reveal a badge with a white gamma sign on a black background. 'This is our emblem.'

'What does it signify?' Alain asked, although he regretted doing so almost immediately.

'The gamma sign is for the astrological sign Aries,' Gerard said. 'It means a new season for France, rejuvenation. And the Führer is a great believer in astrology.'

'The Führer?' said Viviane. 'What the hell are you talking about? You're French, not German.'

'France and Germany are partners now, Viviane,' he said. 'Partners in a new Europe.'

'Poppycock.'

Gerard flushed violently at her reaction. Viviane was not sure if it was his usual embarrassment at being close to her or something more worrying; anger perhaps.

'And I have a gun,' Gerard said. He lifted his pullover to reveal a pistol stuck into his pocket. 'I don't have any bullets yet. We'll get them in a week or so.'

Viviane's eyes flashed angrily. 'You're like a little boy, Gerard. Playing at soldiers.'

'No, I'm not. And I came to ask Alain to join us.'

'Well he's not going to.'

'He should. We get good pay and extra rations. And he'll never be sent to work in Germany.'

'We have no need of better pay and extra rations,' Viviane said.

Gerard gave her a doubtful look. Alain had done better than most people since the start of the war but they still found things difficult.

'Think it over, Alain,' he said. 'Those of us who are in at the beginning will do best. I get a uniform next month.'

'And what are your duties?' Viviane asked. 'Cleaning the German's boots? Teaching children how to salute Hitler?'

Alain gestured to her to stop but she was too angry to keep quiet.

'And will you beat up people who insult the Nazis? Will you round up the Jews and help imprison them or send them to labour camps in Germany?

'That's not fair, Viviane,' Gerard said. His face was white now and his lips compressed. 'I am a patriot and all patriots should stand by our Government. The Maréchal is doing the right thing for France and for Frenchmen. If I am able to help in any way, then I am honoured to do so.'

'By harming vulnerable people?'

'You know as well as I do that Laval and the Maréchal are only arresting undesirables. Jews and criminals.'

Viviane did not answer but stormed out into the kitchen.

'I think you should go now,' Alain said.

'We are still friends, though,' Gerard said. He looked alarmed, suddenly. Surprised at the vehemence of Viviane's reaction. 'We three are still friends?'

'Of course. Of course.' Alain got to his feet. The sooner he got Gerard out of the house the better.

Gerard made for the door but stopped on the threshold. 'You will think about what I suggest,' he said. He took a deep breath. 'Your background, well it makes you a little at risk. You'd be safer as a member of the Milice.'

'I'm not a criminal,' Alain said in surprise. 'I deal in the black-market but who doesn't?'

'I don't mean what you do. I mean what you are. Or rather, what your mother was.'

He held Alain's gaze for a while and then turned and left.

Alain did not answer. He closed the door behind Gerard and leaned with his back to it. He gnawed on his bottom lip anxiously. What did he mean? Was the fact that his mother was a Gypsy going to cause him problems?

And then he shuddered. Was his old friend warning him or threatening him?

He stared at the kitchen where Viviane was making a noise clattering with pots and pans. I'll not tell her, he thought. She has enough to put up with as it is.


### DAVID'S PAPERS
*Grasse, 11 May 1943*


It was a warm and lovely May. Viviane and the children spent a lot of time outdoors. It was not only because it was more pleasant. Viviane had been feeling increasingly trapped in the house and now that David had authentic looking papers she felt more confident in taking him out.

Besides this, the Italian soldiers were very friendly, and especially keen on children. They often gave Celeste and David fruit or a cake. She felt more relaxed with the Italian soldiers than with the more conscientious French police. It was the police who would stop her to ask where she was going or demand to see her papers. It was as if they were trying to prove that they and not the Italians were in control. Whether they were trying to prove it to the townspeople, the Italians or to themselves was not clear.

The French authorities had agreed to meet the German demand for French workers to be sent to Germany and dispatched half a million there in the early months of the year. But this proved not enough. On the 23rd of April the Germans demanded a quarter of a million more be sent in the following two months. The French were swift to obey. Although most men were younger than Alain, he was increasingly worried that he would be included in the quota in the near future. Despite the relaxed nature of the Italians the demands from the French Government were increasingly alarming.

He had other worries as well. Because Marseilles was in the hands of the Germans his usual supply chains had dried up. He spent much of his time in Nice and Cannes but although he got some leads he was unable to make up for the loss of his previous contacts. For the first time since the end of the war he and his family began to go hungry. He looked increasingly gaunt and increasingly troubled.

'Are we right to keep David with us?' he asked Viviane suddenly one evening.

She looked shocked. 'Why do you ask that?'

'Because times are hard now. There is less on the market, less of everything. I get some things from Gabriel in Nice but even he's finding life more difficult.'

'You're not going back to Marseilles.' Her voice was strong and determined.

'I won't. There's no need to worry about that. The biggest criminals, including Carbone and Spirito, are in league with the Gestapo. It's not a healthy place for small fry like me.'

He leaned back against his chair. 'It's because of this that I'm wondering whether we should give David up. Food is getting scarce and I've noticed that you're doing without.'

'It's to keep a nice slim figure for you,' she said with a smile.

'It's not a joking matter,' Alain said. He took her hand. 'We could take David to an orphanage. Maybe with some nuns. He'd be safer there.'

'Would he? A Jew? I thought you were an atheist. I thought you despised the church.'

Alain took a deep breath. 'I do. But not every member of the church.' He recalled the bravery of Père Benoît and his fellow friars.

'And what would Celeste do without David? They're like brother and sister.'

Alain did not answer. He found it difficult to continue arguing whenever Viviane used Celeste to support her case.

'And things are safer now,' she continued. 'The Italians are not harsh masters. And they're not as efficient as the police. Roland says they are continually hampering his efforts to crack down on petty criminals.'

'That's a good thing,' Alain said with a smile.

'So we're agreed then,' she said.

'Agreed?'

'That David stays with us. Where he's loved and protected.'

Alain shrugged. He was not going to argue any longer. Especially as he agreed with everything Viviane said.

Raoul Villiers smiled as he glanced around. Being out and about on such a fine morning was what he liked best about being a policeman.

That and the opportunity to watch the little dramas of life. He grinned as he saw the little boy come tearing down the road in hot pursuit of a cat. The cat almost seemed to be playing with him, slowing to a walk until he got close and then suddenly leaping ahead. Finally it appeared to tire of it all, turned to face the child, made itself look huge and hissed savagely.

The boy took fright and burst into tears.

Villiers chuckled to himself, reached the cat in two strides and landed a kick in its side. It sailed across the road and, howling in pain and outrage, disappeared up an alley.

Villiers bent to the little boy and took his hand.

'No need to cry, little man. You scared the cat. You defeated it.'

'He scared me,' the boy said, wiping his nose with his cuff. 'He was very angry.'

Villiers tousled the boy's hair and glanced around in search of an adult. 'Are you out on your own?' he asked, gently.

At that moment a woman turned the corner at the top of the street, her face frantic with worry. Then she saw the little boy and ran down towards him. A small girl hurried after her.

'You should keep a better eye on him,' Villiers said sternly. 'He shouldn't be running around the streets alone at his age.'

'My daughter fell over,' she said, angrily. 'She cut her leg and while I was tending to her, he ran.'

'I was after the pussy cat,' the boy wailed.

'It's alright, David,' the woman said. 'There's no need to be upset.' She glanced up at the policeman and was suddenly overwhelmed by panic.

'I have his papers,' she said, rummaging in her bag and thrusting them into his hand.

Villiers was surprised and, without really intending to, gave them a casual glance. He was just about to give them back when he stopped, pursed his lips, and looked at them more carefully. Then he smiled although he did not give them back to her.

'I know you, don't I?' he asked.

'I don't think so.' Viviane was suddenly brittle and defensive.

'Yes I do. You're Viviane Loubet.'

'That was my maiden name.'

Villiers shrugged. 'Which means that you are the sister-in-law of Capitaine Boyer, my boss.' His voice took on a cold edge.

Viviane tensed. She was always wrong-footed when Roland was mentioned. Now she felt really concerned. She knew that he could be a real stickler for discipline and if he had been hard on this young policeman then it might mean trouble. He might take dislike of his boss out on her. Even more so if he recalled that she was married to a man who always sailed close to the wind where the law was concerned.

She tried to give a winning smile. 'I haven't seen my brother-in-law for a while. Do give him my regards.'

'A close family, I see.' Villiers laughed. Then his eyes narrowed. 'Wait a minute. Aren't you living with Alain Renaud?'

'We're married,' she said.

'Alain and I went to school together. He was older than me. He didn't like me.'

'Boys will be boys. But then they grow up, of course.'

'As do little girls.'

Viviane's eyes glinted. She was not sure if he was referring to Celeste or to herself. A sick feeling oozed into her stomach. The police were getting more undisciplined with every passing year. They were hungry: for food, cigarettes and for wine. All too often they sought to slake this hunger on the one commodity which was never in short supply. Young women were now more wary of the police than of the criminals they were meant to protect them from.

'My husband works from home,' she said, hoping that this would dissuade him from trying to take advantage. 'He hasn't been sent to Germany, thankfully. Perhaps if you'd like to call round, you can chat about the past over a bottle of wine.'

Villiers tilted his head. 'And I'm sure that he has many fine bottles, Madame.' He gave a wide grin. 'Your husband's entrepreneurial activities do not go unnoticed at the police station.'

She did not know how to respond and said nothing.

'Anyway,' Villiers continued, 'you need to go home and bandage up your daughter's leg.'

She turned to go but he spoke again. 'And do keep a better eye on the boy. After all, he's not yours, you're only taking care for him for a while.'

'Everything's perfectly in order,' she said. Her mouth was suddenly dry as dust. 'The boy's mother was my friend.'

'Of course.' His tone was ironic, mocking.

She was about to leave when she felt his hand upon her arm.

'These papers, Madame,' he said. 'Where did you get them?'

Viviane saw to her horror that he still had the papers in his hand.

'From his mother,' she said. 'Or should I say, from her friend who brought him here from Paris.'

Villiers nodded but there was a deep frown on his forehead. 'And where did this friend get them from?'

'From his parent's home, I presume. Why do you ask?'

Villiers pursed his lips. 'Because they're not actually that good a forgery.'

Viviane felt her head grow dizzy. Her ears were filled with a terrible booming noise, fierce waves crashing on a cliff. She could see the policeman standing in front of her but nothing else. Her whole world had shrunk down to this tiny space of utmost danger.

He pointed out the words at the bottom of the document. 'The ink has run a little, you see. Most people wouldn't notice it, perhaps, but I was trained in the fraud section in Lyons.'

He held the papers out to her. 'You'd be advised to put this right, Viviane.'

She stared at him in terror, unable to speak or to respond in any way. She did not know whether to take the papers or not. If she did, would this be an admission that she knew they were forgeries? Should she pretend to be confused? Should she deny everything?

She felt the tears welling in her eyes and prayed that they would stop. Everything seemed about to collapse around her. She would lose everything, David, Alain, her freedom, Celeste. She heard a sob beginning to sound in her chest.

'Now on your way,' Villiers said. He thrust the papers into her hand. 'And see to these as soon as possible.'

He patted David and Celeste on the head and headed off down the street.

'You'll have to get David new papers,' Viviane said.

Alain scowled. His stomach was still churning from Viviane telling him about the encounter with Villiers. He always got anxious when the Police started poking around in his affairs. It was even more worrying now that David was living with them. He did not know much about Villiers but he needed to find out more about him. He guessed that some of his contacts would have had dealings with him, good or bad.

'New papers!' Viviane repeated.

'I don't know how I'm going to get them,' he said. 'The friar's printing presses were destroyed.'

'Gabriel Chiappe got the last papers,' Viviane said. 'Can't you get you some more from him?'

Alain sighed. 'I don't know. And if he can, I have no idea how much it would cost.'

'It doesn't matter how much it costs.'

Alain looked at her dubiously. She was in a panic, a frenzy. He understood this but money was not limitless, far from it. He very much doubted he would be able to find enough for new papers and he was reluctant to ask for more money from Dorothy.

'Also,' he continued, 'don't forget that the papers Gabriel provided had a flaw. I don't know if he'll get us better ones next time.'

Viviane gave him a cold look. 'You'll just have to make sure that he does. After all, you always boast that he's your friend.'

Celeste clattered down the stairs with a dolly under arm. She was humming happily to herself and tugged at Viviane's apron. 'Maman, can David and me go and play with Monique?'

'No you can't,' Viviane snapped. 'Go and play in the yard. And keep your voices down.'

Celeste was shocked at her mother's angry response. Her bottom lip began to quiver and she had to force back the tears. Then she stomped out into the yard, calling on David to follow.

'You don't need to take it out on her,' Alain said.

'Who should I take it out on then? Pétain, Laval, Churchill, Hitler?'

Alain got up and caught her in his arms. She resisted for a moment, quivering like a hind caught in a trap. Then she gave a tiny cry, part anger, part despair, part surrender. She put her head on his shoulders and began to weep.

## NEW PAPERS AND MORE
*Nice, 12 May 1943*

The next morning, Alain parked his motorbike in a street just off the flower market in Nice. Gabriel had a small apartment in the old town, up a little winding street a little beyond the Cathedral. He would never go there, of course. To arrive there alone would be to invite a shot in the belly from one of Gabriel's trigger-happy cronies. But he knew his old friend's habits and strolled along the nearby streets, peering into every cafe and bar.

For five minutes the only response he got were the cool glances of the cafe owners and the calls of the working girls to come and buy them a drink. Then he heard a shrill whistle and turned towards it. Gabriel was sitting in an ill-lit bar with two girls perched beside him.

Alain pulled up a chair and the girls immediately sidled closer to him.

'Buy me a drink, won't you,' one of them said. She was in her thirties, with a fine figure and a challenging look. The other one was much younger, perhaps only fifteen. She should be in school, Alain thought sadly. She did not say anything but reached out and took his hand.

'I need to speak to you,' Alain told Gabriel, trying without success to disengage the young prostitute's grip.

Something in his tone made the older woman take notice. She dropped all pretence of interest and lit a cigarette, leaning her head against the wall and retreating into a kinder world.

The young girl squeezed his hand a little more tightly, hope defeating experience, until she too realised he was not interested and let go.

Alain stood up and Gabriel swallowed his drink and followed.

'Nice friends you have,' Alain said.

'Profitable friends.' He touched him on the elbow. 'I can give you a special price if you like. You can have both together, if you wish.'

Alain shook his head. 'I've come about business.'

Gabriel opened his hands wide, as if to say, this was business and then chuckled. 'If it's in my power, I'll help, old friend,' he said.

Alain peered around to make sure that no one was within hearing distance. A man was squatting on a step rolling a cigarette, two old ladies were chatting by an alley way but he could see no one else. 'I need more papers for the boy.'

Chiappe looked surprised. 'Why? Have you lost the ones I gave you?'

Alain sighed, wondering how to say it without angering him. 'They had some flaws, too tiny for anyone to notice except an expert. And an expert noticed them.'

'Fraud squad?'

Alain nodded.

'And what did he do?'

'Nothing. Except to tell Viviane to get some better papers.'

Chiappe rubbed his fingers across his mouth, deep in thought. Then he sighed. 'I didn't know about any flaws, Alain. I'm sorry.'

'I know you didn't. There is no blame attached to anyone. The forger may have been a little careless.'

'He's dead now, at the hands of the Gestapo. Fortunate for him, after what you've told me.'

Alain did not respond. He had little doubt that, were he still alive, Chiappe would have been on the next train to Marseille in search of the forger.

'Can you help me again?' Alain asked.

Chiappe shook his head. 'Not in Nice. I don't have contacts with anyone who provides papers.'

Then he clicked his fingers and gasped. 'Oh yes, I do.'

He leaned closer to Alain and whispered in his ear. 'There's a priest or friar or something who has a printing press in an old church near here. He fled Marseilles when the Germans took over. I've heard that he makes passports for Jews.'

'Father Benoît?'

'You know him?' Chiappe asked in surprise.

'I met him once. I thought the Germans might have captured him.'

'Maybe they did, but you know what they say about the power of the Church. The Nazis probably got warned off and let him go. Anyway, I know where we can find him.'

He hurried off, with Alain trailing in his wake. They visited several cafes, where Chiappe had swift, furtive conversations with various people. None of them looked like typical church-goers. Alain began to think their quest was hopeless but eventually one hard-faced man looked from Chiappe to Alain and gave a curt nod.

Chiappe's hands moved so fast, Alain only caught a glimpse of him stuffing some notes into the man's breast pocket. The man sniffed and said a few words out of the corner of his mouth. Chiappe grabbed Alain by the arm and led him away.

'Who was that?' Alain asked.

'Best not to know.'

They trudged up some alleys which wound like a maze into the innermost heart of the old town. The air grew hot and noisome, panting dogs eyed them malevolently, vermin scurried into holes at their approach. Every third doorway had a woman stationed at it, some professional whores, others ordinary housewives driven to sell themselves for food. Drug dealers sat on benches or steps, with a few furtive men making trades.

Not so different from Marseille, Alain thought. And what on earth was Father Benoît doing in such a place?

At last they came to a building which looked as though it had fallen in on itself a couple of centuries ago. The roof was missing most of its tiles, the windows appeared to sag under the weight of the walls and the door was at a crooked angle.

'Here's the Vatican,' Gabriel said with a laugh.

He hammered on the door and stepped back.

It opened a crack and Alain caught sight of a man peering out nervously.

'Vincent sent me,' Gabriel said.

The door opened and a hand gestured to them to enter.

'Lawrence,' Alain said with surprise.

The young man looked at him in terror and then light dawned. He gave a foolish grin.

'This is Gabriel,' Alain said, clapping him on the arm and pointing out Chiappe.

'He told me you're the angel Gabriel,' Lawrence explained.

Chiappe looked confused but shrugged and offered Lawrence a cigarette. He refused it initially, but then glanced around and stuffed it into the pouch on his belt.

'You want to see Father Benoît?' he asked.

'I do,' Alain said. 'And I'm glad to see that you and he are alive and well.'

Lawrence grinned and loped off, gesturing to them to follow.

The printing operation here was tiny compared to what Alain had seen in the monastery in Marseilles. Three men and two women worked at rickety desks and there was only one printer to duplicate the documents they produced. Father Benoît was perched on a high stool at the rear of the room, scrutinising some papers with utmost care.

He looked up when they approached and his brow furrowed. 'I seem to recognise you, my son,' he said to Alain.

'You kindly agreed to produce some identity papers for the little boy we're taking care of,' Alain said. 'Unfortunately, the Germans arrived a few hours later.'

A look of pain slid across Father Benoit's face. 'A terrible time,' he said. 'But with God's will and guidance we continue the work.'

Alain took David's papers from his pocket and showed them to the friar. 'I need these to be replaced,' he said.

'Why do you need new papers when you have them already?' Benoît asked.

'Because there's a tiny flaw in them.' Alain pointed to the bottom of the document.

The friar peered at the document, then picked up a magnifying glass. 'I can see no flaw.'

'Nor can I. But a member of the fraud squad noticed it immediately. He advised me to get new papers.'

'And you think we can do better than this?'

Alain shrugged. 'I hope so.'

Benoît glanced at Chiappe. 'And who is this?'

'My friend. He's an influential man on the coast.'

'Ah,' Benoît said. 'By which you mean a gangster.' He held out his hand to Chiappe.

Chiappe gave a grin which was part human, part shark, and shook his hand.

'You have put yourself at risk coming here, my son,' Benoît said to him. 'At least in this world. Maybe, by doing so, you have saved yourself in the next one.'

'Alain's my friend, father,' Chiappe replied. 'And I am a man of God.'

Benoît gave him an unfathomable look. 'Our Lord works in mysterious ways,' he said, at last.

He called over one of the women at the table. 'These documents have a flaw,' he told her, 'and have been compromised. They are for a little child and he and this man's family are in jeopardy. I would like you to produce new papers immediately.'

'My other work?' she asked.

'Of less immediate need.'

'Then they'll be ready this afternoon,' she said, taking the papers back to her desk.

Father Benoît got off his stool and took Alain's hand in his. 'And now I must leave you, my son. I am grateful for all that you have done for the boy.'

'I am his father now,' Alain said.

Benoit's eyes filled with tears and he gave a little bow.

'Claude,' he said in a gruff voice, 'where is Brother Ludovic?'

One of the men looked up. 'Have you not heard, Father? He has fallen sick with the flux. He's in a terrible state.'

Benoît looked aghast. 'But I need him to translate for me. I am going to see Angelo Donati this morning and I don't speak Italian.'

'I was brought up in Menton and can speak Italian,' Alain said. 'I can translate for you.'

Benoît stared at him intently. Alain almost took a step back, so powerful was his gaze.

Finally the friar said. 'This is of the utmost secret, my son. Can I trust you to never breathe a word of what Donati and I discuss?'

Alain gulped, surprised by the intensity of Benoît's words and manner.

'Of course. You're helping me. It's the least I can do.'

The friar nodded and touched Alain on the arm, almost a blessing.

'Do you want me to come with you?' Chiappe asked.

'Forgive me, my son, but no. I have told Donati that I will come with only one person.'

Chiappe gave Alain a wry glance, suspecting that Benoît was making an excuse. No doubt the friar's faith in redemption was tempered by knowledge of the power of temptation.

Father Benoît led the way to the entrance of the building. Brother Lawrence opened the door, peeped up and down the street and gestured that all was clear.

They stepped out and Benoît led them away at a furious pace. 'It's best not to be seen near the building,' he said. 'Prying eyes and ears.'

'I could arrange protection,' Chiappe said, to his own surprise.

Benoît considered this. 'I would normally say that God's protection is sufficient but maybe he has asked you to lend a hand. Let me pray tonight regarding your offer.'

'Why would you want to do that?' Alain whispered in Chiappe's ear.

He shrugged. 'I'm not sure. Maybe it's some form of insurance.'

Benoît led them down the narrow streets of the old town. Chiappe said goodbye and the friar led Alain onto the Promenade des Anglais, which ran for seven kilometres beside the beach.

'Who is this man Donati?' Alain asked as they hurried along the promenade.

'I don't know much about him,' Benoît replied. 'He's said to be an important member of the Italian business world, in banking and other enterprises. But my concern with him is because he is helping Jewish people to gain places of safety.'

They passed the Hotel Negresco and turned right into the Boulevard Gambetta. Benoît stopped a little further along and then darted into a doorway, dragging Alain along with him.

'You remember your promise to me,' he said, his voice stern and commanding. 'Not a word of what we discuss is to pass your lips.'

Alain nodded.

Benoît hurried up the stairs and gave a soft knock upon a door.

It was opened by a well-dressed man in his fifties. His hair was receding with traces of grey close to his ears. He had a long, fine handsome face with a large nose framed by deep grooves on either side which might have made him look miserable were it not for a huge, warm smile. He shook Father Benoît's and Alain's hands and then, in perfect French, invited them to take a seat.

Benoît gave a look of astonishment. 'I was told you could not speak French,' he said.

Donati smiled. 'I lived in Paris for twenty years and have been in the south since the Germans arrived. My French is, I believe, quite adequate. Although, in these troubled times, I am careful who I allow to know it.'

'My apologies,' Benoît said, 'I was misinformed.'

Donati waved his hands as if to say it was nothing to worry about.

Alain wondered if he should leave as there was now no need for him to translate. But the two men began an intense discussion about the situation of the Jews and appeared to almost have forgotten him. He decided to stay.

It was a revelation to him. For a start Donati told them that he was himself of a Jewish background. Then it became clear that he had been astonishingly active in aiding his fellow Jews. His extensive networks meant that he had been able to send Jewish families to secure havens in Saint-Martin-Vésubie and other towns. He had spirited others out of the country to Switzerland and Italy.

All of this, it appeared, was possible because the Italian military were reluctant to take any measures against the Jews, countermanding Vichy orders to imprison them and even, on one occasion, surrounding a Gendarmerie barracks with troops until the French reluctantly freed their captive Jews.

More recently, because of German pressure, the Italian authorities claimed that they were taking stringent measures against the Jews. This, however, appeared to be nothing but a ruse. The Jews were safer with the Italians than they had been under Pétain's Government. Donati made full use of his countrymen's reluctance to harm the Jews.

But he was not content with this. He had an even more ambitious plan which was why he had asked Father Benoît to meet him.

'My people feel a little safer now,' he said, 'but it is not enough. Now, I want to ship all the Jews in southern France first to Italy and from there, onward to North Africa and the safety of the Americans and British.'

Benoît gaped in amazement when he heard this.

'How will that be possible?'

'We will need more than the support of the Italian military over here. We must get the Italian government to agree.'

'That's impossible. Mussolini will never countenance it.'

Donati leaned back in his chair and eyed Benoît with searching eyes. 'Mussolini is not as impressed by Hitler as he pretends. He is frightened of him, yes, but like a child who lives in fear of a violent father will seek every chance to prove to himself that he is not afraid. Mussolini is not beyond conniving at measures to wrong-foot Hitler.

'But he will need additional encouragement. That is where you come in, father. I want you to persuade your Pope to intercede with Mussolini and his ministers to insist that the plan goes ahead.'

Benoît pulled at his long nose. Pope Pius XII believed that he needed a harmonious relationship with the Fascists in Rome, which was understandable. Yet there were other rumours which were more troubling, rumours that he had been less forthright than he might have been in condemning German persecutions of the Jews.

Yet, as he considered this, Benoît realised that here was an opportunity to put all such rumours to rest. If the Pope supported the plan to transport Jews to North Africa, then suspicions that he turned a blind eye to persecution would be proved wrong.

'I'll do it,' he said, taking Donati's hands in his. 'I shall go to Rome to seek the support of the Pope.'

Donati got to his feet and shook Benoît's and Alain's hands. He opened a bottle of the very best Italian wine and poured three glasses.

Alain sipped his thoughtfully. 'If the plan goes ahead,' he said, finally, 'would my little boy be able to go to North Africa?'

Donati shrugged. 'How old is he?'

'Four and a half.'

Donati sighed. 'That is young. Would your wife be able to go with him?'

'She's not a Jew. The boy's not really ours. We took him in. And there's my daughter to consider.'

Donati sat down and nursed his drink for a while. 'If your wife were to go with the boy, the authorities might conclude she is a Jew. That is a perilous risk for her to take.'

'Perhaps the whole family could go,' suggested Benoît.

Donati shook his head. 'I don't think so. This would take the places needed by Jews who are in mortal danger.' He did not say what was also on his mind, that this option might be seized by unscrupulous people as a way to escape from France.

'But you'd take the boy on his own?' Alain asked.

'Perhaps,' Donati said. 'If we can find a family to take him with them. But I'll be honest, Monsieur, it is not that likely.'

Alain nodded. It might not be likely but Donati had not ruled it out.


## ABANDON HIM?
### *Grasse, 13 and 14 May 1943*

Alain pondered what Donati had told him throughout the journey back to Grasse. What puzzled him most was why the man had so recently come up with the plan to send the Jews to North Africa. It seemed that the Italians were more humane than the French had proved, so what on earth was the hurry?

His face must have betrayed his emotions because Viviane immediately picked up that something was troubling him.

'You didn't get the papers?'

'No, I have them here.' He produced the papers and passed them to her.

'So Gabriel really is a friend,' she said.

'In a way. Although he wasn't able to get them for me.' He told her all that had happened that day.

'And Father Benoît's papers are better than Chiappe could produce?' she asked anxiously.

'I presume so. I can't see the sort of flaw which Villiers pointed out, at any rate.'

He took her hand. 'I have other news, though.' He glanced at the children. 'I think they should go out to play.'

She looked alarmed and ushered the children out into the yard. Alain poured some wine.

Viviane listened intently as he relayed all that he had learnt about Donati's plan. She remained silent after he had finished, her mind replaying every comment, weighing every word.

'So they would take David if he went with another family?'

'I think so. But Donati couldn't guarantee it.'

'And do you trust him?'

Alain thought back to his impressions of Donati. 'Yes, I do. He didn't strike me as a pious man like the friar. He's just an ordinary person, but one who is doing what he can to fight a great wrong.'

'Just like us,' she said. Her voice was matter of fact.

He nodded. He hadn't thought about it in this way but it was the truth. And he would never have considered that he might do such a thing. Perhaps he wouldn't have done so were it not for Viviane. Were it not for David.

'So what should we do?' he asked quietly.

Viviane's eyes filled with tears. 'I don't know, Alain. I really don't.' She gazed out of the window, listening to the noise of Celeste and David playing. 'He's become part of our family. Celeste loves him.' She paused. 'And I've come to love him, as well.'

Alain nodded. 'Me too,' he said quietly.

She gave a tiny smile at his admission that he felt the same.

'I know it might be for the best,' she continued. 'David would be safer away from here. Physically safer, at least.'

The image of his mother's desperate pleas flashed into her mind. 'But he's already lost one set of parents. Is it fair for him to lose a second?'

No sooner had she said this than thoughts of her own parents came to her. She had lost her mother to her sister long ago. But not her father. Perhaps thinking on this would give her the answer.

'Maybe we should sleep on it,' she said at last.

'Maybe.' Alain rubbed his mouth vigorously. 'But what bothers me is why now? Why is Donati seeking to transport the Jews now? He said himself that the Italians are treating his people better than Pétain and his crew.'

'Perhaps Donati thinks the Italians won't do so for much longer. Or that they'll begin to do what Hitler wants.'

Alain shrugged. It was beyond him. The world appeared to have lost its mind. He had never placed much faith in the institutions of life: country, government, religion, laws. But even this small amount had been revealed to be futile.

Finally, he had an idea, if only the glimmer of one. 'Perhaps we should ask Dorothy,' he said. She looked confused. 'Why?'

'Because she knows more than we do. About what's happening in the war. And most importantly, she can tell us how the Americans might respond to hordes of Jews arriving in the middle of a war in North Africa.'

She heaved a sigh of relief. 'Good. We'll sleep on it and then see what Dorothy thinks.' The burden of decision already seemed a little lighter.

Viviane managed to get a baguette from Monsieur Blanche's boulangerie. It was still warm when she got it home and the whole family wolfed it down.

Alain had been finding it harder to get as much food since the capture of Marseille. Imports from North Africa had dried up and the German Occupation west of the Rhone sucked up most of the surplus from there. The family's stock of food was getting very low and they were all getting gaunt and thin. This was the first breakfast Viviane had eaten in days.

Alain disappeared after breakfast in search of more petrol. It was in very short supply and it took him several hours and visits to many of his suppliers before he managed to get as much as he needed. He finally roared up to the house at twelve o' clock.

Alain hurried into his store-room while Viviane and the children clambered onto the motorbike and sidecar. It was not as powerful as the one he had abandoned in Marseille. The sidecar was smaller and uncomfortable but the children did not complain. It was amazing how adaptable they were, Viviane thought, taking some comfort from this.

Alain came out of the store, padlocked it shut and thrust a bottle of wine beside Celeste's feet.

'No drinking it,' he said, waving a finger in admonishment. 'This is for Madame Pine.'

Celeste giggled at his jest. 'We don't have a cork-screw,' she said.

Alain wiped his forehead in mock relief. 'Thank goodness for that. I don't want you arriving at Madame Pine's drunk.'

He climbed into the saddle, kicked the bike into life and started off.

It was gone twelve when they arrived at the villa. Viviane cursed herself for not thinking to come in the afternoon. It might look to Dorothy that they had come at this time in order to get some lunch.

She need not have worried. Dorothy rushed out of the door the minute they arrived.

'Come in, come in,' she cried.

Viviane and Alain had never seen her so excited. They exchanged puzzled glances and followed her into the house. The children were already scampering after Groucho, Dorothy's cat, shrieking with pleasure as he raced away from them before stopping and purring, enticing them to chase him.

Dorothy led them, not into any of the living rooms but into the kitchen and then into a tiny, windowless pantry. The handyman, Pierre Sorel was there, fiddling with something on a shelf. He turned when they entered, a look of alarm on his face, then put his fingers to his lips.

So this is how she gets her news, Alain thought. It was a very modern radio, capable, he thought, of hearing news from sources his old set would not be able to tune into. Perhaps sources like the Allied military.

Dorothy approached Pierre and he held up a pair of headphones. She took one of the earpieces and pressed it to her ear, while Pierre did the same with the other one.

They stood like that for several minutes, as silent and immobile as statues in a graveyard. Viviane and Alain looked on with growing concern.

Suddenly Dorothy gave a yelp and kissed Pierre on the cheek. She thrust the headphones at him and gave Viviane a fierce hug.

'Great news,' she cried. 'Wonderful news.'

'What is it?' Alain asked.

'The last of the German and Italian forces in North Africa have surrendered to the Allies.'

She gave a little skip of delight. 'Unconditional surrender. The Italian General had tried to cut a deal but the Allies demanded unconditional surrender.' She clapped her hands with joy.

'What does this mean?' Viviane asked.

Dorothy gave a whoop of delight.

'It means no good for the Italians,' she said. 'Perhaps not much better for the Germans, either. The Italians have lost all of their African conquests and as for the famous Afrika Korps...' She rubbed her hands vigorously as if wiping away some dirt.

'This calls for a drink,' she said. 'You too, Pierre.'

'Might there be more news?' he asked.

'I doubt it,' she said.

He nodded and began to hide the set.

They followed Dorothy back into the morning room. She gestured to Lucile to follow her and yelled for Marie to bring some bubbly and six glasses.

'Here's to Ike,' she said, sipping at the wine. It was an Italian bottle for she had run out of champagne.

'Who's Ike?' Viviane asked.

'General Eisenhower,' she replied. 'His nickname's Ike. He's the head of the Allied forces in North Africa and he's really trounced the bastards.'

'So what will this mean?' Alain asked. 'For the war?'

'It's good news, obviously?' Viviane said. There was a trace of doubt in her voice. She had grown wary of expressing hope.

'In the long run, sure,' Dorothy said.

'In the long run?'

Dorothy did not answer immediately. She worried that an Allied victory in North Africa might lead to the Germans and Italians consolidating their hold on Europe. This was not a thought she wanted to ponder too deeply.

'Well we'd be foolish to think we'll win the war overnight,' she said. 'But it's a big step forward.'

She gave a consoling smile to Marie and Lucile. Pierre raised an eyebrow in a sardonic manner.

'You'll stay for lunch?' she asked Viviane to change the subject.

'No, we couldn't —'

'Yes you could. There's nothing fancy but you're very welcome.'

Lucile and Marie went to the kitchen to prepare lunch while Pierre disappeared.

'So he's a radio operator?' Alain quipped.

'He's my handyman,' Dorothy said, sharply. 'And none of you say anything about the radio.'

The meal was vegetable soup with croutons, followed by apple tart. Dorothy may have said it was nothing fancy but it was tastier than anything the family had eaten for months.

The moment they had finished, Celeste begged to go out to play.

'But don't get dirty,' Viviane called as she and David disappeared in search of the cat.

'They're lovely kids,' Dorothy said. 'You must be very proud.'

Viviane was unnerved by this comment. It was almost as if Dorothy had guessed the reason they were here. She looked at Alain who stared back in silence.

Viviane sighed, realising that Alain would not say why they had come and that it was down to her to broach the subject.

Hesitantly she began to relate the possibility of sending David with other Jews to North Africa.

Dorothy listened in silence. It seemed to her that it was an almost impossible dilemma. Keeping David was a never-ending peril for the family. Sending him away was risky and might be upsetting for him. But if it guaranteed his safety it might be a course worth taking. And not only his safety but theirs.

Viviane fell silent at last and gazed at Dorothy.

Dorothy took her hand and squeezed it gently. 'It's a terrible choice to have to make,' she said. 'I'm glad it's not me who has to make it. David's been with you what, almost a year?'

'A year in August. Yet he thinks of us as his parents now.'

Dorothy did not answer but her face looked a little doubtful.

'You don't think he does?' Viviane asked in surprise. 'He calls us Maman and Papa.'

'I don't know what he thinks, Viviane. And neither do you, I guess. If he does think of you as his parents then maybe he'll come to think of others in the same way in just as short a time.'

Viviane was shocked and upset by this suggestion. But at the same time, she realised how true it might be. She closed her eyes a moment, trying to work out if she wanted to keep David for his sake or for her own.

She looked from Dorothy to Alain. They both appeared as tortured as she felt.

'You think we should let him go?' she whispered to Dorothy.

'I can't make that decision for you, Viviane. But I can say that the Allies will look after him. New York is full of Jews and they'd be happy to take such a little fellow in.'

'But he's safe here,' Alain said. 'The Italians are not like the Germans. Or like the bastard government in Vichy.'

'I agree. The Italians are much less dangerous than the Germans for the moment. But who knows what may happen if the war turns against them?'

'You think it will?'

'I'm sure it will.'

All three of them fell silent. The weight of what they had to decide seemed impossible to bear. A thought came to Dorothy and she made to say it, then thought better of it.

'What?' Viviane said immediately. 'What were you going to say?'

Dorothy sighed. 'Don't take this the wrong way, Viviane. And don't get alarmed. But it seems to me that you have to think not only about David but about yourselves.'

'What do you mean?'

Dorothy shook her head. 'The Italians may be more tolerant of the Jews but they don't love them. And the French are the same. If things get worse what might happen to people who are shielding them? What might happen to your family?'

Viviane burst into tears. This was the thought that had been gnawing at her, unacknowledged for the last ten months. She wept and wept and nothing that Dorothy or Alain could do could stem her tears.

Finally, exhausted, she lay her head back against the chair. She felt drained and empty. She seemed to have no fight left in her, no strength at all. The world was slipping away from her, leaving her behind, and she lacked the will to try to keep up with it. A cold despair seized her but even that now held no terrors. The world was nothing more than blood and ash and she doubted that she could wade through it any longer.

But she had to, she knew.

She took a deep breath. 'Then David goes away,' she said.

Alain nodded. 'But we must say nothing of this to Celeste or to David until the day comes for him to leave.'

## HEAT AND FEVER
*Grasse, 17 July 1943*

The town panted under ten days of fierce sun and still air. The streets were hot underfoot and children dared each other to place their hands on walls as hot as ovens. Wherever people walked it felt like they were wading through air which resisted every step. Bakers had always worked in the early hours of the morning but now they worked from midnight, desperate to avoid the heat. It did little good for the night was almost as stifling as the day. Many other shopkeepers shut up shop.

Viviane poured some water in a basin and rinsed her face. It made little difference for her face was hot and the water was tepid. She was envious of Alain for he had gone to Nice for a few days and would enjoy its sea breeze. There was rumour that a dozen trucks carrying Tuscan olive oil had gone missing on the road. He hoped to procure several cases of the precious stuff. Most French oil was now dressing German salads and, although the French thought Italian oil a poor substitute, many were willing to pay a high price to get it.

David hopped down the stairs. He had just discovered how to hop and preferred it to walking. 'Not on the stairs,' Viviane said. 'Anywhere else but not on the stairs. It's dangerous.' Even to her own ears she sounded tired and listless.

She put some water on to boil and shook the jar of coffee beans. There were just enough to make a cup for herself with a drop left over to flavour the children's milk. She had a sudden thought, went to the pantry and sniffed at the bottle of milk. Her gorge rose. It had gone rancid. She glanced at the cheese which lay in a saucer sitting in a bowl of water. It had gone as soft as butter, oozing across the saucer as if trying to make an escape for freedom. It wouldn't last, she decided; they may as well eat it this morning.

'Where's Celeste?' she asked David when she returned to the kitchen.

'She hurts,' he said. 'In her head and throat.'

Viviane looked surprised, Celeste was rarely ill and if she was, she would always insist on coming down. A sudden pang of fear hit her. She ran up the stairs and into the bedroom. Celeste was laying on the bed with the sheet screwed up on the floor.

Viviane felt her forehead. It was burning with heat.

'Maman, I've been sick,' Celeste said. There was a pool of vomit on the floor beside the bed.

'Never mind, darling,' Viviane said. 'Maman will clear it up in a jiffy.'

'My throat hurts,' she said.

Viviane felt her throat which made her whimper a little. The glands were up.

'Stick out your tongue,' she said. It was red and bumpy with patches of slick white. She peered more closely. Celeste's face and neck bore a red rash. She touched it gently and it felt like sandpaper. Her first thought was that she had got sunburn although she had not been in the sun for days.

Her hand went to her mouth. A couple of children at the far end of town had developed polio. She racked her brains thinking of the symptoms of this. She couldn't be certain but she thought they were similar. She fought down the terror which gripped her.

'I think we'd better take you to see Doctor Langeis,' she said, trying to sound bright.

'I don't want to,' Celeste wailed.

'Don't be silly, he'll make you feel better.' Celeste began to cry but got out of bed and pulled her clothes on. She was shaking a little and Viviane had to help her with her buttons.

'I don't want any breakfast,' Celeste said as they reached the bottom of the stairs.

'That's fine, darling. We'll go now. Come on David.'

'I want breakfast,' he said, sticking out his bottom lip.

'We'll get some bread from Monsieur Blanche,' she said. 'Stop complaining.'

As they left the house Viviane remembered to plonk hats upon the children's heads. Celeste usually complained about this but now she was strangely acquiescent. Viviane's fears rose even higher.

To her surprise, the Doctor's door was locked. She hammered loudly on it and finally, Madame Langeis opened the door. She was in her early fifties, a lovely woman. Now she looked frightened. She had obviously just been crying.

'Are you alright, Madame Langeis?' Viviane asked in alarm.

'I am. But my husband has been taken for questioning by the police. They think he is one of the Maquis. But he isn't, I swear it.'

Viviane nodded in agreement although she too had heard this rumour. She couldn't believe that the portly, genial doctor would have been involved in any acts of resistance but she thought that he might well visit nearby Maquis camps to deal with their sick and wounded.

'My little girl is ill,' Viviane said.

'I can't help you,' Madame Langeis said. 'You'll have to go home.' She glanced at Celeste and then frowned and bent down to examine her more closely. 'I'm no doctor, Viviane, but I think Celeste should go to the hospital.'

'Do you think it might be polio?'

'I think you should go to the hospital.'

Viviane's heart leapt into her mouth. She nodded her thanks and headed down the street.

I can't take David, she thought. Too risky to have him there when I'll be looking after Celeste. She turned left at the next street, hurried down to Sylvie's house and hammered on the door.

It did not open but the next door neighbour's door did.

'She's gone away,' the old lady said. 'Went off with a fancy man to the mountains. Took Monique with her. Sylvie's fortunate. I wish I still had my looks.' She shook her head ruefully and shut the door.

'Now what?' Viviane muttered under her breath.

She glanced up the street. She was close to her mother's house. She took a deep breath. She had no choice. She would have to leave David with her.

Viviane saw her mother in her usual place, eyes glued to the window to watch whatever might be happening on the street. Viviane pushed open the door and stepped in.

'To what do I owe this pleasure?' her mother said, coldly.

'I need your help, Maman.'

Marthe raised an eyebrow. 'Why am I surprised? You only ever come when you need something.'

'Celeste is very ill,' Viviane said, in too great a hurry to bother to respond. 'I must take her to hospital.'

'What's the matter with her?' Her tone softened a little.

'I don't know. She's burning and her skin is red.'

'We're all burning with this heat. You shouldn't let her go out in the sun.'

Even now she has to criticise, Viviane thought.

'I need to go to the hospital.'

Marthe shrugged. 'So go. Why are you telling me?'

Viviane pushed David forward. 'I can't take David; we may be at the hospital a long while. Would you look after him?'

'A stranger? In my house?' She shook her head.

'Please Maman.'

'Go to one of your fine friends. That whore, Sylvie if she can clamber out of bed.'

'I tried her. She's not in town. Please Maman.' She hated that she had to beg but had no choice.

'Let the boy stay,' came Georges' voice from the back room.

Marthe's face grew angry. 'It's all right for you, old man,' she called. 'You won't have to look after him all day.'

'I'll take him down to the river. Show him the fish.'

'And break your neck trying to get there?'

Georges came into the room on his crutches. He looked skinnier and more care-worn than ever. 'He'll be all right with us, Viv, don't fret.'

He gazed at Celeste, carefully. 'Your mother's probably right, it looks like sun-stroke. But get her checked over at the hospital.'

Viviane kissed him on the cheek and then did the same to her mother, although with visibly less enthusiasm. Then she grabbed Celeste by the hand and hurried out of the house.

Marthe and Georges stared at David. He stared back at them. 'I'm hungry,' he said.

Georges patted him on the head and laughed. 'Me too little feller. Let's see what Grand-mere can get for us.'

'I'm not...' Marthe began but then thought better of it. She went into the kitchen, muttering to herself every step of the way.

They had a breakfast of bread and jam with warm milk almost on the turn. Georges' military pension was small but he was a popular man and many of his friends would leave a little food on his doorstep. He had been surly about this at first, ashamed that they thought him in need of charity. But lately, as food got ever scarcer, he was grateful and thought himself lucky.

Needless to say he did not take David to the river. The trip would have been too arduous for him at the best of times but was unthinkable in this heat. Instead he took him into the back yard and let him tinker with an old clock which he had always intended to mend but never got around to.

It was relatively cool out here and as Georges helped the little boy dismantle the clock, he found a peace he had not experienced for a long time. It was interrupted a little later when Odette arrived. Even out here he could hear the excitement in her voice as she loudly regaled her mother with some juicy piece of gossip.

'You don't say,' Marthe kept saying. But Odette did, at great length and volume.

The sun crept over the back wall at ten o'clock and Georges decided that they should go inside. He allowed David to take in the clock-face and some of the larger components. His face shone with excitement as he followed Georges inside, his arms overflowing.

Odette looked David up and down as if he were a stray dog, unable or unwilling to keep the contempt from her face. Georges scowled at her but kept his counsel. He had learnt long ago that sparring with his eldest daughter was hard and painful and, at best, he would only ever scrape a draw.

'Don't start,' he contented himself with saying and then picked up a book.

'Look at that,' Marthe said to Odette. 'Nose in a book as usual when he was the one who offered to take the boy in.'

'How long will she be gone?' Odette asked.

Marthe shrugged. 'There's a lot of illness around. The boy could be here all day.'

It was as if her words sparked something in David. 'I want a pee-pee,' he announced.

'The toilet's in the yard,' Marthe said.

'Can you manage, little feller?' Georges asked.

David nodded. 'I'm a big boy now.' He started towards the kitchen.

Then Odette said, 'We don't want him to make a mess of himself,' and darted after him.

Georges looked surprised as she went past. Perhaps she's discovered her caring side, he thought.

He found his place in the book and Marthe seated herself at the window, staring in turn at the street and her husband.

Odette appeared at last, holding David tightly by the hand. She had a look of triumph on her face.

'You'll never guess what I discovered in the toilet,' she said. 'The little guttersnipe is a Jew.'

Marthe's hand went to her mouth in dismay.

Georges gave a groan. This could be dangerous and it had to be dealt with.

He flung down his book. 'Whether he is or not, doesn't matter. The boy's been taken in by Viviane. He belongs to her and so he belongs to us. I never want to hear you repeat this outside these walls. Either of you.'

His voice had taken on a hard and decisive edge, the sort that had carried across the killing fields of Verdun and the Somme.

Marthe bowed her head in acquiescence. Odette looked as if she might argue but thought better of it.

Viviane returned later on that afternoon with better news than she had feared. Celeste had scarlet fever, not polio. She could go home, although the doctors told her to have David sleep in their room until Celeste had recovered.

'So that's good news,' she said.

Then she caught a wary look in her mother's eye.

'We know,' Odette cried triumphantly. 'We know the boy's a Jew. I've seen that he's been circumcised.'

Georges struggled to his feet and slapped her face. She crouched to the ground, as if she were about to leap at him.

'And I said that it doesn't matter,' Georges cried. 'David's family and we should all remember it.'

Despite his words Viviane felt the fragile bonds that held her to her family beginning to unravel before her eyes.

'Thank you, Papa,' she said. Then she grabbed David and ran out of the house.


## HIGHS AND LOWS
### Grasse, 25 July 1943

The summer was as lovely as the spring. The only thing which dampened Viviane's spirits were her worries about Odette. What might she do now that she had discovered that David was a Jew? Her father's adamant decision to embrace David as part of the family would ensure her mother said nothing. But Odette might be a different matter.

Alain had been in touch with Father Benoît who promised that he and Donati would search for a Jewish family to take David with them to North Africa. They waited anxiously and at the end of July they got a message that an elderly couple were willing to take him with them.

Viviane was unhappy about him being cared for by older people but Alain persuaded him that it was probably only a temporary measure. She still had misgivings but agreed to the arrangement. There was no indication of when the ships would make the perilous journey across the Mediterranean, or indeed, if Donati had managed to arrange the transport. As the weeks drew on they decided to put all thought of David leaving out of mind.

Dorothy invited the family for a picnic on the last Sunday of the month. She seemed to have more food and wine once again and she was very generous with it so Viviane was more than happy to accept. Besides, Alain often pointed out how important it was to hear the point of view of a foreigner. Particularly one who was as well informed as Dorothy.

She was remarkably knowledgeable about what was going on across France and beyond. She used her radio to pick up foreign transmissions but Alain wondered if she was also in touch with elements of the Resistance.

It was a glorious day. The sky was a vivid blue with a few fleecy clouds floating high over the distant mountains. The sun was hot but a cool breeze blew off the Mediterranean which made the temperature more bearable. The cicadas were chirping without pause and there was the sound of birdsong from the tall trees sheltering the villa. Butterflies skimmed across the lawn and fat bumble bees sampled the vintage of the nectar from the flower-beds.

Dorothy and Marie had arranged the garden furniture under the shade of a huge old Cedar of Lebanon. Pierre had clambered up to its lowest branches to fasten a swing for the children to play on. Lucile had been hard at work all morning preparing the food.

'I don't know how she does it,' Viviane said to Dorothy when she saw the food spread out on the tables.

'Nor do I,' Dorothy said. 'Things are getting harder to find, as I'm sure Alain will tell you.'

Alain nodded. 'I'm having a bit better luck with the Italians. Are you as well, Dorothy?'

She blushed a little. 'If you're referring to my admirer, then yes. Emilio Marinelli is a delightful old darling.'

She gave him a defiant look. 'In fact, he's heard about our little get-together and invited himself to join us.'

Alain and Viviane exchanged glances. They knew that Dorothy was on good terms with the captain but were not sure that they wished to be. It was one thing for an American to fraternise with the enemy, quite another for them to do so.

'Ah well,' Alain said. 'I suppose we're supposed to be on the same side. Germany, Italy, France. All part of the brave new world order.' He squeezed Viviane's hand. 'And if he brings some Chianti…'

No sooner had he said the words than Marinelli's car raced up the drive. The driver opened the passenger door and the captain bounced out, holding two bottles of wine in his hand. He dismissed the driver who cast an envious look at the food before getting back in the car and driving off.

'Buongiorno,' Marinelli cried as he approached. He placed the two bottles on the table. Chianti, Alain was pleased to see.

The Italian took Viviane's hand and kissed it in a polite and proper manner.

Then he beamed at Dorothy. 'Ciao Bella,' he said. He lifted her hand to his lips and kissed it, rather more intently than he had Viviane's and certainly for a longer time.

'There's plenty of food, Emilio,' she said, pulling her hand away. 'No need to eat me.'

He gave a good-natured chuckle and flung himself into a chair. 'Where are your beautiful bambini, Signora Renaud?' he asked.

'They're playing on the swing, Capitano.'

He turned and watched the children for a while. Viviane felt he looked a little sad as he did so. Alain took the opportunity to examine the wine labels. They were a good year. He wondered where he stored them.

'Beautiful bambini,' Marinelli repeated as he turned back towards them. He gestured to the laden table. 'This is a delightful feast, Dorothy. I am flattered that you invited me.'

'I could hardly not,' Dorothy said. 'After all, you provided the ham and the desserts.'

'We have desserts?' Viviane gasped.

Marinelli kissed his fingers. 'A fine Italian one, Signora, Torta Barozzi. It's a coffee and chocolate cake, although sadly this one lacks the chocolate.' He raised his hands in an apologetic manner. 'The war.'

'I wish this darn war were over,' Dorothy said. 'I crave chocolate.'

'We all wish it, Signora. But we have hopes that the Allies will sue for peace. The war is not going well for them.'

Dorothy gave him a thoughtful and considered look. 'I've heard they did OK in North Africa.'

'For the moment.'

'They've kicked out the Germans and the Italians.' She offered Marinelli a piece of bread. 'And I hear rumour that they've invaded Sicily.'

She gave a long, dramatic pause. 'And, of course, your king has sacked Mussolini.'

Marinelli said nothing, almost as if he had not heard. But his face betrayed him, an incredible range of emotions. Shock, disbelief, doubt, anger, fear.

'I would like a drink,' he said, at last.

Alain stared at Dorothy in amazement. Mussolini had lost power? What would this mean for the war? For the people of their town?

He pulled the cork on one of the bottles, filled one glass and passed it to Marinelli. Then he filled the remaining glasses.

Marinelli stared at the wine as if he did not know what it was. He was too overwhelmed to drink it.

'What do you mean?' he stuttered, at last. 'About Il Duce?'

'It's just a rumour,' she said, airily, 'nothing more. I can't recall who told me it, to be honest.'

She took a long sip at her drink, enjoying the Italian's discomfort. 'My, but this is good Chianti, Emilio. You've done us proud.'

'About Mussolini?' he repeated.

Alain and Viviane exchanged glances. It seemed that Dorothy knew more about the war than Marinelli.

'Well,' she drawled, 'I hear that Patton and Montgomery have given your General Guzzoni a good whopping. Your army won't be able to hold Sicily much longer. Because of this the Grand Fascist Council voted to give the King back his constitutional powers. And this afternoon, the King dismissed Mussolini.'

Marinelli wiped his mouth a couple of times and forced a smile to his face. 'As you say, Dorothy, this is rumour. I have heard nothing of the sort.'

'Then I must be mistaken,' she said with a self-deprecating air. 'I should learn never to listen to gossip. I must say, I had my doubts when I first heard it.'

Viviane wondered if Marinelli would ask Dorothy who she had heard the rumour from but he said nothing. Either he didn't want to know or he was too unnerved by the news to think to ask.

'Anyway,' Dorothy said, with a clap of her hands. 'Let's put all this miserable talk of battles and war behind us. We should enjoy the day. Time for the picnic.'

'I'll get the children,' Viviane said.

She ran over to get Celeste and David, bringing them back, still chattering with delight at their time on the swing. But once they saw the food on the table, they stopped their noise and stared wide-eyed in wonder.

The sight of them seemed to shake Marinelli out of his stupor. 'Such lovely bambini,' he said. 'Let us pray that they live in more peaceful days.'

'Amen to that,' Dorothy said. 'Come along children. Sit down and tuck in.'

Viviane reached over and filled their plates.

Marinelli sipped his wine, every so often stealing a glance at Dorothy.

The picnic was a great success. Marinelli seemed to have convinced himself that the talk of Mussolini's fall was false and he proved the life and soul of the party. In his youth he had spent some years working as a conjurer and he entertained the children and adults with magic tricks.

Early in the evening his car returned. Marinelli seemed surprised. It was much earlier than he had ordered.

A lieutenant climbed out of the car and hurried towards them.

'Capitano,' he said. 'There has been an announcement on the radio. Il Duce has resigned.'

Marinelli turned to stare at Dorothy, his gaze unfathomable.

'Resigned?' he asked.

The lieutenant nodded. 'And he has been arrested. Marshal Badoglio is now Prime Minister.'

'And the war?' Marinelli could not keep the hope from his voice.

'Marshal Badoglio and the King have declared that Italy will continue to fight against the Allies.'

Marinelli opened his mouth to speak but for a moment no words came. 'Go back to the car and wait for me,' he said at last. The man looked surprised but marched off.

Marinelli stared at the ground for a long while. When he looked up, his face was a sea of emotions. 'Do you have some cognac?' he asked, quietly.

Dorothy passed a bottle to him. He filled a glass to the brim, drank half of it off in one gulp.

'Are you disappointed by the news?' Dorothy asked softly.

Marinelli shook his head. 'I don't know. Shocked, I suppose. Mussolini has led our country for twenty years. I was a young man when he came to power. What will happen now?'

'Do you think Italy will continue the war?' Alain asked.

'What choice do we have?' he answered miserably. 'I doubt the Allies will allow us to surrender with honour. And Hitler will never let us give in. The war will carry on, there is no doubt of that.'

His mind was in a whirl. He had no love for the war and little liking for Mussolini. But he knew well that the fallen leader was the only Italian with any influence with Hitler. Now that he had been ousted, anything might happen.

He drank off the rest of the cognac and got to his feet.

'Won't you stay a little longer?' Dorothy asked.

'Alas no. I have duties to attend to.' He kissed Dorothy's hand and strode to the car.

'Emilio's a good man,' Dorothy said as she watched him climb into the car. 'I get a lot of food and wine from him. And more information than he realises.'

Viviane wondered what he got in return but said nothing.

Alain drank the last drop of his wine and stared at the dregs for a moment. Then he gave Dorothy a shrewd look. 'Where did you hear about Mussolini?' he asked. Then he held out his hands. 'But please, don't tell me if you don't want to.'

'I won't. It's safer that way. But it's a trustworthy source.' She poured three glasses of cognac and passed them around. 'Believe me, the Germans are not doing as well as they claim.'

'But they've taken over the south of France,' Viviane said. 'Or west of the Rhone, at any rate.'

'Because they had to. They're alarmed now that the Allies are in North Africa. And, for all that he dances to their tune, they don't respect Pétain. And nor do they trust Laval. I can't say I blame them. I doubt he even trusts himself.

'That's why they raced south to take over the country. They've lost whatever faith they had in the collaborators. They trust only themselves to fight the Allies.'

'Then let's drink to the Allied success,' Alain said.

'Yep,' said Dorothy. 'But it's going to be a long road yet. Winston Churchill once said that the war might last twenty years or more.'

Viviane shuddered at the thought.

'But the Yanks are here now,' Dorothy continued. 'It will be over sooner than that. Six or seven years is my guess.'

'1950,' Viviane said. 'Celeste will be fourteen by then. All her childhood will have been spent in this wretched war.'

'At least we're together,' Alain said. 'Which is more than we can say for David and his parents.

## WEISER HEADS TO GRASSE
*8 September 1943*

Weiser stood outside the door to General Blaskowitz's office. He glanced in a mirror to check his appearance. He had been summoned by the General on numerous occasions recently but this was the first time that the order had come with no forewarning and no explanation of its purpose. He felt a prickle in the back of his neck and was not sure if it was excitement or apprehension.

He knocked on the door, a little louder than he intended, and took a deep breath as the door was opened by an orderly.

The General was sitting at his desk, which was crammed with papers. He did not look up but gestured to Weiser to approach.

'Sit, Ernst,' he said.

Weiser was astonished by the General's use of his first name. It suggested that what he was about to say was either wonderful or horrifying.

Blaskowitz scribbled his signature on the document he was reading and flung it onto the pile to one side of his desk. He gestured to his orderly to take the pile away. Only when the man had left did he turn his attention to Weiser.

'The bastard Italians have capitulated,' he said. 'We had our suspicions once they'd imprisoned Mussolini, although they swore that they would continue the war. But today, the Allies announced that an armistice was signed five days ago.'

'Five days?'

Blaskowitz nodded. He threw the translation of the armistice across the table towards Weiser.

He scanned the document with growing astonishment. 'What does this mean for the war?' he asked.

Blaskowitz shrugged. 'The Italians have proved useless friends. We will not miss their military prowess. But it means that we've had to move troops into the whole of Italy.' He sighed. 'I fear it will stretch us too thin.'

'And for us in France?'

'That's why you're here. We are to take over the Italian zone, starting today. The Italians are now enemies and their forces are to be disarmed or destroyed.

'I want you to take a regiment into the Riviera. We're already stationed in Cannes, and I want you to go north to Grasse. From there, we'll be able to command all the coast from Saint-Tropez to the Italian border.'

'And the French? What is to be their status?'

'Conquered peoples. There's to be no pretence like with the Vichy Government. Conquered.'

He paused and glanced out of the window at the port. 'But treat them with civility if possible. Make sure your men don't engage in any rough stuff. That's why I chose you for this task.'

He handed Weiser his instructions and dismissed him.

Weiser was pleased to be leaving Marseille. The local criminals were cosying up to the Gestapo and he didn't trust either. Better to be fighting a clean battle. He sent for Otto and packed his few belongings into a kit bag. They reached Cannes five hours later.

The regiment he had been allocated were a sorry spectacle. Most of the men were very young, some appeared little more than children, and they seemed forlorn. Others looked more than twice their age. Weiser was less worried about the older men for he knew he could rely on them. The youngsters, however, might not perform well.

'It's a good job we're only fighting Italians,' Mundt said.

'I wonder if they'll put up much resistance,' Weiser said. 'They've been our allies for years and I think that few will want to start a fight with us.'

'And the French?'

Weiser shrugged. He had no idea how they would react to a German occupation on the heels of the Italian one.

'I think they've been completely demoralised,' Mundt said. 'France has given up, lost all sense of honour.'

'Let's hope so,' Weiser answered. 'I don't relish guerrilla warfare.'

It was almost midnight when they reached Grasse. Weiser decided that it was too risky to attack entrenched positions and stationed his men at all the exit roads in case the Italians attempted to break out. He need not have bothered. Perhaps the Italians did not know that German forces were near or were unsure how to react. At any rate the night was peaceful.

Early the next morning, Weiser and Mundt drove up to the headquarters of the Italian II Corps and demanded their surrender. It was a risky manoeuvre for there were still a hundred Italians within the building and Weiser did not want to attack erstwhile allies. And, besides, he had his doubts about the effectiveness of his troops. He was relieved when the Italians filed out led by their General. He looked abject and distraught and surrendered immediately.

'Well this is proving simple,' Mundt said.

Weiser did not respond. He hated it when things looked too easy. Experience taught him that whenever men thought this, events would too easily go awry.

But on this occasion his fears proved unjustified. A couple of dozen Italians had slipped away in the darkness, fearing imprisonment or reprisals.

'Most of them are from the border area of France and Italy,' one of the Italian officers explained. 'They have relatives in the area and probably hope to blend in with the locals.'

But the rest of the troops showed no inclination to resist the Germans. Weiser imprisoned the officers, disarmed the men and sent them on the seventy kilometre march to the border.

The German troops fanned out across the city throughout the rest of the morning. Grasse appeared to be a ghost town. Nobody was on the streets and all the shops and houses had their shutters drawn.

'I would almost prefer to be shot at,' Mundt murmured.

Weiser gave him a wry look. A death at the hands of some jittery householder was the last thing he wanted.

They had reached the Town Hall by this time and Weiser gestured his men to take up positions in front of the building. The door remained firmly closed. He glanced at his watch. It was almost noon. He would wait five minutes before making his next move.

The minutes inched by and then he gave a signal to a corporal. The man cocked his machine gun and sprayed the door with bullets.

Five minutes later the door was opened a crack and a stick with a white flag appeared. The corporal darted forward and flung open the door.

'A pity it wasn't like this at Stalingrad,' Mundt said.

The Mayor approached them slowly, his hands fluttering with anxiety.

'There's no cause for alarm,' Weiser said. 'The Wehrmacht are here for the protection of your city and its people.'

The Mayor licked his lips, tried to speak but could only managed a strangled gasp.

'You will cooperate fully?' Mundt asked. 'You and the other officials? Including the police. We wish to avoid any unpleasantness.'

The Mayor nodded. 'Of course, of course. Full cooperation. From all my officials and all citizens.'

'You can't guarantee the latter,' Weiser said.

'True —'

'But we shall hold you to account for any trouble, nonetheless.'

The Mayor looked as if he was going to vomit.

Weiser pushed past him and into the Town Hall. It was an imposing building with large rooms and high ceilings. But the light from its windows gave little light to the interior and the few light bulbs still working cast a feeble glow.

'Is this where you will be located?' the Mayor asked, nervously. 'The Italian officers were at the barracks.'

'I shall lodge one of my senior officers here,' Weiser said. He had formed an instant dislike to the place. It was surrounded by nearby buildings, and too dark and gloomy. He wanted to spend as little time in it as possible.

He handed the Mayor a document. 'This is a proclamation concerning our occupation of the south. You will print copies of it and display it at every street corner. I don't want people claiming they don't know their responsibilities towards the Reich.'

He pointed to the final paragraph. 'You will take note that any opposition will necessitate the execution of the guilty parties. Please make sure that all your officials know this.'

He turned on his heel and strode out of the building.

'That's given them food for thought,' he said to Mundt.

Mundt gave a grim smile. 'Will we stay here or at the barracks?' he asked.

'At the barracks, initially. And then we'll see how the townsfolk settle down.'

Mundt glanced around the streets. 'This is a fine town,' he said. 'I hope we stay here a while.'

'I hope we can go home soon,' Weiser said.

Mundt sighed. Neither of them thought that was likely any time soon.

'I miss Hilda and the children,' Weiser said.

He said the words more forcefully than ever before and, now that the thoughts were given substance, he felt a sudden desolate pang. 'I haven't seen them for two years,' he said.

Their troops had secured the barracks by the time they got there. The Italian weaponry and equipment were being catalogued and the sergeants were already allocating sleeping quarters for the men.

Weiser poked his nose into the room the Italian General had used. It consisted of a large office with a desk, three filing cabinets, a couch and some chairs. To the rear was a small bedroom with a narrow bed, a chest of drawers and a washstand.

Weiser bridled at the sight of it. Over the course of the war he had slept in far worse places but now that he had started to think about home and family he was suddenly aware of how grim his life had grown. He took a deep breath and told himself to snap out of it. He was an officer of the Wehrmacht and not a child.

But, nevertheless, he thought he might look for somewhere more pleasant to spend his time in Grasse.


**A FIERCER REGIME**

The townsfolk ventured out of their homes the following day. Alain forbade Viviane or the children to leave the house and said he would go out to see what was happening.

'Don't do anything foolish,' she whispered, clinging on to him tightly.

He shook his head. There was not the slightest chance that he would take any risk. He had seen the Germans at work in Marseille.

It was late morning when he slipped out of the house. There were a few souls out on the streets but not many. As if by mutual agreement no one communicated to anyone else apart from giving the briefest of nods.

He made his way to the Place aux Herbes. There were a few more people here although none of the market stalls had been set up. One cafe, Le Terminus, was open. Two old men sat at a table outside sipping their morning coffee. Alain wasn't sure if they were stupid, defiant or merely captives of their own routine. One was Theo Joubert, so it could have been routine or defiance but most certainly not stupidity.

'Bonjour Alain,' Theo said as he approached.

Theo had run a cheese stall on the market years ago and they had become friends. Alain did not know the other man by name but gave him a polite hello.

'Come join us,' Theo said. 'Unless you have something better to do.' He gave an ironic laugh, revealing his few brown teeth as he did so.

Alain pulled out a chair. A woman appeared beside him, Isabelle Blois, the owner of the café. 'What will you have?'

'A coffee,' Alain said. 'And croissants for my friends and me.'

Isabelle laughed at his joke. 'Croissants? I can't remember what they are.' She disappeared into the cafe.

'A fine looking woman,' Theo said.

Alain nodded. 'Wasted on that idiot, Maxime.'

Like most men, Alain had something of a crush on Isabelle. She flirted outrageously with all her customers because it increased her profits. Why she remained so loyal to her ugly, curmudgeonly husband was a topic of lewd discussion amongst half the town.

She brought out three cups of coffee and took a seat beside them, lighting up a cigarette and blinking in the morning sun.

Alain tasted his coffee. It was bitter, and weak, mixed with chicory and acorns. A few years ago he would have thrown it down the drain but now he sipped at it with something not far removed from pleasure.

A couple of German soldiers appeared at the street opposite them and glanced nervously up and down the open square in front of them. One was little more than a boy, the other, a sergeant, might have been his father.

The older man stared at them, appraising Isabelle with great interest.

'Come on over, boys,' she called. 'I'll give you coffee.'

The young boy shook his head fiercely but the older man smiled and approached.

Alain looked at Isabelle in astonishment but quickly masked it. She had her own purposes, no doubt. Most likely they were the need to make money, even from their conquerors. Sensible really, as they were likely to be the only people flush with the stuff.

The older soldier glanced around, perhaps to check for any danger or in case a German officer was watching. Then he took a seat and gestured to his companion to do the same.

For a moment the younger man hesitated, then seemed to remember that the older man was a sergeant, and did as he was ordered.

Isabelle shouted to her husband to bring two coffees and gave the older soldier a lazy smile. He eyed her appreciatively.

Maxime came out with two coffees. He gave no reaction at seeing the Germans. He was, Alain thought, either stupid or a consummate businessman.

'These are on the house,' Isabelle said, pushing the coffees towards the soldiers.

'Danke,' said the young private, curtly. The sergeant merely smiled.

Isabelle glanced at Maxime and he grunted and retreated into the cafe.

'You speak French?' Alain asked the soldiers.

The sergeant jiggled his hand. 'A little. We have been in France for a few years now.' He paused and then gave a cold smile. 'Do you speak German?'

'Not at all.'

'You might do well to start learning it.'

'Is it worth it?' Alain said. 'Will you be here long?'

The young man looked incensed but the sergeant chuckled, silencing his companion with a glance.

'Herr Hitler says the Reich will last a thousand years,' he said. He sipped his coffee. 'So that must be the case because he informs us that he's always right.'

Alain smiled. 'All politicians are the same.'

'The Führer is not a politician,' the young man said, angrily. 'He is far more than that.'

Alain and the sergeant exchanged glances but said nothing.

'My name is Wilhelm Ferber,' he said. 'This is Private Alphonse Dahn. He is imbued with the ardour of youth. Me not so much.'

He gave a deep sigh and looked the buildings up and down. 'This is a fine town,' he said, as much to himself as to them. 'I come from Darmstadt, in Hesse. We have a market-place much like this, the Schlossplatz.'

'Perhaps you should go back there,' Alain said.

'Believe me, I want to. Just as soon as you Frenchmen admit defeat, hey.' He slapped the table and laughed at his own jest.

'It's the British and Americans who aren't admitting defeat.'

'Their time will come,' snapped the young man.

Wilhelm swallowed his coffee and got to his feet. 'Thank you, Madame,' he said. 'I shall come again.'

'You'll pay for the next one,' Isabelle said.

Wilhelm smiled. He very much doubted that.

The young private also stood but as he did so he knocked both his and Wilhelm's cups on the ground. Then he stamped on them, his face contorted with fury. He glared at the Frenchmen, as if daring them to do or say anything in response.

They looked at the ground.

'Accidents will happen,' Isabelle said brightly. She called to Maxime to fetch a broom.

Wilhelm opened his mouth, perhaps to apologise, but thought better of it. He contented himself with glaring at the boy and pushing him away. As he left, he turned and gave a small bow to Isabelle.

Alain stared at the broken shards of the cups. The young soldier had ground them into the smallest pieces. He felt sick at the sight of them. He was not sure why but images of the German round-up in Marseille filled his mind.

'Free coffee?' Theo scolded Isabelle. 'You'll have the whole army sniffing around the place. You'll be seen as an easy touch.'

'I doubt it. The old man is too shrewd to tell anyone else that I gave him a coffee for free. I think I can look forward to a good working relationship with him.'

'Why would you do that?' Theo's friend asked.

Isabelle did not answer but looked at Alain.

'It's business,' he explained. 'The Germans are here in Grasse. We can't do anything about it except to make the best of it. And to rob them blind without them noticing.'

'I don't see how giving them free coffee is robbing them blind.'

'A farmer chooses one cow to lead the others to the slaughter-house,' Alain said. 'Wilhelm is our chosen cow.'

'But what about the boy?' Theo said. 'Is he a young bull or is he the slaughter-man?'

None of them answered. It was not a question they wished to consider too deeply.

## THE WOLF AND THE WEASEL
*Grasse, 12 September 1943*

Gerard Pithou had been waiting in the forecourt of the Police Station for almost two hours. He felt honoured by being chosen for the task, and the long wait did nothing to diminish his enthusiasm. The Gestapo were setting up an office in Grasse with Kriminaldirektor Heinrich Schorn as their head. Gerard had been given the task of welcoming him and acting as his official liaison. He had settled himself on a bench beneath a plane tree where he could get a good view of the road leading up to the building.

He was desperate for a cigarette, had been for the last hour, but he'd successfully fought off the desire. Now, finally, he succumbed to temptation. He pulled a packet from his jacket pocket and lit up. He inhaled deeply and felt a sudden sense of calmness. All was right in the world. Birds cheeped in the trees above him and the sun dappled his head.

He had been selected for this honour because of his enthusiasm and dedication. It was, he thought, an appropriate reward. He had, at some risk to himself, already spied on members of the police who he believed to be lukewarm in their support for Maréchal Pétain and Prime Minister Laval. Raoul Villiers was the chief of these. Gerard had even gone to the length of befriending him, a task he found most distasteful. Villiers was a loud-mouth and a fire-brand. Gerard thought he might even be a communist. So far he had discovered nothing incriminating about the man but he remained convinced that he would find something sooner or later.

His fingers fondled the revolver at his lap. He was no great master of it, with an aim which was distinctly feeble, but it gave him a feeling of immense importance. He took a long drag on the cigarette, closing his eyes so that he could savour the taste more thoroughly.

Suddenly he heard a screech of tires and car doors opening. He leapt to his feet, throwing the cigarette to the ground and grinding it into the earth. He wondered whether to rush to open the gate but, while he was hesitating, the Gestapo officers pushed it open and entered.

He stood straight and saluted, searching the men for any indication of who might be the Kriminaldirektor. It was impossible to say. There were four men, who looked to be in their early forties, all dressed in civilian clothes of good quality. One wore a bowler hat, two were bare-headed and one wore a trilby.

The man in the bowler hat approached. His face was long and lean, putting Gerard in mind of a bloodhound. 'Who are you?' he demanded. He spoke atrocious French in a heavy German accent. His air of authority was palpable.

'I am Militiaman Pithou,' Gerard answered, cursing inwardly that he had angered the Kriminaldirektor. 'I have been ordered to welcome you, to see that you are made comfortable and to act as liaison while you settle in. It is an honour to meet you, Monsieur.'

'You have been smoking,' the German said in reply.

Gerard thought for a moment to deny it but the man's manner told him that he would be foolish to oppose him in any way. There was a hard edge to him, the feel of a man who might be ruthless in squashing any dissent or failings.

'I have, your honour,' Gerard admitted. 'It was a long wait.'

The man turned towards the others. 'You see how this Frenchman berates us for our tardiness,' he said.

'I didn't mean to sound critical —' Gerard began.

'I want no excuses,' the man said. 'If you are to serve the Reich adequately you would do well to learn this. And smoking is a disgusting habit, one more suited to the criminal class.'

The man in the trilby approached. Gerard realised that he was actually considerably younger than the rest of the men, possibly in his early thirties. But he was very overweight and it gave him the appearance of an older man. His face was round and flushed, and his breathing sounded laboured.

He touched Gerard gently on the arm. 'We do not mean to be so fierce,' he said. 'But if your wait has been long then our journey has been longer. We too are fatigued and, if truth be told, a little bad-tempered. Forgive us.'

He spoke excellent French with only a trace of accent and he sounded friendly and good-natured.

'There is nothing to forgive.'

Gerard turned towards the Kriminaldirektor and gave a little bow, holding out his hand to indicate that he should go first into the building. 'Please, after you, Herr Kriminaldirektor.'

'Herr Schorn,' said the man in the bowler hat, bending to whisper in the fat man's ear.

The young man gave a little chuckle, causing his jowls to quiver.

Gerard was aghast. He had mixed the two policemen up. The Kriminaldirektor was not the hard, lean-faced man, He was the fat young man.

'A thousand apologies,' he stammered. 'I had not realised.'

'There is no need to be contrite.' Schorn said, his face bright with amusement. 'You will not be the first to make this mistake nor the last.'

He indicated the lean man in the bowler. 'Herr Buchner is my deputy. He looks like a detective, does he not? Whereas I...' He patted Gerard on the hand. Gerard almost recoiled for Schorn's hand was cold and wet. It was like being touched by an octopus.

Schorn grinned and entered the building.

Capitaine Boyer was waiting with three of his senior staff. He snapped to attention and his men, after a moment, did likewise, none of them in time with any other.

'Slovenly,' Buchner said. 'Have you no pride?'

Boyer swallowed. 'Welcome to Grasse,' he said.

'You must improve the appearance and attitude of your men,' Schorn said. 'Or Kriminalinspektor Buchner will do the job for you. He will enjoy it. Your men will not.'

Boyer did not know how to answer so dipped his head in acknowledgement.

'Let us proceed,' Schorn continued. 'Where is your office, Capitaine?'

Boyer pointed to a door with his name upon it.

'That is mine, I suggest,' Schorn said. 'You must now find yourself somewhere else. With your sergeants, perhaps, or your Gendarmes.'

Boyer looked astonished but merely nodded. Schorn stepped into the office, leaving the three other Gestapo officers with Boyer.

'I shall need an office,' Buchner said, 'as will my colleagues.'

Boyer nodded and told Sergeant Lassals to install the Gestapo men in the sergeant's office.

'But where will we go?' Lassals hissed.

'The typists' room. They will have to find somewhere else. Just do it.'

'Capitaine Boyer,' called Schorn.

Boyer gestured Lassals to go, took a deep breath and went into his old office.

Schorn was sitting in Boyer's chair, behind his desk, as if he had been here for years. 'Do take a seat, Capitaine,' he said.

Boyer pulled up a chair and sat opposite the Gestapo official. It felt decidedly odd to be looking at the room from this perspective.

'This is a very spartan room,' Schorn said. 'I thought you French would have liked something softer, more comfortable.'

'Like you Germans, we want our offices to be clean and uncluttered. Formal.'

'Not me,' Schorn said. 'Arrange for some vases of flowers. And a cushion for this chair. I find I work most effectively when I am comfortable.'

'I shall see to it at once,' Boyer said.

He could not help but stare at Schorn. He was the exact opposite of how he imagined a member of the Gestapo would look. He might have been a bank manager, a salesman of women's garments or the owner of a café. Someone at ease with himself and the world. He found this dichotomy extremely disquieting.

'Let us proceed,' said Schorn. 'My function here is twofold. One is to assist you and your colleagues in maintaining law and order. We are particularly concerned with the black-market, crimes against the Reich and political insurrection.

'The second function is to support the Final Solution of the Jewish Question.' He gave a wide grin, like that of a child who finds that the birthday gift he has been given is the one he has yearned for all year.

'The Final Solution?' Boyer asked.

'Tut, tut, Capitaine. Surely even here in the fat and indolent south you have heard that all Jews are being moved to work camps in the east. The war is not just a matter of soldiers. Weapons must be manufactured, roads and railways maintained, homes destroyed by Allied bombers rebuilt. This is the task of the Jews of Europe. Part of my role is to help facilitate it.'

'And how will you do that?'

'How will we do it?' corrected Schorn. 'You are under my authority now, Capitaine Boyer. You also will have a part to play in the identification and transportation of the Jews in this area.'

He leaned back in his chair and contemplated the ceiling before continuing.

'First you will give my staff access to all records of births and marriages. In particular, you will specify who is of Jewish blood, including any who have Jewish grandparents.'

'And what will happen to them?' Boyer asked.

'I have told you. They will be sent to our eastern territories and put to essential war-work.'

'All of them? Even women and the elderly?' He paused. 'And children?'

'Everyone can offer something to the Reich. Those who are strongest will perform the more arduous duties. Those who are weaker will be given tasks appropriate to their physical attributes and abilities. Children are particularly adept at working in the fields, I gather. Picking fruit and vegetables, collecting manure and such-like. It sounds quite fun, actually.'

'There are rumours —' Boyer began.

'And that is all they are,' Schorn said. 'Do you actually think we Germans work the Jews to the point of exhaustion? What is the sense of it? Really, Boyer, you surprise me.'

Boyer did not say any more. He was desperate to leave the office. Schorn was polite and affable but so were any number of villains that he had dealt with in his career. But with those he had held all the cards. Now, he realised, he no longer had power or authority.

'There is another matter,' Schorn said. 'The south of France is noted for the numbers of its Gypsy population. I also want you to provide information regarding them.'

'They are to be sent to work-camps?' Boyer asked. He was gripped by concern for Alain, Viviane and Celeste but tried to sound insouciant.

'You know as well as I do, Boyer, that Gypsies are loath to undertake honest work. Criminals and swindlers, every one of them. I doubt that they will be useful labourers. The Reich will find another way to deal with them.' His hand made a slicing gesture across his neck.

Boyer tried neither to agree nor disagree. Schorn noticed this and looked amused by his discomfort.

'Anyway,' he said lightly, 'to work, my dear Boyer. I sense we shall be excellent partners in this endeavour.'

He dismissed him with a wave of his hand. Then he said, 'Boyer, send in the man from the Militia.'

Boyer seethed at being used as a messenger in this way but gave a curt nod. Schorn watched this with a cold smile.

He looked around the room as he waited. He would examine it carefully when he got the chance. You could learn a lot of useful things about a person from his work-space. And he wanted to learn everything he could about Boyer.

A knock sounded on the door.

'Enter,' Schorn said in a voice honed to dominate.

Gerard opened the door and stood hesitantly on the threshold.

'Come in, man,' Schorn said. 'No need to be nervous.' He indicated the chair which Boyer had just vacated. 'Your name is?'

'Gerard Pithou, Excellency.'

He sat down and stared anxiously at the German. What on earth could such an important functionary want from him?

Schorn steepled his fingers, stared at Gerard in silence and let the seconds tick by. He watched the beads of sweat begin to form on the Frenchman's face. It was pudgy, he thought, the Frenchman must like food and have access to the black-market. Two bits of knowledge he would be able to put to good use.

'You are wondering why I sent for you,' he said, eventually. It was an assertion rather than a question.

Gerard nodded.

'I have heard excellent reports of you,' Schorn continued. It was a lie but a useful one.

Gerard flushed with excitement.

'I am new to this town,' Schorn continued. 'I need eyes and ears to help me in my task. You know what the chief of these tasks is, I assume?'

'Of course,' Gerard said, although he had no idea what it was.

Schorn eyed him for a minute, toying with him, not caring in the least whether he knew or not. This was all about snaring the Militiaman, terrifying and binding him.

'I presume that you have no liking for Jews?' he said at last.

'None at all.' Gerard said it in as firm and decisive a tone as he could.

'Nor criminals, traitors, idlers? Negroes, Arabs, Gypsies?'

'I dislike them as much as the Jews.'

'Tut, tut, my friend. Not quite as much, surely?'

Gerard inclined his head in a contrite gesture.

Schorn smiled.

'So my task,' he continued, 'or should I say our task, is to search out these undesirables. They have flaunted themselves for too long, rubbed the noses of you French in the dirt too long, insulted the honour of the Reich too long. It must come to an end, my friend.' He paused. 'I'm sure you agree.'

'Absolutely.'

Schorn stared at Gerard so long that he began to blush a fierce red.

'Do you have a girlfriend?' he asked, finally.

'Not for a while,' Gerard answered.

Schorn suspected that he may never have had one but let it pass. 'But you like girls?'

Gerard nodded.

'Anyone in particular?'

Viviane's face and figure leapt into Gerard's mind. 'Yes. The wife of a...' He stopped himself mid-flow and blushed even more.

'Don't be embarrassed,' Schorn said. 'It is quite normal for a man to desire his friend's wife. Quite common in fact. What is her name?'

'Annette Dubois,' he lied. 'They live in Antibes. I don't see them often.'

'Probably a good thing, ah?' Schorn said heartily. 'Too great a temptation?' He gave a sigh.

'But if you like any other girl,' he continued, 'just let me know her name. I will make it my business to ensure that she becomes a very good friend of yours.' He gave a conspiratorial smirk.

Gerard nodded, mutely.

'Good. Now go and see my assistant, Kriminalinspektor Buchner. The man you thought was me. He will tell you of your duties.' He waved a hand of dismissal and opened an attaché case.

Gerard slipped out.

A weasel, Schorn thought, but a useful one, no doubt.

# WHAT ABOUT DAVID?
*Grasse, 12 September 1943*

Viviane had barely left her chair all morning. Alain had gone out to see about the food situation and had been longer than she'd expected. They still had coupons in their ration books but since the arrival of the German troops there had not been enough food in the shops for her to use them. The black-market had always provided extras, enough to eke out the food on ration. Now, they realised that it might be essential for them to survive.

Viviane had sent the children out to the yard to play. They seemed to sense her mood for they were not their usual boisterous selves. Even if they had made a lot of noise, she would not have heard them. Monstrous thoughts crowded her head. Some of it was about how to find food for the family. On top of this was the generalised anxiety about what life would be like under German occupation.

But most tormenting of all was what might happen to David. Would Father Benoît and the banker Donati still be able to secure ships to take the Jews to North Africa? Would the couple who were going to take him there still be willing to do so?

Her fingers drummed upon the table. It was seventy kilometres to the Italian border. It would take four or five hours to get there on the motorbike. If they had to walk with David it would take two days. And then they would have to get to some port in Italy. Genoa was the only one she knew of and Alain said that was two hundred and fifty kilometres distant. And, with the roads crammed with Italian soldiers fleeing the Germans, it would take three days by bike and over a week to walk. And what if the ships were going to sail from elsewhere in Italy, even further away?

She wiped a tear from her cheek. This was no good. She would have to get a grip on herself, have to stay strong.

She picked up her bag and pulled out the identity cards: hers, Celeste's and David's. She placed them next to each other and began to study them. Then she had an idea, leapt up and rooted around in a drawer which was full of things which the family had once thought important but were rarely used or needed. At the back of the drawer she found it, a small magnifying-glass which Alain had used as a child to look at bugs and clues in make-believe crimes.

She returned to the table and pored over each of the cards with agonising care. Even with the magnifying-glass she could see no differences between the three cards. Father Benoit's forger had been more skilful or less slipshod than the criminal Chiappe had used. The thumping ache in her head grew a little less intense. She leaned back in the chair and exhaled wearily. If the worse came to the worse, if they were not able to procure a place for David on a ship, then his card might be enough to protect him.

A knock sounded on the door. Viviane leapt to her feet in alarm, her momentary sense of relief overturned immediately.

'It's only me,' came a familiar voice.

'Sylvie,' she said, as she opened the door to her friend.

'I can't stay long,' Sylvie said. 'Could you look after Monique for the day?' She licked her lips anxiously. 'I have some work.'

Viviane told Monique to find Celeste in the yard. Then she gave Sylvie a suspicious look.

'You look worried,' she said, taking Sylvie's hand in hers. 'Please tell me you're not getting involved in something perverted. It's dangerous, Sylvie.'

They both knew that some women provided rough services to vicious men. It paid well but left them with bruises, black eyes and sometimes even broken bones. One woman had disappeared from the town completely, either murdered or held captive somewhere.

'It's not that,' Sylvie said. 'Even I'm not that stupid.'

She said nothing more for a while but then suddenly blurted out: 'The fact of the matter is that I'm entertaining some of the Germans. Some young officers, not riff-raff. They're pretty decent.'

'Sylvie, how could you?' Viviane looked at her aghast.

'I don't want to,' she snapped. 'I thought at least you would be sympathetic.' She began to cry. 'We've got hardly any food, Viviane. Monique is skin and bones. If I don't do this, we don't eat.'

'You could have come to me. I could have given you something.'

'I have my pride,' she said, bitterly.

Viviane almost told her that sleeping with the enemy was a peculiar way to prove it but kept silent.

She opened her purse and thrust some money into Sylvie's hands. 'Don't argue,' she said, as soon as Sylvie opened her mouth. 'At least it will allow you to have Sundays off.'

'To go to confession?' Sylvie said.

They both laughed at her jest. It started quietly but all too soon verged on the hysterical. Yet it gave them both a little relief.

'I can't remember when I last cried with laughter,' Viviane said.

Sylvie nodded. 'Me neither. Most of mine are tears of despair.'

A heavy gloom threatened to overwhelm them.

But then Sylvie gave a long, contended stretch. 'Don't think I don't appreciate the money, Viviane,' she said. 'But a glass of something wouldn't go amiss.'

Viviane went to the cupboard and brought back a bottle of local wine. It was thin and rather tasteless but, at that moment, it tasted like nectar.

Suddenly the door was thrown open and Alain stepped into the room. He gave Sylvie a nod and then took hold of Viviane's hands.

'I've just had a message from Signore Donati,' he said.

She grabbed his hand. 'The ships are ready?'

Alain shook his head. 'They never will be. The Germans have occupied most of Italy and nobody's going anywhere.'

Viviane took a deep breath. To her astonishment she found that she was relieved.

'So we get to keep him?'

Alain nodded. He looked bleak with dismay for a moment but then forced a smile on his lips. 'So it's turned out alright. He'll be better with us.'

Viviane nodded. She picked up the magnifying-glass. 'I've only just looked at his identity papers. They're perfect. Nobody will suspect a thing. And, anyway, the German soldiers won't be interested in checking people's papers.'

She glanced at Sylvie and smiled. 'In fact, they may not have the time or energy.'

Alain looked confused but neither of the women chose to enlighten him.

'Will you stay for something to eat, Sylvie?' Alain asked. He put a bag on the table and pulled out a can of haricot beans, a length of saucisson and three onions. 'Here's the makings of a casserole.'

Sylvie nodded gratefully and followed Viviane into the kitchen.

Viviane stared at her as she entered, wondering at the expression on her face.

'I've guessed about David,' she said.

Viviane gave her a wary look. 'Guessed what?'

Sylvie sighed. 'Isn't it obvious? I know David's a Jew.'

Viviane took a deep breath. 'How long have you known?'

'To be honest, soon after you got him. And it was more obvious every time I saw you grow more anxious. And now, after what Alain's just told you…'

Viviane wrapped her arms around Sylvie, hugging her close. 'I didn't want to tell you. I didn't want to incriminate you.'

'I guessed that. I was a little hurt but I knew the reason.'

'You'll keep it secret?' Viviane shook her head, angry at herself for even asking the question. 'Of course you will. How stupid to even ask.'

'Better than Alain at any rate,' Sylvie said. 'I hope he's never as foolish with others as he was just now in front of me.'

'He thinks of you as family. And perhaps he thought I'd already told you.'

Sylvie picked up an onion and began to peel it, her face growing ever more thoughtful.

'Isn't it odd how we've all started keeping secrets from each other,' she said quietly. 'And we don't even question it anymore. You kept David's Jewish background a secret from me, Alain thought you had told me, and you never told him that you hadn't. What is this bloody war doing to us?'

'It's breaking us, that's what,' Viviane said. 'I wonder if we'll ever be able to put the world back together again.'

'At least we've got each other,' Sylvie said. 'Those we love. Family, friends.'

Not my family, Viviane thought. Her mother had been even more unpleasant than usual when she saw her two weeks before. And she couldn't recall when she had last seen her sister.

'And,' Sylvie continued in a more optimistic tone, 'if all the Germans are as nice and polite as some of my officers then things won't turn out too bad.'

A loud knock sounded on the door and Viviane held up a finger to silence her. They heard the creak as Alain opened it a fraction. Then the door shut once more and Alain called to her.

'Viviane, Roland is here.'

'Roland?' Sylvie mouthed. She had no wish to be in the same room as Viviane's brother-in-law.

'You stay here,' Viviane said. 'He won't be long.'

Viviane went into the living room. Alain was already pouring two glasses of wine.

Roland perched on a chair in his uniform, looking uncomfortable. He took the wine with a word of thanks and took a swig.

'Is Odette all right?' Viviane asked. She was surprised to discover that she was a tiny bit concerned. Perhaps family meant more than she imagined.

'She's fine,' Roland said. 'Perfectly fine. That's not why I've come.'

He swallowed the rest of the wine in one gulp. Viviane felt her heart begin to pound at the sight of this.

He took a deep breath and the words came tumbling out. 'I've come to tell you that the Gestapo have established themselves in Police headquarters. Five of them. And they're on the hunt for Jews.'

'What's that got to do with us?' Alain asked.

Roland looked astonished.

'David,' he said. 'I know about David.'

Viviane cried out, vainly trying to stifle her words.

'How do you know?' Alain said, signalling to her to keep silent.

'It was a guess at first,' Roland said. 'I've been a policeman all my life and I can sense when things are amiss. But then Raoul Villiers told me that David's papers were forgeries.'

Viviane gasped aloud but Roland held up his hand to try to calm her.

'Villiers did it for the best of reasons, Viviane. He's no friend to the Germans, quite the contrary. Nor to our own government to be frank. He thought it best that I knew. In case of…well, just in case. He thought I'd be able to protect you.'

'And can you?' Alain asked.

Roland avoided his gaze. 'I've no idea,' he said at last. 'I'll do what I can, I really will. But this Gestapo Chief appears clever and devious. I doubt it will be easy to pull the wool over his eyes.'

'So what should we do?' Viviane asked.

'Keep quiet. And keep out of the way.' He paused. 'I'm concerned about the flaws in David's papers.'

'Alain got better ones.' She handed him the identity papers and magnifying-glass.

He studied the papers carefully for a couple of minutes. 'They look fine to me. But would it be alright if I asked Villiers to come over to check them out? He's trained in this sort of thing.'

'I suppose…' Viviane began.

'Can we trust him?' Alain asked.

'Absolutely,' Roland answered. 'The only other one I'd say this of is Henri Lassals, my old sergeant. He's honest and loyal to me.'

'Can we trust honest men?' Alain asked. 'Might not their honesty incline them to give us away?'

Roland sighed. 'Perhaps. You may be right.' He closed his eyes for a while.

'I always believed that I was honest,' he said at last. 'That I would do what the law required, exactly as it stipulated. But now?' He climbed to his feet wearily. 'Now I'm not so sure.'

He kissed Viviane on the cheek and shook Alain's hand.

'Keep David out of circulation as much as possible,' he said. He went to the door and paused. 'And, if I were you, I'd not visit Odette. Or your mother.'

Viviane felt sick at his words. Alain closed the door behind Roland and leaned against it, as if by doing so he could keep the whole world at bay. But nobody could. Not anymore.


### DEATH OF GEORGES
*Grasse, First week in October 1943*

The family sat mute around Georges' bed. His breathing was shallow now, the sound of his breathing faint in the morning air.

I thought I would feel more pain, Viviane thought as she gazed at her father. But then she realised that she had been waiting for this moment all her life. Her father had always been an invalid, always been frail, a man who had ever seemed caught in death's unforgiving clasp.

She wondered, for the first time, if he had lived his life in constant pain. It was said that when some people lose a limb they never escape the feel of it. Like an unforgiving ghoul it haunts the body it once belonged to. Was this so for her father? And if it was, then did the phantom leg still hurt? Did he constantly feel the agony of the bomb blast which shattered his leg, the ordeal of hours in a shell-hole, the torture of the amputation without anaesthetic?

Her mother sniffled and, almost immediately, Odette did the same. Her mother's grief was genuine, of course. Viviane was less sure of her sister's.

Her mother stared at Viviane with a reproachful look, as if to say: it is wrong of you not to cry as your sister and I do, not to display your hurt, not to parade your feelings in an obvious manner.

Viviane bowed her head, partly from grief but mostly to hide the fact that it was secreted so deep within her she could not display it.

She knew that she had always been her father's favourite and had relished this. He always allowed her more freedom than he ever did Odette.

But no, she suddenly realised, that was not the case. It was not that he didn't allow Odette licence, more that she never asked it of him. Odette was content to play the dutiful daughter, perhaps at the same time resenting it.

Viviane, on the other hand, delighted in the fact that she was the wild daughter, the one her father expected would break the rules and never punished with any great enthusiasm when she did.

But her father and she never presented such a united and implacable front as did Odette and their mother. Had they and not the Maginot Line been blocking the advancing German armies, France would still be free.

Viviane smiled at this thought, which brought the ire of her mother down on her head.

'You find your father's death a matter of amusement?'

'Not at all. I was thinking of happy memories. That's all.'

Her mother grunted, disbelieving her daughter's words.

The priest stood up and leaned over her father. He was more adept at sensing the arrival of death than any doctor. He opened the Bible although he had no need to for the ceremony was part of his being. He began to intone soft words.

Finally, he fell silent and made the sign of the cross.

'He has passed,' he said, his voice filled with wonder, an emotion which never changed. Mankind might be frail and predictable, he thought, but God never was. He was always able to surprise mere mortals.

The priest gave the final offices, bowed to the dead man and then made to retire from the room. He had liked the old man but never cared much for Marthe nor her family.

'I'll find you in a moment,' Odette told him. 'You'll take a drink and a little something for church funds?'

The priest inclined his head with great politeness. The rituals must be observed in every particular.

The funeral was held two days later. Viviane decided it would be best if the children did not go.

Sylvie offered to take them to the woods to look for mushrooms, an adventure which would help dispel any sadness. They were very excited, and Celeste was adamant that they might chance upon fairies as well as mushrooms. Her friend Monique looked a little doubtful of this; she was three months older than Celeste and considered herself more worldly-wise.

David was agog at the thought of seeing such magical creatures and asked Celeste to describe the fairies again and again. She smiled with the condescension of greater knowledge and told him all she knew about fairies with ever greater elaboration.

Viviane kissed them goodbye, shut the door behind them and gazed at Alain. 'You'll be too hot in that.'

Alain demurred. 'I always wear my overcoat to funerals. It looks appropriate.'

'But I know you,' she said. 'You'll get too hot, take if off and trail it around like a piece of rag. You'll look better in just your suit.'

Reluctantly he agreed. He knew that however he looked, the rest of the family would find fault with it. He had even been denied the role of pall-bearer. That honour had been allocated to Roland Boyer and three of Marthe's cousins, two of whom the old man had actively disliked.

It was one of those October days which paraded its beauty, with a bright sky dotted with fragile clouds and a sun as warm as that of June. The trees waved gently in a breeze, their leaves like flame and embers.

It would be better if the day were dreary, Viviane thought as she looked about her. This was a day which seemed more suited to celebration, not the sorrow of a funeral.

But then she smiled a little. Perhaps this was as her father would have wished. He had experienced too much sorrow in his life. He would not wish it at his funeral.

There were over seventy people in the church, for her father had lived in the town all his life and was well-liked. The priest looked at ease, this is my house as much as God's his manner seemed to say. Odette would not like that at all, Viviane thought.

The funeral went with all possible dignity. Somewhat to her relief, Viviane felt tears begin to flow the moment the coffin was lowered into the ground. It would not have been seemly if she had been dry-eyed when her mother and Odette appeared racked with regret and anguish.

But even as she wept, she wondered who her tears were for. Were they for her father, tears of sorrow at his passing or tears of joy at his release from pain?

Or were they for her, for now she felt the last link with her family had been completely severed. And, if so, were they tears of sorrow or of release?

The funeral feast was held at her father's house. She looked at the food on the table ruefully. Alain may not have been invited to be a pall-bearer but Odette had been insistent with her demands on him to provide as much food as he could.

He had certainly done that. Although annoyed at the way he had been snubbed, Alain had procured an amazing amount of food and drink. He had spent a fortune in doing so but he had no regrets. Although the guests thanked Marthe, as was appropriate, most realised that it was he and Viviane who had provided and were careful to quietly acknowledge this.

Viviane was sitting alone near the window when Odette approached. Her face was hard and bitter. 'I suppose you think you can buy your way into mother's good books with this gross feast?' she said.

Viviane looked shocked. 'It's Papa's funeral,' she said. 'You asked us to provide the food. We were happy to do it for him.'

'Happy to flaunt your good fortune,' Odette snapped. 'My husband earns a modest salary from upholding the law. Whereas Alain…' She stared at Viviane, all too aware that both of them knew how the sentence was meant to end.

Viviane's temper flared but she managed to keep it in check. 'If you didn't want us to contribute then you shouldn't have asked.'

'I shouldn't have had to ask,' Odette said. 'You should have offered. As it was, I had to plead and cajole.'

'That's not true.'

'Maman knows it is. The whole of the family knows it.'

Viviane clamped her mouth shut. This was not the time for an argument.

'Not that it cost him that much,' Odette said quietly. 'Yesterday, when Alain left after delivering the wine, I found that money had gone missing from Maman's purse.'

Viviane gasped in astonishment. 'What are you insinuating?'

'I'm insinuating nothing, just relating facts. When Alain came into the house there was money in Maman's purse, coins and notes. When he left there were a few coins only.'

'Perhaps Maman gave money to him. For the food.'

Odette shook her head. 'Maman was in bed. I was in the kitchen. Alain was alone in the room.'

'He would never do such a thing.'

'Wouldn't he? Admit it, Viviane, it's in his blood. Gypsies cannot help but steal and swindle.'

'And bitches like you can't help but lie and spread falsehoods.'

Odette looked at her in rage. Her hand flashed out and she raked her fingers across Viviane's cheek, drawing blood. 'A mark of shame,' she snarled as she headed back to their mother.

'I'm never going back to that place,' Viviane said when they had returned to their house. She dabbed at her cheek with a rag dipped in iodine. It stung but was like nothing to the pain caused by Odette's behaviour.

Alain did not answer. He was lost for words.

'People will say it was my fault,' Viviane continued. 'That I goaded her when she was vulnerable in her grieving.'

'You don't know that —'

'I do. For that's precisely what Odette and Maman will say.' She began to weep softly.

'Why would someone be so cruel?' she said. 'To her own flesh and blood?'

Alain pursed his lips, thinking it best not to answer.

'How could she?' Viviane said.

Alain sighed. 'You may be sisters,' he began, 'but you were never close.'

'But to do this!' She pointed at her cheek. 'It's monstrous.'

She closed her eyes. She had never much cared for Odette and knew that she felt the same about her. But she was truly shocked at how she had behaved.

Alain started to speak once more but thought better of it. He feared that Odette's behaviour might prove to be merely the start of something even more cruel and vicious.

## VIVIANE AT VILLA LAUREL
*Grasse, 21 October 1943*

The trees were beginning to turn red and a golden haze had settled in the skies. October was normally one of Viviane's favourite months and, in the past, she would often have taken Celeste for long walks in the hills surrounding the town. Now, the month had been tainted by the death of her father.

She could only watch the skies from the house for she feared going outside with David and dared not leave him alone at home. She would go out shopping when Alain was at home, keeping up appearances and taking Celeste with her. But she kept herself to herself far more than in the past and tried to avoid conversations.

She kept thinking of her father, and how much she missed him. And then her hand would go to her cheek. The scars from Odette's nails were beginning to fade but the memory of them was intense and burning.

Whenever she thought about her family she felt as though she had been kicked in the stomach. And she imagined that they would watch her as she writhed on the floor in agony and laugh.

'Maman,' yelled Celeste one day from the living room. 'It's Auntie Dorothy.'

Viviane came out of the kitchen, wiping her hands. Dorothy was at the window peering in.

'I didn't want to knock too loud,' she announced as Viviane opened the door to her. 'I know what gossipy neighbours can be like.'

'I'm not sure that standing on the street and starring into my window will stop the gossip,' Viviane said, in a more annoyed tone than she intended.

'Apologies, darling,' Dorothy said, not at all offended. She swept into the house and threw herself in a chair. 'I've come to ask you a favour.'

'What is it?' Viviane asked, embarrassed that she had been so curt. 'I'll help if I can.'

'Lucile's mother has fallen ill and she's had to leave my employ to look after her. I can't cook a thing; I've had people do it for me this past thirty years. Would you take her place?'

'Can't Marie?'

Dorothy reddened and shook her head. 'Marie has neither the skill nor the inclination to cook.'

Viviane was dumbfounded. 'I'm not trained. I couldn't do what Lucile does.'

'I know that, darling. But I've eaten what you've made, don't forget. It's not haute cuisine, I admit, but you simply do wonders with whatever you lay your hands on.' She gave an outrageous pout. 'But don't trouble yourself if it's too much bother, of course. Not if you'd like to see me starve to death.'

Viviane laughed aloud. 'I can't promise you great wonders.'

'Just an egg or two on a plate would suffice, darling. You know I have simple tastes.'

Viviane smiled. Simple was not how she would describe Dorothy's appetites. 'How often will you want me?'

'Three times a day, of course. I believe that a regular health and dietary regime is of the utmost importance.'

'Breakfast, lunch and dinner?'

'Not breakfast, I couldn't possibly do with people at breakfast. But lunch and dinner, yes. And possibly morning coffee and afternoon tea. Not every day, though. On occasion you can leave the fixings out for me.'

'What about the children?'

'Bring 'em with you.'

Viviane stared at Dorothy for a moment. She suspected that her request was not entirely self-centred. The American had a warm heart. If the children were there they would be fed, as Dorothy probably intended, all along.

'I wonder if you can afford me,' Viviane said with a smile.

'Tosh. I could buy your little house, motorbike and husband and still have change in my purse. Anyway, don't fret, the wages will be minimal as suits your lack of training. But in addition to this pittance you can dine with me. You and the children. And Alain if he brings you over.'

The tears started in Viviane's eyes and she knelt on the floor in front of Dorothy, taking her hands in hers and kissing them.

'How very Medieval,' Dorothy said. 'I bet Doug Fairbanks could have made something of this.'

Viviane got to her feet, face crimson at what she had just done. She was going to say something, some words of thanks and gratitude, but none seemed large enough. All she could do was stare speechless at her friend.

Dorothy insisted that she start straight away. 'All I've got,' she said, 'is a stone hard piece of bread and some butter which has lingered on the plate so long it's returning to its milky provenance.'

'Do I need to do any shopping?'

'Nope. Marie has that in hand. Come on, get your things and tell Alain he can come for lunch.'

Viviane scribbled a note for Alain telling him what had happened. She scanned it briefly when she had written it. She suddenly felt shocked. This was an innocent message but she found that she was scrutinising it for anything which might be incriminating.

A feeling of alarm swept over her but then she saw how excited Celeste and David were at the thought of playing with Dorothy's cat, Groucho. She helped David into his coat and followed Dorothy out to her car.

The roads were empty save for the occasional German military vehicle. David got excited at the sight of them and pressed his nose to the window.

'Let him be,' Dorothy said, sensing that Viviane was about to tell him to get away from the glass. 'He needs a little fun and besides, the Krauts will expect a little boy to want to look at them.'

They drew up at the villa and Groucho ran out to greet them. 'Well that's them taken care of,' Viviane said as the children crouched down and petted him.

Dorothy led the way into the kitchen where Marie was picking the eyes out of two potatoes.

'Thank goodness,' she said, pushing a lock of hair out of her eyes. 'I was not born to be a cook.'

'Me neither, sweetheart.' Dorothy said. 'The only affinity I have with food is to eat it. But Viviane's gonna cook so you can hang up the apron.'

Dorothy and Marie showed Viviane where things were. She stifled a grin. They stumbled upon things by accident rather than design and some of the utensils clearly had them completely baffled. Viviane guessed that Lucile hadn't often let them into the kitchen.

'I think I've got it all, now,' Viviane said, putting away the knife sharpener which Dorothy had hypothesised was a decorative roller for crimping pastry. 'I'll check out the food cupboards and prepare some lunch.'

'Four adults including you and me, Marie and Pierre,' Dorothy said. 'But best make it five in case Alain comes over. And the two children, of course.'

Viviane set to with a will. She was careful with Dorothy's provisions for they were no longer easily replaced. She smiled with pleasure as she worked. It had been a long time since she had been able to put the right ingredients into a meal rather than scraping around for what little was available, suitable or not.

Within an hour she had produced a mushroom omelette, a carrot and haricot bean salad and an apple tart. Alain arrived as it was being served, almost as if he had smelled it from a distance.

'I hope you don't mind me taking Viviane away from you,' Dorothy said as she watched him tuck into the meal with gusto.

'Not at all,' he said happily. 'Anything to help, Dorothy; you know that.'

'And the children can play here, safely,' Dorothy said, casually, almost as if it were an afterthought. 'It will be good for them to fuss the cat and roam around the grounds.'

'I'll bring what food I can,' Alain said. 'Although it's not getting as easy as it was.'

'Whatever you can manage, dear man.' Dorothy gave a little sigh. 'I must admit to missing Emilio Marinelli. Not just for the food but for the company. He was a charming man. I doubt that any of the Krauts will be of similar nature.'

'Not according to my brother-in-law,' Viviane said. 'The Gestapo have moved into Police Headquarters. Their chief has helped himself to his office.'

'Is he surprised?' Dorothy asked. 'After all they've helped themselves to your country.'

Alain frowned. 'You're right. And I can see little end to the nightmare.'

'It will come,' said Dorothy, soothingly. 'I feel it in the water.'

## DENUNCIATIONS
*Grasse, November 1943*

Heinrich Schorn lay on the couch in his hotel room, reading avidly. He had taken two rooms in the Auberge Beauville, keeping one as a bedroom with an adjacent one rearranged as a sitting room. The proprietor, Monsieur Favart, had exhibited no qualms about having members of the Gestapo in his hotel. Business was business and he had always turned his gaze from the assorted lovers, prostitutes and criminals who had enjoyed his facilities. He was, and always had been, a double-dealer, as anxious to keep on the good side of the police as to take money from the nefarious. He had grown wealthy as a result, although he was always careful to hide the fact.

A knock came on the door.

Schorn put down his book and reached for his revolver. 'Enter,' he said.

Favart was tall with a long face containing searching eyes. A man born to spy, Roland Boyer always said.

'There are two women to see you, Herr Schorn,' he said.

Schorn looked perplexed. He was a man of fixed habits. Prostitutes arrived on Tuesdays, Fridays and Saturdays. Today was Wednesday.

'Who are they?'

Favart shrugged. 'They're wearing hoods to conceal their faces.'

Schorn frowned. It seemed to him unlikely that anyone would be able to keep their identity secret from Favart unless he chose to allow them to.

'Send them up,' Schorn said. 'And don't disturb us.'

He sat up and put the book face down on the coffee table. It was a dog-eared copy of The Maltese Falcon. Sam Spade was his hero, the spare, needle prose of Dashiell Hammett a constant delight. He covered the book with a newspaper. It would be unfortunate if these French women were to see him reading a decadent American novel. Besides, he didn't want anyone to cast their eyes upon his most treasured possession.

A second knock came upon the door and this time, Schorn rose to answer it. His hand gripped the pistol in his pocket as he opened the door a crack. He could see only two women but he took one step outside to check the corridor before gesturing them to go into the room. He gave another quick look up and down before shutting the door behind him.

'Pull your hoods back,' he commanded. The women obeyed instantly.

With their drab clothes and pinched, hungry, watchful faces they looked to be in their forties although he thought they might actually be ten years younger. No pleasure to be had with either of them, he thought. Unless he took them to a ditch on some lonely road where he could screw them without having to look them in the face. Where the sound of their screams and the gunshots to their heads would be minimised.

One had olive skin and eyes so dark they were almost black. Her hair was long and untidy, it looked as if she had not washed it in weeks. She might have been attractive in her youth although any charm had long since gone. The other had a pale complexion, blue eyes and blond hair. She might almost have been Aryan. He stared at her for a little longer. Her eyes lacked all warmth and her jaw was set in a manner suggesting anger and truculence.

'Sit, ladies, please,' he said, indicating the couch. He pulled up a straight-back chair, the better to loom over them. 'To what do I owe the pleasure of your visit?'

'We have names for you, Monsieur,' said the olive-skinned woman. 'Black-marketeers, prostitutes, Gypsies, people who secretly support the Resistance.'

Schorn feigned a look of disinterest. It would never to do to show these people they were of the slightest value to him. But his pulse quickened at what she said. He had very few men and only Buchner had any real flair for detective work. As with most Gestapo officers, nine out of ten of his arrests were due to the work of informers.

The Gestapo had a fearsome reputation but it was in reality, a house of cards. Sam Spade could have done the work of two dozen Gestapo without breaking sweat. It was the informers who allowed them to function, who enabled their success and bolstered their reputation.

Why people were so keen to inform was an endless source of debate amongst his colleagues. Some argued that it was for monetary reward, others because of fear or to curry favour with their conquerors.

But Schorn believed that most informers were motivated by one of two reasons. The first was lust for a shred of power. The other was to wreak revenge on someone they hated.

'Names?' Schorn said, holding out his hand. 'Let me see.'

The woman gave him a list written in pencil. It was incredibly neat and easy to read, as if the woman had laboured over it with utmost care. It was headed by the Mayor's name, which was the norm for such documents. Every planning application the man had refused and every regulation he had promulgated appeared to be reason enough for him to lose his life.

Most names were dispiritingly familiar to him. Doctors featured heavily, solicitors and dentists even more. School teachers who were still working were occasionally named, those who had retired much more so. Old grudges rankled more strongly than new ones, it seemed.

Butchers, bakers and grocers featured in the list, as usual, an attempt to get revenge for selling poor produce.

'No Jews?' he asked.

The woman leaned over and pointed out a name. 'I have heard that this man might have a Jewish grandfather.'

Schorn took a pencil and swiftly drew a star against it.

'Gypsies?'

The woman shook her head.

'This is most valuable, Madame,' he said, giving a warm smile. He folded the paper in two and placed it beside the table. Then he reached inside his pocket. The women tensed, wondering what he was going for, fearing it would be a pistol or a blade.

He kept his hand inside for a while longer, enjoying the look of fear on their faces. But then he produced his wallet. They could not disguise their look of relief. He took out a hundred franc note and handed it to the woman. She took it quickly and secreted it in her purse.

'You look aggrieved, Madame,' he said. 'You expected more?'

'Not at all,' she said hurriedly, her voice trembling with fear.

'It would have been more,' Schorn continued, 'if the list had contained more Jews. It is a matter of simple arithmetic.' He smiled. 'But now you know for next time.'

His smile vanished and he gestured to them to leave. He decided that he would have another glass of wine and retire for the night with his book.

The dark woman went to open the door but the blond woman placed her hand against it.

'I know a Jew,' she said.

Schorn stared at her.

'Go on.'

'A little boy. He's being taken care of by a French couple.'

Schorn gave an appreciative nod. 'And how do you know this?'

The woman did not answer for a moment. When she did it was with triumph in her voice. 'Because I know the woman. She's my sister.'

Schorn's eyes glittered. Siblings, the deadliest of rivals.

'And the man,' Odette continued, 'he's half Gypsy.'

Schorn reached for his wallet, pulled out another hundred franc note and gestured them to sit once more.

### THE GYPSY QUESTION
*Grasse, 15 November 1943*

The rain battered the town with greater ferocity than a normal November. The temperatures plummeted and the days grew ever darker and more drear. Viviane swaddled the children in every article of clothing she could but they still complained that they were cold.

It's because they're so thin, she thought. There's not enough flesh on their bones and no warmth in their bellies. She too was hungry. She would sometimes wake in the night with her stomach clenching in painful spasms. Every morning she grasped her wrist to check how much thinner it had grown. And every morning she gave the children the little she should have eaten for her own breakfast. Alain was also getting thin. His ribs were starkly visible and his clothes hung on him. Sometimes he looked like a child who had put on his father's clothing.

They might have starved altogether if it were not for the meals she ate at Dorothy's. And even these were getting smaller. Dorothy gave Marie ever more money for the shopping but it bought less each time. Viviane's ingenuity was stretched to make meals which would beat their hunger. She began to dread the onset of winter.

Dorothy, on the other hand, somehow maintained her sense of cheerfulness. Viviane wondered if it were not sometimes a charade, but if it were, it did the job. Villa Laurel felt like a refuge from the storm, an oasis in an ever more barren desert. Viviane sometimes found herself praying to the Madonna, thanking her for sending Dorothy to them.

It was on the fifteenth of the month that Dorothy's good cheer disappeared. She took Viviane to one side, her face tight with anxiety.

'I've just heard disquieting news,' she said. Her voice was unusually quiet.

Viviane felt that she would vomit. She could not speak, merely nodded for Dorothy to continue.

'Himmler has just announced that Gypsies are to be treated the same as Jews and sent to camps.' Dorothy held Viviane's gaze. 'Gypsies and part-Gypsies.'

Viviane's hand went to her mouth. 'Alain's mother was a Gypsy.'

'I know. Alain told me. He thought that coming here might incriminate me so he told me.'

'But what does it mean?' Viviane grabbed Dorothy's hand so tight it made her wince. 'Dorothy, what does it mean? For him? For Celeste?'

Dorothy did not know how to answer. She took a deep breath and spoke in as calm and honest a way as she was able.

'If the Nazis use the Nuremberg Laws and treat the Gypsies the same way as they do the Jews then Alain is in danger. He will, I think, be considered a half-Gypsy and may be sent to a camp.'

Sent to a camp. The words hung in the air; pestilence heavy.

'And Celeste?' Her voice was shaky and barely audible.

'She will be deemed a quarter-Gypsy,' Dorothy said. 'But I doubt the bastards will target her.'

Viviane wailed in horror. Doubt was not strong enough, nowhere near strong enough. She leaned against the wall, gasping for breath, unable to suck any air into her lungs. She thought she might die.

Dorothy massaged her shoulders, rocked her back and forth, desperate to get her breathing again. Then Viviane gave one almighty sob and began to breathe. She slipped to the floor, weeping inconsolably.

'Get out,' Dorothy snapped at Celeste and David who had come running to see what was wrong.

David screamed and fled but Celeste burst into tears and swooped upon her mother.

'Maman, Maman, I'm here, I'm here. Don't cry, please don't cry.'

Viviane reached out and gathered Celeste close. Dorothy took one look and rushed out in search of David.

She found him sitting at the top of the stairs, shaking with terror. She scooped him up and hugged him tight. 'I'm so sorry, darling,' she said. 'Auntie Dorothy didn't mean it.'

'I want my Maman,' he said.

'She's downstairs, with Celeste. I'll take you to her.'

'Not this Maman,' he wailed. 'I want my old Maman.'

Dorothy held him even tighter. How could this be happening?

They spent the afternoon talking in lowered voices about anything other than the news that Dorothy had told them. The children were calm now and playing board games under Marie's watchful eye. Dorothy talked about her days in Hollywood. It seemed the only thing worth talking about, the only thing safe to talk about. Her words were like stones dropped into a pond. They made a momentary impact and then the ripples died and it was as if they had not been.

Alain came over as the evening drew on.

Viviane threw herself into his arms. She began to sob, almost noiselessly.

'What's wrong?' Alain asked, in alarm. The question was directed not at her but at Dorothy.

For answer, Dorothy rose and poured him a large glass of cognac and placed it on a table beside the couch. 'Come sit,' she said, 'both of you.' She gestured to Marie to take the children to another room.

Alain heard the news in silence. He had been half-expecting this for years so he was shocked less than the others. But an icy void grew in his stomach, little by little, so unstoppable it seemed it would swallow him alive.

'Do you know more?' he asked at last.

Dorothy shook her head.

Viviane looked up and stared into his eyes. 'What will happen to us?'

'Probably nothing,' he said, trying to smile but failing. 'As least nothing serious. Maybe we'll find some shopkeepers less willing to sell food to us but I've still got enough friends to save us from starving.'

Viviane sighed in relief and threw her arms around Alain, kissing him on the cheeks, on his lips, on his nose. It would be alright. Everything would be alright. He would make sure that it was.

At that moment they heard the sound of a car crunching over the wet driveway. Alain went to the window and peered out cautiously, watching as the car pulled up in front of the villa. 'It's Roland,' he said.

He hurried to the door, returning a moment later with his brother-in-law.

Roland Boyer pulled off his hat and bowed to Dorothy. 'Apologies for this intrusion, Madame, but I must speak with my sister-in-law and her husband.'

Dorothy rose from her chair but Alain stopped her. 'Whatever you have to say, Roland, you can say in front of our friend.'

The policeman looked doubtful but gave a shrug.

'Is it about the laws concerning Gypsies?' Alain asked.

Boyer looked flabbergasted. 'How did you know?' he asked.

'Never mind how. I know. That's why I came here. To tell Viviane and Dorothy about it.' He had no intention of letting Roland suspect that Dorothy had a wireless set so powerful it was illegal.

Dorothy poured Boyer a cognac which he swallowed in one gulp, not even thanking her.

'What will it mean,' Viviane asked. 'For Alain and for Celeste?' She surprised them all, even herself, by how calm and strong her voice seemed now.

Boyer took a deep breath. 'Not good, I'm afraid. Alain will be considered a half-Gypsy and be sent to a camp in the east, Poland probably.' His face was tight with sorrow.

They heard this news in silence. The hopefulness of a moment before was now smashed and irreparable.

'And Celeste?' she asked, her voice now beginning to break.

'She will be considered a quarter-Gypsy,' Roland answered. 'It's unlikely that she will be sent to a camp.'

'Unlikely? But not certain?'

Boyer shook his head. 'Alas, I cannot say for sure. But I do know that the Germans didn't want to accept Jewish children for the camps. I'm ashamed to say that it was Pétain and Laval who insisted on that. I doubt the Germans will want to take Gypsy children.'

'But they will take Alain?'

Boyer nodded.

'How will they get hold of me?' Alain asked.

Boyer looked confused.

'Will they come and arrest me? Will they surround my home? Will they hunt for me in the streets and alleys if I'm not found there?' There was a strange, hard note in his voice, a note that none of them had heard before, not even Viviane.

'They will demand that people give themselves up,' Boyer said.

Alain shook his head. 'I won't.'

Roland stared at him. 'Then what will you do?'

'I'll go to ground. I'll get away.'

'And leave us?' asked Viviane aghast.

He began to weep, tried but failed to keep the tears from flowing. 'It's the safest thing to do, Viviane. For you and the children. If I'm found with you it will be dangerous. Deadly dangerous.'

Boyer looked from Alain to Viviane and nodded. 'Alain's right. The best thing for all of you is for him to disappear.'

'And go where?'

Boyer did not answer for a minute. No one spoke, the only sound the soft ticking of the clock.

'To his friend in Nice,' Boyer said at last. 'Either that or go to join the Maquis. They are fighting from their bases just north of here.'

'They're part of the Resistance, right?' Dorothy asked.

Boyer nodded. 'Joining his friend or the Maquis are his only choices. If he is to survive.'

'Could your criminal friend get you out of France?' Dorothy asked.

Alain shook his head. 'I don't know. Perhaps.'

'You must decide quickly,' Boyer said. 'At once.' Then he held up his hand. 'And whatever your decision, do not let us know.'

Alain looked at him, his face stricken. Then he hugged Viviane. 'Tell the children that Papa's gone to visit a friend. Tell them I'll be in London.'

Viviane wailed in horror and clung onto his neck. He removed her hands gently, kissed her on the lips and then made for the door.

'I'll take him to your house,' Boyer said to Viviane, 'let him pick up some things. Then I'll drive him out of town.'

'Isn't that a risk for you?' Dorothy asked.

'He's family,' he said simply. He turned to Dorothy and whispered something in her ear.

Dorothy turned and glanced at Viviane. 'Of course, she can,' she said.

He hurried out to catch Alain.

He returned a few hours later with three suitcases containing Viviane and the children's clothes, personal belongings and toys.

Viviane stared at them blankly.

'You're to stay here,' Boyer said. 'Few people know of your friendship with Madame Pine. Keep it that way. Now, I must go. And you must never return to your home.'

It was only when she looked out of the window that she realised that Alain was waiting in Roland's car. She ran out of the room, desperate to get to him. But the car had disappeared by the time she ran out on to the drive.

# HUNTING
*Grasse, 30 November 1943*

Kriminaldirektor Schorn lifted his head at the sound of the knock. He knew who it would be. He pulled out a cigarette from a pack and lit it, breathed in slowly, deeply, imagining the smoke filling his lungs, curling into every little sac and bronchi. Such pleasure from such a tiny thing, he thought. He took another drag, felt the drying itch at the back of his throat. It was both a pain and a pleasure and that was what he liked most about it.

He stared at the door, thinking about the emotions of the man waiting on the other side. A slow smile crossed his face. After the war, he thought, I should go big game hunting. Africa. Or when the British Empire has been destroyed, India. He chuckled at the idea of it. He didn't even like the sound of gunfire.

'Enter,' he said at last.

The handle turned and Gerard Pithou walked into the room. Schorn stared at him for a little while, exactly like his mother would stare at a herring on the fishmonger's slab. 'Sit,' he said, indicating the chair on the opposite side of the desk.

Gerard sat down and passed a sheathe of papers across to him. Schorn looked as if the action was inconvenient, a bore. But he picked the papers up, nonetheless and began to read them. There were thirty or so names in the list, complete with addresses, places of work and other places where they might be found.

'A good trawl,' he murmured. 'Thirty Jews. You are getting quite efficient.'

Gerard beamed with pleasure.

'And the women I have provided for you?' Schorn asked. 'They have pleased you?'

Gerard thought of the women who had been delivered to his door. Most were prostitutes although he did not have to pay them. A few were not, young girls mostly, terrified and compliant.

'Very pleased, Kriminaldirektor, thank you.'

'But they are not your best friend's wife?' Schorn said with a smile. 'She is still, where is it, Cannes?'

Gerard tried to recall what he had told Schorn about Viviane and where she lived. 'Antibes,' he said, relieved that he remembered his lie.

'And you told me she was called Annette Dubois?'

Gerard nodded. He was sure that was the name he had given.

'We could find her, you know,' Schorn said, allowing a hint of excitement to sound in his voice. 'We could get your friend, out of the way.'

Gerard swallowed hard. 'I couldn't do that, Kriminaldirektor. Much though I desire her.'

Schorn leaned back in his chair. 'And we Germans are told that Frenchmen are great lovers.' He shook his head ruefully. 'I guess it would be different if she lived closer to hand. In the town itself, for example.'

'Sadly, she doesn't.'

Schorn smiled. Pithou's not an idiot, he thought, he knows I am playing with him. He had already found out that the only Annette Dubois living in Antibes was an elderly widow and suspected that the woman he lusted after lived in the town. It was gallant of Pithou to try to protect her and her husband. Gallant but foolhardy. For he could use it against him later, should he have need.

Schorn lit another cigarette and offered the pack to Gerard. He was tempted to take one but thought it best to give a polite refusal. 'I've just put one out,' he explained.

'I admire your self-control, Schorn said. 'I, unfortunately, entirely lack any.'

Gerard's eyes widened. He had never met a man with such steely self-control as Schorn.

Schorn placed the list of names to one side of the desk and picked up a sheet of paper.

'There has been a development,' he said. 'Reichsführer Himmler has announced that all Gypsies and Half-Gypsies will be officially placed on the same level as Jews. They are to be collected together and transported to the east where they will be interned.'

Gerard gave one brief nod. His mind slowed, thoughts struggling jerkily, desperately, like an insect caught in a spider's web.

Schorn stared at him, suddenly alert to Gerard's reaction.

'Do you know of any Gypsies in the area?' he asked.

'Not off the top of my head,' he replied. He heard his voice sounding tense and shrill.

'Then you must hunt them,' Schorn said, 'for me, for Reichsführer Himmler and for the Reich. It is noble work.' He focused his attention on Gerard until the man began to visibly wilt under his gaze.

'I suppose,' he continued eventually, 'there must be some Frenchwomen who have married Gypsies. They, of course, will not be sent to the camps.' He gave a fleeting look of concern. 'Their lives will be difficult, of course, with no man to protect them, no money, no means of support.' Then he laughed. 'But it is their fault, of course, for marrying degenerates.'

Schorn held Gerard's gaze a good while longer. Then he gave a lazy wave towards the door. 'I believe you have work to do, my friend.'

Gerard struggled to his feet and headed for the door. He closed it behind him and headed for the nearest toilet. He thought he was going to be sick.

Early the next day Gerard put on his Milice uniform and made his way to Alain and Viviane's house. The curfew had ended but it was still dark and a biting wind raced through the streets. A trashcan tumbled along the road, clattering and crashing. A dog howled in the distance.

He had hardly slept that night, horrified at the news that Schorn had given him. Alain would be sent to some camp thousands of kilometres away. And as for Viviane and Celeste? And then another thought struck him. Not just Celeste, of course.

For the first time he began to wonder about David. He turned over in his mind the story that Viviane had told him about how he came to be living with her, about the penfriend who was the boy's mother. He had never questioned her account. Doing such a deed seemed entirely in keeping with how Viviane would act. Kindly, caring, decisive, impetuous. It was why he loved her.

He shivered as this thought came to him. Loved her. He very rarely allowed it to surface.

He forced his legs to move more swiftly, hoping that the persistent beating of his feet upon the ground would knock any unwanted imaginings from his mind. It must have worked for he suddenly found himself outside her door.

He stood, unmoving for several minutes. Now that he was here, he realised something chilling; he had no idea why he had come. Was it to warn his best friend of the peril he faced? Or was it to arrest him and bear him in triumph to the Gestapo chief?

He leaned his shoulder against the wall beside the window. How will Viviane react, he wondered. And how will I respond to her?

Still not knowing what he was going to do, he knocked upon the door. It did not open. He knocked again, slightly louder. No one answered. He stepped to the window and peered in. He could see no sign of anyone inside. He frowned. It was still early and a cold and bleak morning; surely they would not have left the house already?

He went back to the door and hammered on it even harder, then pressed his ear to the woodwork. Nothing. Taking a deep breath, he pushed on the handle. It moved and the door opened.

He hesitated for the briefest moment. But he was Alain's best friend and no one would be surprised that he had gone in uninvited. No one would criticise him for it.

He stepped inside. He had a momentary attack of panic. Perhaps they had heard about the new Nazi law and killed themselves. But no, of course they wouldn't do that.

He went from the living room into the kitchen and then out into the little backyard. He returned to the house and stood at the bottom of the stairs.

'Alain,' he called quietly. 'Viviane.'

But no answer came. He glanced behind him, almost as if he feared someone was in the room with him. Then he began to climb the stairs.

He peered into the children's room. The beds were made but something looked different. He could not think what it was for a moment. And then he realised that Celeste's customary Teddy Bear was not on the bed. The one he had given her on her third birthday.

He stepped towards Alain and Viviane's bedroom. He hesitated outside for a long while. He had been inside time without count in his imagination. Now, today, when he had the opportunity and the motive for entering, he found the deed almost impossible.

But finally, taking a deep breath, he entered. The bed was made, there was potpourri in a bowl, there were pictures of the children on a little table to the left of the bed, a book on a smaller table to the right.

His eyes scanned the room. The cupboard doors were open as was every drawer in a small chest. They were empty of all clothes. His heart quailed for a moment. The Nazis had been already. They had taken his friends to their deaths.

One item only lay on the floor, almost hidden in the shadows beside the bed. He bent down and picked it up. It was one of Viviane's handkerchiefs. He put it to his nose and imagined he could smell her scent, imagined he could breathe it in.

Perhaps they've escaped, he thought, desperately. Perhaps they've had warning and fled in time.

He tucked the handkerchief into his pocket and trudged down the stairs.

He wondered how Schorn would feel if they had escaped. He would find out that they were his friends and it would look bad for him. He took a deep breath. He would have to name many more people to outweigh such a disastrous failing. Many more Jews, defectives, Gypsies and undesirables. He closed his eyes. It might prove a terrible burden.


**A VISITOR**
*Villa Laurel, 1 December 1943*

Alain had been gone for sixteen days. Every morning Viviane woke and counted the days. Every morning, Celeste climbed into Viviane's bed and asked when he would return. She was used to him going away but she sensed that this visit to London seemed altogether more long-term.

'I can't say,' Viviane said. 'But he'll be back soon, I promise.'

Viviane dressed and went downstairs. Marie had placed a baguette in the bread-basket. It was yesterday's bread reheated, still warm from the oven. She got butter from the larder, hardly enough to scrape on the bread, and a small pot of preserve. Dorothy's hitherto large reserves of food were dwindling.

She boiled some water and made coffee while Marie took a plate into the morning room where Dorothy liked to eat breakfast alone. Viviane and the children ate with Marie in the kitchen.

It was all that Viviane could do to even talk with the children. Every hour since he had left, she would suddenly stop what she was doing and think about Alain. Where had he gone? Had he travelled to Nice to join Gabriel or had he trekked overland to join one of the Resistance groups in the mountains? Whichever he had done, she knew his life would be in danger. But less danger than if he had stayed here, she tried to console herself.

The Germans had been ruthless in capturing any Gypsies or part-Gypsies in the south of France. Camps had been attacked, men murdered, women raped and beaten. The SS and Gestapo systematically criss-crossed the countryside in search of Gypsies and Jews as well as any others they deemed undesirable.

Yes, Alain's escape might mean he'd be safe.

She took a deep breath. She was grateful that Dorothy had taken her in. She and the children were safer here than in Grasse. No one, apart from Roland, knew they were here.

And then a knock came on the door.

Marie looked up in surprise. 'Who could want Madame Pine at this hour?' she said.

'Perhaps it's not Dorothy they want,' Viviane said. Her mind began to race with fears. That it might be someone with awful news about Alain, a policeman demanding that she return to her home or a member of the Gestapo come to arrest them all.

Marie patted her gently on the arm and went to see who it was.

She returned a moment later. 'It's someone for you, Viviane,' she said.

Viviane glanced at the back door, wondering if she could grab the children and make it into the trees before she was seen.

'It's alright,' Marie continued. 'She said she's a friend of yours. Sylvie Duchamp. And she has a little girl with her.'

'Monique,' yelled Celeste, racing for the door. Viviane was powerless to stop her but ran after her, fearing that it may be a trap.

But Sylvie and Monique were alone at the door, shivering in the cold.

'I've found you at last,' Sylvie said. 'Can we come in? It's freezing out here.'

Viviane gestured them to go to the kitchen. Marie put some water on to heat. 'Would you like coffee?' she asked.

'Yes please,' Sylvie said, sinking into a chair. 'It's a longer walk than I thought.'

'Why are you here?' Viviane said. 'And how did you know I'd be here.'

'I didn't know for sure. I thought that you and Alain had fled the area, gone to Menton where he was born, perhaps.

'But then I remembered that you'd got friendly with some American woman. It took a bit of hunting but I finally found out where she lived.'

'Who did you ask?' Viviane said, her voice cracking with alarm. 'Nobody must know we're here.'

'Don't worry about that. I asked Isabelle Blois at Café Terminus. I said I wanted to ask Dorothy about how much I could charge American boys when they invade.' She glanced at the children and blushed. Marie raised an eyebrow but did not comment.

'So nothing changes,' Viviane said. But she squeezed Sylvie's hand in delight.

Marie gave them coffee then went out to resume her duties. They could hear the sound of a gramophone playing Gershwin from the Morning Room. Dorothy would be lying on the chaise longue, no doubt, dreaming of better places than here.

'There is a change, to be honest,' Sylvie said.

Viviane raised a quizzical eyebrow.

'See how well Monique looks now,' Sylvie began. 'And me as well. Better food, better clothes.'

'You've got married?' Viviane's eyes opened wide in delight.

'If only. No, but I've got the next best thing. A boyfriend. One who's very generous.'

Something in her tone made Viviane feel a prickle of unease.

'Do I know him?'

Sylvie shook her head and pulled out a pack of cigarettes. 'He's a German officer.' Her voice was deliberately matter of fact.

'What?' Viviane looked horrified.

'I had to do it,' Sylvie said. 'Honestly, Viv I had to. The Government stopped paying Louis's salary six months ago and my regulars were running out of money for my services. It was that or starve.'

'But the Germans!'

'Not the whole bloody army.'

Viviane and Sylvie stared at each for a moment and then both burst into gales of laughter.

When they had calmed down, Viviane reached out and held her hand. 'But isn't it risky, Sylvie? Sleeping with the enemy?'

'Not as risky as starving to death. And let's face it, plenty of people down here are happy to be friends with the Bosch. There's more than one way to get into bed with them. Restaurant owners giving them the best tables, wine-growers selling them the best vintages, people eager to fawn and scrape around them. Believe me, there are more rats than we cats playing with the Germans.'

'I don't care about all the others. I care about you.'

'And I care about you,' Sylvie said swiftly. She picked her words with care. 'I heard that Alain had disappeared. After the Germans had cracked down on…you know.'

'I've no idea where he is,' Viviane said.

'I'm glad to hear it. And if you do know, I hope you'd never tell a soul, not even me.'

'I don't, Sylvie, I really don't. I wish I did.'

Sylvie pulled Viviane's hand to her lips and kissed it lightly. 'I'm sure he'll be fine. Alain's always survived setbacks with a smile on his face. And usually a coin in his hand.'

'Until now,' Viviane said bleakly.

'Now and always,' Sylvie said emphatically.

The door opened and Dorothy walked in. 'You must be Viviane's friend,' she said.

Sylvie nodded and offered her a cigarette.

'I don't,' Dorothy said. 'Not unless it's Marijuana.'

'What's that?'

'It's heaven in a roll of paper. Or maybe hell.' She paused. 'Every bit as much as sex.'

Sylvie blushed. 'How did you know? About me and the Germans?'

'I didn't know about that,' Dorothy said. 'But I saw how well you look and realised that you were being looked after by someone very powerful. And nowadays, that means a Kraut.'

'I had no choice,' Sylvie said, sulkily.

'I'm not judging, darling. We all must do what we can to survive. I suspect some folk think I did the same with my little Italian soldier. But the most he got from me was a kiss goodnight.'

'That wouldn't put food on the plate,' Sylvie said.

'No. I'm luckier than most, I guess. When it comes to the readies.'

Dorothy sat down and stared at Sylvie. 'So why are you here, sweetheart? Should we be worried by your presence?'

'If you think I'm going to betray Viviane, you must be mad.'

'I didn't think that at all. Not until you mentioned it, at any rate.' She leaned back in the chair. 'I was thinking more that you might have worrying news.'

'Oh, yes I have.' Sylvie's voice was heavy with sarcasm. 'The Germans are winning the war. We're a conquered people and will be for the rest of our lives. Is that news enough for you?'

Dorothy patted her on the hand. 'The only people who are conquered are those who think they are. Somehow, I don't think any of us are included in that category.'

She got up and made for the door but then paused. 'Stay for lunch, why don't you. It will be nice company for Viviane.' She didn't wait for an answer but left the room, shutting the door behind her.

'Dorothy's been very kind to me,' Viviane said, annoyed at Sylvie's tone.

'I'm sorry, Viv. It's just that I didn't care for her suspicious attitude.' She lit a cigarette. 'I came here for two reasons. One was to see if you were alright. The other was…well.'

She passed a roll of notes to Viviane. Hundreds of francs.

'You can't do this,' Viviane cried.

'I can, and I am. Friends have to stick together, Viv. Now more than ever.'

## WEISER AT VILLA LAUREL
### *Grasse, 2 December 1943*

Oberst Weiser was in a hurry. He had been at Police Headquarters, in conference with Schorn and the other Gestapo operatives. It had not been a successful meeting.

Schorn had been friendly, almost unctuous, but his subordinates had been demanding and insulting. They appeared to believe that the only rationale for the war was the annihilation of the Jews and that the army was there solely to see it done. Weiser had finally lost his patience, cursed them and stormed out.

'That was not altogether wise,' Otto Mundt said as they drove off.

Weiser scoffed at his words. 'If you think that Nazi rats like that are going to worry me, then think again.'

'Nevertheless, Ernst, the Gestapo are a power to be reckoned with.'

'Do you think they can control the Army?' Weiser said.

Mundt did not answer for a moment. 'Adolf Hitler controls the Army. And who on earth would credit that?'

Weiser scowled. He thought of how General Blaskowitz had been treated by Hitler and his accomplices. Awarded an Iron Cross for heroism in the First World War, Blaskowitz had been instrumental in Germany's conquest of Poland. But while Commander-in-Chief in Poland he fell foul of the SS because he made an official complaint about their treatment of Jews and Poles. Because of this, his later assignments were continually blocked and his career had stalled. Now, he was in command of a second-rate army in a third-rate theatre of war.

Mundt was right. The Army was no longer in control of its destiny.

The meeting with the Gestapo had left Weiser feeling unclean and he wanted a bath and some dinner. He leaned over to the driver and told him to speed up.

The soldier put his foot down hard. The wind in the open-top car helped make Weiser feel better and he sat back in his seat with a sigh of relief. But the driver was driving too fast for the winding road and struggled to turn into a sudden curve. He managed to round the bend, only just, then saw to his horror a farm-cart straddling the road in front of him.

He never had a chance. The car collided with the cart and spun off the road, smashing through rocks and bushes on the steep incline to the side. It came to a halt fifty yards below the road.

The driver had been thrown through the windscreen and lay against a boulder with his neck broken. Mundt had been thrown clear but Weiser was still in the car, his foot caught under the seat. Smoke began to pour out of the engine.

Mundt yelled in alarm and clambered to his feet. There was an excruciating pain in his leg and arm and he felt dizzy but despite this he staggered over to the car and clawed the door open. Weiser was barely conscious so Mundt hooked his hands under his arms and dragged him from the vehicle, ignoring his friend's agonised groans.

He was only just in time. He managed to drag Weiser ten feet away when the car burst into flames. He examined his friend. His leg was broken in two places, the bones sticking through his trouser legs. Blood was everywhere. He threw off his uniform, tore his shirt into strips and tied a tourniquet around Weiser's thigh. The pain in his own leg was making him feel faint and he glanced up at the road to see soldiers from the escort racing down towards them. Then he fainted.

He woke in the middle of the night. He was in a bed with his arm in a sling and a bandage on his leg. He glanced to his left and saw Weiser in the next bed. He was not moving and for a moment he thought his friend was dead. But then Weiser turned and gave him a grin.

'Awake at last, Otto,' he said.

Mundt shook his head in confusion. 'The last thing I remember was dragging you out of the car.'

'And you saved my life. The car was consumed by fire.'

Mundt whistled. 'What have I done to myself?'

'Pulled some ligaments in your leg, wrenched your shoulder and given yourself mild concussion. The doctors say you landed on your head. The hardest part of you.' He chuckled, quietly.

'And you, Ernst?'

'My leg is fractured in two places. The doctors have set it but say I'll limp for the rest of my days.'

'A home-going wound?'

Weiser shrugged. 'I doubt it. In any case, I'm not allowed to travel for a while. It seems I'm stuck here for some time.'

Mundt nodded. 'And the driver?'

'Dead. Fractured neck. I suppose it saved him from a court martial. Apparently, he was a substitute driver, not very experienced at all.'

Mundt nodded. He thought it wise not to say that the soldier had driven so fast because he was following Weiser's orders.

A doctor approached their bed.

'How do you feel?' he asked. He was French and his tone was decidedly cool.

'I've felt better,' Mundt said. 'Where the hell are we?'

'In the civic hospital,' the doctor replied. 'One of your officers had the good sense to rush you here rather than leave you at the mercy of your own orderlies. You would have survived if you'd gone there, Major but your colonel would probably have died.' He gave a chill smile. 'May I congratulate you on your tourniquet. It staunched the blood and saved his life.'

Mundt shrugged. 'He owes me money. I need him to live so I can collect it.'

The Frenchman made no response to this jest.

'What happens now?' Weiser asked.

The doctor's eyes narrowed. 'My diagnosis hasn't altered since last I told you, Colonel. You must stay here overnight and then rest for a month at least. No travel, no great exertion, no walking unless with crutches.'

'Can I work?'

The doctor shrugged. 'If you must.'

'And Major Mundt?'

'He has concussion and should stay here overnight. Then he can return with you to barracks.'

'Any pretty nurses?' Mundt asked.

The doctor gave him a look of contempt and turned on his heel.

'This won't do,' Mundt said as he looked in at Weiser the following evening.

The colonel was sitting up in bed in the tiny bedroom behind his office. The bed was small and looked uncomfortable. Although his orderly had rigged up a table so he could work, it proved inadequate for the task. The other problem was that there was no heating and the window was loose, allowing a chill wind to surge around the room. Normally it would not matter but Weiser was shivering from the cold.

'I'm going to have to move you,' Mundt said.

'That's ridiculous.'

'No it's not. And the French doctor agrees. I spoke to him on the telephone.'

'I'm not going back to the hospital.'

'Of course not. But I've sent people out to look for somewhere you can convalesce and work in peace.' He glanced at the paper in his hand. 'They think they've found somewhere suitable. It's called Villa Laurel. It's owned by a wealthy American woman. Apparently, she's still living a pretty good life there. I've told her you're moving in today.'

Weiser started to argue but thought better of it. To be honest, the last few hours had been hell. The room was too small, the bed as hard as iron and the food inedible. He deserved a bit of comfort, he decided.

'And is the American amenable?' he asked.

Mundt laughed. 'Of course she isn't. But what choice does she have?'

Dorothy glared at Weiser as he approached in a wheelchair. His orderly had wanted him to be stretchered in but he was having none of that. Not in front of an American woman.

'You must be Colonel Weiser,' she said as he approached.

'I am,' he said in passable English. He held out a hand. 'And you are Mrs Pine?'

Her eyes narrowed and she did not take his hand. 'And you're going to take over my home? For how long? If it's not a rude question?'

'Not rude at all, Mrs Pine.' He glanced at Mundt.

'The doctor says six months for Oberst Weiser to make a full recovery.'

Dorothy looked aghast. 'And he's going to stay that long?'

'Not necessarily,' Weiser said. 'I plan to leave well before that.'

'If the Oberst is fit enough,' Mundt said.

'And who are you?' Dorothy said. 'His doctor? You don't look like a doctor.'

'I am Major Mundt, Oberst Weiser's adjutant. And I shall be staying in the villa as well.'

'Heaven help me,' Dorothy said, raising her eyebrows as far as they could go. 'You'd better come in then, Colonel, Oberst, or whatever you want to call yourself.'

Weiser smiled and gave a polite nod of his head.

'My title is Oberst in German,' Weiser said. 'But you may call me Colonel if you prefer.'

Dorothy pointed out the morning room down the hall. 'That's your bedroom. I was told you couldn't manage the stairs.'

'That's very kind of you. I hope we haven't inconvenienced you at all.'

'Sure you have. But I haven't exactly got any choice over the matter.'

Weiser inclined his head in a gesture of apology.

'None whatsoever,' said Mundt.

'And I hadn't figured on your bosom buddy coming along to hold your hand,' she said, glaring at Mundt. 'I'll have the servants find him a room.'

'I would prefer it to be close to the Oberst,' Mundt said.

'You'll get what we can find.' She pointed to a door next to Weiser's room. 'Unless you're happy sleeping in the broom-cupboard.'

'Somewhere upstairs will be acceptable,' Mundt said, coldly.

Dorothy nodded. 'And I don't want a pack of soldiers trooping around my home and gardens,' she said.

'There will just be a few guards,' Weiser said. 'They will bivouac in the far end of the garden.'

Dorothy was not mollified by this but gave a curt nod of agreement before heading for the kitchen, yelling for Marie.

Weiser and Mundt went into the morning room. It was rectangular in shape with high ceilings. There was a large window looking east and a patio door leading to the garden.

'I'm not happy about that,' Mundt said, pointing to the door. 'Partisans could get in through there. We'll have to board it up.'

Weiser shrugged. He would have preferred not to have done this but did not argue because Mundt, as his adjutant, had responsibility for his security.

'I'll make sure it can be made good when we leave,' Mundt said. He gave a chuckle. 'I'm not sure I would want to cross Frau Pine too much.'

The room contained a small bed with soft pillows and a thick patchwork quilt. It looked warm and inviting, far better than anything Weiser had slept on since he had last been home, three years before. There was a bedside cupboard beside the bed with a candle stick. At the foot of the bed was a small table which was to serve as a desk. A straight-backed chair stood beside it. Someone had clearly gone to some trouble to make him comfortable.

An armchair was set against the narrow wall, facing towards the patio door and giving a lovely view of the garden. A small cupboard had been cleared of various items, ready for Weiser's clothes and other effects. These were in a case which one of the soldiers had dropped in the centre of the floor.

Mundt summoned Weiser's orderly. 'This room is suitable?' the man asked when he arrived. He scrutinised the door doubtfully.

'Yes,' Mundt said. 'Put away the colonel's clothes.'

Weiser sank into the armchair with a sigh of relief and stared out at the garden. 'This is a lovely view,' he said. 'I'm not sure I want it boarded up.' He glanced at Mundt. 'There will be guards, presumably? In the gardens. And the bed is out of the line of fire.'

Mundt went to the door and squinted towards the bed. 'I suppose you'll have to die sometime,' he said, with a shrug. 'It might as well be here as on a battlefield.'

Weiser laughed and watched as the orderly put away his clothes. He pulled his Luger out of its holster and placed it on a side table. He had not expected to find such a haven of peace. It was almost worth having a broken leg.

Marie knocked on the door. 'Your room is ready, Monsieur,' she said to Mundt.

'Go and take a look,' Weiser said. 'Then we'll have some schnapps and consider what to do about the Gestapo.'

Mundt followed Marie. She was a pretty little thing, he thought, as he followed her up the stairs. Nice figure, nice backside.

He expected to be led to one of the rooms on the second floor but she made for a second, smaller flight of stairs and led him up to a third floor in the roof.

'The servants' quarters,' she explained.

'And you are a servant?' he asked.

'Yes.'

'Then we shall be neighbours.'

Marie did not look the least bit concerned at his words which intrigued him a little. She pointed out his room. He glanced inside. It was tiny, with a window he could only look out of when standing. There was a small bed with a couple of blankets folded up on the old mattress. A table and chair were behind the door.

'Wonderful,' Mundt said, his voice thick with sarcasm. 'Can I trouble you to make my bed.'

Marie gave a curt nod and bent to her task.

Mundt watched her for a moment before heading for the stairs.

'A good room?' Weiser asked.

'It has walls and a ceiling,' Mundt said with a sigh.

'You wanted to come with me,' Weiser said with little sympathy. 'You could always return to the barracks.'

'Not for a while. Not while you're so infirm. It would be like leaving my grandfather to fend for himself.'

Weiser smiled and indicated a bottle of schnapps. Mundt picked up the bottle and then glanced around. 'There's no glasses.'

He stepped out of the room and saw a figure hurrying to the kitchen. 'You there, bring two glasses to Oberst Weiser's room.'

He went back inside and glanced at his friend.

'Still seething over those Gestapo swine?'

Weiser nodded. 'They treat us with such contempt. And they are fools, as well. They are so blinded by their fanaticism they cannot see the perils they create. It will encourage the populace to be difficult. They're as bad as the SS.'

'Careful, Ernst. Walls have ears. And besides, since when has anybody in any country lifted a finger to help the Jews? Even the British and Americans made it difficult for them to emigrate there before the war. And Laval and his mob worked like demons to rid France of them.'

'Not everyone is like that,' Weiser said. 'Some are sympathetic to the Jews and do all they can to help them. I think it is folly to attack them like this. Cruel folly. The country will rise up against us, sooner or later.'

He glanced up suddenly. Viviane was standing in the doorway with two glasses in her hand. She looked thoughtful, almost perplexed.

'You wanted some glasses,' she said, holding them out.

Mundt eyed her appreciatively. 'Yes,' he said. 'For our schnapps. Put them on the table. And leave the door open.'

She did as she was ordered, gave Weiser a little bow and then left the room.

'A pretty woman,' Weiser said, almost to himself. 'And well-mannered.'

He watched her as she disappeared, while Mundt poured the schnapps.


### THE HUNTER AND THE PREY
*Grasse, 2 December 1943*

The day broke in a riot of colour. The sky was azure blue with fingers of flame on the eastern horizon. The sun was a pale yellow but was growing in power with every second. It looked more like a June day than a December one.

A flock of geese sped past in a vee-shaped formation. Gerard followed their flight. He thought, this is how the skies of England must have looked in the Battle of Britain. Except instead of geese there would have been Messerschmitts and Spitfires.

As he had done every day for the past two weeks he slipped into Viviane and Alain's house. There was still no sign of them.

He was less nervous of being found here now. For the past week he had found himself following the same routine. He had been amazed the first time he did it, self-aware and embarrassed on the second and third occasions. Now he could not stop himself.

He went up to the bedroom and pulled back the sheets on the bed. He lay down upon it, where Viviane would have slept. He closed his eyes and her image wafted like mist into his mind, solidifying into a shape which leaned over him with tender gaze. Close, so very close. He gasped as she untied her hair, shook it free over her shoulders and began to unbutton her blouse.

He allowed himself to stay like this for a little while then got up and walked down the stairs. He went to the kitchen and poured some water into the sink. This is what she must have done every morning, poured water in the sink to wash herself, before she set about her daily tasks, feeding the family, cleaning the house, making coffee, sipping it slowly as she pondered the future.

He stepped into the courtyard and gazed at the tin bath hanging from the wall. She would use this once a week, perhaps even twice, filled with hot water from a pan on the stove. She would sit in a cloud of steam in the middle of the kitchen, humming to herself perhaps. He imagined her curves, saw her soap herself gently, saw her bend her head to wash her hair.

He returned to the kitchen, ran his fingers along the table, pulled open a drawer and straightened the knives and forks and spoons. Would she have done this, he wondered. Was she fastidious in this matter or slapdash? It pained him suddenly that he did not know.

He strolled into the front room. Here was her favourite chair, a low, comfortable one, with a throw her grandmother had made over the back. Alain's chair was harder, made of leather, stained and cracked by the years. Celeste favoured a little stool which doubled in her games as a pony, a Princess's throne or a motorbike like her father owned. Another stool was close by, presumably the one for the little boy.

He touched the back of Viviane's chair, stroked it gently. Then he went and sat in Alain's chair. Except if things worked out as he hoped, it would be his chair, and Viviane his wife.

He closed his eyes.

The pain was too much to bear. He missed her dreadfully. Yet he missed Alain as well. He felt guilty about what he was doing, what he was thinking. But he could no more stop himself than kill the breath in his throat.

Wearily he climbed to his feet. Another day beckoned, of knocking on doors and laying hints with passers-by. It was getting more difficult with each day. The townspeople seemed ever more reluctant to talk to each other. And with him it was worse still.

Once they would have viewed him as familiar old Gerard. Now he was Gerard of the Milice. The only people willing to speak to him were those who were keen to betray their enemies. And there seemed fewer and fewer enemies to betray. He had been too effective in this matter, it seemed.

He left the house and wandered aimlessly along the streets. He patted his pockets, searching in vain for a pack of cigarettes. He turned left at the next alley, came out in the Place aux Herbes and headed for Café Terminus. It was almost empty inside, although there was a thick pall of smoke from the three or four old men sitting alone at tables. Maxime Blois was wiping one of the tables but the ash dropping from his cigarette undid most of his toil.

He went to the counter and nodded at Isabelle Blois. 'A beer and a packet of cigarettes. Gauloises, if you have them.'

She stared at him coldly then flung a packet on the counter. 'I'll bring the beer over,' she said. He decided to ignore her discourtesy.

He sat at a table near the door. He considered himself a smoker rather than a drinker so he was mildly surprised that he had ordered a beer so early in the morning. His mother had got up before dawn as usual to prepare him breakfast. These were much better since he had joined the Milice. Monsieur Blanche refused to give them any special treatment but his rival baker Madame Pichot set aside a fresh baguette for his mother every morning.

It was the same in the rest of the town, his mother said. In half the shops she was treated the same as everyone else. In some she was given better food and more of it. A few refused to even serve her. Gerard had pressed her for the names of these last but she refused to tell him. The war would not continue for ever, she reasoned, and she would have to live with these people after it ended.

Isabelle Blois flung a beer mat on the table and plonked the glass on top of it. She gave him a cold look. She was well aware that she treated the German soldiers better than she treated the members of the Milice. The Germans were merely the enemy. The men of the Milice were traitors to France.

'Keeping yourself busy, Gerard?' she asked, her voice heavy with sarcasm.

Gerard sipped at his beer. 'Upholding the law, if that's what you mean.' He was surprised at his own response. In the past he would have been tongue-tied in front of her. Now he thought he sounded authoritative and determined.

'Playing at soldiers,' she sneered. 'I've a good mind to go and tell your mother about it.'

'Maman knows what I do,' he said. Her goading was beginning to make him angry.

'I bet she doesn't, little man. Not everything at any rate.' She strode back to the bar.

Gerard watched her as she began to polish the glasses. You may be high and mighty now, he thought, but there will come a day.

He opened the pack of cigarettes and lit up. The smoke soured his mouth for an instant and then he began to relax. He stared at the smoke wafting from the tip, then glanced at the packet with its new design of a Gypsy dancing girl swirling in smoke.

He imagined Viviane in her bath. Thought of Alain, hiding because he was a Gypsy.

He believed he might never see Alain again, especially if he had gone to join the Maquis, as he suspected. But he could not live without seeing Viviane again. He took out a second cigarette and lit it from the tip of his first. He was smoking with intensity now, sucking down the smoke as if it were life itself.

He wondered if he should go back to Viviane's mother again and demand that she tell him of her daughter's whereabouts. The old woman had been reluctant to talk to him, knowing that he was a friend of Alain's. The little she said was useless. It was clear that she had not seen her daughter for a while and cared little about what was happening to her.

Then another thought struck him. What about Viviane's sister?

The thought of speaking with Odette made him uneasy. She used to torment him when he was a child and even now he could not bear the look of contempt she assumed whenever she saw him. As well as this, he had always been reluctant to have dealings with her pious, pompous husband. Capitaine Boyer suspected that he engaged in petty crime and Gerard could not stop from looking guilty in his presence.

He cursed to himself. All other leads had come to nothing, so there was no alternative. He stubbed out his cigarette, swallowed a mouthful of beer and strode out of the bar.

Isabelle watched him go. He had forgotten to pay but it was a price worth bearing to see the back of him. She never understood why Alain was his friend.

Gerard knocked loudly on Odette's door. There was no answer, although out of the corner of his eye he saw the curtains twitch and an eye examining him. The curtain closed again and he remained at the door, hands in his pockets. Two could play the waiting game.

Again the curtain twitched and again the eye peered out. Then he heard a soft exclamation and the door was thrown open.

'What do you want?' Odette demanded. 'You have no business here.'

'I am a senior member of the Milice,' he answered, his sense of dignity wounded. 'I decide whether I have business here or not.'

'You know who my husband is?'

'Of course, Madame.'

'And he knows who you are. Nothing but a petty thief and accomplice to Gypsies.'

'You mean the Gypsies that your family has married into?'

She scowled at him, surprised at his quick and pointed response.

'My husband —' she began.

'Is under the authority of Kriminaldirektor Schorn as am I. You would both do well to remember this.'

She gave him a venomous look and held the door open wider. Schorn was not a man to be antagonised. 'You'd better come in,' she said.

He took a seat at the table although she had not invited him to. Then he took out a pencil and notebook crammed with notes.

Despite herself, Odette was curious to see what was in the book. She took a seat beside him. He moved it away a little, as if they were children taking a test and he feared she was trying to copy his answers.

'What's in your book, Gerard?' she asked. 'Love poems to my sister?'

He looked horrified at her words, his face blushing a deep red.

Odette laughed. 'I know you, Gerard Pithou and I know my sister. You're pathetic and transparent. You've itched for her ever since you first clapped eyes on her. Don't try to deny it. And she probably encouraged you.'

'She did not,' he said, angry at her insult to Viviane.

Odette chuckled quietly, pleased she had hit her target so deeply.

'So what do you want, Romeo?'

'I want to know where…' he stopped himself in time. 'I want to know where Alain Renaud is.'

'And why would I know that?'

'He's your brother-in-law.'

She shrugged.

He licked the tip of his pencil and made a note, ostentatiously.

'Your scrawls don't frighten me,' she said, leaning back in her chair as if to prove her lack of interest in what he wrote.

'Even if you don't know where Alain is,' he said, 'what about Viviane? You must know that.'

He glanced up as he said it and saw the blank look in her face.

'You don't know that either,' he said, in surprise.

'I don't. And I care even less.' She ran her fingers across her lips. 'I suspect they've run into the hills. Or gone to Marseille to join Alain's criminal friends. You'd know more about them than I do.'

Gerard did not respond. Despite his pleas, Alain had never taken him to see his contacts in Marseille. He was not going to admit this to Odette, though.

'I doubt that Viviane would have taken the children to anywhere as dangerous as that,' he said.

Odette laughed. 'You're a bigger fool than you look. The most dangerous place for her and the brat is here.'

'Brat? You mean Celeste?'

'No, you idiot. The boy.'

Gerard looked confused.

'So you don't know,' Odette said, her face triumphant. She made a scissors movement with her fingers.

Gerard shook his head. 'What does that mean?'

Odette grinned. 'The boy's been circumcised. I've seen it myself. He's a Jew. Surely you didn't believe the story she made up about him?'

Gerard snapped his notebook shut. 'Thank you, Madame, you've been most helpful.' He marched out of the house with Odette's laughter following him.

## OVERTURES
*Villa Laurel, 5 December 1943*

Weiser spent his first few days at the villa working from his bedroom although he could do very little, falling asleep almost as soon as he tried to read anything. He grew weary of the effort and spent long hours gazing out of the window at the mountains in the distance.

His leg pained him and he was extremely tired. This was partly from the trauma of his accident and the operation to put his bones back together. But it was also because of the Gestapo.

The first letter he had received after he was installed at the villa was from Kriminaldirektor Schorn. It pointedly informed him that his convalescence should in no way interfere with the army's hunt for Jews and Gypsies. Weiser had railed and raged at the effrontery of the man. Even Mundt could not calm him.

'Perhaps we should get rid of the bastard,' Weiser said, finally.

'An excellent idea, Ernst,' Mundt said. 'As long as you don't get caught.'

Weiser did not answer. It was, of course, unthinkable that a German officer would murder a fellow German.

And he knew that the death of any senior German official, whether military or Gestapo, was inevitably blamed on the French and led to horrific reprisals on the local population.

He marvelled at his thoughts. Was he really thinking of murdering a colleague? And was he stopped only out of concern for enemy civilians? He shook his head. Morphine did peculiar things to the mind, it seemed.

A few days later he felt strong enough to leave his room. He curtly told his orderly exactly where he could put the wheelchair he brought for him and told him to find some crutches instead. He cursed that a mere road accident had led to this situation.

He was in a foul mood by the time the orderly returned with the crutches. He put them under his arms and started off. But it was far more difficult than he imagined. Swinging his whole body after the crutches was unnerving and the movement caused him pain in his leg. But he persevered, ignoring the orderly's anxious gaze.

'Are you sure you wouldn't be more comfortable with the wheelchair, Oberst,' the man ventured at last.

Weiser shot him an angry glance and told him to fetch Mundt. He fled the room, gratefully.

'Ah, you must be Long John Silver,' Mundt said, when he arrived.

'Don't be so disrespectful,' Weiser snapped.

'Sorry, sir,' Mundt said although he did not appear the least bit so.

'Walk with me,' Weiser said. 'I want a report on everything.' He gave a wry smile. 'Are we still winning the war?'

Mundt lowered his voice. 'It's all according to how you define war. For example, I heard a report that eighty of our soldiers were executed by guerrillas in Greece so we slaughtered a thousand civilians in retaliation. If that is winning the war then, yes, we're doing really well.'

Weiser looked shocked, remembering his earlier thoughts about murdering Schorn. 'Was it the SS who killed the civilians?'

Mundt shook his head. 'A regular army division. They destroyed a whole village, smaller settlements and churches. And captured a thousand sheep and goats.' He did not bother to hide the contempt in his voice.

This war is driving us mad, Weiser thought. For a moment he wished he had been killed in the car crash. But then he remembered his wife and family and recalled what he was really fighting for.

'Any other news?' he asked.

'Berlin has been bombed by the RAF. Naturally, there was no damage whatsoever. Except to the British planes, of course.' He spoke in a sceptical tone.

Weiser stared at his friend. 'Careful Otto,' he murmured. 'As you said to me a few days ago, walls have ears.'

He had no sooner said this than he realised that someone was indeed close by and may well have overheard all that they had been discussing.'

'You girl,' he said, 'come here.'

The girl came over. 'You want some more glasses, Colonel? For your schnapps?'

Weiser stared at her, astonished at the trace of impudence in her tone. She did not flinch from his gaze.

'Did you hear what we were saying?' he asked.

'No, Colonel. And even if I had, I cannot understand German.'

Weiser grunted.

'You are one of Madame Pine's servants?' Mundt demanded.

'Her cook.'

'So why aren't you in the kitchen?'

'I came to call my children in from the garden. It's time for their lunch.'

Weiser felt his heart ache. He missed his family dreadfully, especially now that Christmas was near.

'How old are your children?' he asked.

'Eight and five.'

'A delightful age.'

'They're a handful. I shall make sure they keep out of the way of both of you. Is there anything else?'

Weiser did not reply but Mundt shook his head.

She turned to go.

'One thing,' Weiser said. 'What is your name?'

'Madame Viviane Renaud.'

'And where is your husband?'

'I'm not sure. He disappeared some while ago.' She paused. 'It's not the first time.'

Weiser nodded. These Frenchmen were ruled by their loins. Little more than beasts in the barnyard. He was sure of one thing. If he were this woman's husband, he would never leave her to go in search of other women.

'You may go,' he said.

'So you don't want any glasses?' Viviane said.

Weiser shook his head and she hurried off.

'A bit of a vixen,' Mundt said appreciatively.

Weiser did not answer which was answer enough of itself.

Viviane pounded the meat to soften it; pounded harder than she actually needed to.

'Something wrong?' Marie asked as she entered the kitchen.

'It's those Germans. They make my flesh creep.'

Marie shrugged. 'Some of them are pleasant enough, though. I quite like the Major.'

'Mundt?'

'Yes. He's always friendly.'

'He's got his eye on you, Marie. That's the only reason.'

Marie glanced at her reflection in the glass door in a cupboard. She had never exactly had many admirers. Only a couple of boys had been in any way serious and Mathieu, the one who she liked most, was in the Vichy army in the Indo-China. He might be dead now, for all she knew. And nowadays, she rarely gave him or any man a passing thought.

'And Colonel Weiser is very polite,' she continued, suddenly keen to change the focus of the conversation. 'I feel rather sorry for him, actually. With his broken leg.'

'I don't,' Viviane snapped. 'It's a pity it was only his leg that was broken.' She flung the meat into an oven dish. 'I just wish they'd leave.'

Marie nodded sympathetically. 'Do you think they have any idea? About David?'

'No. They're too stupid or too busy making plans to conquer the world.' She closed her eyes. How she missed Alain and his calm, good sense.

She placed the meat in the oven. One good thing about the German presence in the villa was that food was now plentiful. Most of it was eaten by the Germans themselves, of course. With the two officers and men to guard the villa, there were a dozen gaping mouths to feed. But there was enough left over for Viviane to augment Dorothy's dwindling supply.

The food for the soldiers had been cooked by her at first but Dorothy had told Weiser that this led to long delays. So an army cook had been brought over from the barracks. He was a clumsy, clueless man, who tried to monopolise the kitchen so much that Viviane complained to Dorothy.

Dorothy didn't bother to talk to Weiser about it but marched straight into the kitchen. The image of the cook cowering before her wrath was one of the few happy memories Viviane had. Now he worked in a corner of the kitchen, avoiding her as much as possible. All he seemed capable of cooking were stews.

'Do you want help with the vegetables?' Marie asked.

'If you'd like to stay and talk that would be good,' Viviane said.

The two young women had grown close over the last month and they stood together at the counter, peeling and chopping the vegetables. They worked for the most part in companionable silence. They both found there was little to talk about, less and less with each passing day. So many topics seemed not out of bounds. Talk of friends, love, the children, the war seemed too fraught with pain. Even gossip about the townspeople felt dangerous, nowadays. And talk of the future was too full of anguish to even contemplate.

The door was flung open and Dorothy walked in. She marched over to where the huge stew-pot was bubbling on the range. The German cook flinched under her gaze. She signalled to him to lift the lid and he obeyed with alacrity. Viviane and Marie watched all this with amusement.

'It smells disgusting,' she murmured.

She looked the cook in the eye. 'Your Colonel and Major have been complaining about your food,' she said. 'I've decided that you're no longer to cook for them. My cook will prepare their food. Savvy?'

The German didn't understand a word but he nodded eagerly, desperate for her to leave him alone.

She nodded and approached Viviane and Marie. 'Is that alright with you ladies?' she asked.

'If you say so,' Viviane said. 'But I'm not sure I understand why.'

'It will please them and put them in my favour,' Dorothy explained. 'Give me a little leverage over the bastards.'

'The way to a man's heart is through his stomach,' Marie said. She glanced at Dorothy and blushed a little, sorry that she had said it.

'I doubt either of them have much heart left,' Dorothy said. She sighed. 'And not because they're Germans. Because they have to fight this wretched war.'

She gave a huge sigh but then shook herself. 'What are you cooking, Viv?'

'Roast lamb and vegetables.'

'Enough for the Krauts?'

'I could add more vegetables.'

'Then do that. I'll go and tell the Colonel.'

It was the first good meal that Weiser and Mundt had eaten since leaving Dijon. Dorothy had decided that they would eat with her, to try to build a relationship. They seemed very pleased. They must crave female company, she realised.

They conversed in French, chiefly about films, which she discovered was something of a passion of Mundt's. Weiser was more interested in literature. Dorothy decided to keep the fact that she had been a scriptwriter to herself for a little longer. She always found that book-lovers were fascinated by the idea of writing for films, often because they thought it was a bastard craft rather than an art. She had the feeling that Weiser would think the same.

'Your chef is very good,' Weiser said, as he put down his knife and fork. 'Where did she train?'

'At her mother's side, I imagine. She's French. All French women cook well.'

Mundt smiled at Weiser. That was not the only reputation that French women had. Weiser studiously ignored his glance.

'She tells me that her husband has disappeared,' he said.

Dorothy grew tense. What had he heard?

'She told me it was not the first time,' he continued.

'I guess so,' Dorothy said cautiously, unsure why Viviane would have said such a thing. Perhaps she feared the Colonel would suspect Alain was in the Resistance. She nodded vigorously. 'I've heard the same, to be honest.'

'I assume he is a philanderer,' Weiser said.

'I couldn't say. More vegetables, Colonel?' She heaped some carrots on his plate.

'The children are very well behaved,' Weiser continued.

Dorothy swallowed hard. This conversation was getting too perilous. She suddenly regretted her decision to dine with them.

Weiser felt inside his tunic and passed her a photograph. 'These are my children. And their mother. My wife.'

Dorothy looked at the picture. Her fears began to ease.

'You have a lovely family, Colonel.'

'Thank you.' He bobbed his head.

'And you Major Mundt?' she asked. 'Do you have family?'

'Alas not. My fiancée was…' he paused. 'My parents did not think my fiancée was suitable.'

Weiser stared at him in surprise. He had not realised that his friend had been engaged.

'That's sad,' Dorothy said, after a few moments of silence. 'I wish my mother had thought the same about my husband.'

Mundt smiled but both of his companions could see that it was a forced one.

'I think there's dessert,' Dorothy said. 'I'll go and check.' She left the room, closing the door behind her.

'I don't want to talk about it,' Mundt said, avoiding Weiser's glance.

'I wasn't going to ask,' his friend replied. 'It's your business, not mine.'


# FOUND HER

*Villa Laurel, 8 December 1943*

Gerard got off his bicycle and propped it against the wall of Villa Laurel. It had taken painstaking work but one of Viviane's neighbours had let slip that she was friends with an Englishwoman. There were no Englishwomen in the area, of course. But he had soon found out that there was an American.

He rang on the doorbell and a maid answered. He was a little overawed by the fact of anyone having a servant but he rose to his full height and made his voice stern.

'Is your mistress in?'

'Madame Pine? She's taken the children for a walk.'

'Children?'

Marie regretted what she'd said. 'What's it to do with you anyway?' she asked suspiciously.

'I'm a member of the Milice,' he said. He could not hide the smirk on his face. 'If I ask a question, you must answer.'

Marie swallowed, hard. She did not like the idea of the Milice at all, and even less the fact that she was talking to a member of it. She felt sure she might give away something she shouldn't.

'Their mother's here,' she said. 'Perhaps you should talk to her.'

'And what is her name?'

'Viviane Renaud.'

Gerard gave a shrug as if he were barely interested in speaking to her. But his heart turned somersaults.

'Wipe your feet,' Marie said as she let him enter.

He paused as he was about to step inside, imagining that he had caught a glimpse of a man in uniform going into a room. But he shook the notion away and followed Marie into the house.

'Viviane,' Marie said, as they reached the kitchen. 'There's a visitor.'

Viviane turned and gasped in surprise. 'Gerard. What are you doing here?'

'I might ask the same about you,' he said.

He gave Marie a pointed look. She took the hint and left.

'I work here,' Viviane said. 'I'm Madame Pine's cook.'

'I didn't know you were a cook.'

'It appears I am.' She was curious about why he was here, a little suspicious even.

Gerard pointed to a chair at the table and she nodded. She went over to the oven to check that the pan of vegetables was simmering slowly and then sat down opposite him.

'You've come to ask about Alain?' she asked.

Gerard nodded.

'I don't know anything. I haven't seen him for the past six weeks.' Six weeks and three days, she thought.

Then a horrible thought came to her. 'You don't know anything, do you? He's not hurt or anything?'

Gerard was about to answer no, but then thought better of it. Her reaction showed that she really didn't know where Alain was. But he might be wise not to say anything one way or another. Keep her in the dark. Give her the feeling that he knew more than she did. It might give him some leverage over her, some power.

'Not that I've heard,' he said.

She heaved a sigh of relief. His heart pained at this. She still loved him, then.

'He's not in the town,' he said, more harshly than he intended. 'My superior, Herr Schorn, thinks he may have joined the Maquis in the mountains. Or perhaps gone over to one of the criminal gangs in Marseille or Nice.'

Viviane did not respond. 'Would you like some coffee?' she asked after a moment.

'Please. If you're having one.'

She poured two small cups of coffee. He took a sip and gave an appreciative grunt. It was the best he had tasted in years.

He felt his heart begin to pound and was not sure if it was from the coffee or the thought of what he had come here to say. He stared at her in silence for a while. He could not think how to begin.

Then he blurted it out.

'Let me take care of you.'

Viviane gave him an incredulous look. 'Take care of me? And how would you do that, Gerard?'

'You could move into my house. We could be happy. Maman would be happy.'

He was amazed at how the words came tumbling out. They had been in his brain so long they tumbled out in one wild rush. Yet at the same time his voice sounded strangled, as if the words were actually too alien to utter.

And then he said: 'We could even get married.'

Viviane looked astonished. 'But I'm already married. To your best friend.'

'But we don't know what's happened to him. He might not return, he might be dead or wounded.' He was sounding ever more desperate. 'He may even have found another woman.'

She gasped. 'How could you even –'

'I'd be a good husband to you, Viviane.' He placed his hands together as if in prayer. 'And a good father to Celeste.' He fell silent; pleading with his looks and gestures, imploring.

Viviane's hot anger now turned icy cold. 'Only Celeste? What about David?'

Gerard could not bear the look in her face and his eyes dropped to the floor. 'I know about David, Viviane. I know that he's a Jew.'

He looked back up at her. 'You should not be looking after him, Viviane. He's a danger to you and to Celeste.'

'A little boy? A danger?'

'Yes.' He gave a decisive look. 'When we're together we shall have to give him up.'

'To who? The Nazis?'

'They will take care of him —'

'Of course they will, you bastard. Like they've taken care of all the Jews, the Gypsies and poor disabled folk. Take care of him by a bullet in his back.'

He searched for a reply but could find none. His words, hitherto so powerful, appeared to have deserted him.

'I want you to leave now,' Viviane said.

Gerard looked anguished and snatched at her hand. 'You'd be safe with me, Viviane. I'm an important man in the Milice.'

'Get out of my sight,' she screamed, leaping from her chair and going to the window.

He got up but did not leave.

As if in a dream he followed her, stood behind her, and placed his hands upon her shoulders. She tensed, tried to free herself from his grasp.

'Let me go,' she cried.

'I love you Viviane,' he said. 'I always have.'

'Let me go.'

He was in despair, so close yet so far.

He reached out and took her breasts in his hands, kneading softly and moaning as he did so.

'Stop it,' she cried, 'let me go.'

She managed to wriggle free of his clutches. But he could not let her leave and backed her into a corner. He reached out to grab her once again.

Her eyes grew wild and desperate. He lunged, his hands reaching out to catch her.

She raked her nails across his face, drawing blood.

He cried out in pain and grasped her hands. She tried to push him away, kicked at his ankles but he was relentless. She kneed him in the crotch.

He doubled over and she slipped free. But he reached out as she tried to run past, grabbed her leg and pulled her down beside him. He was up in a moment and straddled her but the pain in his groin slowed him down.

She reached for a chair and slammed it against his arm. But he grabbed it from her and threw it against the table, sending the coffee mugs crashing to the floor.

He bore down upon her now but she fought him every inch of the way, pummelling on his chest, spitting on his face. It inflamed him even more and he tried to find her lips with his. Drawl from his mouth dripped on her face and she screamed more loudly.

Suddenly the weight was gone from her. Someone had pulled him off.

She sat up, gasping for breath, and saw Colonel Weiser dragging Gerard across the floor. Gerard lashed out blindly, punching him hard in the eye.

Weiser groaned but didn't let go. Then his leg gave out and he crashed to the floor. Gerard kicked him on his knee, in a frenzy, making him yell in pain and fury.

Then, suddenly, Gerard stopped himself, realising his adversary. He was assaulting a German officer. He cried out in terror and fled.

Viviane clambered to her feet and went over the Colonel who was writhing on the floor.

'Are you hurt?' both asked at the same time.

'I'm not,' Viviane said.

'Well I am.' Weiser said. 'But my pride most of all.' He gave a feeble grin.

She helped him to his feet and onto a chair. Then she burst into tears.

Major Mundt flew into the room, pistol in hand, his eyes searching everywhere for danger. Viviane watched events unfold as if in a dream. Marie ran into the room; her hand going to her mouth at the scene. Dorothy was hot on her heels, spoke to Marie then hurried over to Viviane and threw her arms around her.

Mundt was tending to the Colonel and bellowing at the top of his voice at the same time. Four soldiers ran through the door and Mundt sent two of them off to hunt for Gerard. Then he put his friend's arm around his neck and got him to his feet.

'Help me get him to his room,' he barked at one of the men. 'You, take a motorbike and fetch a doctor from the barracks,' he told the other.

Viviane collapsed into Dorothy's arms, weeping uncontrollably. Years of resentment, years of trying to keep control, years of powerless anger overwhelmed her, flooded through a shattered dam.

'I'm all alone,' she cried, 'I don't know what to do.'

'I'm putting you to bed,' Dorothy said. 'Marie, give me a hand. No, better still, you take care of the children. I left them in the garden with Pierre.'

Dorothy grabbed Viviane firmly round the waist and began to walk her towards the door. But Viviane's legs were shaking and it looked like she might not make it. Luckily, Pierre appeared, his face wide with concern. Without a word he slipped his arms under Viviane and hoisted her into the air.

'Let's get her to her room,' Dorothy said. 'The children?'

'They're with Marie,' he answered. 'She sent me in to help.'

Pierre carried Viviane up the stairs quickly but carefully and laid her on her bed. She was still weeping and was shaking as if in a fever. He stood by her side, wringing his hands with anxiety.

'Get her some cognac,' Dorothy told him. 'One for me as well. And bring some weapon, anything.'

He rushed from the room, grateful to be given a task he could easily do.

Dorothy turned to Viviane and stroked her gently on the forehead, as if she were a sick child. 'Everything is okay,' she said. 'There's no need to worry.'

But her mind raced with concern. What the hell had been going on? She'd no sooner got back from her walk with the children when Marie collared her to say that a member of the Milice was here and was talking to Viviane. Her heart had hammered at the news and she called to Pierre to take the children back into the garden. Then she heard a crash from the kitchen and raced after Marie to find out what it was.

She was desperate to ask Viviane what had happened but thought better of it. Pierre arrived a moment later with a bottle of cognac and a cudgel. He pulled two glasses from his pocket and swiftly filled them.

'Help me sit her up,' Dorothy said.

They pulled Viviane into a sitting position and Dorothy put the glass to her lips. She coughed and spluttered as she swallowed a drop and then gestured to Dorothy to stop.

'Lay her back down,' Dorothy said to Pierre.

'No,' Viviane cried, swinging her legs to the floor. 'The children —'

'They're safe with Marie.'

'That's not safe.'

Dorothy glanced at Pierre. 'Go and find the kids. Bring them back to the house. And don't leave them.'

She held Viviane's arm firmly, keeping her on the bed. 'Come on, darling,' she murmured. 'Stay here a while. Everything will be okay. Pierre and Marie will look after the children. You just rest up for a little. I won't leave you.'

Viviane was too weak to argue.

Dorothy leaned her back against the pillows and gave her another sip of cognac. 'You're not hurt?' she asked, softly.

Viviane shook her head. 'I don't think so.' Tears began to well once more. 'He tried to rape me, Dorothy. And he said that Alain might be dead.'

Dorothy squeezed her hand. 'Do you know who he is?'

Viviane nodded. 'Gerard Pithou. He's been Alain's friend since they were at school.'

Dorothy sucked in a breath. That figured, she thought. A man who'd probably always desired her and only just managed to bury it because of his friend. She'd seen in any number of times, written about it a couple, in fact. It was a can of worms and this war was opening plenty of them.

'The colonel saved me,' Viviane said. Her voice was distant, matter-of-fact.

'He's a gentleman,' Dorothy said. 'It's lucky he was here.'

Viviane looked surprised at her words for a moment but nodded in agreement.

They were silent for a little while.

Then Viviane looked up. 'Gerard knows about David,' she whispered. 'And he's in the Milice.'

Shit, Dorothy thought. Then the game's up.

But she gave a comforting smile and told Viviane not to worry about it. 'Everything will be okay, honey. Don't fret. I'll look after everything.'

Yet even as she said these words, she knew they were straws in the wind.


## AN AGREEMENT
*Villa Laurel, 8 and 9 December 1943*

Dorothy knocked on Colonel Weiser's door. She heard a muffled conversation and then Major Mundt opened it.

'The Colonel says you can come in,' he said, his voice dripping with resentment.

Weiser was sitting on his chair with his leg resting on a stool. A German medical officer had just finished examining him and was packing up his case.

'Nothing broken,' Weiser told her, 'although my knee's pretty knocked about.'

He took a deep breath, fighting the pain. 'How's the girl?'

'She's pretty done in,' Dorothy said. 'I've put her to bed. She's in shock.'

'Do you want my doctor to see her?'

Dorothy blinked in surprise. 'Can he give her anything?'

'Something to calm her,' the doctor said. 'A sleeping draught, perhaps.'

'Okay.' She stared at the man and then turned back to Weiser. 'But I'm going with him.'

'Of course. But please come back here afterwards.'

She returned a little later. She had been surprised at the gentle, caring way the doctor examined Viviane. His manner was almost as calming as the drink he gave to her.

'That was kind of you,' she said as they walked down the stairs.

'I was a junior doctor when the war started,' he said. 'I go back to my hospital when it's over.' He gave a huge sigh and headed out of the house.

She knocked on Weiser's door again and this time walked in without waiting. Mundt looked as though he was about to remonstrate but kept his mouth shut.

'Who was the man who attacked her?' Weiser asked.

'A friend of Viviane's,' she answered. She had decided it would be best if she spoke as truthfully as she could safely do.

Weiser glanced from Mundt to Dorothy, perplexed. 'So why did he attack her?'

'It's obvious,' Mundt said. 'He's probably always lusted after her for years and now he thought he saw the chance to satisfy his desires. I presume her husband is no longer around?'

Dorothy looked at him in surprise. 'You should come to Hollywood after the war, Major. Help me write some scripts. You're a real student of mankind.'

Weiser laughed. 'A student of womankind, more precisely,' he said.

She stared at him a moment, saw him now as a man and not an enemy. Then she glanced at Mundt who looked almost sheepish, gave a little shrug and smiled at her.

She took a deep breath. This was certainly turning into one strange day.

'I know about the little boy,' Weiser said.

Dorothy's mouth fell open.

'How?' She cursed herself for saying this but there was no way of going back now.

'I saw him in tears a few days ago,' he explained. 'He was asking for his mother. The little girl consoled him by saying their mother would be with him shortly. He said he didn't want her; he wanted his real mother.'

He glanced at Dorothy to catch any hint that he had been correct. She had grown poker-faced, which suggested he was right.

'I'm guessing the boy is a Jew,' he said, quietly.

Dorothy swallowed hard. Out of the corner of her eye she saw that Mundt looked as startled as she felt.

'Don't worry,' Weiser said. 'The secret is safe with us.'

'Absolutely,' said Mundt with surprising vehemence.

'What about the Frenchman?' Weiser said. 'Does he know about the boy? Is there anything we need to know about him?'

Dorothy licked her lips. They were as dry as sand.

'He's in the Milice.'

'Damn,' cried Mundt. 'Then the Gestapo will know.' He gnawed on a finger-nail.

Weiser leaned back in the chair. He was silent for a good while, running over the problem in his mind. 'Madame Pine, who else knows the boy is a Jew?' he asked.

'My maid, Marie,' she answered. 'And my handyman, Pierre. We decided to tell them to ensure they kept David away from...' She paused. 'Well from you and your men, to be honest.'

'It's the Gestapo we must keep him from,' Mundt said.

Weiser nodded. He drummed his fingers on the table beside him. 'The young woman must stay here, with the children,' he said finally. 'Under our protection.'

Mundt nodded and appeared to relax.

'Can you protect them from the Gestapo?' Dorothy asked.

Weiser stared at her. 'Let's pray to God I can.'

Dorothy made for the door but paused on the threshold. 'One thing more, gentlemen,' she said. 'Please don't tell Viviane that you know about the boy. It would worry her too much.'

The sleeping draught was very effective, Viviane slept the rest of the day. Dorothy spent the time in a very different state. She had been surprised by the reactions of the two German officers, pleasantly surprised. But they were still Germans and she wondered how much she could trust them.

It was the avowed policy of the Nazi government to deal with what they saw as the Jewish problem and she had heard alarming rumours of how they were going about it. The work-camps people were being shipped to were places of misery, it was said. There was little shelter from the elements, little food and no medicines. The adults were worked until they dropped, sometimes until they died.

If she had heard this, then the Germans surely must have as well. How much could she trust men who might know such things yet still support Hitler?

And yet the Colonel had fought to protect Viviane, even to the extent of being injured. And neither he nor his friend liked the Gestapo, it was clear.

Her mind returned to the reaction of Major Mundt once again. He appeared even more determined to protect the boy than the Colonel was. She was surprised by this for Mundt had hitherto seemed colder and more antagonistic than his superior. There's a story there, she thought. She smiled to herself. She would wheedle it out of him. It would be a challenge she'd enjoy.

Coping with Viviane would be an even greater challenge. The fact that Pithou knew about David would trouble her greatly and she'd soon come to realise that her rejection of him would only make things worse. And he had displayed a viciousness which boded no good at all.

Viviane would be terrified of the Gestapo coming to arrest them. Terrified of all Germans, in fact. It was this that made her change her mind about what she would tell her.

She had a troubled night and rose just before dawn to make herself a cup of coffee. She took it in to Viviane's room and watched her as she slept. She looked peaceful, young and innocent. She never looked like this when she was awake. An anxious watchfulness shadowed her now, especially since Alain had left.

She pondered anew the decision she had come to. The last thing she had asked of Weiser was not to tell Viviane that he guessed correctly about David. Now she had determined to do the opposite, to tell her the truth. It would alarm her at first, no doubt, but then she would come to see that it afforded the only hope she had. A slim hope, at that, she thought, although she would never admit this to her friend.

Viviane turned over on her back and opened her eyes. She smiled at Dorothy and then immediately a frantic look came over her face.

She sat up in bed and clutched Dorothy by the arm.

'Why are you here?' she demanded. 'What's happened? Where are the children?'

'They're sleeping soundly,' Dorothy said. 'Marie slept on the chair in their room.'

'Because they're in danger?

Dorothy shook her head. 'Because you were too sedated to wake if one of them called for you.'

Viviane relaxed a tiny bit. 'You're not lying?' she asked. 'You're telling me the truth?'

'Of course.'

Dorothy felt queasy at her words, knowing what she had planned to tell her later that day. But then she thought, maybe this is the best opportunity and she should seize it.

She took Viviane's hand. 'There's something else I need to tell you, honey.'

Viviane stared at her wide-eyed. 'Alain?' she whispered.

'No. It's about David.' She took a deep breath. 'Colonel Weiser has guessed that he's not your son. He overheard Celeste and David talking and it made him put two and two together.'

Viviane's hand went to her mouth. Dorothy's eyes filled with tears but she knew that she could not stop now. She had to press on.

'And he's guessed that David's a Jew.'

'What?'

Dorothy placed her hand on Viviane's knee. 'The Colonel's not a fool. He reasoned that it was the most likely reason you'd take David in.'

'But he could be the son of a relative. Or a friend. Which he is.'

Dorothy forced herself to speak more forcefully. 'David's mother wasn't your friend, Viviane. And even if that were the case, then the boy would have been taken in by an orphanage. Weiser knows that. You don't become a colonel if you're an idiot.'

'Will he betray us?'

'He's vowed not to. He hates the Gestapo, it seems.'

She gazed at Viviane. And maybe he likes you rather more, she thought.

'What about the other one, his friend? He's a much nastier man.'

'So I thought,' Dorothy answered. 'But when Weiser said that he knew about David the Major grew very fierce. Surprisingly so. I'd put money on it that he'll never give you away. Never, ever.'

'But he's a German.'

'But not necessarily a Nazi. Neither of them are, I guess.' She could not help her mind from wandering back to Mundt's angry, determined reaction. What was it about that?

'But Gerard…' Viviane began.

'Hush now, sweetheart. Gerard will be too ashamed to do anything about it. And besides, when he's calmed down, he'll probably feel contrite and ashamed. He won't do anything to hurt you.'

At the precise moment she said these words, Gerard was walking into Gestapo Headquarters.


### BETRAYAL
*Grasse, 9 December 1943*

Kriminaldirektor Schorn sat back in his chair and studied his visitor.

'You seem agitated, Pithou,' he said, at last. 'Please, sit.'

Gerard slumped into a chair and, without realising he was doing it, patted his pockets.

'You want a cigarette?' Schorn asked. He pushed a pack across the desk.

'Lucky Strike,' he said. 'American cigarettes. Do you know that the GI's get nine cigarettes in their rations? Our soldiers get six at most, and they're usually foul weeds taken from Russian corpses. These were confiscated from Red Cross packs for American airmen.'

Gerard took a cigarette, lit it and went to pass the pack back across the desk.

'Keep it, my friend,' Schorn said. 'It looks like you're in need of it.'

He waited until Gerard had taken two long puffs and then leaned forward in his chair.

'Now, Gerard, my friend. Tell me what is troubling you?'

'I'm not troubled,' Gerard said, quickly.

Schorn shrugged. 'My mistake, forgive me. But you have news?'

'I found a Jewish boy yesterday.'

For a moment, Schorn looked surprised. Then he gave a slow hand-clap. 'Bravo, Gerard. I shall telephone the Führer and give him the news. The end of the war is now that much closer.'

Gerard flushed a deep crimson.

Schorn chuckled to see his discomfort. He took out another packet of Lucky Strike, lit one, and took a long drag on it.

'The child has been taken in by a French woman,' Gerard said. 'Her husband has fled because he's a Gypsy. I believe he is with the Maquis or maybe criminal elements in Marseille.'

'And why is this so important that you bother me with it?' Schorn said, his voice with a trace of contempt. 'Tell Kriminalinspektor Buchner. He will deal with it.'

Gerard did not answer, only looked even more uncomfortable.

'I see,' Schorn said at last. 'This is some personal grudge. You do not like this woman.'

He paused and an amused look came to his face. 'Or perhaps you like her too much. Don't worry, my friend, I understand this.'

He stubbed out his cigarette, for the conversation now promised much greater pleasure than even a Lucky Strike. 'You want me to arrange to deal with the child?'

Gerard gave a slow nod.

'And then you want more?'

Again Gerard nodded. 'I want her, sir. I want her to be given up to me.'

'Of course you do. But you realise that she will not welcome your advances.'

Gerard recalled how she had reacted at the Villa.

'I do. That does not matter.'

'I suppose you relish it, in fact. Enjoy the thought of making her accept your advances.'

Gerard gave the briefest of nods.

Schorn chuckled. 'Then you will require some equipment, no doubt. Handcuffs, a gag, a riding crop, a whip?'

Gerard did not answer although the tip of his tongue licked his lips.

'Consider it done,' Schorn said. 'Now, where can we found this woman of your dreams?'

'She's at a villa a few kilometres north of the town. It's called Villa Laurel and is owned by some American bitch.'

'An American? And she's still in France?'

Gerard nodded.

'Excellent. Two birds with one stone. You shall have your paramour and I shall have the American. I am fond of all things American.'

'She's an older woman.'

Schorn shrugged. 'I only want to interrogate her. Unless she's a comely matron, of course.'

'And the boy?' Gerard said. 'The Jewish boy?'

Schorn sighed. 'I can't lay on transport to the camps for just one boy. He'll have to be dealt with here. Buchner will be happy to do it. It only takes a bullet.'

'Could the woman watch?'

Schorn's eyebrow rose to his hair-line. 'Watch the little boy being executed? My, but you have been wounded.' He gave a fulsome smile. 'Yes, if that's what you wish. Now, tell me where is this Villa Laurel?'

The Gestapo car gunned up the narrow road and screeched into the driveway of Villa Laurel. Showers of pebbles cascaded from its wheels as the driver revved the car up even faster. Schorn liked this driver because he knew how to drive in the most appropriately dramatic manner.

The car skidded to a halt outside the entrance. Schorn scrutinised the villa carefully. Envy licked at his soul.

'She must be a very rich bitch,' he murmured. 'Do you know how she came by this wealth, Pithou?'

Gerard shrugged. 'Some people say she's a film star from Hollywood but I don't know if that's true.'

Schorn's interest was piqued even more. Officially, the Nazi Government condemned decadent American films but that rarely stopped aficionados such as he from watching them. The image of Greta Garbo came to his mind, swiftly followed by Mae West, and he wondered who the owner of the Villa would look like most.

The driver leapt out of the car and opened the door for Schorn who headed straight for the villa. Gerard joined him at the front door. He was torn. Part of him wanted to scurry away from the place but part of him was excited at returning in such powerful company.

Schorn glanced at him. 'Aren't you going to ring the bell?'

Gerard hurried to do his bidding. He listened to the ringing of the bell sounding in the hall, imagined what effect it might have on the listeners.

The door opened and Marie peered out.

'You —' she hissed at Gerard.

Schorn pushed open the door, almost knocking her to the floor in the process.

'Where is your mistress?' he demanded.

'I'm here,' came a voice from the morning room. Dorothy stepped out and confronted Schorn. 'Who are you?'

Schorn scrutinised her from top to toe. His lip curled. 'I was told you were a Hollywood star. A character actress, perhaps?'

'Who the hell are you?'

Schorn gave a little bow. 'I am Kriminaldirektor Heinrich Schorn. The chief of the Gestapo for the area.'

'I see.' Dorothy made her voice friendlier. 'How can I help you, Herr Schorn?'

Schorn took off his gloves and slapped them against his palm in an impatient rhythm. 'You have a woman here.' He paused, realising he did not know her name, and glanced at Gerard.

'Viviane Renaud,' he mumbled.

Schorn nodded. 'As my friend said. And Mademoiselle Renaud has two children with her. One of them a member of a proscribed community. A Jew.'

'Viviane is here,' Dorothy said. 'But the boy is not a Jew. We have the papers to prove it.'

Schorn scoffed. 'Papers. French papers aren't worth the paper they are written on.' He smiled at his own joke. He had been waiting a long time to say it. He turned to Gerard who forced a laugh.

'Send this woman to me,' Schorn said, pushing past Dorothy into the sitting room. 'With the children and the papers.'

Dorothy swallowed hard. She wondered if she could alert Viviane and give her the chance to make a run for it. But she dismissed the thought as soon as it came to her. Fleeing with the children would be impossible and, even if they got away, they would not escape their hunters for long.

'Bring them here, Marie,' she said quietly. 'And then go to the kitchen and prepare some lunch for the Kriminaldirektor.'

Marie looked astonished at the notion but hurried off to do it.

'You'll have a drink, Herr Schorn?' Dorothy said. 'I'm afraid I don't have any schnapps.'

'I can't abide the stuff. Do you have any Bourbon?'

Dorothy gave a look of surprise. 'Not many Germans appreciate American drinks.'

'I appreciate all things American, Frau Pine.'

He watched her appreciatively as she went to the drinks cupboard to find some Bourbon. She was more Mae West than Greta Garbo but, despite his earlier jibe about her being a character actress, handsome enough. In his experience, older women were often more satisfying than younger ones.

'You were an actress, I'm told.'

She handed him a large glass of Bourbon. 'You were told wrong, Herr Schorn. I was a script-writer.'

Schorn looked impressed. 'You must know many actors and directors. Authors, perhaps? Dashiell Hammett? I greatly admire his books.'

'Never met Hammett. He's kind of a private guy. I worked a little with James Cain, though.'

'The writer of The Postman Always Rings Twice?'

Dorothy nodded.

Schorn raised his glass in salute and took a sip. 'You appear to have kept good company in the past, Frau Pine.'

The door opened and Viviane walked in with the children.

Schorn got to his feet. 'Mademoiselle Renaud, I presume.'

Viviane's eyes flicked to Gerard and then back to Schorn. 'Madame Renaud,' she said. 'I'm a married woman.'

'Of course. And these are your delightful children?'

Viviane clutched hold of their hands tightly. 'Yes. Celeste and David.'

'The little boy is very dark.'

For a moment Viviane almost said that her husband was as well but she checked herself in time. 'He's not my natural child. He's the son of a good friend who was killed in a bombing raid by the British.'

Schorn gave a sympathetic look. 'What terrible cruelties the British inflict on you French. The poor boy.' He came over and rubbed his hand across David's hair. 'Very dark. Almost oriental.'

'I think his father's family may have come from Corsica. It's the Italian influence.'

'Our erstwhile allies,' Schorn said with a sigh.

He held out his hand. 'Your papers please. The children's as well as yours.'

Viviane fumbled in her bag. The room was chill but sweat appeared on her brow. She prayed that Schorn would not notice.

'Are you unwell, Madame Renaud?' he asked. 'Have you a temperature?'

'I've been busy in the kitchen,' she replied. She held out the papers. 'Here they are.'

Schorn took the papers and examined hers carefully before handing it back to her. He looked at Celeste's, grunted and returned it as well.

Then he glanced at David's, rather more casually.

'All in order,' he said, and made to hand it back.

Viviane gave a sigh of relief and closed her fingers on it. But she was too late. Schorn had snatched it away.

A frown appeared on his face. He looked at the document again, turned to the light from the window and scrutinised it with painstaking care.

'There is some irregularity here, Madame,' he said at last.

A lump blocked her throat. 'What do you mean?' she blurted out, finally.

'Alas, I'm not at liberty to tell you,' he answered. 'But I can tell you that there is a serious irregularity. A very disturbing one.'

'Nonsense,' Dorothy said. 'His papers have been checked by the police.'

'By Captain Boyer, perhaps?' Schorn said. 'The buffoon?'

He folded up David's papers and put them in his pocket.

Then he stared at Viviane for a long time. When he spoke again his voice had lost all trace of friendliness. It was hard, official, naked with power.

'I believe that the boy is a Jew. I shall have to take you into custody, Madame Renaud.' He looked stern, almost angry. 'It is clear that you are an unfit custodian of children. I shall arrange to have both of them taken to some place of safety.'

'No,' screamed Viviane.

'But you said you'd only take the boy,' Gerard said. 'Only the Jew.'

'Tut tut,' Schorn said. He suddenly grew tired of the charade. 'I haven't time for such distinctions. One bullet or two makes very little difference to the Reich. And without their distraction your girlfriend will have more time to attend to your needs.'


## JURISDICTION
### 9 December 1943

Viviane leapt at Gerard, snarling in fury. He just managed to fend her off.

The door opened and Major Mundt entered the room.

'What's going on?' he demanded.

Schorn gave him a disdainful glance. 'It is none of your business, Major. Please leave.'

'I shall it make it my business, Herr Schorn. Why are you here? What are you doing with this woman and her children?'

'Doing my duty.' He pointed at David who was clinging on to Viviane's skirt. 'If you must know, this creature is a Jew. He is to be taken into custody. As will the woman and her daughter.'

'I think Oberst Weiser will have something to say about this,' Mundt said. He poked his head out of the room and called out. 'Marie, fetch the colonel.'

Marie returned a moment later with Weiser. Curiosity overcame her fear and she slipped into the room.

'What is the meaning of this?' Weiser demanded.

Schorn sighed and shook his head. 'I have already told your Major. This boy is a Jew and the woman has been hiding him, illegally. She will be taken into custody.'

He glanced at Gerard. 'Not by the Gestapo but by the French Milice.'

Gerard's eyes flared and he took a step towards Viviane.

'And the children will be taken into a place of safety,' Schorn continued.

'Not the girl,' Marie said. 'We can take care of her, can't we Madame Pine?'

Before anyone could answer, Schorn waved his hand dismissively.

'Very well. But the boy, the Jew boy, he comes with me.'

Weiser limped over to Schorn and stood inches from him.

'Surely you can't think that one little boy poses a threat to the Third Reich?' His voice was little more than a murmur.

'The idea of him does,' Schorn said. 'And those who try to protect such scum pose an equally great threat. No matter what their rank or station.'

Weiser smiled. It was bleak and unforgiving. 'Do you seek to threaten me, Herr Schorn?'

'If you feel threatened by my legal actions that is your concern, not mine.'

'Oh I don't feel threatened by you, Herr Schorn. I fought at Minsk and at Stalingrad. Nothing on earth can threaten or frighten me.'

Schorn glared at him. 'I have legal authority in the town and the area.'

'But not here,' Mundt said. 'This is a military base.'

'Don't be preposterous,' Schorn cried. 'The child comes with me. And if you argue I shall take the whole family.' He stared at Dorothy. 'And all who have collaborated with them.'

'The boy stays here,' Weiser said. 'And so does everyone else.' He turned to Viviane. 'Madame Renaud, you and the children may leave us now.'

'You have no authority to do this,' Schorn said. 'I have jurisdiction here.'

Weiser frowned. 'Now where have I heard that phrase before? "I have jurisdiction here." Where did we hear that Mundt?'

'In Rostov. From a communist commissar ordering us to leave.'

Weiser clicked his fingers. 'Of course it was. Remind me, Mundt, what happened to the commissar?'

'I shot him.'

Weiser nodded and turned to Schorn. 'You were saying, Herr Schorn?'

Schorn did not reply.

Weiser bowed towards Viviane. 'I trust you are completely recovered, Madame Renaud?' he said.

'I am, Colonel, thank you.'

He smiled, turned his back on Schorn and limped out of the room.

'Madame Pine,' Mundt said. 'Perhaps you could send for Sergeant Ferber to escort the Kriminaldirektor to his car.'

Schorn glared at him and strode out with Gerard hurrying in his wake.


Viviane spent the rest of the day in a daze. Marie looked after the children while Dorothy sat Viviane in a chair in the kitchen and prepared lunch.

'I didn't think you could cook,' Viviane said, after a while.

'I can't. But I'll make a better fist of it than you will after your shock.'

Viviane closed her eyes. Her anger and fear had dissipated completely, replaced by an emptiness which seemed to crawl crab-like from her heart towards her flesh. She thought she would soon become hollow, a thing dead on the inside.

'Why did he do it?' she asked at last.

'Who? The Colonel?'

'Yes.'

Dorothy tossed a badly peeled carrot into the pot and came to sit beside her.

'I don't know, honey. I guess he's old school and doesn't care for the Gestapo. Maybe he doesn't even care for the Nazis.'

'I thought all Germans are the same.'

'Are all French people the same? We Americans certainly aren't. There's good and bad in every nation.'

She took Viviane's hand in hers and was surprised how chill it was. 'Do you want some fresh coffee?'

Viviane shook her head. The cup beside her was untouched. She turned eyes devoid of life to her friend. 'What will happen, Dorothy? Will the Gestapo come back for us?'

Dorothy shook her head decisively. 'Not while Colonel Weiser and Major Mundt are here.'

'But the Gestapo man said that he had jurisdiction over us all.'

'I think that the jurisdiction of a squad of armed soldiers will prove more powerful.' She peered at Dorothy. 'Are you sure you shouldn't go to bed? Maybe take more of that sleeping draught?'

Viviane shook her head violently. She had to stay awake.

Dorothy leaned back in her chair and watched her quietly. After a while she got up and made her way back to the oven.

'Lunch won't get fixed by itself,' she said. Then she groaned, loudly. 'Wow, this is going to take some digesting.' She glanced back at Viviane. 'Hey hon, you couldn't give me a hand could you?'

Viviane started out of her stupor and walked over to her. She peered into the pan bubbling on the hot plate. It resembled a sink of grubby dishes.

'Shall we start again?' Viviane asked.

'That's my girl,' Dorothy said, pleased that her ruse had worked.

Viviane poured the liquid down the sink and retrieved the vegetables with a spoon. 'I'll peel the carrots again,' she said. 'And the potatoes and turnips.'

'Whoops,' Dorothy said, 'I think I forgot to peel the turnips.'

'And you left half the field on them.' A little smile came to her lips.

I may not be a cook, Dorothy thought, but I can still work magic.


## CHRISTMAS GIFTS
### *Villa Laurel, 24 December 1943*

Pierre Sorel put the final decoration on the Christmas Tree. He never understood the point of it but Dorothy was adamant that they have a tree and would always choose which one for him to dig up and pot. This year a small fig tree stood proudly in the sitting room.

'That's not right,' Dorothy said. 'Put it on that branch, to your left.'

'If Madame would like to do the job herself —'

'Madame would not. What's the point of employing a handy-man if he refuses to be handy?'

Pierre pretended to grumble but put the final bauble on the tree.

'The kids will love it,' Dorothy said.

Pierre stretched and gave her a pointed look. 'Do you think the children are alright?'

'They don't know anything: the Gestapo, the threats. And they never will.'

'But the boy is a Jew?'

'He is. Does that bother you?'

Pierre considered it for a moment. 'It might have done five years ago,' he said, at last. 'Nobody in France liked the Jews then. We blamed them for the hard times, the unemployment, the Depression. But I grew to like Leopold Blum after he became Prime Minister. Just think, a Jew as Prime Minster of France. He looked after ordinary people. And now...'

He fell silent. Dorothy stared at him with curiosity.

'Now, look what's happening to them,' he continued. 'They have their possessions stolen, they are dragged away to camps, they are murdered in the streets. It's not right. Not right at all. And the poor little lad. He's a good boy.'

She went to the sideboard and poured two glasses of wine.

'I have no liking for the Bosch,' he said. 'But I'm glad that the Colonel and Major are here. I dread what will happen when they leave.'

Dorothy gave him a glass. 'Me too, Pierre. I've been racking my brains about how to prevent it. But Colonel Weiser's leg will be better anytime soon and then he'll return to barracks.'

'And afterwards, the Gestapo will come back for the family.'

Dorothy pursed her lips. She didn't want to think about it.

'The tree looks good,' she said, determined to cheer herself up.

'I've made some gifts for them,' Pierre said. 'A little horse for David and a doll for Celeste.'

'That's very sweet of you. Now I'm gonna see what's cooking. Get the car will you please?'

Dorothy had cajoled Lucile to come over to help Vivian with the preparations for dinner and the kitchen smelled wonderful.

'Wow, ladies,' Dorothy said, 'this looks fantastic.'

'I shall have to go very soon,' Lucile said. 'I have to prepare supper for Maman.'

'I know. And I'm very grateful.' She went to the sideboard and retrieved two parcels. 'Gifts for you and your Maman. Toilet water and some very nice soap.'

'You shouldn't have done, Madame. I have no gift for you.'

Dorothy snorted. 'You don't call this dinner a gift? It's a magnificent one.'

'It is,' Viviane said. 'I couldn't have made anything as lovely.'

'Now get on home,' Dorothy said. 'Pierre's got the car at the front, he'll take you.'

'You're so kind, Madame,' Lucile said, so grateful she gave a little curtsy.

Dorothy gazed at the food on the sideboard. The meal had cost her an absolute fortune on the black-market. There were oysters, three for every adult and thin sheets of smoked salmon. Pierre had shot a brace of pheasants and they were resting in a cool part of the oven. Boulangère potatoes were simmering and some green beans were waiting for a quick reheat.

Major Mundt had provided a hearty German sausage and a smoked cheese, both of which Lucile pronounced inedible but Dorothy had insisted be served. There was also a small Bûche de Noël.

'Marie,' Dorothy said, 'go and ask the Colonel and Major to join us in the sitting room for drinks. And fetch the children. You come as well.'

She glanced round the kitchen. 'Is everything in order here?'

Viviane nodded. 'Lucile is a wonder. She's given me instructions on what to do. The potatoes will take forty five minutes and the pheasant will keep hot until we're ready.'

'Come on then, apron off, you've got to look your best.'

Viviane was surprised that she said this and for a brief, desperate moment, she wondered if Alain had arrived. But she dismissed the thought immediately. No good would come of hope.

'I need to get the children's presents,' Viviane said, 'and put on something more presentable. I'll be back down in a minute.'

Dorothy glanced at the food once again. Yes, it was a lovely meal, considering the circumstances. But she couldn't help but contrast it with the festivities in Beverly Hills. She took a deep breath and headed back to the sitting room.

The room looked lovely. A warm fire flickered in the grate, holly and laurel festooned the mantle-piece and the tree was decorated with baubles and trinkets. The side-board was laden with drinks.

Marie came in with the two children who gasped in astonishment. David ran to the tree and stared at it with wonder.

The two German officers entered, dressed in their best uniforms. Mundt clicked his heels together.

'Alas I cannot do the same,' Colonel Weiser said pointing at his leg and giving a wry grin.

Viviane arrived, having changed into her best frock and tidied her hair.

'Maman, look at the tree,' David called, running up to it and staring, wide-eyed.

Mundt glanced at Dorothy, Viviane and Marie and bowed. 'The Lord may have been visited by three Kings but we are blessed with three beautiful ladies.'

Marie giggled with delight and the others exchanged smiles.

'A drink, Colonel?' Dorothy asked. 'We have some spumante left by your Italian predecessor.'

'That is very kind, Madame Pine,' Weiser said. 'But Major Mundt has brought some champagne.'

'Krug,' Mundt said. 'The best of both worlds. A German name and a French flavour.'

'Talking of names,' Dorothy said, 'we should knock all this formality on the head. I'm Dorothy.'

Mundt glanced at Weiser who gave a nod.

'Then I am Otto,' he said. 'And the Colonel is called Ernst.'

Weiser turned to Viviane who found herself blushing at his look.

'I'm Viviane,' she said. 'And this is Marie. You know the children.'

'We do indeed,' Weiser said. 'It is a joy to share this day with you all.'

There was an embarrassed silence, broken only by the arrival of Pierre.

Mundt opened the champagne with a pop which made the children squeal with delight. Weiser gave a toast to Dorothy. 'And may next year bring peace,' he added, his voice tight with emotion.

Major Mundt cleared his throat. 'Now is the time for gifts,' he said.

'We have no gifts,' Dorothy said. 'Other than the fine food and wine we're about to share.'

'For the children,' Mundt explained. 'It is the German way.'

'And the French way, too,' Pierre said quickly. 'I also have gifts for the children.'

Celeste took hold of his hand, her face shining with anticipation.

He reached behind the tree and retrieved two packages wrapped in brown paper. The children fell on them.

'Children,' Viviane said, 'thank Monsieur Sorel for your gifts.'

'Thank you, Pierre,' both of them said, tearing the wrapping paper off.

'A dolly,' Celeste cried, hugging it to her chest.

'A horse,' David said in wonder, holding it up for Viviane to examine.

'And you have something, gentlemen?' Dorothy asked.

Weiser gave a parcel to David. He shouted with pleasure and began to tear at it.

His gift was a little toy drum, with two yellow drumsticks. He began to beat it immediately.

'We may all come to hate you for giving him this,' Dorothy said with a smile.

'And for Celeste,' Weiser said.

Celeste gave him a nervous glance and began to open it. She gasped with astonishment. It was a pair of red shoes.

'How did you know?' Viviane asked.

'Marie said that she yearned for red shoes,' Mundt said. 'I found these.'

'Thank you,' Viviane said.

Celeste immediately put on the shoes and skipped up and down the room.

'Have you got us anything, Maman?' David asked.

Viviane smiled and gave them their gifts, a book about fairies which she had been given when she was a child. It was a little dog-eared but was precious. For David she had a toy fire engine which had once belonged to Alain. He gasped in astonishment and promptly sat on the floor to examine it.

The adults watched them play while they sipped their champagne.

'One last gift,' Weiser said. He produced a little box from his pocket and gave it to Viviane.

She looked bewildered but he gestured her to open it. 'You have been greatly troubled,' he said. 'It is the least I could do.'

She opened the box and blinked in amazement.

'It was my mother's ring,' he said. 'One she wore for the theatre.'

Viviane stared at the ring. It was beautiful, lovelier than anything she owned. She ran her little finger along it, feeling its smoothness. Then she held it out to Weiser.

'I can't accept this.'

'But you must. I fear that with the perils of war I may come to mislay it.'

'But it should go to your wife.'

He shook his head. 'My mother and wife hated each other with the utmost passion. Mother would erupt from her grave to curse me if I were to give it to Hilda.'

Viviane stared at him, wondered at the look in his eyes. There was sadness there but something else. Something too elusive for her to capture.

'It's lovely,' Dorothy said, firmly. 'Thank the Colonel, Viviane.'

Viviane stared at her in surprise.

'It would be ungracious to refuse such a lovely gift.' She gave Viviane a determined look.

'Thank you, Colonel,' Viviane murmured at last. 'I think it's beautiful.'

She put the ring on her right hand. The room fell silent around them. Viviane held her hand up to the light. It looked lovely on her.

Weiser and Mundt exchanged glances. Neither wanted to make the obvious comment. In Germany people wore their wedding rings on the right hand.

And then David began to beat a rhythm on his drum.

'That seems an appropriate signal for dinner,' Dorothy said. 'Take your places, everyone.'

Marie and Viviane hurried out to bring the food. At the door to the kitchen, Marie took her hand. 'They're nice men,' she said. 'Honestly.'

Viviane did not reply. She had her doubts about that.

## WEISER'S THOUGHTS
*Villa Laurel, 5 January 1944*

The first week of January was miserable, with grey skies, a searching wind and persistent drizzle. The children were forced to spend much of the time inside but Pierre found them an old jig-saw puzzle in the store and they became engrossed in this.

Viviane awoke each morning and would drowsily reach out for Alain before remembering that he would not be there. Her heart clenched at the realisation.

Her next thoughts were always about the Gestapo officer and the threat which she believed he still presented. She felt sure that he would return for them as soon as Colonel Weiser left. She concocted plans of fleeing the villa, going to ground somewhere secret and secure. But she knew that this was futile. There was nowhere to run to, nowhere to hide. She would be better off staying here with Dorothy and, if the worst come to the worst, hope that her brother-in-law would be able to protect them.

But she wondered if Roland would show any loyalty or compassion for her. He had always been pleasant enough but distant. And Odette's influence would surely make him wary of helping her.

She glanced out of the window in the direction of the town. There were so few people she could trust now.

The image of Gerard slid into her mind and she shuddered. She wondered if she had ever actually liked him. Wondered if she had ever noticed that he lusted after her. Wondered, to her shame, if she had ever done anything to encourage him.

Her mind replayed their dealings over the years. She could honestly think of nothing she had done which might have given him the wrong message. And besides, even if she had been flirtatious, that was no reason for him to attack her. Not even reason enough for him to make demands upon her.

She rubbed a hand across her eyes and got out of bed. The water in the ewer was icy cold but she poured some into a basin and sprinkled some dried lavender into it, breathing in the scent which rose wraith-like from its surface. She dipped a hand-cloth into the water and gingerly rubbed it over her face, her neck and arms. Then she slipped out of her night-dress and washed herself more thoroughly. She shivered as she dried herself and wondered what the day might bring.

She went into the kitchen and was surprised to find Dorothy sitting by the stove.

'You're up early,' she said. Dorothy was normally a late riser.

'I was freezing cold so I came to warm up,' she said. She held her hands out to the warm air wafting from the oven. 'It's a beautiful day outside but it feels really cold. I miss California on mornings like this.'

'I'll make some coffee,' Viviane said. 'Has Marie brought the bread?'

Dorothy pointed to the baguette upon the table. It was, for a change, fresh this morning.

The children drifted into the kitchen and soon they were all tucking into breakfast. They halved the baguette, saving the rest for later. Dorothy still had enough cash to buy in the black-market but bread was not always available.

The children were growing fractious and Marie suggested taking them into the garden.

'Make sure they have their coats,' Dorothy said.

Viviane tidied up the kitchen and glanced outside. It was a beautiful day and she realised she had not left the house in over a week. She made up her mind and grabbed a coat. For a moment she wondered whether to follow Marie and the children. But she thought they deserved a bit of space without her glooming over them so instead she headed to the far side of the garden, where a grove of magnolias and fig trees grew.

It was very cold but she welcomed this. The wind seemed to blow the webs of doubt and despair from her mind. I should do this more often, she thought.

There were dozens of magnolia trees, many of them already beginning to bloom. Little clumps of primroses were showing, crocuses were peeping through the soil and there were a few stands of snow-drops dotted around. Half a dozen mimosa bushes were already bright with yellow blossom.

Then she saw a movement behind the bushes. Her heart hammered in terror. It must be the Gestapo, she thought. Who else would be in the gardens at so early an hour? They had come to spy on her, or worse.

She stepped slowly towards the figure, trying her best to keep silent. She had to see if it was the Gestapo, risky though it was.

Then she stopped and sighed. It was the colonel. Her heart began to quieten.

He was sitting on a tree stump, gazing at the mountains to the north. He was clutching a book although it was not open.

She made to move away, wishing not to disturb him, but she stepped on a twig and he spun around at the noise. He struggled to his feet the moment he saw her.

'Please, Colonel,' she said. 'There is no need for you to get up. I didn't mean to disturb you.'

'You did not disturb me, Madame Renaud. I was in a dream but not a very engrossing one.' He paused a moment, his mind working. 'Please join me. Reality is so much better than dreams.'

She meant to refuse him but thought it impolite and risky to do so. She came over and gave him a little curtsy. He chuckled at it and shook his head slightly.

'You are on your own?' he asked.

'Yes. I wanted some fresh air after being cooped up in the house.'

'Me too. And I wanted some peace.'

Silence dropped between them.

'You like the mountains?' she said, after a while.

'Very much. I was brought up in Leipzig and I liked to hike in the mountains to the south. Would you care to walk, Madame? It's still quite chilly.'

She meant to refuse but thought it would look impolite. He picked up his walking stick and led the way towards the more level ground further from the house.

'What are you reading?' she asked.

'This? It is called Melancholie, by Ernst Keil. He was one of my ancestors. But he is better known for the magazine which he owned, Die Gartenlaube. Have you heard of it? For many years it was the most popular magazine in the world.'

She shook her head.

'It means Gazebo in French,' he continued. His voice sounded proud. 'The title was, let us say, camouflage. He intended the magazine to spread liberal and democratic ideas in the German states but he hid such notions by producing the magazine like an encyclopaedia, with articles designed to educate the readers. But he carefully chose the articles to espouse his views.'

'And what were they?'

'Democracy, liberalism, kindness. It must have worked because the Prussians banned it until Bismarck rescinded the ban. Perhaps Bismarck's support explains why Ernst was an advocate for a united Germany.'

He gave her a swift, sidelong glance, worried in case he was boring her. On the contrary, she appeared to be listening with the greatest interest.

'In the beginning,' he continued, 'under Ernst's leadership, the magazine was very sympathetic to the Jews. After he lost control it became anti-Semitic. Now it is owned by the Nazi party. It no longer has many readers, I'm glad to say.'

She inhaled sharply. This man was full of contradictions. All her life she had thought of Germans as the enemy. The people who had wounded her father in the first war, ruined his life. Yet Weiser, despite being a German officer, did not seem the sort of savage brute she imagined he would be. And he was certainly not like a Nazi. She shuddered. Not like that Gestapo officer. Not even like Gerard.

In fact, the colonel showed nothing but scrupulous correctness towards her. More like English gentlemen in films, in fact. She glanced at him. How old is he? she wondered.

He stopped suddenly and turned to her. She was embarrassed to see that his eyes were wet. 'I'm so sorry about what is happening to you, Madame Renaud. About how my compatriots treat Jews. Sometimes, I am ashamed to be German.'

'Then I think your ancestor would be proud of you,' she said, touching the book.

He smiled. 'Well I am certainly suffering from melancholy.' He avoided looking at her. If one thing was combating his misery it was whenever he caught sight of her.

'I hate this war,' he continued. 'I wish it were over.'

'We all do. Do you think that France will be treated more generously when Germany wins?'

He looked at her in surprise.

'You think we will win the war?'

She nodded. 'That is what we hear all the time. Britain has been bombed to rubble and even the Americans are planning to capitulate.'

He shook his head in disbelief. 'Herr Goebbels would be pleased to hear that his propaganda is so effective.'

'But isn't that the case?' She felt confused; hopeful and yet distrustful.

Dorothy was convinced that the Americans would defeat the Germans but that was understandable, of course. Nobody else believed it. The Resistance might fight and die but theirs was a hopeless cause.

The image of Alain came to her mind but she pushed it away. She had convinced herself that he was in Nice with Gabriel Chiappe, not fighting some futile battle as part of the Maquis.

Weiser gave her a thoughtful look. 'You really do believe Germany will win?' he repeated.

She nodded.

He sighed. 'Well I have my doubts. I have been on the Russian Front, Madame Renaud. The communists will never surrender. They have fought us to a standstill and now they are pushing us back. And look at North Africa. Even Rommel has been defeated there.'

'But that's only deserts.'

'Good men can die in deserts. Tanks and guns and supplies can be lost.'

He bent his head and a sudden shudder went through him. 'We have destroyed the world.'

Without realising she was doing it, she reached out and touched his hand. Without realising he was doing it, he took hers in his.

They stood like this for a long time.

Silent.

Lost.

Found.

# CONFRONTATION
*Villa Laurel, 26 February 1944*

Viviane put the casserole into the oven and began to make some coffee. She called it a casserole but that was a stretch as it contained nothing but vegetables and those mostly small and of poor quality. With so many men sent to work in Germany there were fewer crops being grown. Recently even the Germans seemed to be having difficulty procuring sufficient food.

Christmas felt a long way behind them. Spring was hovering on the horizon but seemed reluctant to pluck up the courage to arrive.

She frowned. February was the shortest month but always seemed to her to be the longest. And this year was a leap-year so would be longer still.

Sylvie had joked that she might take the opportunity to propose to her latest lover, a jovial, rotund German Major. Viviane had been furious at her for saying this, reminding her that she was still married. She blushed at the memory of her vehemence.

'Don't kid yourself that I'm the only one to think this,' Sylvie had said, blowing her a kiss. Her words often came back to her.

She finished making the coffee and took a cup into the study.

'Thank you, Viviane,' Dorothy said. 'Just what I need.' She pointed to a small pile of paper beside the typewriter. 'Look, I'm getting on really well. And a lot of it is due to you.'

'What do you mean?'

'I thought my writing days were behind me but since you and the children arrived, I've felt inspired again. Not dark subjects like I used to write. I'm working on a frothy comedy for someone like Cary Grant. Something to make the world laugh again.'

Marie poked her head into the room.

'Viviane, will it be alright if I take the children for a walk? They're sick of being indoors.'

'Where will you take them?' Viviane asked in alarm.

'Down to the woods. Not far. Pierre says there are herons nesting by the pond.'

Viviane hesitated for a moment but then agreed. The children had to live as normal a life as possible. They called goodbye from the hall, so keen to go they could not spare the time to come to kiss her. She heard their excited cries as they ran outside.

'How is Colonel Weiser this morning?' Dorothy asked.

'I have no idea,' Viviane answered. 'Why would I?'

Dorothy picked up her coffee. 'I thought you might have taken him a cup.'

'I asked Marie to take him one before I brought yours,' she answered. 'After all, she is the maid.' She made for the door.

Dorothy smiled to herself. One could find amusement in even the darkest of days, she thought. And people should. She rolled another sheet of paper in the machine and began to type.

Viviane was putting the finishing touches to an apple tart when she caught a glimpse of Marie racing up the path to the house. She was calling at the top of her voice.

Viviane dropped the tart on the floor and ran to the door.

'What's the matter?' she cried. 'Is one of the children hurt?'

It was only then that she realised that Marie was carrying Celeste who was sobbing silently to herself.

'What's happened?' Viviane said, shaking Marie by the arm. She reached out to Marie's face. It was red with blood and her clothes were torn.

'They took, David,' she gasped. 'I tried to stop them but I couldn't.'

Celeste climbed into Viviane's arms. 'Horrible men,' she said. 'And Uncle Gerard.'

Viviane looked at Marie.

'Yes, the fat young man. Your friend. He was one of the men.'

Viviane's free arm waved as if she were a swimmer trying to keep her feet in a rip tide. She heard a wail come from her mouth, a long, deep animal cry of distress.

The French window to the study crashed open and Dorothy raced across to them. 'David?' she gasped.

'Some men took them,' Marie said. She began to cry. 'I tried to fight them off, Dorothy, but there were three of them. That bastard was in charge.'

'Which bastard?'

'The one who tried to rape Viviane.'

Dorothy took both Marie's hands. 'It's alright, darling,' she said, 'everything will be fine.' Yet even as she said this, she knew it would not be.

'Did the men say where they were taking him?' she demanded.

Marie shook her head. 'But the man who attacked you had a gun.'

Viviane staggered against Dorothy at these words.

'Think, Viviane,' Dorothy said harshly. 'Where would he have taken David?'

'I don't know,' Viviane said. 'Maybe his house.'

'Do you know where that is?'

Viviane nodded.

Dorothy turned to Marie. 'Take Celeste into the house and give her some milk. And tell Pierre to get the car.'

She squeezed Viviane's arm. 'Don't worry honey, we'll find him.'

Viviane did not answer. She was remembering Schorn's threat to shoot David.

They followed Marie back into the house. Dorothy just remembered to grab their coats from the stand. They might spend hours trying to find the boy.

All Viviane could think was that she had not kissed David goodbye.

Pierre skidded the car to the door and leaped out. 'They've taken David?' he cried. His face was screwed up with anxiety.

'We're gonna get him back,' Dorothy said.

Viviane was in a daze but felt Dorothy shove her towards the vehicle. And then, out of the corner of her eye, she saw Mundt running towards her.

'Madame Pine,' he called. 'Is there some problem.'

'Yes, Major,' she said. 'Some men from the militia have kidnapped David.'

Mundt looked shocked. 'Where have they taken him?'

'That's what we're gonna find out.'

She hustled Viviane into the back of the car and threw herself next to her.

'Wait here a moment,' Mundt said to Pierre. Then he turned, yelled to one of the soldiers and raced into the house.

A moment later he returned with Colonel Weiser who yanked open the door and leaned in towards the two women.

'Do you have any idea where he may have taken David?'

'We guess maybe his house,' Dorothy said.

'Do you know where it is?'

'Viviane does.'

Weiser glanced at Viviane to see if she was in any state to direct them. 'Very good,' he said. 'We will follow.'

His staff car screeched around the house and came to a shuddering halt. The driver leapt out and held open the door. Weiser waved to Pierre to lead the way.

If she had been more conscious Viviane would have been alarmed at the way Pierre threw the car round the twists and turns of the road. Dorothy was holding on to the armrest for grim life. Weiser's car clung to them like a limpet, though, and they both reached Gerard's house safely.

Viviane seemed to have recovered her wits now and leapt out from the car before it had even stopped. She hammered on the door, yelling at the top of her voice for Gerard. The door was opened a few minutes later by an elderly woman.

'Madame Pithou,' Viviane gasped. 'Have you seen Gerard?'

'He's gone to work.' A look of fear came to her face. 'Is he hurt?'

'I hope he is,' Viviane said bitterly.

'What do you mean? Has he done something wrong?' She threw her arms in the air. 'I pleaded with him not to join those horrible people.'

'He's taken my child,' Vivian cried. 'Stolen my little boy.'

Madame Pithou looked shocked. 'The Jew boy?' she mouthed.

Viviane stared at her speechless.

The old lady took her hand and squeezed it. 'Perhaps the Gestapo.' Tears filled her eyes. 'I'm so sorry.'

'The Gestapo,' Viviane cried, racing back to the car.

Mundt blocked her path. 'Madame Pine must not be seen by the Gestapo,' he said. 'Nor you. Colonel Weiser and I shall go alone.'

'I'm going,' Viviane said.

'No, Madame Renaud —'

But his words came too late. She was already climbing into the back of the car.

They reached the police station five minutes later. Weiser grabbed hold of Viviane and bent close to her face.

'It is right that you come with us, Viviane for you are the boy's carer. But let me do the talking.'

Viviane's face screwed up but she nodded in agreement.

He undid the strap on his holster. 'Come, Otto,' he said.

A clerk rose to try to bar their way but one glance made him think better of it and he sat down again.

'Where is your commanding officer?' Weiser demanded.

The man pointed to a corridor behind him.

Weiser hurried off, pushing himself fast despite the pain in his leg. He waited a moment for the others to arrive and then nodded. Mundt kicked the door savagely and it flew open.

Schorn was standing behind his desk, berating Gerard. His face was filled with contempt.

Gerard was red-faced with embarrassment.

David was nowhere to be seen.

'Now look what your stupidity has led to?' Schorn said to Gerard.

He wiped the scowl from his face and turned to Weiser. 'Can I help you, Colonel?' he asked.

'I'm sure you can. This Frenchman has just kidnapped a child. I have come to fetch him back.'

'A full Colonel acting like a baby-sitter?' Schorn said. 'Wonders never cease.'

'The boy...' Weiser said.

Schorn took his seat and stared at them all. 'The boy is a Jew, Colonel Weiser. As I believe you know. The Milice have taken him into custody.' Here he gave Gerard a withering glance. 'For some reason they brought him here to be dealt with.'

'Dealt with?' Viviane said in horror.

Schorn smiled. 'I could say that he will be taken to an orphanage, in order to make you feel better. Or I could say that he will be taken to a work camp and reunited with his real mother. But this is war, Madame, and we have no time for such niceties.'

He pulled out a cigarette. 'You'd be surprised, I'm sure, but some of my assistants are actually recruits from the criminal class. Poachers turned gamekeepers, if you like. Burglars, ruffians, murderers. They will have no scruples about dealing with the boy.'

He lit the cigarette but then froze. Weiser's pistol was pointing at his face.

'I'm not going to allow you a final cigarette, Schorn,' he said. 'If you don't produce the boy, you're a dead man.'

'You can't threaten me,' Schorn said.

'I assumed that an educated man like you would know the difference between a threat and a promise.' He cocked the hammer of his gun. 'Now telephone for someone to bring the boy.'

Schorn's hand shook as he reached for the phone. He snapped an order into it and slammed it down. His eyes returned to the gun which pointed unwavering at his face.

'You won't get away with this, Weiser,' he said. 'I have jurisdiction in the matter of the Final Solution.'

'But not if you are in your grave, Herr Schorn. And here's my promise. You will be.'

'I've broken better men than you.'

'And I've killed far better than you.'

The room fell silent. The only sounds were the ticking of a clock and Schorn's laboured breathing.

The door opened and Viviane cried out in joy. She scooped David into her arms.

Mundt stepped forward and leaned over Schorn's desk. 'It was so kind of you to take care of the boy,' he said. 'You haven't completely forgotten the role of the police.'

'My only role is to act in the interests of the Reich,' Schorn snapped. 'And that includes ridding the world of Jews.'

Mundt punched him in the face. He was thrown from his chair and crashed against the wall. He groaned and tried to get to his knees but was unable to.

'My friend can sometimes be a little too direct,' Weiser said. 'But I'm sure you'll forgive him. For if you'd remained in your chair I would have shot you.'

He turned and led the way out of the office and to the car.

**THANKS**
*Villa Laurel, 26 February 1944*

To everyone's astonishment, David seemed little troubled by his ordeal. He had stared open-mouthed at Weiser threatening Schorn with his gun and even more when Mundt had punched him hard enough to send him flying.

He chuckled with pleasure as Viviane took his left hand and Weiser the right and headed to the street.

'Do you want to come in my car, David?' Weiser asked.

'Yes please.'

'It's safer for both of you,' Weiser explained to Viviane. The driver opened the door for her and the boy.

'Otto, you go with Madame Pine,' Weiser said. 'And keep right behind us.'

Viviane cuddled David as the car sped through the streets. David wriggled out of her grasp, climbed over her and put his nose to the window. 'We're going so fast,' he yelled with delight.

A smile came to Weiser's face and he leaned over to the driver. The man nodded, put his foot down and the car hurtled down the road even faster.

Viviane was thrown about a little and Weiser took her arm.

'Thank you for rescuing David,' she whispered. 'I'll be forever grateful.'

He smiled but could find no words to say.

Once back at the house, Dorothy took charge. She ordered Weiser and Mundt to go into the sitting room and told the driver to join them. He looked nervous and stared at Mundt to know what he should do.

Mundt simply told him to do as she said.

'Cognac for all of us,' Dorothy said as she followed the Germans into the sitting room. 'Pierre, please do the honours.'

They heard footsteps pattering down the hall. It was Marie and Celeste. They screamed with delight when they saw David.

'I've been in a soldier's car,' he yelled. He clenched his fist and waved it in the air. 'And Major Otto punched a nasty man, wham.'

'Major Otto?' Dorothy said. 'How delightfully informal of you, Major.' She indicated Weiser.

'He calls the Oberst by his first name as well,' Mundt explained with a shrug. 'So does Celeste.'

Pierre passed around with a tray of tumblers brimming with cognac.

Dorothy raised her glass to the room. 'To everybody here,' she said. 'Humanity at its best.'

Viviane sipped her cognac. Over the rim of her glass she saw Weiser regarding her with a warm and comforting gaze.

She spent the rest of the day in a daze, worn out by the ordeal. She and Marie were told to sit down and do nothing. Dorothy bustled about, ably supported by Pierre who showed himself well able to perform the role of cook, barman and server.

The German officers brought a welcome addition to the lunch - two big bars of chocolate.

'Where on earth did you get these from?' Dorothy asked. She studied them askance. 'They look British to me.'

'Chocolate is in short supply in Germany,' Mundt said. 'We rely on our British friends to supply it.'

'Taken from the Red Cross, I assume.'

'We ask no questions,' Mundt said.

She undid the wrapping and broke it into squares. 'Knowing the provenance, I can't say I'll enjoy this overmuch. But I'll try hard to.' She bit on a piece of the chocolate. 'You Germans really can be bastards.'

'We know this,' Weiser said. 'War makes villains of us all. Enjoy your chocolate, Madame Pine.'

Dorothy grinned. 'Touché, Colonel. I'm suitably chastised.' She popped another square into her mouth.

Viviane took a piece and nibbled at it a sliver at a time. It was milky and there was little taste of chocolate.

Celeste and David crammed several squares into their mouths.

'What do you think will happen now, Colonel Weiser?' Viviane asked.

She had gone over this question continually since they had returned to the villa. Gone over it without the slightest hint of an answer.

Weiser leaned back in his seat and glanced out of the window. 'Hopefully, nothing. Men like Schorn are bullies. He won't dare bother you when Otto and I are around.'

'But how long will you be around?' she asked. 'Surely you cannot stay here forever? As soon as your leg is better, won't you have to return to your barracks?'

'If I keep charging around the place looking after your children my leg will never get better,' he said.

But he did not answer her question.

Later that night, Viviane lay in her bed and listened as the house drifted into silence. The last one to retire was Dorothy, humming very low to herself as she moved along the corridor to her room. Tonight, unusually, she paused outside Viviane's room.

Viviane smiled, certain that her friend was listening to make sure that she was alright.

Reassured by the silence, Dorothy resumed her humming and went to her room.

Viviane tried to relax but without success. The events of the day circled around her mind, as they had for the last ten hours. Marie running screaming into the house, the panic and sense of despair she felt as they raced off in search of David, the sight of Schorn and Gerard. The cold, shattering despair when Schorn told her that David would be murdered.

And then, more fleetingly, she saw Weiser point his pistol at Schorn, saw Mundt punch him so hard she thought his neck might have broken. She sighed. She wished it had.

What would happen to them now, she wondered. She could not believe they were of any real interest to Schorn and his contempt for Gerard in bringing David to him seemed to underline this. But things might be different now that he had been so humiliated by the German officers. Her heart began to pound.

Maybe Schorn would thirst for revenge. Maybe he would come for her and the children. Memories of the day slithered around her head. Only Weiser and Mundt could keep her safe.

She heard the sound of movement in the corridor. It was Groucho the cat, on the hunt for mice. It seemed so normal a sound, so familiar. Yet the rest of their lives were in turmoil.

What had they done to deserve these terrible times? Were every last man, woman and child in France secretly monsters and being punished because of it? Were the British, the Dutch and the Jews?

And the Germans? They might be winning the war, but she wondered at what cost to themselves. Their fate might be every bit as awful as the people they conquered.

She thought of Weiser and wondered what she could do to repay him. What she could do to show her thanks.

The clock in the hallway began to chime. She counted them. One, two, three. It was the middle of the night and she had not slept a wink. Her thoughts went to Colonel Weiser once again. If it hadn't been for him then David would have been killed.

A wild desire to thank him seized her. But what if it were too late? He had threatened a senior Gestapo officer. Perhaps Schorn would arrange for his dismissal. Perhaps he would even be executed.

She got out of bed. She had to thank him. She had to do it now, immediately.

She lit the candle beside her bed and opened the door. She rehearsed a speech of thanks in her mind, struggling to find the words to convey the immensity of her gratitude. It was cold in the corridor and, as she made her way down the marble staircase, she realised that her feet were bare. But she did not pause, she had to thank him.

She stopped outside Weiser's door, listening as Dorothy had done at her room four or five hours earlier.

Then she took a deep breath and walked in.

She was surprised to find that he was sitting up in bed, reading by the light of a candle.

He glanced at her in astonishment. 'Is there something wrong?' he asked.

'No. Nothing's amiss.' She stepped closer to him.

'Is that your ancestor's book?' she asked.

He shook his head. 'Huckleberry Finn. It's about an American boy. I love him. His wayward spirit, his kindness and honesty.'

She shook her head. 'I've never heard of it.'

He held it out to her. 'Take it. Keep it.'

She shook her head. 'You've already done so much for me. I can't accept anything else.'

She managed a fleeting smile. 'In fact, I came here to thank you. I've been fretting about it for hours.'

'I need no thanks,' he said.

But she realised, trembling, that his eyes said different.

Without a word, without a thought, she pulled off her night-gown.

He gasped, blinked repeatedly, and then drew back the sheets.

She slipped in beside him. His lips were warm, the touch of his hands gentle and consoling.

She lay on her back and pulled him onto her. Opened her legs and felt him lower himself. She held her breath, waiting for him to move inside her. But he didn't.

He made a little sound, a soft sound, like the mewing of a cat or a frightened child.

'I can't,' he said.

'But it's alright,' she said. 'I want you to.'

'I don't mean that.' He shook his head. 'It's not you, Viviane, believe me. I've wanted you since first I met you.'

'Then why —'

'I can't,' he said. 'I'm aroused, believe me. Everywhere but where I want to be...'

She reached between his legs and felt the truth of what he said.

A rush of feelings crashed over her, part relief, part resentment. When she came to his room, she had no intention of offering herself to him, but she had. And he was unable to respond.

His head dropped on her shoulder and he began to weep.

'It's this war,' he said. 'It changes you.'

She did not answer for a long time.

'I know,' she said at last. 'I know.'

## THE COOLEST LOVE
### *Grasse, Spring 1944*

Viviane made up her mind to avoid Weiser after that first night. She was ashamed of herself, horrified at her betrayal of Alain. She began to wonder if Odette's view of her was justified.

Weiser acted scrupulously towards her, the perfect gentleman. She fretted that he was becoming more distant, that he might decide to leave the villa. Leave her and the children defenceless.

A week later she went back to his bedroom. She returned most nights after that. But Weiser, although he longed to, could not respond to her.

'Is it me?' she asked nervously, one night.

He shook his head. 'How can it be? You're beautiful and utterly desirable.' He looked away. 'I don't deserve you.'

One night in May she managed to arouse him sufficiently for them to begin to make love. But he could not sustain it and soon rolled away from her in tears.

She held him close and whispered consoling words in his ear. It was only later in the night, as she lay awake, that she thought how lucky she had been. The last thing she wanted was to fall pregnant with another man's child. Especially that of a German officer.

She was not sure if Dorothy knew what was going on, although she suspected that she had guessed at the liaison. If she did, she never made any comment. Of course, she had lived in Hollywood with its wild parties and loose morals. And for this, Viviane was grateful.

She felt certain that Marie suspected, however. Sometimes she had slipped from Ernst's bedroom in the hour before dawn and found Marie nearby. She was certain that on one occasion Marie had actually witnessed her leaving. Yet she never said anything about it.

But then again, Viviane was a little suspicious of Marie. She was very friendly with Major Mundt and not above flirting with him. This was especially the case whenever Dorothy was near, almost as if Marie were doing it to get some reaction from her.

She wondered if Mundt was as unresponsive a lover as Weiser. It would be a shame if he was, she thought. After all, Marie had lost her boyfriend long ago. And Viviane still had Alain.

She closed her eyes at the thought. He had been gone for six months now and she longed for him to return. Whenever she thought about him, she grew hot with shame at her attachment to Weiser.

She knew that she would be at the mercy of Gerard and Schorn were it not for Weiser's feelings for her. And, of course, she had grown more than fond of him. She was living in a quandary and the torment and guilt wrenched her heart.

'How's the colonel?' Dorothy asked her one day, out of the blue.

Viviane blushed and turned her face to hide it. 'As far as I know, he's alright,' she answered. 'Why do you ask?'

Dorothy shrugged. 'He seems kind of troubled. Has he spoken to you about what may be worrying him?'

'Why would he? I'm only the cook. He'd be more likely to tell you.'

Dorothy did not answer but gave her a look so shrewd Viviane almost confessed there and then.

'If you get the chance, ask him, would you?' Dorothy continued. 'The last thing we want just now is for him to get the jitters.'

In truth she was concerned that Weiser might be planning to leave and return to the barracks. If that were the case then it would not be long before Herr Schorn came knocking.

'I'm not sure why you think that I —' Viviane began

Dorothy touched Viviane's arm. 'Just be a darling, would you, and ask him what's wrong?'

As usual, Viviane waited for the clock to strike eleven before slipping out of her room. It was the middle of May and there was enough light for her to see without a candle. She opened Weiser's door and closed it silently behind her. It was a warm night and he was sitting staring out of the open window, chin in hand.

She came behind him and caressed his shoulders. 'You look thoughtful,' she said.

He turned and half smiled. She bent and kissed him gently on the lips.

He reached out and took her hand.

She sensed an unease about him, a tense anxiety. 'What's the matter?' she asked.

'The war,' he answered, after a long silence. 'For a long while now I've yearned for it to end. Now, I think that something is happening, something I can't quite understand. It's the final throw of the dice, I think.'

He reached out and pulled her onto his lap. 'Perhaps Germany is on the verge of losing the war. There's been a huge increase in Allied bombing raids this last few weeks. In the north mainly but also on the south, especially Marseille and Avignon. I wonder what may be afoot.

'Yet, at the same time, we constantly hear that we're about to unleash wonder weapons on our foes, weapons so powerful they will bring the Allies to their knees.' He shook his head wearily.

She lifted his chin and stared into his eyes. 'And what do you wish for, Ernst? For an end to the war or for German victory?'

'I'm not at all sure, to be honest. And whatever happens I fear for what it may mean for us.'

She drew him into bed and there, for the first and last time, they consummated their affection.

She lay awake for hours, wondering at what had just happened. Part of her felt contented. But more of her was petrified at what the future may bring.


## BEST OF FRIENDS
*Grasse, May 1944*

The man stopped and crouched down. He tilted his head this way and that, listening for any sound, the slightest sound. The dark streets loomed around him, empty.

But as he listened more intently, he realised that the streets were not silent. Water gurgled in drains, two tom cats hissed at each other, a fox barked on the edge of town. But there was no sound of footfalls. No sign of any person abroad apart from him.

He slipped across the street and went into the house. He was there a long while. When he came out he seemed perplexed and troubled.

He looked up and down the street, uncertain what to do next. The moon came out from behind a cloud and he checked his watch. Half past three.

He came up with an idea and hurried off to the edge of town.

There was no problem finding the house, even in the dark, for he had been coming here for most of his life. He knocked quietly on the door and pressed his ear against it. There was no sound from within. He knocked again a little louder. Again no response.

He bent and scrabbled in the gutter, then stepped into the middle of the road. He weighed the stone in his hand and threw it against one of the upstairs windows. Then another and another.

The window opened and a head peered out and searched the street below.

'Let me in,' he whispered to the figure at the window.

The head disappeared from view.

A few minutes later the door was flung open and a familiar figure beckoned him in, shutting the door behind them both, staring at him in astonishment.

'I thought you were dead?'

'Don't be so stupid, Gerard. What on earth could harm me?' Alain flung himself into a chair. 'Have you got any wine?'

Gerard stared at him in silence for a moment. 'Where have you been, Alain? With the Maquis?'

Alain shook his head. 'No. With Gabriel Chiappe in Nice. I'm a full time black-marketeer now.'

Gerard chewed over this news in silence. 'Why are you here?' he asked, finally.

Alain did not answer immediately. He had come to Grasse because Chiappe had persuaded some friends in Corsica to take Viviane and the children there. The Italian and German forces had been pushed off the island and it was now in the hands of the Free French.

Chiappe had winced when Alain asked how much this act of persuasion had cost him but refused to divulge the price. But he also made it clear that Alain would have to remain in Nice to work for him.

'Why did you risk coming back?' Gerard repeated.

There was something odd in his tone, some edgy eagerness. He's nervous at my being here, Alain thought and decided it would be best not to tell him the real reason.

'To see Viviane. But she's not at home. I realised she might still be at the American woman's villa but I wanted to be certain before I went there. That's why I came to you.'

Gerard did not answer.

'Do you know where she is, Gerard?' Alain asked.

'Yes I do.' Gerard paused for a moment and ran his fingers through his hair. 'And I'm afraid you're not going to like what I tell you about her.'

It had been Schorn who first put the notion in his head by calling Viviane a whore.

From that moment, everything had become clear to him. She was whoring herself to the German officer. This was the reason she had remained at the villa so long. This was why she and the children appeared relaxed and well-fed.

This explained why she had rejected his advances so forcefully.

He had mulled over all of this in the long, bitter days ever since.

Fleetingly, a part of him understood why she had done this. Then he had berated himself for not offering his help and protection to her before.

Most of his thoughts, however, were far angrier. How could she do such a thing? Why hadn't she come to him? How on earth could she prefer a German to a true-born Frenchman, a man who had loved her all his life?

Alain's voice intruded on his thoughts. 'What are you trying to tell me?' he said.

Gerard forced a sorrowful look upon his face and began to speak.

Alain listened to his tale stone-faced. Stone-faced and silent.

A growing contempt for his friend curled around Gerard's heart. This was all Alain's fault. Viviane would never have been forced to whore herself if he hadn't deserted her. He had left her alone and afraid, and she must have thought she had nobody else to turn to except the German. Alain had driven her to it and had only himself to blame. He was not a fit husband, never had been.

If only I'd married her, he thought. I should have married her. It should have been me.

'We need to rescue her,' Alain said, the moment Gerard had finished speaking. 'Need to get her away from that German's clutches.'

Gerard looked astonished. 'You want her back? After what she's done?'

Alain nodded. 'She would have had no choice, Gerard. She must have thought I was dead. Or perhaps the man forced himself on her or even threatened the children.' He pressed his fingers to his forehead as if seeking to keep the thoughts from spilling out. 'It hurts, I can tell you. But I understand why she did it. And I must get her back.'

Gerard swallowed his dismay. He had been scheming all day about how he might win over Viviane. He had been certain that Alain was gone for good, almost certainly killed. He thought there would be no impediment to his dreams from that direction.

Then, when the German got tired of her, he would be waiting. A senior member of the Milice, ready to offer his support and devotion. She might not be keen at first. That was understandable, to some extent. But she would not, could not, turn down him for ever. Not when he had risen even further in the Milice. He would be a powerful man. A great man. She would no longer be able to resist him. When the war was over, they would be happy together. Man and wife. Lovers.

But now all these dreams began to unravel. Alain had returned and he was willing to take Viviane back. Desperate to, in fact.

Perhaps he even doubts my words, he thought, doesn't believe that she has prostituted herself to the German.

For a moment, Gerard realised that this might be the case, that he had no proof that Viviane had done what he had spent days and nights fearfully imagining.

He dismissed the idea as soon as it had arisen. She had to be whoring herself, she must be, there was no other explanation possible.

Alain turned to him with a searching look, almost as if he had read his mind. 'Do you even know this for certain, Gerard?'

Gerard shuffled in his seat, trying to work out an answer.

'How could you know?' Alain continued before Gerard had time to answer. 'How could you know that she has slept with this man. Did she tell you?' He shook his head in disbelief. 'Even if she was forced to do so, I can't imagine she would tell you. That she would admit to doing such a thing.'

'It wasn't Viviane who told me.'

'Then who?'

Gerard licked his lips. 'A friend.'

He glanced at the clock. 'We can go and see the man in a couple of hours. Here, have some more wine and I'll get us something to eat.'

He filled Alain's glass to the brim and put the bottle on the table besides him. 'There's plenty more where that came from. I guess you have need of it.'

Alain mumbled his thanks and swallowed most of the wine. 'You're right Gerard. I may need another bottle.' He gave a weary grin. At least, in Gerard, he still had one true friend.

An hour later, Gerard grabbed his coat and told Alain that they should be on their way.

They were shown into the police waiting room and told to wait. After an hour, Gerard excused himself saying he wanted to go to the toilet. He was a long while and when he returned he did not sit on the bench next to Alain but in a chair opposite. He seemed very edgy, Alain thought.

They had been in the police waiting room for two hours now.

Alain glanced at his watch. It was almost eight. He assumed that Roland Boyer was the friend Gerard had mentioned. Knowing his brother-in-law, it was likely he would be punctual.

He smiled when the door opened precisely on the hour, pleased that his surmise had been correct.

But it was not Roland.

'Welcome, Monsieur Renaud,' the man said, advancing to Alain. 'Your friend, Gerard, has just informed me that you are a senior member of the Resistance. I am Kriminalinspektor Schorn and I have the pleasure of interrogating you.'

He smashed Alain across the face.

Alain yelled when the bucket of icy water was thrown over him. He was naked on a chair and the cold sliced into his body like icicles splitting wood. He had no idea how long he had been in the cell; he had lost count after the third dawn.

The Gestapo man picked up another pail and wafted it in front of him, to his left, to his right, taunting as to where he would throw it. Alain stared at the bucket knowing that the straps that bound him to the chair meant he could not move to avoid the water. But at least he could anticipate the throw and clench his teeth to prevent himself crying out.

The man stepped closer and poured the water on his groin, one slow, steady stream which made him gasp.

'That's enough Gort,' Schorn said. 'Take a break.'

Schorn lit a cigarette and loomed over Alain, blowing the smoke in his face. 'Cigarette smoke is fascinating, is it not,' he said. 'It is a pleasure when you inhale it yourself, less so when someone else spits it in your face.'

'I like it,' Alain says. 'It costs less than buying my own.'

Schorn stared at him, coldly. 'You are proud of your sense of humour? Still?'

Alain shrugged.

Schorn smiled and pressed the end of his cigarette into the back of Alain's hand.

Alain yelled as the heat seared into his flesh.

'Not quite so amused now, I see,' Schorn said.

He extinguished the cigarette in Alain's flesh and pulled up a chair.

'I ask again,' he said.

His voice was quiet, his words slow as if he were tired or bored.

'You are a member of a Resistance group. Where is their camp? Who commands it, who are its members?'

'I told you, I am not in the Resistance.'

'Of course you say this, my brave friend. And that buffoon Pithou believed you when you said that you were a member of a criminal gang in Nice. But my colleagues there say they have no record of a Gabriel Chiappe.'

'Of course they don't. He won't be going by that name, now. And besides, he will have bought your colleagues off.'

'Please, my friend, do not make such vile insinuations. We Germans are not sneaks and liars like you French. We cannot be bought off. And we will not give up our quest for the truth.'

He cocked his head suddenly, struck by an amusing thought. It should prove an amusing diversion.

'Tell me, Alain,' he said with a grin. 'How many Wehrmacht soldiers has your wife slept with? How much do you think she charges for her sexual services?'

Alain shook his head. 'She doesn't. She's not like that.'

'But you know that she is Colonel Weiser's whore. At the American woman's villa.'

Alain stared at him with contempt. He understood his tricks.

'I'm afraid you've been misinformed, Monsieur Schorn.'

Schorn shook his head. 'No doubt she started the affair for laudable reasons.' He smiled. 'But now, I think she must be enjoying it very much.'

He bent down and stared into Alain's face.

'She's a pretty woman, Alain. Can you picture what she gets up to in bed? All those little tricks and techniques she was never willing to allow you.'

Alain rocked against his bonds.

Schorn chuckled gently. 'How submissive she must be. How willing to do whatever is demanded of her.' He chuckled. 'And not just with the colonel. With anybody.'

He sighed, as if beguiled, and grinned at Alain. 'Anyway, enough of these pleasant thoughts.'

He rose and beckoned to Gort. 'No more water, for now. But his finger-nails need attention. I am worried that he might scratch himself with them. Remove them please. And then afterwards, use the cosh.'

He closed the door behind him to muffle the agonised screams.

Five days later, Gerard sat in Schorn's office, twisting nervously in his seat. As usual Schorn had spent the last half hour ignoring him, poring over documents, signing some, amending others, speaking brusquely on the telephone.

Finally he yawned, leaned back in his chair and gave a wide grin.

'I have a task for you, Pithou,' he said.

'Anything,' Gerard said. 'Obviously.' He felt relieved at his return to favour.

'I'm glad to hear it. Especially as it rather poetically finishes an amusing entertainment.'

He yawned once again. 'There is a body in one of the cells below. I want you to dispose of it.'

Gerard blinked in confusion.

'You won't recognise it for Gort is very heavy-handed. But don't worry, I can vouch for the identity. Your friend Renaud was a defiant one, I'll give him that. But sadly, he gave nothing away.'

He frowned. 'I think that perhaps he had nothing to tell.'

# MESSAGES
*Grasse, May 1944*

Odette Boyer tapped the baguette against the kitchen counter. The bread and the counter seemed equally hard. She cursed bitterly. Her husband's position had once been well-paid and respected. That had all changed with the arrival of the Germans. He had been thrown out of his office and sent to an annex with his sergeants. And his pay had been cut in half. She could hardly bear to look at him anymore.

He sat at the table, waiting silently for his breakfast. As if he were still a bread-winner of any merit.

She flung the baguette on the table.

'This is stale,' he said. 'It's like rock.'

'Then dip it in your coffee,' she said. 'Be a man, can't you?'

She was about to sit down when she saw an envelope sliding beneath the front door. She was surprised. They rarely had letters anymore.

She picked up the letter and held it up to the light. It was addressed to her.

Intrigued, she opened it and began reading. Her face went from surprise to amazement, to joy, to cunning.

She sat down at the table and began to read it over again, managing to keep her emotions in check more this time.

'Who is it from?' Roland asked.

She did not answer him, chose instead to read it a third time.

He sighed and dipped some bread in his coffee. He would not give her the satisfaction of asking a second time. He really did not care that much.

'If you must know,' she said abruptly, 'the letter is unsigned.'

He raised an eyebrow, his interest piqued by this information.

'But it does contain some very interesting information. About my sister.'

He shrugged, as if he was not interested, knowing that this was the best way to get Odette to tell him everything.

'To be honest, I'm not really surprised,' she continued. 'Poor Maman. At least Papa is no longer with us. It would break his heart. Kill him probably.'

Roland did not respond.

Odette placed the letter down on the table as if it were something precious and fragile.

'This letter says that Viviane is a whore.' She stared at her husband, triumph in her eyes. She always knew things would come to this.

'And the letter is unsigned?' Roland asked.

Odette frowned, wondering what abstruse point he was trying to make.

'It doesn't matter whether it's signed or not. It's certain to be true. It says that she is living at some villa north of the town. The villa is occupied by a German colonel and she is fornicating with him. Openly, in front of the owner of the house, in front of the servants, in front of Celeste.' She bowed her head. 'My poor little niece. To know such things about her mother.'

Roland heard all this in horror. He had kept Viviane's whereabouts secret from everybody. The fact that the letter-writer knew where she was boded no good. It was accurate about where she was. Did this mean that it was accurate about all the rest?

'Let me see the letter,' he said, holding out his hand.

She pulled it to her chest. 'Going to use your detective powers on it? Discern the personality of the writer from the way he shapes his letters?'

'Give it to me.'

She passed the letter over, a smirk playing across her face. He had always liked Viviane, rather too much, she sometimes thought. So now let him find out what filth she was getting up to.

'I don't believe it,' he said, flinging the letter on the table. 'It's just some malicious fool trying to cause trouble.'

'Sneer if you want to,' she said, snatching up the letter. 'I'll find others who will corroborate it.'

With your slew of harpies, he thought, not troubling to hide the disdain from his face. He got up, put on his hat and left.

Odette hurriedly cleared the table, leaving the dishes unwashed in the sink. Then she put on her coat, pocketed the letter and scurried off to her friend, Jeanne Greuze.

'Well I must say, I'm not over-surprised,' Jeanne said after she had read the letter three times over. She placed a hot hand on Odette's in a show of sympathy.

'Nor am I,' Odette said. 'Thank God Papa is no longer with us. He hated the Germans.'

'His leg,' Jeanne said, knowledgeably. She was already considering who amongst their friends she would tell first, preferably before Odette could do so.

'Do you know of Villa Laurel?' Odette asked.

'Oh yes,' Jeanne said. 'Don't you?'

'I wouldn't be asking you if I did,' Odette said, tartly.

'It's owned by an American woman,' Jeanne said. 'A vaudeville artist, I believe. Yvonne Robinne's daughter works there, I believe.'

'Claudette?'

'The younger one. Marie.'

'Well she'll know the truth of it.'

'Or her mother will.' Jeanne rose and got their coats.

'I don't know anything about such a thing,' Yvonne Robinne said. 'And I don't believe a word of it.' Her eyes narrowed. She did not care for the two women who had come uninvited to her house.

Odette snorted. 'You don't know my sister.'

'That's a terrible thing to say about your own flesh and blood,' Yvonne said.

'But Viviane Renaud is staying at the villa?' Jeanne asked.

For the briefest moment, Yvonne did not answer. 'I haven't the slightest idea,' she said.

'Haven't the slightest idea of what, Maman?' came a voice from the door.

Marie walked in with a basket over her arm. 'Madame Pine sent over some cheese,' she said. 'She knows how partial you are to Brie.'

Her mother's eyes flashed a warning at her but Marie did not see it.

'What a lovely young girl your daughter is,' Odette said to Yvonne.

'Yes indeed,' said Jeanne. 'It must be a worry for you.'

'What do you mean?' Marie asked, mystified.

'You working at the villa,' Odette said. 'With all those Germans.'

Marie swallowed and glanced at her mother, who gave a tiny shake of her head.

'Oh that,' Marie said, thinking quickly. 'There's only one there now. The colonel. And he's very old, on his last legs. I doubt if he'll see the spring. He's no threat to me.'

'From what I gather,' Odette said, 'he has no interest in you, child.'

'I don't think he has much interest in anything except how to make his peace with God.'

'That's not what we've heard,' Jeanne said. She glanced at Odette who gave a nod for her to continue.

'We've got it on good authority that Viviane Renaud is sleeping with the Germans.'

Marie's eyes grew wide with alarm. Perhaps they had heard about her, too.

Odette saw how flustered the girl was and gave a thin smile of triumph.

'That's nonsense, madame,' Marie said. 'Idle gossip.'

'Perhaps you're right,' she said. 'Oh, how I hope you are. For the sake of all the family.'

Marie wasted no time in finding Viviane when she returned to the villa. Viviane listened to her tale with growing alarm.

'Thank you for telling me,' she said when Marie had finished.

'Do you think it will it be a problem?' Marie asked, anxiously.

'I expect so.' She sighed. 'My sister has always hated me. She'll be glorying in this. I guess that half the town will know about it soon.'

'Not necessarily,' Marie said. 'And anyway, if people know that you and your sister don't get on, they may just think it's spite on her part.'

Viviane looked a little more hopeful. 'Do you think so?'

'I'm sure.'

Viviane hugged her fiercely. 'You're such a good friend, Marie.'

'Well,' she laughed, 'in that case, you can make me some coffee.'

Viviane began to prepare the coffee when the doorbell chimed.

Marie put on her apron and hurried off to open it.

It was Gerard Pithou.

'What do you want?' Marie snapped. 'You're not welcome here.'

'I know,' he said. 'I know that full well. But I've come to give Viviane a message.'

'She won't listen to any messages from you.'

'I think she will to this,' he said.

And he pulled out a revolver and shot himself in the head.


## WHISPERS
*Grasse, 6 June 1944*

Roland Boyer was summoned to Schorn's office later that day. He stared impassively at the Gestapo officer. Schorn had hoisted his feet on the fine oak desk, partly in emulation of the American detectives he adored, partly to annoy Boyer.

'There's been a death,' Schorn said airily. 'A member of the Milice.'

'Retaliation?' Boyer asked.

'No. If it were then I would investigate it. This was merely a suicide so I'm giving the case to you. It's high time you pulled your weight around here.'

Boyer did not respond to the jibe. He leaned forward, pleased that at least he could now do some real police work.

'It's someone you know,' Schorn continued. 'Gerard Pithou, a friend of your brother-in-law.'

'Gerard?' Boyer said in surprise. 'Why on earth would he kill himself? Was there a message?'

'Not on him. Except maybe the death was the actual message.'

Boyer frowned, puzzled.

Schorn gazed at him intently, eager to see his reaction. 'He went to find your sister-in-law, you see. Killed himself at her door.' He chuckled. 'I imagine that was some kind of suicide note, don't you?'

Boyer did not give an answer other than an icy stare.

'Does his mother know?' he asked, eventually.

Schorn shrugged, picked up a sheet of paper and pointed at the door.

The first thing that Boyer did was to visit Madame Pithou. He knocked on the door with a heavy heart. Gerard was her only child and she had always doted on him.

The interview was one of the more painful ones he had ever experienced. He left the old lady weeping bitterly. He was none the wiser as to a motive.

He climbed on his bicycle and began to ride towards the villa. He looked straight ahead as he rode. Being thrown out of his office by Schorn had been a humiliation but few of the townspeople saw this. But the replacement of his car with a bike was a different matter. When he struggled up cobbled streets on the old bike his humbling was plain for all to see.

He propped the bicycle against the front door of the villa and rang the bell. It was opened a moment later by the handyman.

'The ladies are upset,' Pierre explained. 'I had to prepare lunch for them, although only Madame Pine ate any of it.'

'Are they too upset to talk?'

'Of course they are. A man killed himself at the door, for God's sake. It was horrible.' He sighed. 'But you must do your duty, I suppose. Better you than that Gestapo pig.'

He showed Boyer into the sitting room, returning a minute later with Dorothy. She sat in a chair and indicated for Boyer to do the same.

'I'm sorry to trouble you, Madame Pine, but I am here to investigate the death of Gerard Pithou.'

'Suicide, Captain.'

'That remains to be seen.'

'Don't you think that blowing your own brains out is suicide?'

Boyer took out his notebook. 'If that was indeed the case, then yes.'

'You think somebody else shot him?' she said in disbelief.

'There are many armed men at your house, Madam. Germans.'

Dorothy raised her eyebrows in exasperation. 'Marie saw him fire the gun.'

Boyer made a note. 'I shall have to talk with Marie, I'm afraid. And Viviane. Are they calm enough of mind?'

'Viviane more than Marie.' Tears sprang to her eyes. 'Witnessing such a dreadful thing was terrible for poor Marie. The doctor's given her a sleeping draught. I doubt she'll wake for a couple of hours.'

'I won't disturb her for now, then. But I'd like to speak with my sister-in-law? In private, if I may.'

Dorothy got out of her chair with great reluctance. 'Be gentle with her, Captain. She may not have seen what happened but she's had a shock.'

At first Viviane was guarded in the answers she gave to him. He grew increasingly exasperated but hid it with practised ease. He was a firm believer that a slow and kindly approach gave quicker results.

'Have you any idea why he came here?' he asked.

Viviane swallowed hard. She did not want to be implicated in any way. She thought it best to act completely innocent.

'Perhaps he found out that I was here and came to ask about Alain.'

Boyer nodded.

'He was Alain's best friend,' she said.

'And you told him that you were here?'

Viviane paused. 'No. He found out for himself.'

Boyer made a note.

'Why do you think he think he did this?' he asked. 'It must have taken him time and trouble to locate you.'

'I've no idea, Roland. None whatsoever.'

'But he was in love with you, of course.'

She blushed furiously. 'What makes you say that?'

He gave no explanation.

She did not press him for one which made him certain that he had guessed correctly.

She ran her fingers through her hair nervously and glanced at the door.

'So if he loved you, did he try to force himself upon you?'

'Who told you that?'

'Nobody actually.' He paused. 'Until you did just now.'

She cursed herself for the mistake. She had never been that enamoured of her brother-in-law but she never underestimated him. She was right not to, it seemed.

'Yes, Roland, he did come here and he did try to force himself on me.'

'And what happened?'

She paused, wondering how to answer.

'Did you fight him off? Did somebody else? Or did he have his way with you?'

'Certainly not,' she cried. 'I tried to fight him off but he was too strong.'

'So he raped you?'

'No.'

'Then…?'

Viviane took a deep breath. 'If you must know, Colonel Weiser came to my assistance.'

Boyer nodded and made a lengthy note of it.

'Do you think Alain may have been complicit in Gerard Pithou's death?'

'How could he be?'

'He may have threatened him. Made him terrified.

Viviane looked shocked. 'Do you think Alain would threaten his best friend? Threaten him so much that it drove him to suicide?'

'If he heard that he had attacked you?'

Viviane paused and then shook her head. 'Even then, Alain would never do such a thing.'

'Have you seen Alain lately?' he asked.

'I haven't seen him since he went off in your car. More than six months.'

'And not a word from him?'

She shook her head and tears began to form in her eyes.

Boyer patted her on the arm. 'That's good news, Viviane. It means he's still in hiding. Still safe. Take comfort from that.'

The door opened suddenly and Dorothy walked in.

'I think you've been questioning her long enough, Captain. She's tired and still upset.'

Boyer snapped his notebook shut. 'Of course.' He got to his feet and spoke quietly to Dorothy. 'May I see the body?'

Dorothy looked surprised. 'It's gone. I've no idea where.'

Boyer looked incredulous. 'It's gone? How can a body just disappear?'

'Don't ask me.'

Boyer suddenly realised. 'Madame Pine, where can I find the German officer?'

Weiser was the height of civility and helpfulness. Boyer marvelled that he was so unlike Schorn. It was as if they were a different species.

'We removed the body, immediately,' Weiser explained. 'We didn't want the ladies to be more upset than they already were.'

'So where is the body?'

'I've no idea. My men moved it.'

'And you didn't tell them where to remove it to?'

Weiser gave him an incredulous look. 'I don't have time for such details, Captain.'

Boyer's eyes narrowed. He sensed there was something wrong here. 'Of course, if you had shot him then you would be quick to destroy the evidence.'

'But he shot himself, Captain. The maid saw this. And why on earth would I do such a thing?'

'Because he attacked Viviane Renaud, perhaps?'

Weiser's foot began to tap gently on the floor. He was not aware of it but Boyer was. A sign of nervousness, perhaps. Or duplicity.

'Yes, he did, Captain Boyer, and it was a vile act. But hardly a motive for me to kill him.'

Boyer shrugged. He sensed that Weiser was saying less than he might.

'That's as maybe, Colonel,' he continued. 'But disposing of the body is rather suspicious, is it not?'

'To suspicious minds, Captain Boyer. To a policeman. I, fortunately, am merely a soldier.'

'And where do soldiers dispose of those who have died?'

'In the heat of a battle, they are left to rot. If there is time they are burnt or buried in a pit with their fellows.'

'And Gerard Pithou?'

'I told you, I don't deal with such matters.' He held Boyer's gaze. 'I'll send for my sergeant.'

The sergeant was very precise in his answer. He had taken the corpse to the barracks and burnt it in the incinerator.

Boyer sighed and put away his notebook. There was no point in pursuing anything more here.

He decided not to question Marie. The easiest thing to do was to accept it was a suicide. Now the case had become merely an enigma. In the past he would have kept it open and investigated it, for years if need be. But now it was just one death out of millions.

But as he climbed onto his bicycle, he decided he would keep the case open after all. Justice had to be done and seen to be done. Gerard Pithou's mother deserved that at the very least.

When he returned home that evening, he found Odette pacing the room in wait for him.

'Have you been investigating the Pithou murder?' she demanded. 'I've been waiting to hear since this morning.'

Boyer raised an eyebrow. He knew that such things could not be kept quiet for long but this had got out very quickly. The body must have still been warm when news of it spread across town.

'It's not a murder,' he said. 'It was suicide.'

Odette gave a doubtful look. 'Was there a note?'

'It's under investigation,' he snapped. 'I don't want to discuss it.'

Yet despite his protests he knew very well that she would find out some details of the case. Partly because she would not rest until she managed to inveigle some information out of him. But it also because her network of informers was every bit as good as his and he hoped that he might learn something from her.

She opened a bottle of wine and poured him a glass.

'I didn't think we had any left,' he said.

'I managed to scrape together some money to buy it,' she said with a smile.

She took a seat beside him. 'So if it was a suicide,' she said almost to herself, 'what would have prompted it?'

Boyer sipped at his wine but did not answer. It was very good wine, the best he had tasted in a long while.

He leaned his head against the chair back and closed his eyes.

'Of course Gerard always had the hots for Viviane,' Odette said.

'I didn't know,' Boyer said.

'Oh yes. Perhaps he tried it on with her and got nowhere. He was an ugly specimen and I guess even Viviane draws the line somewhere. Maybe he shot himself in despair.'

Boyer was surprised at how quickly Odette had arrived at this conclusion. He wished that some of his sergeants were as skilful.

He heard her adding more wine to his glass but did not open his eyes. He wanted to listen to her ruminate undisturbed.

'Or maybe she was so incensed that she killed him. She's always had a fiery temper.'

'Where would Viviane get a gun?' he asked, still without opening his eyes.

She did not answer. Her fingers drummed rapidly on the table. He reached for his wine and took another sip.

'She could have got it from the Germans,' she said. 'I hear there are some at the villa.'

'And she wrestled with the Colonel to seize the gun?' He gave a snort of derision.

Odette gazed at him. So there was a colonel at the villa? She hadn't known that.

Her mind began to race like a hare. This way, that way, veering from side to side, sniffing at different concepts, different notions.

'Have you seen the Colonel?' she asked after a while.

He nodded. 'I questioned him this afternoon.'

'Is he an older man?'

'In his forties, I should think. Why do you ask?'

Odette filed away the fact that Marie had lied to her about his age.

'A man in his forties,' she said, 'hundreds of miles away from any wife and living in the same place as Viviane. And she with Alain out of the way for months. Why do you think I asked?'

Boyer sat up at her words, his mouth wide in surprise.

'Pah,' Odette said. 'I should have been the Police Captain and you should have kept house.'

'It's only your guess,' he said, aggrieved. 'It wouldn't stand up in court.'

'It's a well-informed guess,' she said. 'I know my sister, the little tart.'

She got up and put on her coat.

'Where are you going?'

'To see Jeanne.'

He groaned. The news of Gerard's death had spread very quickly. Odette's gossip about Viviane would spread quicker than the plague.

'I don't think you should talk to Jeanne,' he called.

But he was too late. By the time he'd got out of his chair, she was gone.


## HOPE KINDLED
*Grasse, 7 June 1944*

Viviane smiled at Weiser as he lay sleeping. She was still shaky from hearing what Gerard had done but she felt a new sense of safety because of it.

She stepped out of the room and saw Dorothy sitting in a chair opposite.

She put her fingers to her lips and beckoned to Viviane to follow her into the kitchen. The sun was just breaking above the horizon and the walls began to turn a muted rose colour.

'I don't know why I sleep with him,' Viviane said. She was embarrassed that Dorothy had seen her leaving the room but realised that there was now no point in denying what had been going on.

'I'm not interested in your love life,' Dorothy replied. 'I've got news. Important news.'

She tip-toed to the door, led Viviane outside and closed it softly behind them.

'The Allies have invaded France,' she said.

'What?'

'Allied forces landed in Normandy yesterday morning. Americans, British and Canadians. We're gonna be liberated.'

She threw her arms around Viviane and hugged her tight.

'How do you know?' Viviane asked when Dorothy finally let her go.

'The radio. Pierre hid it from the Germans. He keeps it in a shack up in the woods. He's just heard the news.'

'Was the message genuine? Could it be propaganda?'

'Don't be foolish. Why would the Germans admit that they'd been invaded?'

'I mean Allied propaganda, not German. Ernst says that the Nazis have developed new wonder weapons so maybe they're winning the war and the Allies are growing desperate.'

Dorothy was silenced by this news for a moment but then shook her head with great determination. 'I don't think that President Roosevelt would lie.'

Any doubts were swiftly dismissed during the course of the day. A steady stream of soldiers came to Weiser with messages. Late in the morning he and Mundt travelled down to the barracks and only returned late in the evening. They looked tense and careworn.

Viviane prepared them a late, light supper but Marie brought it back to the kitchen virtually uneaten.

Everyone retired to bed. Viviane lay restless, wondering whether or not to go to Weiser. He had seemed so exhausted that maybe it would be better to leave him on his own for the night. In the end she convinced herself to go to him. She might be a comfort to him and besides, if she didn't go it might make him suspicious.

Most important of all, she wanted to find out what was happening.

She crept along the corridor which was well lit by the light from a full moon. Just as she was about to pass Dorothy's room, she heard a loud crash and a groan.

She opened the door in alarm and saw Dorothy lying naked beneath the window. At the same moment a second naked figure leapt from the bed and bent down beside her. It was Marie.

'She's fainted,' she said. 'She's been celebrating too much. Help me get her back in bed.'

The two women lifted her between them and settled her against the pillows. She opened her eyes and grinned. 'Here's to Ike and Monty,' she said in a slurred voice. 'I want another cognac.'

'You've had enough,' Marie said.

'Then let's make love again.' She pulled Marie closer.

Viviane stared at them open-mouthed.

'I'd better go,' she said, at last.

'Thank you,' Marie said. 'She's done this a few times before. She'll be alright.'

Viviane closed the door behind her and shook her head in surprise. We get our love where we can, she thought with a growing smile. Then she went down the stairs.

Weiser was sitting at his table, poring over a map of France. He looked up as she entered, almost went to fold up the map, but immediately returned to his scrutiny.

'Where are you looking for?' she asked with an innocent tone.

He stared at her for a moment and then sighed. 'You'll know soon enough, I suppose. We found out yesterday that Rome has fallen to the Allies.'

Then he pointed to the northern coast of France. 'And there's more. The Allies have invaded Normandy. Thousands of ships, tens of thousands of men.' He paused. 'Actually the Allies claim a hundred and fifty thousand men were landed.'

She pursed her lips, wondering at the implications of this. Dorothy clearly believed that the end of the war was in sight, with victory for the Allies. But she wondered if this view was shared by Ernst.

'What do you think will happen?' she asked.

Weiser gave a swift laugh, a bark. 'If I knew that I'd be a Field-Marshal.

He pointed to the map again. 'Many of the High Command thought any invasion would be at Calais. Normandy is too long a sea-crossing to keep supplied and is too far from Germany. I wonder if the Allies may have made a strategic blunder.'

He used a pair of compasses to measure the distance from the landing site to the German border, shaking his head in disbelief.

'It will lead to untold bloodshed in France, I'm afraid. Of soldiers and French citizens.' He paused. 'Maybe even British and American citizens.'

'But you said that Germany could no longer bomb Britain.'

'Not with planes. But if these wonder weapons are more than figments in the mind of Adolf Hitler then the war may turn in our favour once again.'

She clenched her hands and placed them in her lap. If that were the case then David would continue to be in peril. And so would Celeste and her. There would be no end to fear. Panic seized her. She might never see Alain again.

Only this morning the world had seemed much more hopeful. Now all of this optimism felt like rubble and dust.

'I don't know what it will mean for us, either,' Weiser said. His voice sounded strange to her ears. Cold, hollow, with not a trace of warmth.

She shook her head, uncertain if she could control her voice.

'General Blaskowitz has been appointed head of all German forces south of the Loire,' he continued. 'But he's a very accomplished commander and if things go ill for us in Normandy he may be sent there. And I would probably go with him.'

Her heart began to race. A cold sweat sprang to her forehead. Ernst was her only sure protection against the Gestapo. The only chance for David to survive.

And she suddenly realised that she had fallen a little bit in love with him. It was not like her love for Alain which was absolute and unbreakable. It was more like the flame of a candle, insubstantial, wavering but still able to hurt.

Ernst forced a smile on his face and took her hand. 'It's ironic isn't it. We both want this wretched war to end but the ending of it may tear us apart. Part of me, Viviane, hopes the war will go on forever.'

He gazed once more at the map of France and his fingers caressed the south coast. 'Perhaps we should pray that the Allies invade here as well. And then I won't be sent to Normandy. I'll be able to stay here and fight.'

'Fight and die,' she cried. Her face was stark with terror.

'I'm too wily an old soldier to be killed,' he said. 'And I have something precious worth living for.'

He took her face in his hands and kissed her gently and then with mounting fervour.


## OPERATION DRAGOON
### *Grasse, Mid-August 1944*

Viviane now heard news of the war every day, either from Dorothy's radio reports from London or from what Weiser told her. It seemed that the initial high hopes of the Allies in Normandy were waning because of the tenacious fighting of the German troops there.

But the Allies poured men and materials into the battle and gained the upper hand. By the beginning of August, they had managed to conquer much of Normandy and Brittany.

Viviane remained anxious that Blaskowitz would be summoned north but Weiser grew increasingly confident that he would be kept in the south.

'It's good news,' she told Dorothy. 'It means we're safe from the Gestapo.'

But it was not all good news, by any means. Dorothy had decided not to tell her what Marie heard every day in her visits to the town. Viviane's relationship with Weiser was now common knowledge. Odette and her friends spread the news with relish and each retelling added more details and more embellishments.

She comforted herself that Viviane had a strong personality and with the end of the war it would all start to be forgotten.

She hoped that Alain would forgive her.

She sighed wearily. This war would end one day but the repercussions might go on for years.

She went into the sitting room and opened her last bottle of Bourbon.

When this bloody war's over, she thought, I'm going to pack up the villa and take Marie with me to California.

Two weeks later, the world turned upside down. Thousands of Allied bombers filled the sky to the south, raining terror upon the coastal towns. Viviane ran to the top of the house. The whole coast appeared to be on fire. She ran back down to join the others.

Dorothy stood in the hallway, her face glowing with joy. Marie stood behind her, shaking with fear. Pierre held a thick club in his hand and the look on his face showed that he intended to use it if necessary. The children looked alarmed and Viviane pulled them close to her.

Nearer to hand, they heard explosions along the roads snaking north from the coast. Telegraph and telephone wires dipped and swayed and fell to the earth.

'That's the Resistance at work,' Pierre said with grim satisfaction.

More bombers crawled across the sky.

Mundt came racing into the house, his face tight with excitement.

'The car is here, Colonel,' he called.

Weiser limped out of his room, clutching a document case. He paused on the threshold when he saw Viviane. He hurried across to her, threw his arms around her and kissed her passionately.

'The Allies have landed on the coast. We're going to try to push them back.'

She held on to his hand as he pulled away. This is the day she had dreaded. 'Take care, Ernst,' she said, trying to hold back the tears. 'Keep safe.'

He winked at her reassuringly and made for the door.

It was only then that she noticed a sergeant standing outside with two young soldiers on either side.

'I'm Sergeant Ferber,' he said. 'Colonel Weiser has commanded me to stay here with a small platoon until he returns. I don't suppose he'll be away for long.'

Viviane thanked him profusely.

Dorothy spent much of the day in the shack with Pierre listening to the radio, trying to find out what was happening. But events were moving too quickly and chaos reigned everywhere so she gleaned little from that source.

Later that night they heard gunfire from the town, not the haphazard noise of fighting but half a dozen shots one after the other.

'Are they fighting in the town?' Dorothy said in alarm.

'More likely executions,' Pierre answered. 'Either the Milice settling scores or the Resistance dealing with them.'

That night they gazed towards the Mediterranean and could see a red glow above the coast. They listened to the sound of gunfire on the breeze.

They spent the next day wondering what was happening. Sergeant Ferber and his two soldiers grew increasingly edgy.

'It's the Resistance, Madame,' he explained to Dorothy. 'The thought of them scares my lads half to death. Poor boys. They should be in school, not waiting to fight for their lives.'

The next morning they heard a car skidding up the driveway, sending gravel high in the air. Weiser and Mundt leapt out and hammered on the door.

Weiser took Viviane's hand. 'We've been ordered to retreat,' he said. 'The Allies have beaten us back and our headquarters have been surrounded.'

Viviane could not find her voice for a moment. At last she whispered: 'Where will you go?'

'West. To cover Marseilles and the valley of the Rhone.' He fell silent. 'I'm afraid I shall have to take Sergeant Ferber and his men with me.'

'But the Gestapo?' She began to tremble. The thought of them coming for her was too much to bear.

'You won't have any need to fear them,' Weiser said. 'I promise.'

He kissed her again, bowed to Dorothy and climbed into the car beside Mundt. As they made for the road he turned once more and raised his hand in farewell.

But the car did not immediately head west. The driver careered at break-neck speed towards the town and screeched to a halt outside the police headquarters.

'Keep the engine running,' Weiser told the driver. Mundt and he headed towards the building.

They found Schorn in his office, together with his assistant, Buchner. They were frantically stuffing documents in a suitcase.

Schorn stared at Weiser in surprise and then smiled. 'You've come to help us evacuate,' he said. 'Good. We're almost ready to leave.'

'You're absolutely right,' Weiser said. He cocked his pistol and shot Schorn through the skull. Mundt dispatched Buchner a moment later.

'We'll take the case with us,' Weiser said. 'It may contain evidence which could incriminate our friends.'

They got into the car and headed west.

Later that afternoon there came a knock on the door of the villa. Viviane and Dorothy looked at each other in alarm. Marie got up to answer the door but Dorothy stopped her.

'No, honey, I'll get it.' She did not need to say who she feared it might be.

But it was not the Gestapo. It was Roland Boyer.

'You've heard the news?' he said.

Dorothy nodded. 'The Allies have landed.'

'They've taken several towns and are beginning to move inland. The Germans are putting up a strong resistance but I gather they're being overwhelmed.'

'And the Gestapo?' Viviane said.

'The little rats have all fled,' he said. 'But I found Schorn and his assistant myself. They'd both been shot, clean through the head.'

'Was it the Resistance?' Dorothy asked.

'Not according to eye-witnesses,' he answered. He glanced at Viviane but refused to say more.

'I can't stay,' he said. 'But I advise you most firmly not to leave the house. There may still be a few stray Germans hiding out and the Resistance are hunting them down.'

Then his face screwed up with anger. 'And already the criminal elements have crept out of the dark. There's been instances of looting and assaults.'

He handed Dorothy a pistol. 'This should scare off any crook fancying his hand at a spot of burglary.' He bowed to them and hurried away.

Dorothy weighed the pistol in her hand. 'As if we'd not had enough of evil deeds,' she murmured.

# LIBERATION
*Grasse, August 1944*

American troops arrived in Grasse two days later. Their commanding officer, a grizzled veteran whose grand-father had fought at Gettysburg, swiftly secured the town, eradicating small pockets of Germans who had got left behind in the headlong German retreat and had been hiding in the surrounding woods.

Then his column moved on, pursuing the enemy to the west. He left behind a platoon of men led by two young officers who could speak a little French. Captain Tom Dunkley had never fired a shot in anger until he landed on the beach a few days before. Lieutenant Niall Johnson was fresh out of school. The first time he had journeyed outside of Kansas was when he was sent to his enlistment camp.

Despite his youth, Dunkley was no fool, and the first person he called on was the mayor. He wore a troubled look on his face when he left the office.

'I don't like it,' he said to the lieutenant. 'The old man said that there would be trouble ahead but seemed unwilling to do anything about it.'

'What sort of trouble?' Johnson asked.

'He refused to say. Let's go find a sheriff.'

Sergeant Henri Lassals looked up from his paper-work when the two Americans walked in. He ran out from behind the desk and shook their hands vigorously.

'We've come because your mayor said there might be trouble ahead,' Dunkley said. 'But he didn't feel inclined to tell me what kind of trouble.'

Lassals frowned. 'There's been a bit of house-breaking and assaults on the street. I guess that's what he means.'

'Can you tell me more? You're in charge here.'

'No, I'm only the sergeant. Capitaine Boyer is normally in command but the mayor asked him to go to Nice to liaise with headquarters there.'

He leaned closer to them and spoke in a low voice. 'The mayor was a good man until the war started. But he lost both his sons in battle and then the Germans imprisoned him. They treated him badly, I'm afraid, and he's a shell of a man.'

Johnson shook his head sympathetically.

'When will your boss come back?' Dunkley asked. He had a sudden sinking feeling in his heart.

'Who knows?'

'Then you're in charge here, I guess.'

Lassals frowned. 'Yes, I suppose I am. Of me and my three men.'

'Is that all? For the whole town?'

'Most of the young ones went to join the Resistance when the Germans came. There's only us old ones left.'

Dunkley whistled in surprise and concern.

'Well we'll do what we can to help. We're going to billet in the German barracks. But I'll leave a couple of men here with you.'

The following morning there came the sound of hammering on the door of Villa Laurel. Marie opened it to three armed men. They were led by a young man who had worked in the library. He was well-dressed and extremely polite. The others were scruffier and dangerous looking.

The young man took a deep breath. 'I need to see the owner of the house, Mademoiselle. And all the people living here.'

He pushed past her before she could reply and led the way into the hall.

'Madame Pine,' Marie called. 'Some men have come to see us.' Her voice trembled with anxiety. She recalled what Roland Boyer had said about looters.

Dorothy appeared in the hallway, fiddling with something in her pocket. She too recalled what Boyer had told them. She doubted she would be able to shoot the pistol but she might be able to use it as a threat.

Viviane appeared behind her and Pierre, with his cudgel visible in his hand.

'There's no need for that, old man,' one of the men said.

Pierre did not answer but tapped the cudgel against his palm.

'To what do I owe the pleasure?' Dorothy asked.

'Is it true that you have entertained Germans here?' the librarian asked.

'Who are you to question me?' Dorothy said.

'That doesn't matter, Madame. Answer the question, please.'

Dorothy took a deep breath.

'If you must know, we did not entertain the Germans. Their colonel was injured in a road accident and took over the villa in order to recuperate somewhere quiet.'

'For six months?' the man said. 'That's a very long recuperation if you don't mind me saying.'

'Well go look for him and ask him why he stayed so long.'

'We don't have to,' the most dangerous looking man said, with a sneer. 'We know you were all whoring yourselves with the Bosch.'

That's enough Dubois,' the librarian said.

'You a wife and mother,' Dubois continued, pointing at Viviane. 'And you, Mademoiselle, a young girl who should have been content with a nice French boy-friend instead of fucking every German in sight.' He wiped some spittle from his lips. 'All of you are traitors, all of you disgust right-thinking people.'

He glared at Dorothy. 'And you, bitch, disgust me most of all. You're old enough to be a grand-mother yet you gave your body to the enemy.'

'No she didn't,' cried Marie, stepping between them. 'Madame Pine is my...my girlfriend. We are lovers.'

Viviane was amazed at her volunteering this information. Dorothy tried to quieten her. Pierre did not seem surprised in the slightest.

The librarian blushed. Dubois eyed Marie and Dorothy up and down. At first, he looked astonished but this was immediately followed by a lascivious regard.

'Perhaps you'd better tell us what the two of you get up to in bed, Mademoiselle. If you want me to believe it.'

'There's no need,' the third man said. 'My wife knows the cook's mother. It's common knowledge that the American and her maid are lovers.'

'So much for trying to keep it secret,' Dorothy said. 'I'm going to cut Lucile's wages when she comes back to work.'

She patted Marie on the arm and pulled her closer.

'So, gentlemen, we're just a pack of lesbians, not interested in the Krauts at all. So, if you're done, I'll wish you au revoir.'

'I'm afraid not,' the librarian said. 'We have good evidence that Madame Renaud was the lover of the German Colonel.'

'Good evidence?' cried Viviane. 'What evidence?'

'I'm not at liberty to tell you. But it is of the highest probity. Madame Pine, it appears that you and your maid are innocent of sleeping with the Germans. But Viviane Renaud must come with us.'

They dragged Viviane out to a waiting car. Dorothy waited until they had disappeared then turned to Pierre.

'Get the car,' she said. 'We're following those bastards. Marie, stay here with the children.'

'I don't want to leave you,' she wailed.

'You must.'

'I don't agree,' Pierre said. 'It will be dangerous for the little ones to stay here with only Marie to guard them. We'd all be better keeping together.'

'We haven't got time to argue,' Dorothy said. 'Come on then, Marie. And Pierre, bring your shot-gun.'


## ROUGH JUSTICE?
### *Grasse, August 1944*

Viviane was taken directly to the town.

'You're a pretty little thing, aren't you,' Dubois said. 'I can see why the Nazi took a fancy to you.'

'Leave her alone,' the librarian said.

Dubois chuckled and fell silent. But all the way into town he kept his eyes glued on Viviane, scrutinising her from her head to her waist.

The car came to a halt behind the church. The place where Viviane and Sylvie used to go to escape the worst heat of the summer. The librarian got out and opened the door for Viviane to leave. She felt Dubois stroke the back of her leg as she did so. She just managed to stop from crying out in disgust.

There were half a dozen women standing in the shade of the church, guarded by three men with rifles. Sylvie was one of them.

She pushed past the guards and embraced Viviane. 'What are you doing here?' she asked.

Viviane shook her head. She could not speak.

'This one's the last,' the librarian said.

A thick-set man nodded and gestured to the guards. 'Then let's begin,' he said.

The women were herded down the steps into the open space on the other side of the church. Despite the hot sun beating down on them, many shivered, although not from cold.

Three men sat at a table, with papers stacked in front of them. The women were paraded in front of them. One of the men, a failing notary by the name of Albert Mignard, read out the charges. They were all identical. Sleeping with the enemy.

Sylvie and Viviane were the last two in line. A man pushed Sylvie forward. She stared at Mignard with a look of defiance. Unlike with the others, he refused to look her in the face.

'Guilty,' he said, although more quietly than before.

'But I'll still see you later, as usual?' Sylvie said, loudly. 'Just after lunch, when your wife takes her nap?'

Several people in the crowd began to laugh but a glance from the men guarding the women soon put an end to it. Mignard gestured for her to be taken away.

A guard thrust Viviane in front of the tribunal.

'Sleeping with the enemy,' Mignard said.

'Who accuses me?' Viviane demanded.

The three men looked disconcerted by the question and began to glance at the papers.

'Who accuses me?' she repeated.

'I do,' came a voice from the crowd.

Odette stepped forward and folded her arms. 'I accuse the whore of sleeping with the German Colonel.'

Viviane stared at her in horror. They had never got on but surely she could not be this cruel?

A long hiss came from the crowd. A stone skittered at Viviane's feet and then another. Gerard was not the only man in the town who had been frustrated by her lack of interest in them. A few more men picked up stones.

'We should stop them,' Lieutenant Johnson said.

Captain Dunkley shook his head. 'We've had our orders. The French must deliver their own justice. It's not our affair.'

'But the girl might be stoned.'

'I don't believe so.'

He was right. The half dozen men who had picked up stones to throw at Viviane found themselves the focus of hundreds of angry eyes from the crowd, men as well as women. The square fell silent and then came the pitter-patter of the stones being dropped.

'She's still guilty,' Odette said. She banged herself on the chest. 'And I say this, who am her sister.'

The crowd stared at her. Few were taken in by her charade.

'Guilty,' Mignard cried, eager to defuse the situation.

But Viviane turned to the waiting crowd, her eyes bright with anger.

'How dare you?' she cried. 'Am I to be condemned because I chose to survive? Chose to protect my daughter?'

The crowd stared at her sullenly. A stone hit her on the head.

She bent immediately and flung it back.

'Or is it because I chose to protect a Jewish child who many of you would have betrayed? Yes, I slept with a German. And I'm proud I did. Because I did it to save a little boy's life.'

The crowd fell utterly silent.

Then Dubois walked towards her, seized her arm and marched her off to join the other women. There were eight of them. None had been able to answer the accusation. No one stepped forward to speak in their defence.

Three chairs were placed in the middle of the square and three women were forced to sit on them. Three men approached, scissors in hand, and began to hack at the women's hair.

The women bent their heads in shame. Most of the crowd began to cheer at the sight of the locks drifting to the ground but many were subdued and silent.

Three more women were given the same treatment. Then it was the turn of Sylvie and Viviane.

Sylvie glanced at the man behind her chair and smiled. 'It's nice to have it short for the summer,' she said. 'Perhaps I'll get you to style it when autumn comes.' A ripple of laughter came from the crowd.

Viviane was pushed into the chair. She was silent. She could see only two things. One was her sister who wore a look of triumph. The other was the priest who stood in the church doorway, looking anguished and powerless.

She felt the scissors shearing her hair, felt the locks falling past her face. She refused to lower her head in shame.

Then she heard a voice beside her. 'Cut mine, you bastards.' The accent sounded more American than she had ever heard before.

She turned and saw Dorothy standing beside her. Behind her, the men from the tribunal rose and shook their heads, gesturing the men with the scissors not to move.

Dorothy snatched the scissors from one of them and began to hack at her own hair. She had sheared most of it before Viviane cried out in anguish.

'You and me, baby,' Dorothy said. 'You and me.'

She continued to hack.

'She's American,' Johnson breathed.

Dunkley didn't reply but gunned his jeep into life, sweeping into the square.

'Enough he bellowed. Enough.'

Dorothy stared at him. 'The cavalry,' she said. 'But not quite in the nick of time.'


## AFTERMATH
### Grasse, 1945

General Charles de Gaulle was now head of the French Government. He swiftly ordered an end to summary executions and all other punishments but some women still experienced surreptitious beatings or worse.

Roland was convinced that those who were most active in acts of retribution were collaborators themselves, attempting to hide the fact with their fervour in dealing out punishment.

He still shared his house with Odette but refused to speak with her.

Viviane wanted to return home, wanted to be reunited with Alain. But Roland advised her against it. Emotions were still running too hot.

It took months for Viviane and Dorothy's hair to grow respectable again.

Dorothy insisted that Viviane and the children stay with her and Marie at least until Christmas was over. Food was more plentiful now that the German army had retreated and Dorothy made the most of the fact. They enjoyed the best Christmas since the war had begun.

On the last day of the year, Dorothy took Viviane into the dining room and poured two large glasses of cognac.

She seemed almost embarrassed as she gave one to Viviane.

'I'm going to leave for the States once there are ships available for civilians,' she said. 'I'm taking Marie with me. She'll love Hollywood.' She took Viviane's hand. 'And I'd like you and the kids to come with me.'

Viviane was speechless at the offer but she shook her head. 'I can't Dorothy. I've got to wait for Alain to return. The children and I miss him dreadfully.'

On New Year's Day Roland called on them.

'I think Hitler's goose is cooked,' Dorothy said as she poured him a drink. 'The end of the war's in sight.'

'I think so too,' Roland said. 'Things are getting back to normal. And that's one of the reasons I'm here.'

He looked at Viviane. 'I've decided to leave Odette. I cannot forgive her for what she did to you.'

'So will Odette go back to Maman?' she asked.

Roland shook his head. 'She refuses to do so. She'd consider it capitulation. Besides, I have too many unhappy memories of our house to wish to stay there. I shall move out.'

'But where will you go?'

He cleared his throat. 'I was wondering if I could stay in your house.'

Viviane gave a tiny smile and nodded. 'I was planning to return soon, anyway.'

'Then I can be your lodger,' Roland said, his voice betraying his relief. 'I have a little camp bed I can set up downstairs.'

'That's wonderful,' Viviane said. 'I'll feel safe if you're around.'

She moved out of the villa at the end of the month. Roland had already moved into her house. She was amused and pleased that he had used neither her nor the children's room even when he was alone in the house. His camp bed was tucked away in the corner with a few sparse belongings on a table beside it. Her bedroom was exactly as she had left it, more than a year before.

The people of Grasse were not exactly as they had been when she had left them. Now they were like strangers to her.

Some sought to befriend her because she had protected a little Jewish boy. Other shunned her because of it.

As much as possible she kept to herself.

On the eighth of May, Germany surrendered. The war in Europe was over.

Dorothy called at Viviane's house a few days later. She gave Celeste and David a chocolate bar to share and then took Viviane's hand. Her eyes were wet with tears.

'Marie and I are going to Le Havre to make the crossing to the US,' she said. 'There are berths on the ship still available. We'd love it if you and the kids came with us. I'll pay for you.'

Viviane burst into tears. 'That's such a generous offer, Dorothy. But my home is here. And so is my husband. I've got to wait for Alain. Who knows, maybe when he returns, we'll all come to join you.'

A sudden desire to do so came over her. She had lost all love for Grasse and no longer felt at home here. Maybe it would be good to make a new life in America.

'When Alain returns, we'll see.' She embraced Dorothy tightly. 'I'll never be able to repay you for what you did,' she whispered.

'We all pay our debts in the coin of love,' Dorothy said. 'That's more than enough for me.'

She ruffled the children's hair, turned and left.

Spring went by and summer came. But still Alain did not return.

Viviane spent long months scanning reports of members of the Resistance who had been killed or wounded. Alain's name was not among them. Finally, she decided to go to Nice to try to find out for herself.

It took her days to track down Gabriel Chiappe. He was doing very well for himself; he liked Nice and was now a big boss here.

He made her very welcome and immediately asked how Alain was.

'That's why I'm here,' she said. 'I thought you'd know where he is.'

He looked anguished and shook his head. 'But he returned home to you. Eighteen months ago.'

She stared at him speechless.

Chiappe's mouth moved but he could find no words. A look of heartfelt pity came to his face and he reached out and held her hand. It was answer enough.

Viviane began to sob, soundlessly, but with terrible anguish.

She did not know how she managed the journey back to Grasse.

She stood outside her house for a while, summoning up the courage to go in. She went into the empty room. She picked up a picture of Alain from the sideboard.

Holding it very carefully, she hung it on the place where the picture of Maréchal Pétain used to hang.

Life in Grasse began to grow normal again. Roland met a young widow and they decided to get married. The woman insisted that he move out of Viviane's house and he lodged with his old friend Lassals until the wedding.

Without him the house seemed even emptier. If it were not for the need to put a bright face on things, Viviane would have fallen into despair.

At the beginning of July there came a knock on the door.

Viviane's heart leapt as it did every time this happened. Every time she thought it would be Alain, knocking as a joke, to surprise her at his return.

She opened the door. It was Roland. Beside him was a young woman. She was gaunt and frail-looking. Her arms were as thin as sticks and the skin stretched tight against her skull.

'I've come back for him,' she said, quietly.

Viviane shook her head in confusion.

'For my son,' the woman continued. 'I'm David's mother.'

Viviane stared at her, unable to speak.

'I've been in the death-camps,' the woman said. 'But I survived.'

Viviane felt the ground sway beneath her feet. This could not be happening. She had lost her husband. Was she now about to lose David?

Then she took a deep breath, one so deep and terrible she shuddered with its fury.

'Come in,' she said, finally. 'We can both get him ready to go with you.'

It took only a quarter of an hour to gather together David's possessions. A woman from the Red Cross took them out to a waiting car.

David looked at his mother in confusion. He could recognise her voice, just about, but she looked like a stranger. He clung to Viviane's skirt until she gently unlocked his fingers.

'This is your real Maman,' she said. 'She's come to take you home.'

David looked up at her. 'But this is my home.' He began to weep.

Viviane hugged him tightly. 'Your home is with your Maman,' she said. 'But I'll always be here, my darling. And if your Maman lets you, then you can come back to see Celeste and me.'

She straightened up and gazed into the woman's eyes. Both knew that this could never happen.

Rachael held out her hand for David's and grasped it tight. She turned and headed for the car but then stopped and came back. She did not speak but she reached out and touched Viviane on the arm. Her hand was thin and bony, almost like a claw. But it pulsed with warmth and life.

Viviane watched until the car had disappeared from sight.

She looked at Celeste who was sitting on the ground weeping. She pulled her to her feet and held her tight.

'David won't forget us,' she whispered. 'And we'll never forget him.'

Nor Alain, she thought. Nor Ernst.

And then she smiled. And nor her very good friend, Dorothy.


## CHARACTERS IN CRY OF THE HEART

Viviane Renaud
Alain Renaud
Celeste Renaud
Rachael Klein
David Klein
Marthe Loubet, Viviane's mother
Georges Loubet, Viviane's father
Odette Boyer, Viviane's husband
Capitaine Roland Boyer, Odette's husband
Gerard Pithou, Alain's friend, member of the Milice
Jeanne Greuze, Odette's gossipy friend
Sylvie Duchamp, Viviane's friend
Monique Duchamp, Sylvie's daughter
Madame Canet, shopkeeper
Monsieur Blanche, baker
Gendarme Raoul Villiers
Sergeant Henri Lassals
Dorothy Pine
Marie Robinne, Dorothy's maid
Yvonne Robinne, her mother
Lucile Arnauld, Dorothy's cook
Pierre Sorel, Dorothy's handyman

Isabelle Blois, cafe owner
Maxime Blois, her husband
Theo Joubert, Alain's older friend
Sergei Guizot, hotel owner in Marseille
Gabriel Chiappe, Marseille criminal and friend of Alain
Le Taureau, Marseille criminal boss
Capitano Emilio Marinelli, Italian Army
Oberst Ernst Weiser, German Wehrmacht
Major Otto Mundt, Wehrmacht
General Johannes Blaskowitz, Wehrmacht
Private Wilhelm Ferber
Private Alphonse Dahn
Gestapo Kriminaldirektor Heinrich Schorn
Gestapo Kriminalinspektor Karl Buchner
Gestapo operative Ludwig Gort
Admiral Carlo Leonetti
Père Benoît, Capuchin monk
Brother Lawrence, a young monk
Angelo Donati, Member of the Jewish Resistance
Captain Tom Dunkley, US Army
Lieutenant Niall Johnson, US Army

## THANKS AND ACKNOWLEDGEMENTS

Thank you for buying Cry of the Heart. I hoped you enjoyed it,

No book is solely the work of the writer. It needs inspiration and nurturing, as does, often, the writer.

This book is inspired by the story of a Jewish friend. His mother was being hunted by the Nazis through the streets of Antwerp and she gave her tiny child to a stranger to hide. It was a terrible and desperate decision for her. I was intrigued by the woman who risked everything, including her own liberty and life, to take in and protect a little child.

In the writing of this book I have had the unstinting support of my wife, Janine, who also read it and gave me many points and suggestions. I ever grateful for all she does.

Some members of my writing group were also kind enough to read early drafts of the novel and make suggestions, improvement and point out errors I had missed. So a big thank-you to Shirley Medhurst, Charlie Baddeley and Heather Lounsbury. Historical novelist Carol M. Cram gave generous and unstinting advice in the final draft of the novel. Any mistakes still remaining after this are solely down to me.

Finally, I must pay tribute to all the courageous people who risked everything to protect children and others in the terrible trauma of the Second World War. Some of them figure in this book, others are fictional and can only represent the unknown saviours of so many people.

The recommendations and comments of readers make all the difference to the success of a book. I would be very grateful if you could spread the word about the book amongst your friends.

It would also be a great help if you could spend a few moments writing a review and posting it on the site where you purchased the book, Goodreads or any other forum you are active in.

To post a review on Amazon please click, tap or paste here: viewauthor.at/MartinLake

## OTHER BOOKS BY MARTIN LAKE

Here are some other books which you may wish to take a look at.

**A Love Most Dangerous.** Her beauty was a blessing…and a dangerous burden, As a Maid of Honor at the Court of King Henry VIII, beautiful Alice Petherton receives her share of admirers. But when the powerful, philandering Sir Richard Rich attempts to seduce her, she knows she cannot thwart his advances for long. She turns to the most powerful man in England for protection: the King himself.

**Very Like a Queen.** The King's favor was her sanctuary—until his desire turned dangerous. Alice Petherton is well practiced at using her beauty and wits to survive in the Court of King Henry VIII. As the King's favorite, she enjoys his protection, but after seeing the downfall of three of his wives, she's determined to avoid the same fate. Alice must walk a fine line between mistress and wife.

**The Viking Chronicles:**
**Wolves of War.** Leif Ormson lived a pleasant and uneventful life. Until the sons of Ragnar Lothbrok threw him into a storm of war, danger and destruction.

**To the Death.** The Viking army, with Leif a reluctant leader, does battle against the kingdom of Wessex.

**The Saxon Chronicles:**
**Land of Blood and Water.** Warfare and warriors mean nothing to Brand and his family. But then King Alfred of Wessex chooses their home for his last-ditch defence against the Vikings.

**Blood Enemy.** Ulf, son of Brand, has risen high in the service of King Alfred. But when he shows himself a berserker he loses everything. Can he redeem himself and return to favour?

**The Lost King Books:**
**The Flame of Resistance.** The battle of Hastings is over. The battle for England is about to begin.

**Triumph and Catastrophe.** Can a 17 year old boy with an ill-equipped army challenge William the Conqueror for his birthright, the throne of England?

**Blood of Ironside.** Betrayed by friends and family, Edgar Atheling refuses to submit and vows to take the battle to the Conqueror's homeland.

**In Search of Glory.** Edgar grows accustomed to Norman rule, although he berates himself for his failures. Then events occur which cause him to continue the fight.

**Outcasts: Crusades Book 1.** Jerusalem has fallen to Saladin. Three newly knighted men journey through a perilous, bitter world to rescue a captive wife and family.

**The Artful Dodger.** The adventures of the Artful Dodger in Australia and London.

**For King and Country.** Three short stories set in the First World War.

**Nuggets.** Fast fiction for quiet moments.

**Mr Toad's Wedding.** First prize winner in the competition to write a sequel story to The Wind in the Willows.

**Mr Toad to the Rescue.** After losing his betrothed to his cousin, Mr Toad and his friends are called upon to rescue her from an even bigger rascal.

**The Big School.** Three light-hearted short stories about a boy's experience of growing up.

You can find my books easily by clicking here: viewauthor.at/MartinLake

I have a mailing list with my new release, news and exclusive stories. To be the first to hear about new releases, please sign up below. I promise I won't fill up your mailbox with lots of emails. I won't share your email with anybody.

If you would like to subscribe please click here:
http://eepurl.com/DTnhb

You can read more about my approach to writing on my blog:
http://martinlakewriting.wordpress.com

Or on Facebook at https://www.facebook.com/MartinLakeWriting

Or you can follow me on Twitter @martinlake14

Made in the USA
Columbia, SC
21 April 2020